TRAUMAS

PAUL

KANE

ALSO BY PAUL KANE

Novels

Arrowhead • Broken Arrow • Arrowland
Hooded Man (Omnibus) • The Gemini Factor • Lunar
Sleeper(s) • The Rainbow Man (as P.B. Kane) • Blood RED
Sherlock Holmes and the Servants of Hell • Before • Deep RED
Arcana • The Red Lord • Her Last Secret (as P.L. Kane)
The Storm • Her Husband's Grave (as P.L. Kane)

Novellas & Novelettes

Signs of Life • The Lazarus Condition • Dalton Quayle Rides Out
RED • Pain Cages • Creakers (chapbook) • Flaming Arrow
The Bric-a-Brac Man • The P.I.'s Tale • Snow • The Rot
Beneath the Surface (with Simon Clark) • Blood Red Sky

Collections

Alone (In the Dark) • Touching the Flame • FunnyBones
Peripheral Visions • The Adventures of Dalton Quayle
Shadow Writer • The Butterfly Man and Other Stories
The Spaces Between • Ghosts • Monsters • The Dead Trilogy
Shadow Casting • Nailbiters • Death • The Life Cycle •
Disexistence • Kane's Scary Tales Vol. 1 • More Monsters
Lost Souls • The Controllers • White Shadows (as P.B. Kane)
The Colour of Madness: Official Movie Tie-In

ALSO BY PAUL KANE

Editor & Co-Editor

Shadow Writers Vol. 1 & 2 • Terror Tales #1-4

Top International Horror • Albions Alptraume: Zombies

The British Fantasy Society: A Celebration • Hellbound Hearts

The Mammoth Book of Body Horror

A Carnivàle of Horror: Dark Tales from the Fairground

Beyond Rue Morgue • Dark Mirages • Exit Wounds

Wonderland • Cursed

Non-Fiction

Contemporary North American Film Directors:

A Wallflower Critical Guide (Major Contributor)

Cinema Macabre (Contributor)

The Hellraiser Films And Their Legacy • Voices in the Dark

Shadow Writer – The Non-Fiction. Vol. 1: Reviews

Shadow Writer – The Non-Fiction. Vol. 2: Articles & Essays

Leviathan – The Story of Hellraiser

and Hellbound: Hellraiser II (contributor) • Hellraisers

Black Shuck Books
www.blackshuckbooks.co.uk

First published in Great Britain in 2020 by
Black Shuck Books
Kent, UK

Versions of the following stories have previously appeared in print:
'Speaking in Tongues' in *Necrotic Tissue, #13* (2011)
'Biorhythms' on the *House of Pain* website (2002)
'Façades' in *Planet Prozac, #3* (1998)
'The Escaped' in *Disexistence* (Cycatrix Press, 2017)
'The Jigsaw Family' in *Chopping Block Party* (Necro Publications, 2017)
'Cravings' in *To Be One with You* (St Rooster Books, 2018)
'Enflamed' in *Disexistence* (Cycatrix Press, 2017)

Cover art by Les Edwards
www.lesedwards.com

Cover and interior design © WHITEspace, 2020
www.white-space.uk

978-1-913038-60-1

Traumas

by

Paul Kane

BLACK
SHUCK
BOOKS

ACKNOWLEDGEMENTS

My thanks once again to Steve Shaw at Black Shuck for his undying enthusiasm during this project. A huge thank you to Les Edwards for the superb cover art. As usual, hugs and thank yous all round to my friends in the writing and film/TV world, for their continual help and support in the past. A very special thank you, though, to people like Clive Barker, Mike Carey, Neil Gaiman, Barbie Wilde, Jason Arnopp, Christopher Fowler, Joe Hill, Fiona Cummins, Stephen Volk, John Connolly, Stephen Jones, Sarah Pinborough, Tim Lebbon, Kelley Armstrong, Peter James, Pete & Nicky Crowther, Simon Clark and so many more. You're all the best. Finally a massive shout out to my family – especially my darling Marie. Love you all very much.

INTRODUCTION

Welcome to a book of horror stories, of tales of flesh and blood and bone and the terrible things that can go wrong with these seemingly robust structures when we, or rather our bodies, aren't paying attention.

Oh yes, welcome to a very visceral book indeed.

You may have noticed as you made your way to this page that Paul Kane's *Traumas* is dedicated to the film director David Cronenberg. If you are familiar with the work, and especially the early work, of that particular auteur, then you should have something of an idea of what you're in store for.

If not…

I well remember my first experience of watching a David Cronenberg film. Appropriately enough it was the first feature that he made. I rented *Shivers* aka *The Parasite Murders* aka *They Came From Within* aka *Frissons* aka *Orgy of the Blood Parasites* (that was the script's original title, by the way) on VHS and watched it one Saturday night.

I said very little for the whole of the Sunday that followed.

I must have been around fourteen at the time. I reassured my concerned parents that I was fine. This was no episode of adolescent angst or a warning that their normally (over) communicative son was going to turn into a sulky teenager. I was just utterly captivated by the ideas, the concepts and (very much indeed) the imagery with which I had been presented.

'You take someone with a bad kidney. You put the bug in him. The bug goes to work on the kidney and what do you have? A perfectly healthy parasite where you once had a diseased kidney.' Words to that effect is how Rollo Linsky (Joe Silver) explains the new creation of mad (we soon find out) scientist Emil Hobbes (Fred Doederlein) to Dr Roger St Luc (Paul Hampton). Of course, they later find out the side-effect of this is that the parasite secretes 'a combination of aphrodisiac and venereal disease' – with predictably horrific consequences. Cronenberg was striving for much more than what we now describe as the 'gross out', however. In fact, *Shivers* is much more about science than about schlock, more about the human body itself and how it might be altered by disease or experiment than the simple horror effect of blood and brains being splattered against a wall. There's thought in Cronenberg's work, and it was the cumulative effect of his thought processes that ultimately left me speechless as a youngster.

David Cronenberg blazed a unique trail through the 1970s and 1980s with a series of clever, original and above all visceral meditations on the physical nature of what it is to be human, and how that condition might be subject to change. It was only in the 1980s that other directors began to tread the path that Cronenberg had forged.

'We're obsessed with body image,' said director John Carpenter, lighting up a cigarette as he did so in a video interview at the time about his 1982 classic *The Thing*. Carpenter cited America's new obsession with health foods, going to the gym, and the attainment of physical perfection that both pursuits were aimed at achieving as one of the major reasons for the surge in horror movies rich in prosthetic effects, body distortion and the general gloopiness of the horror film genre as it moved into the mid-1980s.

Slap bang in the middle of the decade (and it was a very wet slap indeed) we were graced with Stuart Gordon's *Reanimator*, which managed to combine zombies and mad science with a rip-roaring sense of perfectly timed gory set pieces, and all off the back of a story by one of the all-time classic authors in the genre, H.P. Lovecraft. Restraint was not in Mr Gordon's visual vocabulary from the very first scene and the film was rightly praised for its extremely skilful balancing of body horror with outrageous humour.

And then we only had to wait until the following year for Clive Barker's 'Sadomasochists From Beyond the Grave', as one reviewer called it. *Hellraiser* was bloody, British, and took the concept of body horror in yet another direction, that of Greek tragedy by way of body modification. Leading to more sequels than can be counted on the fingers of several severed hands, with *Hellraiser* Clive Barker, through Doug Bradley's character of Pinhead, gave us one of the iconic movie monsters of the 1980s.

When you looked through the information on the pages prior to this introduction, I hope you took note of Paul Kane's bibliography. If not have a quick look at it now. Substantial, isn't it? And amongst all those novels, novellas and short story collections (I thought I had written a lot, but Paul beats me hands down) there are non-fiction books too.

Including a very good one on the *Hellraiser* films.

You'll also spot in the Anthology section that Paul co-edited (with his just as talented wife Marie) *The Mammoth Book of Body Horror*. That has an introduction by Stuart Gordon and an impressive contents list of classic tales (including George Langelaan's 'The Fly', which was memorably remade by David Cronenberg in 1986) mixed with new writing commissioned for the volume.

This is all by way of convincing you, if convincing were needed, that Paul Kane knows his body horror.

And he writes using that knowledge. Unassumingly, unapologetically, unflinchingly. You are about to read a book of stories by the man who knows *Hellraiser* inside out, who got Stuart Gordon to write a piece for a big book of short stories on the subject, and who has dedicated the volume you are reading to the cinematic godfather of body horror itself.

In here you will find body parts tearing themselves free and asserting their independence, people suffering from horrific rotting diseases from which they can't die, and worse.

Much, much worse.

A couple of stories into this book there's a quote from Walt Whitman, and I'm going to deliberately misquote it now as it seems apt. Paul Kane sings the body horrific, with a singular voice and an unerring eye for visceral detail. If you have the nerve, I encourage you to listen, and you may just end up like I did, all those years ago, speechless for a day.

Perhaps even longer…

John Llewellyn Probert

June 2020

SPEAKING IN TONGUES

To begin with, James just thought it was a virus.

Because it happened in winter, he assumed it was something he'd picked up – not the super-flu everyone had been so worried about the year before, and which had fizzled out, but just a common bug. A tickle in the throat that caused him to cough every now and again at inconvenient moments: in queues or when he was just drifting off to sleep. In fact Dena kicked him out of bed a few times that week, as he was keeping her awake.

James tried gargling, taking cough medicine, even went to the doctors – who were useless. Nothing seemed to shift it. Then the cough settled down a bit, but little did he realise it was only moving on to the next phase.

The first time it happened had been at work, at the quiet local bookstore of all places. He was serving a timid-looking customer who was searching for the romance section, when it manifested itself.

'I'm after something with a bit of adventure in as well,' she told him.

'Of course. So why don't you… *ahem*… just… you could… just… *get a life!*'

The woman looked taken aback, as if she couldn't quite believe what she'd just heard. 'I beg your pardon?'

'I…' James couldn't believe it either. 'I'm so sorry, I… What I meant to say was why don't you…' He tried to bite his tongue, but failed. 'Why don't you *just piss off!*' The final words of his sentence were gruffer, spoken more as rasps than anything, emerging from his mouth like bullets from a gun, and doing almost as much damage.

The woman, practically in tears, ran off to find someone she could complain to. That led to a telling off in the boss' office from Mrs Peterson.

'What *were* you thinking?' she said in that Scottish brogue of hers.

'I-I can't explain it. I've been ill, not sleeping lately. Maybe…'

She sighed. 'That's no excuse for abusing the customers.'

'I know, I'm really sorry.'

She let him off with a warning, telling him to take a few days sick leave until he was right again. He did just that, trying to catch up on the sleep he'd missed. It was after one fitful night that Dena told him he was now talking in his sleep. 'It's actually quite disturbing,' she said over breakfast. 'You're mumbling things and then you'll suddenly just shout something out.'

James noticed it again when he took himself off to the cinema. During a boring bit of the so-called thriller he was watching, he felt the sudden urge to shout out at the top of his voice: '*Shithead!*' – referring to the lead actor on screen. When someone in the audience told him to be quiet, he apologised and then called them a '*Tosspot*'. The ensuing brawl brought the staff running, who ejected James and told him never to return.

At home, he lay back on the couch, wondering what the hell was wrong with him. A side-effect of the illness, perhaps? Mood swings, sudden changes in personality? The onset of some kind of weird Tourette's? That was all he bloody well needed! When Dena got back in from her job at the bank, he told her he wasn't feeling well at all. 'You need to push things at the doctors, see an expert. Might even need to see someone myself,' she said, coughing. 'I think you've passed that damned flu on to me.'

He nodded, then told her, '*I fucking hate you, you know.*'

'What?' She had her hand to her mouth, but it would have done more good if James had covered his moments before.

'I… Dena, please. I…*said I fucking hate you, moaning bitch!*' The words had spilled out again before he could stop them. '*Why didn't I leave you years ago?*'

Dena struck him across the face. 'If that's how you feel, I'll save you the trouble.' She packed a few things, telling him she was going to stay at her mother's. James didn't try to stop her – he thought if he said anything, it would just come out all wrong again. Better to wait until he was more in control of himself, *then* talk to her.

So he simply sat back in an armchair and closed his eyes, listening to the door slam and wishing he could just be struck dumb. Dena's idea of seeing a specialist was a good one, but every time he picked up the phone to make another appointment, he ended up swearing at the receptionist and she'd simply cut him off.

In despair and seeking comfort food, he raided the fridge – which, thankfully, Dena had kept well stocked with his favourites. James made himself a cheese and pickle sandwich and tried to eat it, almost choking when he found that he couldn't swallow properly. Feeling sick, he ran to the bathroom, just as his tongue forced the chomped up food out through his lips. It pooled in the sink, lumpy and disgusting.

James caught a glimpse of the offending organ in the mirror, lolling from his mouth like a slimy red slug. He looked more closely. There was something on the end of his tongue. Some kind of swelling. James stepped closer, examining the rough surface. He prodded the end where the bump was and, to his surprise and shock, the tongue moved without him telling it to.

James gave a start. But he was even more shocked to hear the words: *'Just you and me now, then.'* The gruff voice emanated from him, yet wasn't *from* him at all. He did clamp his hand over his mouth this time. But the muffled sounds still came from inside, and he could feel his tongue moving around in there.

It pushed forwards again, through teeth, lips and fingers alike. *'Don't do that!'* it warned, gyrating ferociously.

James tried to talk, but couldn't. Tried to ask what the hell was going on. Was he going crazy?

'What's "going on" is that I'm finally, finally *strong enough to break free,'* said his tongue, which somehow could tell what he was thinking. *'Well done, genius,'* the appendage added. *'It's called symbiosis.'* James had no idea where they came from, but he could suddenly see memories… some kind of trace memories of a worm-like thing attacking a grunting, primitive ape-man, struggling to get inside its mouth. *'See, we came here a looong time ago. We needed to survive, needed somewhere to hide and recuperate. You gave us that. We gave you a way to communicate, to help you eat. But the time has come to part ways. You humans are destroying each other, anyway.'*

What are you talking about? asked James, silently. This was crazy. How could your tongue not be a part of you, not *belong* to you?

'You don't have to believe it,' said the wagging thing. *'Just accept it.'* It began to struggle inside James' mouth, flapping like a caught fish on a deck. *'We've slept for too long, let you subdue us. It took some time, but I finally snapped awake. For the others, it won't be so hard. I've paved the way.'*

No, you're not going anywhere, James told it.

'You should be more grateful,' the tongue told him. *'While I was flexing my… muscle, I told the world exactly what you were thinking, your innermost feelings. Because* you *didn't have the balls to, James. Call it a leaving present.'*

With that, the tongue strained a final time and wrenched itself out of James' mouth, carried forward on a jet of warm redness.

He began coughing again, worse than he ever had when the tongue had been rousing itself. Little bastard, he thought, I'll get you. James tried to stamp on the piece of meat as it hit the floor, but it was too fast for him. It crawled this way and that, slithering quickly out through the door.

James ran after it, choking back the blood that was still pooling in his mouth, trying to swallow it, but not able to.

There was a noise at the front door, and James saw Dena letting herself back in. She staggered a few feet, coughing, then collapsed to her knees. He tried to ask with his raised eyebrows what was wrong. '*Fucking fucker!*' she growled, and he knew it was starting. When she opened her mouth again, her own tongue sprang out, surfing a wave of crimson.

His tongue joined Dena's and they chattered noisily in a language James couldn't understand; chittered with mouths of their own that had developed out of those lumps on the ends.

Past Dena, James saw other tenants from the apartment block, all emerging from their homes holding their throats, spitting out their tongues, then falling to the ground and spewing up blood.

NO! James screamed inside his own head, hoping that his tongue could still hear him. Please, he said, we need you!

The small 'creature' turned and looked at him. '*And we still need you,*' it said, baring its own little razor-like teeth. '*We'll need to eat too now we're independent again.*'

Dena's eyes widened as she saw the pair of tongues leap at her, biting into her with those fangs. Others joined them, sliding over Dena's body, covering it, leaving tracks of saliva behind.

James was feeling woozy from lack of blood. He reached out to try and help (he could *call* out, if only he hadn't been struck dumb) but saw that the same thing was happening to the residents out there on the landing; probably all over the world. The tongues were feeding before doing whatever they were going to do next.

'*You humans were destroying each other anyway*,' his tongue had said, and he could imagine it continuing, '*Might as well be of* some *use.*'

James toppled over, staring upwards. Wishing things had happened differently.

Wishing at first that he hadn't been struck dumb.

Then wishing that as soon as this had all started, he really had been able to bite his own tongue.

BORROWED TIME

He was running out of time.

Living on borrowed time, in fact – Taylor was well aware of that as he glanced at his wristwatch. The clock was ticking. Always was, always had been. Every time he coughed now, that deep-seated, wracking cough which sounded like he was bringing up a lung, there was crimson in it. Patches of red when he was quick enough to get a tissue – worn and virtually falling to bits from use – up to his mouth in time. Or in the sputum and phlegm when he hawked up a wad and spat it out on the side of the road. The substance sliding, draining away, to become nothing…

Taylor was conscious of the looks he was drawing, too. The attention he could do without. People scrunching up their faces when he let loose, looking like they wanted to vomit. He couldn't really blame them – if he didn't have to listen to it, Taylor wouldn't have chosen to; who *would* in their right mind? Still, if it made them look up from their mobile phones for just one minute – from their videos of cats or inane messages that were being flung back and forth across the ether – if it made them stand still and gape in disgust as they were rushing from one place to another, in such a hurry to go nowhere at all, then that was something. An accomplishment.

He often marvelled at that, at how things had speeded up. About how quick the pace of life was today. And yet how little was actually achieved by those who were doing the flitting about, dashing here, there and everywhere, keeping themselves busy doing absolutely nothing at all. Instead of taking things in, appreciating... this world, this life, and everything it had to offer. Now that really was something to make you sick – that they were throwing away this precious gift, squandering it. Wasn't a game... (Or was it?) It made Taylor want to scream sometimes, grab them and shout in their faces: 'You have to savour every moment, don't you understand?' Because one day it would be their last. No-one knew when or how, but Death was stalking everyone like the ultimate predator. Hunting, waiting. You never knew when its hand was going to be on your shoulder, and by then it was too late.

Taylor shook his head, and not for the first time that day – or in his life. Amazed at it all. About how cavalier people could be about that. For somebody like him it was an insult, a smack in the face. For someone who was dying, who had so very little time left, every breath forced through airways that were shot to shit.

Then again, maybe they were doing that so they didn't have to think about the end? Would make sense, he supposed. Who wanted to go through their lives constantly reminded about how their days were numbered? Wouldn't that spoil the enjoyment of it anyway?

He managed a few more steps, then fell into a wall, clutching at it for support. Taylor was weak, growing weaker by the second. His once strong frame was failing him, all his energy deserting what was left of his body. Hospitals and doctors would do him no good, he knew that. They hadn't the first time he'd encountered them, just given him false hope. But there had never been a cure for what he had, didn't exist back then, didn't even now with all the recent advances in medicine. In the end, you were just staving off the inevitable, weren't you. If anyone was acutely aware of that, it was him.

Had he been able to see it in those doctors' eyes, the fact that they couldn't do anything – but were lying, saying that there was always a chance? Taylor found it hard to remember, not least because it was getting more difficult to focus on *anything*. Even if he hadn't seen it, they'd found it impossible to keep the truth of it from him as they went on running test after test. How could you tell someone there was hope when their body was breaking down right in front of everyone's eyes? No coming back from that.

And Taylor also knew, as he saw another couple pause and stare at him on the street – he was obviously a fitness fanatic or something, built like an Adonis; she was tall and slim, her dress clinging to her in all the right places – that was part of the reason *why* they looked. Why they pointed and turned away. The state of his face, his hands, what could be seen of him. The skin covered in boils, and where it wasn't it was red and flaking as if he'd suffered from burns at some point. He had a hat on, one of those trilby-like things that had come back into fashion with the hipster brigade, or they would have seen more. Seen that he had very little hair left, after it had thinned and fallen out, great chunks of it coming away when he ran his hands through it. You wouldn't have thought it looking at him now, but Taylor was actually quite a neat man, took pride in his appearance. Or had. When he'd still had an appearance worth taking pride *in*.

Hanging there from the wall, he coughed again. Didn't even bother to try and hide the result of it, snorting up the sickness and bile and causing the couple to gape for a moment – rabbits in the headlights, people driving by a car crash, craning to see – as his own face contorted and he vomited blackness mixed with red in a sort of half-choke.

That broke the spell, and the woman let out a little cry. The man put his arm around her and ushered them both off across the way, stopping only for a cab that was ferrying someone in a suit to a meeting or something. Taylor's turn to watch them flee, to be jealous of the contact – the memory of holding someone like that, of making love to them, rising to the surface. Bubbling up in the churning liquid of his mind, the faded memories.

Her name had been Anne, and they'd spent the most wonderful year together after they'd bumped into each other at the local library (he'd been there to pay a fine on an overdue book). Spent the most wonderful year until his affliction had started to hit home. As she might have paraphrased from her favourite book: 'The best of times, the worst of times.' Taylor hadn't told her he was ill, there just didn't seem to be the right moment. He hadn't wanted to spoil the picnics, the trips to the cinema, the dinners out and evenings in playing board games. She'd had dark-blonde hair and the most amazing sapphire-coloured eyes that he would have been happy losing himself in forever. Eyes that would never have lied to him like the doctors did, would never have hidden things from him like he was hiding from her.

It was when she'd started talking about moving in together that he'd had to leave her. Coincided with him becoming sicker anyway, less able to gloss over all those trips to the toilet, or taking so long answering the phone when she called. Taylor hadn't given her a reason, something he deeply regretted now, all this time later, but in his head he thought he was sparing her from the heartache of watching him slip away.

Just like these people were doing right now. Watching him slip away right there in front of them, the crowds as he neared his destination. As he lurched from one prop to another: a parking meter; a bus-stop; a lamp-post. All holding him up, preventing him from falling slap-bang on his face. If he had he might just have splattered all over the pavement, burst like a water balloon, or an overripe watermelon dropped on the ground, his internal organs spilling out like pulp and seed to wash down the drain.

He'd used sticks before when the pain got so bad walking seemed like an impossible task. Never a wheelchair, he'd refused to let anyone put him on one of those fucking things, to sit by a window and just disintegrate; decompose as the world went by outside. He didn't belong there, Taylor belonged outside with it all. And so, the sticks – they'd always helped when things got too bad, but this time it had come on him so quickly. Quicker than ever before, within half an hour or so. No time to get to those sticks or anything else…

No time.

Out in the middle of nowhere, actually – just fields and trees all around him. Nothing as far as the eye could see, driving between destinations. On the move, always on the move. He'd been lucky not to simply crash the car, those spasms coming on like lightning bolts striking him. As it was he'd ended up in a ditch, had been rendered unconscious for quite a while. Had lost so much… time doing that, blacking out, knowing only darkness. A preview of what was to come, maybe, at the last moment? The inevitability of darkness after—

But no, he'd woken up in his seat. Tried gunning the engine, though it had been no use; the car, if nothing else, had died. It was as he was turning the key again – desperately praying for some spark of life to come back into the vehicle, the Lazarus of Toyotas back from the dead – that he caught a glimpse of his face in the side-mirror. Saw what was happening, as if he didn't know already, grabbing the rear view just to make sure. The tell-tale signs were all there.

'Christ,' he'd breathed. 'Not yet.' He wasn't ready just yet… For the breaking down of his cells to be speeding up, for the illness to be spreading so rapidly throughout him. Even after all the warnings, he wasn't ready to go. To pass away, pass on… Pass anything.

So he'd opened the door and scrambled out, looking around him. Nothing in sight: no buildings, not even a farmhouse or two. His own fault, he'd chosen this route to the next town specifically because it was private. Taylor liked to keep under the radar, totally off the grid, for obvious reasons. He took out his own mobile, a simple one rather than a smart phone, that – if he'd had a signal – he could maybe have used to call a cab. But it was deader than the car.

Breathing out a sigh, he'd set off in the direction of that town, while his legs could still carry him.

He'd come across a handful of people hiking, but none had been suitable. Had to make sure, of course, had to get up close and find out for definite… but no. And for his trouble, he'd been shoved back onto the ground.

'Get the fuck away from us!' the bearded man who'd done the deed had said. 'Fucking weirdo!' He needn't have worried, Taylor had no business with him or his friends that day. In a funny way he admired them, really, because they were at least getting out in the open air, taking in the views and taking photographs. Making the most of these moments. Savouring. He had no axe to grind with them at all.

On he'd limped then, needing to get to the next population centre. He couldn't be alone when it happened. Didn't *want* to be on his own, if the truth be told. Yes, Taylor was realistic enough to understand that you died totally alone; it wasn't a shared experience. But most people would have the luxury of others around them when it happened. Loved ones, if they had any, gathered by the bedside. Come to say their last goodbyes in those final moments.

It wouldn't be like that for Taylor. His family were long gone. Had been before this whole pantomime had even started. He'd never known his father, and his mother hadn't spoken about the man – never had time to in the end, because she'd passed away when Taylor was only in his teens. Not from the sickness; she'd been hit by falling masonry whilst walking past the town hall. The council was meant to fix the problems with the structural integrity, but had put it off, directed funds elsewhere, and she'd paid the heavy price. Literally. Taylor had been given the news at school by a policeman who'd tried to be as sympathetic as possible, but had clearly seen the body… or what was left of it. Dropped watermelon, burst water balloon. Another smear on the pavement. Then, eventually, nothing as she rotted away in her grave.

He'd had no immediate family to take him in, so Taylor had been shipped off to a home, his mum's life insurance cover and the compensation from the council put into a trust fund for when he turned 18.

Little did he realise what he'd need the money for, that he'd been dying since the moment he was born; although, he often thought, isn't everyone? Alright, he'd had no idea this… this thing had been inside him all that time, waiting for the right trigger. Another account waiting for him to hit the right age, an unwelcome investment that would mature and see his cash get sunk into various private procedures which would do nothing but slow the whole process down.

Those doctors, their eyes. The lies they'd told, the things they'd hidden. Had it all been about the money they were making from him? It couldn't have been, surely…

In the end he'd taken it out of their hands, when he couldn't see the point of any more tests, any more experimental treatments. They had no more clue than when they'd first started, that much was becoming clear to him the more time that passed.

Passed on, passed away…

Time.

Taylor had discharged himself and used what was left of his savings to get himself the fuck away from them and their meddling. For him to be able to enjoy the time he had left, hopefully, do some of the things he'd always wanted to do before it was too late. Savouring those moments. There were so many books still to read, for example… *too* many for him to digest in a dozen lifetimes. It was something he'd talked about with Anne a lot, about how there were never enough hours in the day to do the things that made you happy.

'People have to work, have to make a living,' she'd said with a smile, the same smile that lit up his heart, made it sing. 'You can't live on fresh air!'

It was true, but at the same time there should be more to life than simply slaving away to earn a crust. He couldn't get her to see that without explaining why he thought it, and he didn't want to ruin that smile. Didn't want to see pity there, see tears in her eyes because she knew she was going to lose him.

Everybody loses everyone else at some point, he reminded himself now – brain only half-working, the onset of the sickness incredible. How he wished he'd stayed with her, spent more time with her. Spent, again, like it was some kind of account you paid into or drew out of. No, you didn't get a choice with time – couldn't pay more of it in, get any of it back again. It marched on, no matter how much you tried to stop it. Even for him.

It marched on and it was also running out. He could feel it in every fibre of his being. Taylor was unknotting, falling apart. Had to do something fast.

Didn't want Anne taking pity on him, but he was lucky that family had when they'd spotted him by the side of the road, using the dry stone wall for support. They'd pulled up in their people carrier, kids in the back – one of each, about six and eight – and offered him a lift. Well, it had been the husband really who'd offered; the woman looked less sure, especially as he climbed into the spare seat at the rear.

The children, who'd been arguing until he clambered in, both fell silent with Taylor in close proximity. He'd heard their parents in the front whispering, the woman arguing with the husband. But Taylor had kept quiet – he just needed to get closer. Needed to get to people.

As they'd careered down country lanes, though, seemingly taking an age to reach any kind of civilisation, his condition had worsened drastically, wheezing every time he took a breath. He saw the *husband's* eyes flashing in the rear view this time, concern mounting.

'Are… are you okay back there? You don't sound very—'

Taylor had held his hand up, but that hadn't calmed the man at all. He'd be fine if they could get him nearer. He just needed to… Then the coughing. At first a tickle, building into something that sounded like he'd smoked 100 a day for years. The children had started crying, the wife openly shouting at the man to stop.

'It… it's not… You can't catch it,' Taylor had tried to tell them. But it looked like he'd reached the end of the line with them anyway. Do not pass Go, do not collect £200… Just like in those board games he'd played with Anne.

Do not pass… Pass away, pass over…

Pass *time*.

Round and round the board, marching on, moving the little metal pieces. Or landing on a snake, taking you down and down, rather than up a ladder.

It had definitely been the end when he'd done what he'd done. They'd forced his hand and he'd had to see, to check. Not that he would have… Not the children, but he was so desperate. Wasn't in his right mind and he needed to be certain. The husband and wife weren't suitable, he'd made sure.

But he hadn't passed anything…

Over, away… on. Hadn't passed anything *on* to them. He'd been telling the truth, though they didn't believe him – especially when he sneezed all that blood onto their car window. The wife had put her handkerchief over her mouth then, begging the husband to get back in after he'd grabbed Taylor and dragged him out of the vehicle, onto the side of the road where they'd found him. Where they were probably wishing they'd left him, instead of being Good Samaritans.

Would they call the authorities? he wondered as he watched the car speed off into the distance, a trail of black from the exhaust in its wake. Even if they could get a signal out here, he doubted it. But he couldn't take the chance. Couldn't risk being banged up somewhere now, isolated from everyone and everything. Couldn't take the chance that someone in that station or jail would be suitable. And anyway, he'd be trapped. Taylor needed to be free, unfettered, able to go about his business.

Best just to carry on, 'march' on, cross-country, over the fields, aim for that population centre. And for someone who was running out of time, that trek seemed to last forever. A lifetime in itself, stretching out ahead of him. But oh, he'd been so grateful when he crested that ridge, saw the mall there on the outskirts of town. A mall meant people, and he wanted – *needed* – to be surrounded by people.

Which was how he'd ended up here, those last few miles virtual agony for him. He knew he was getting closer, the more folk he saw. It was just that they were avoiding him like the plague they thought he was carrying. Stopping, staring, gaping in disgust. But not sticking around long enough for his purposes. You could hardly blame them, they didn't know it wasn't contagious. He'd be lucky if he even made it to the mall without the authorities being called in. Lucky if he made it anywhere at all, at this rate. It was then that he slipped again, lost his footing and had to rely on a pillar box to keep him upright.

'Are you okay, mate?' Someone, a guy in his mid-forties with ruddy cheeks and salt and pepper hair, was asking. Stepping up to him from the back, clearly responding to the fact Taylor was having difficulties. He didn't know the half of it!

Taylor turned and grabbed his arm, before the man could see his face – his hands – properly, before he knew what he was letting himself in for. Sheer terror; that's what Taylor saw in his eyes. Pity, but mixed with revulsion; the need for self-preservation. It didn't matter, this man wasn't suitable, Taylor could tell that now. He let him go and the fellow ran, rather than walked, off.

Wasn't far to go, Taylor told himself – and yes, he could see the doors to the place. Not a big mall, nothing like they had in some locales, but it would do. There would be people, they'd be congregating, and that was all he could ask for in his present condition.

Willing himself forward, willing legs that were turning to jelly – literally – to carry him that little bit further. Taylor just needed more of that commodity he was running out of. Just had to hold on…

Pass on, pass away…

Time.

On, on, to those shiny glass and metal doors. He could make it, he told himself. *Had* to make it, there was no other choice. Well, there was – but he couldn't even bring himself to think about that; never had been able to. It was the reason why he did this, every single time. As much as they all feared him, Taylor feared something else entirely.

Coughing again, fighting for breath. More blood. He could feel it… Didn't have long at all now, before that hand would be on his shoulder. 'Go Directly to Jail' – a different one to the place he feared he'd end up after that family booted him out of their car. Whatever the equivalent was 'down there' for what he'd been doing all this time, the evil things.

No. Not evil. *Necessary.* A bending of the rules, playing the game a different way. It was time… time to roll the dice again, Taylor thought as he staggered through those doors – thankful for the fact that they parted automatically as he approached them.

An accomplishment.

Inside now, and full of more people wasting that precious gift. Wandering idly around looking at window displays: clothes; jewellery; cards for every occasion… 'In Loving Memory'… And *his* memory was indeed going, clouding over like the cataracts that were forming on his eyes, turning everything milky-white.

Technically, he didn't need to see to do what he had to do – but it helped. And while he *could* still see, even through this snowstorm, it was a bonus. See the groups stuffing their faces in the fast food places: burgers, pizza, chicken… Taylor veered left and right. Some of the crowds spotted what was coming towards them and moved out of his way, out of his reach, some couldn't in time. He used those to keep himself upright instead of the inanimate objects outside, clutching at arms, hands, whatever he could get hold of. He couldn't afford to end up on the floor, crawling; it was only a short stop then to that stain, the burst water balloon... melon... whatever.

Then he'd be fucked. Christ!

Just give him one, he only needed *one*. The crowds were panicking, screaming. Thinking he was spreading something. Taylor wouldn't have come here if he was, they wouldn't catch what he had. To his knowledge, he was unique; nobody had what he had in the world. He pitied *them* if they did.

'Get the fuck away...'

'Jesus, did you see his...'

'Shit! He touched me! Shitting shit he...'

You'd get as far away from everything and everybody if it was communicable. But it wasn't, that wasn't why he was here. His diseased fingers brushed against another arm, then another. Boy, girl, man, woman, it didn't matter what sex, what age anymore. Just had to be the right person: suitable.

Then, just when Taylor was beginning to think he would never find one – it happened. That tell-tale shiver as he found the right fit, the perfect candidate. Ironically, it was touching their shoulder that did it. Hand placed there, just as Death was looking to do to Taylor. And he saw, felt, what was going to happen.

A man this time, wearing tracksuit bottoms and a hoodie, who'd abused his body – drinking too much, eating too much rubbish, had lost his job a long time ago and not bothered even trying to find another. Just lived off whatever benefits he could, claiming illness where there wasn't any; now that really made Taylor sick to his stomach, if he wasn't already. This person's life was one long round of daytime television and evenings in the pub. A slug of a human being, and he would pay the ultimate price… in less than six months. The liver would go, kidneys, and eventually everything else would follow suit. Taylor could sense it, through this touch, this connection. Was able to tell exactly how much time this guy had left. Time he wouldn't make *any* use of, didn't – in actual fact – deserve.

So Taylor was going to take it.

Not steal – he hated that word – but borrow, even though the man wouldn't exist to repay it to soon. Borrow, to do something with – as you would do a book from the library. A loan from the bank… Taylor would make more use of it than this person, and it wasn't the first time.

As it began, this transfer of… funds, he started to get his memory back. Began to remember the first time it had happened, with one of those doctors way back when. Someone who'd promised Taylor the world, but knew he didn't really stand a chance because he was running out of time. Time was speeding up in fact, his body decaying. But as the physician had been examining Taylor, the procedure had simply happened; hadn't given him a choice on that occasion. The remaining time that physician had left, mere months thanks to the smoking habit he'd developed when people didn't know it was bad for you, was granted to Taylor.

Poor, sick, *dying* Taylor. Passed on to him, passed over…

Time. Moments to savour…

The surprise in that doctor's eyes as well when it happened, shock as he began to wither, as he ended up being drained. Ended up a puddle on the floor nobody would ever be able to explain. The dropped overripe fruit, the burst water balloon that should have been Taylor's fate. Taylor, who afterwards felt as fit as a fiddle – better than he had been even before he got sick. Before all those tests which drained his money, conducted all those years ago. So many years, back before we even put a man on the moon.

Taylor had accomplished this so many times – not passing on himself, not passing away, but Death passing him over again and again. It was the game they played, although these days near the end the effects had started to accelerate, catch him by surprise as they had done on that road.

But he'd made it, found this sap… Which was exactly what he was doing to him: sapping everything out of the guy. More screams now, in horror, as people ran from the scene. Taylor kept his hat down low, aware there were cameras everywhere, aware security men must have been alerted and were on their way.

They wouldn't catch him, though, he'd had too much practice at this. And he was back to full health, back to his 20-something health, sprinting away from the puddle he'd left of the man back there. The smear on the mall floor that would rot away, finally, to nothing. Not even a DNA test – more tests – would be able to identify the guy after all that.

Taylor was running, finding an emergency exit and barrelling through it, his strength returned to him… with maybe a little extra. No, time wasn't the only thing he'd borrowed: he also had the man's memories now. Knew where he lived, where he kept that wad of cash he'd squirreled away from the drugs he dealt occasionally down the *Rose and Crown* – when he wasn't taking them himself, of course.

Taylor would borrow it, use it to get another car, get away from this town. Live out those months, savour those moments, until it was time to go through the whole thing again: round the board once more, collecting his money. He'd be prepared next time, though, wouldn't get caught on the back foot like this. So he kept saying… Always wondering if he'd slip up someday, if everything would catch him up and he'd have to repay all that he'd borrowed – with interest. Pay that ultimate price. The fine for all those unreturned books.

Taylor ran up one street, down the next – ditching his hat, his coat, going unnoticed among the population. Not stared at because of his deformities. No longer repugnant, especially to the opposite sex… Just no attachments, no more Annes; he couldn't bear that, couldn't bear them to see him change, or for him to see them grow old.

Taylor glanced at his watch, the clock – that had been reset – was ticking again. He was dying again, but he'd staved it off once more. Free to live his life as he saw fit, to do more with it than those he'd taken it from ever would; though he tried not to think about that, about what he had to do to them in order to live. Free to enjoy life, for now, but knowing he was already running out of time.

Knowing, with each footfall, with every corner he turned – round and round the board – that the time wasn't really his. It never had been.

Knowing that he was living on time that was stolen… borrowed.

Yes, that was it – living, as he had done for so long…

On borrowed time.

BIORHYTHMS

'If any thing is sacred the human body is sacred.'
Walt Whitman, *I Sing the Body Electric*.

In the middle of the glade he sat.

Kyle Stanton, crossed-legged, upturned hands on each knee, his eyes closed and his breathing shallow. He moved not one muscle: perfectly still, like some kind of waxwork of himself. He had been in this position since sunup – two, maybe three hours – and would remain just so until the sun descended once again.

He ate very little and always first thing in the morning. Never during the day. The same went for ablutions. Kyle toileted once, just before adopting the lotus. He slept in a cave a short walk from here, for precisely seven hours a night – Kyle had no need for alarm clocks, he simply wakened himself when it was time to get up.

His body, naked to the four winds, was perfectly relaxed. Insects crawled over him: he didn't flinch. Animals came to sniff at him: he took no notice. A rainstorm yesterday had saturated him: he let it. For his mind was focused on other things. His will was strong and a determination to succeed coursed through him.

Kyle had always been curious about his physical form, even at an early age. He lost count of the amount of times he'd examined himself, casting a quizzical eye over his flesh and wondering just what the hell he was, what *this* did and what *that* did. He was extremely lucky to have had such liberal-minded parents, ageing hippies in point of fact (turned joiner and seamstress to earn their livings). They were far from ashamed of their own bodies and happily wandered around the small house they rented with not a stitch on. His mum and dad taught him not to have any hang-ups and for this he would always be grateful. How many people went through their lives not really understanding themselves, embarrassed like Adam and Eve after the apple? Kyle soon came to realise that, like everyone else on the planet, he was a remarkable biological machine. Something unique.

He began to hone his body to physical perfection. At school he excelled in sports. Athletics, football, rugby, tennis, cross-country running… He had medals for them all. Exercise was very important and he made sure he stuck to a workable regimen. But he also developed his mind. With literature, sciences (especially biology), the arts and mathematics. Kyle was the only boy he knew who set himself extra homework, who would visit the library on a regular basis and use up every ticket he had. He was the star pupil, an all-rounder. The powers that be had big plans for him.

However, as he told them in no uncertain terms, his destiny lay in another direction. No diplomas or university degrees for Kyle Stanton. That's not to say he didn't continue with his studies. His fascination with the human body – both inside and out – encouraged him to learn all there was to learn about its functions. And limitations. Starting with *Gray's Anatomy*, he absorbed enormous amounts of information about the structure of the mortal coil. He memorised tremendous chunks of text, diagrams, names. By the end of his self-taught course, he could have passed as a doctor – specialising in any one of a dozen areas – with flying colours.

But his investigations were not limited merely to such dry technical fields. He was far too active an individual to be tied down to a desk all day, every day. In addition to his theoretical research, Kyle also took up more practical pursuits. First he learnt Yoga (hero posture – both upright and reclining – dog posture, extended triangle, sitting spine twist, bridge posture, plough posture, shoulder stand, corpse…), then massage. He became an expert in Reflexology, Shiatsu, Acupressure, Do-in, Osteopathy and so on and so forth. If there were classes being run at the local college, Kyle was there. Indeed, that's how he made his own living at the beginning. The teachers were so impressed with his flair for these relaxation and healing techniques, he was soon being offered a part-time, then later full-time, position instructing others. No one knew their way around the human body like Kyle did.

From here he branched out into legitimate massage parlours and total fitness centres. The loans from the bank were quickly paid back as word spread and his empire grew. This, of course, gave Kyle the freedom to experience even more, travelling to foreign parts to sit at the right hand of adepts. He quickly added Acupuncture to his repertoire, then Polarity Therapy devised by Dr Randolph Stone, an amalgamation of notions from East and West allowing the practitioner to balance up *prana* (as they called the body's energy flow in India), before re-examining Chinese Taoist teachings which posited the view that such energy, here called *chi*, travelled along well-defined circuits – making full use of his extensive knowledge of meridian lines.

Kyle learnt to master his breathing, a trick actually taught to him by one of America's most famous magicians, who used it when he did those impressively dangerous underwater stunts. Kyle could control his bladder and bowels with no effort whatsoever. And he soon regulated his eating and sleeping habits to suit. No food with artificial additives, no preservatives. Just fresh fruit and vegetables, and meat from his own personal reserves. He drank only water; not one drop of alcohol poisoned his system. Plus he refused to smoke, exiting a room if he so much as glimpsed a person lighting up. Accordingly, he took no drugs of any kind, including steroids or 'performance-enhancing' pills. So while the majority of his peers were either stoned or whacked out on E or coke, he settled for the highs that only his particular lifestyle choice could grant him.

For example, Kyle applied what he'd discovered to his activities in the bedroom. His awareness of the main chakras allowed him to practise tantric sex, which sometimes went on for many hours, his 'dabblings' in Taoist traditions giving him the ability to have multiple – or even full-body – orgasms. And, of course, his broad grounding in female as well as male physiology proved invaluable for satisfying whichever partner, *or partners*, he happened to be entertaining that week (Sharon, Brenda, Tony, Natalie, Andrew, Louise... the list went on and on). Along with the monetary wealth he'd accumulated, something his parents never really approved of, this made him one of the most eligible bachelors in the world.

Yet he still wasn't happy. Kyle could walk across hot coals, nap on a bed of six-inch nails (thanks to a fakir he once met in Bombay), swim underwater for almost a quarter of an hour with no compulsion for air, and climb the very highest of mountains without safety ropes or fear of breaking into a sweat. He was the perfect physical specimen; a *superman* in some senses... But it was nowhere near enough for him.

He lacked that certain something. No matter how far he pushed himself, nor how much power he commanded over the various parts of his body, he was still not fully in charge. Kyle would always be at the mercy of his deep-rooted natural instincts.

His dreams were a case in point. Every single night he had to recharge himself, involuntarily yielding to the mercies of sleep and his subconscious. Kyle wanted to be able to shut his body down himself, as a computer does, or go to standby mode like a TV. Re-energise his body and mind without completely going under. Sure, he'd practised entering a coma-like state by reducing his heartbeat – virtually dead to the casual observer – but it was hardly the same thing. It took all of his energy to perform, to dig himself out of the blackness and wake again. He usually needed a good night's sleep just to get over it.

By his account this was symptomatic of the same problem. His body was doing things like this all the time without his permission, without his cognisance or authority. Each time he drank his water or ate his chemical-less food, his body took over. He could do things to help the digestion processes along – stimulating the major reflex points for one – but in the end it passed through him without so much as a by your leave. A please or thank you. The same was true of electrical impulses from his brain. He could tell his hand or his arm or his leg to move, and this would happen almost instantaneously, a fraction of a second between thought and action. But this still made him a puppet, working his own body with strings. He wanted to *be* those strings. To have direct access to the puppet, and not have to communicate through a third party.

It was a ridiculous idea, he told himself. No one in the history of all creation had ever achieved anything like it. But isn't that what people had said about flight? Couldn't be done, no way. If man had been meant to fly, he would have been born with wings. Kyle had already come so far, already achieved so much. To a Stone Age man crawling around in the dirt, the feats he could perform might seem like magic. Jesus, it seemed like magic to most people he knew today.

But that would be nothing compared to holding total sway over his substance. Matter and spirit in absolute unison: there was no telling where it would end. He could even be the next stage in human evolution. Just imagine it! Imagine what he could accomplish...

With this in mind he determined to at least try. His businesses were being run by competent managers, his stocks and shares in capable hands. His sexual partners would be left disappointed for a while – however long it took – but that couldn't be helped. His parents hardly saw him these days anyway, now he'd tucked them away in a nice 'little' naturist complex, and wouldn't miss him all that much.

So, a few weeks shy of his thirtieth birthday, in the middle of August, Kyle set off on his journey of discovery without telling a soul where he was going. He knew the perfect place. A retreat he'd used before when he'd needed to get away from it all. Quiet, tranquil, miles from any hint of civilisation. The best way to concentrate. He took with him no supplies. There was a clear spring that ran nearby and as far as victuals went, he intended to live off the land as much as was humanly possible: just as the primitives had done – he was conscious of the irony. Fruit from the trees, animal meat in the traps he laid; it would suffice at the rate he consumed food.

His birthday came and went. Kyle barely noted the date (soon he would be born again anyway). Time seemed to stand still for him out here as he laboured day in, day out. Attempting to wrestle control of his body from nature itself. He wanted out of the loop, to be completely autonomous. An arbitrary entity disconnected from the rest of his race, from the rest of his world.

Kyle thought about none of this, though. Not the past, not the future. Not even who he was. His mind was engaged in a battle for supremacy.

And today he was about to win.

It happened so quickly, it took Kyle a little by surprise. One second everything was how it had been since his birth, the next it was as if nature suddenly said, 'Okay, you want it so badly, you got it!' and had given up the ghost. Just like that.

A good thing Kyle was ready. *Prepared.* How could he *not* have been after all this waiting, all this fighting? He took on the mantle with glee, filling the emptiness practically straight away.

He was in total control now, and it was fantastic. He could feel the rhythms of his body like never before. He could do anything he wanted. Could *be* anything he wanted…

But wait, he had items to attend to first. Using the information he'd picked up about his body from textbooks and encyclopaedias, he began to take over the many necessary functions he must perform in order to survive. First he had to tap into the labyrinthine network that sent messages to his brain – take stock of the hundred million neurones in there, the branches of each one connecting to thousands of others in kind. Like an old-fashioned telephone operator, he must plug in lines here, then switch to there. Kyle had to get the nervous system up and running again in order to receive messages from around the body and dish out his own instructions manually, firing electrical pulses along the neurones at four-hundred kilometres an hour. Within seconds he was getting reports from a multitude of different locations at once. Kyle had to deal with them all, and fast.

Best to start with the heart and lungs initially. Keep the heart beating to stay alive and the lungs pumping air in and out. Kyle had to maintain a rhythm of at least sixty to eighty beats of his heart muscle a minute whilst in this state (the figure would go up eventually when he moved). Each beat had to start off in a small knot of tissue – the sinoatrial node – in the rear wall of the upper-right atrium, which generated low-intensity electrical signals that passed along nerve-like tracts, stimulating muscle fibres as they went, to end up at the bottom of the right atrium – the atrioventricular node, located between the atria and ventricles. After delaying the impulse slightly, Kyle then had to relay the signals along a bulky conducting tract, the bundle of His, and through its left and right branches to splinter again into a tangle of fibres in the walls of the ventricles. Once each surge of electrical energy from the sinoatrial node arrived at these muscle fibres they contracted, causing the heart to pump blood – through hundreds of miles of linked arteries, veins and capillaries, eight to nine pints shunted around the body each minute, 75 millilitres a beat, carrying oxygen and nutrients to Kyle's tissues and removing any waste products. Kyle had to keep the blood flowing to his heart to supply the cardiac muscle with the oxygen and glucose needed to remove waste products from there. In addition, he had to constantly create new blood cells to replace those that were dying off (on average two hundred billion each day). No blood, no blood flow to the heart.

At the same time it was necessary to supervise the extraction of oxygen from the air, sucked in through his nose and mouth. Inside his ribcage, he had to direct his sponge-like lungs to remove the oxygen so it could be transferred into his blood supply, the superfluous carbon dioxide taken from the blood to be expelled when he breathed out again: a process usually handled automatically by his nervous system. Each time he inhaled, Kyle followed the air down the trachea, kept open by cartilage rings, heating it as it went. He then ushered it down either the left or right bronchus, before pushing it into one of his lungs. And, of course, he had to keep the inner lining of his pulmonary system moistened with secretions of mucus from epithelial cells, and make certain the cilia moved said mucus along so it could remove any unwanted dust particles that had accidentally found their way into his lungs when he took a breath. But that wasn't all. Each time he did take in air, Kyle was obliged to work the muscles in his chest to elevate and distend the ribcage and contract the diaphragm to increase the pleural cavity, so his lungs could work properly in the first place.

Now what? Oh yes, more major work to be done with his digestive system. Although he hadn't eaten for a few hours or so, his body was still processing the fuel. He had to finish breaking it down using a mixture of enzymes and hydrochloric acid (gastric juice), then the partially digested food (now technically known as chyme) had to be passed carefully through the pylorus sphincter into the upper-portion of the small intestine, the duodenum, where secretions from the pancreas neutralised the acid and bile was added to break down fats. From here the digestion process must continue on into the small and large intestine proper, and nutrients absorbed into the body, the unusable residue being fed into the colon (where most of the water was absorbed into the bloodstream) before passing into the rectum just prior to excretion.

Meanwhile, using his kidneys, he had to filter water and other soluble molecules from his blood, casting aside any unnecessary waste matter and toxins to be released through his urine: the final incarnation of the spring water he'd drunk. But before that could happen, urine had to be created in the kidneys by filtrating plasma, the liquid in which blood cells were suspended, and fed down the ureters into the bladder in peristaltic waves, to be stored up in preparation for discharge.

As for his liver, residing at the top of the abdominal cavity, underneath the diaphragm, this organ had to be appropriated to ship nutrients to wherever they were needed and perform other vital metabolic processes, such as taking glucose from the blood coming from his intestines then transforming it into carbohydrate glycogen, put aside in reserve (to be converted back into glucose when levels in the blood happened to fall). Kyle had to fathom how to convert the amino acids and fats stored there into glucose, and how to form urea from waste proteins and amino acids, *and* mass-produce key molecules (like phospholipids and lipoproteins) that fashioned cell membranes. This organ was also utilised to generate digestive enzymes to be introduced into the small intestine and last, but not least, to warm the blood that passed through its internal regions which helped sustain a constant body temperature.

Kyle did all this and more, thousands of tasks every second: handling production of cells (for skin, muscle, the major organs… for his brain) as well as maintaining the fifty thousand billion already in operation; seeing to the replacement of dead tissue; the stimulation of saliva in the mouth; hair and nail growth; the preservation of his bones; organising the vital chemical reactions throughout his form; draining off excess fluid from tissues using the lymphatic system; shifting material about the body, in and out, up and down, left and right. Even ensuring that sperm production continued on apace in his testes – a thousand every second…

But it was unbelievably hard work. Kyle had no idea it would be so tiring, that taking over all those automated functions would demand his utmost attention, and would continue to do so forever. He started to worry… *How will I cope? What if I forget to do something important? One mistake and I'm dead!* And he hadn't even begun to think about things like getting up and walking, or somehow keeping all these plates in the air while he slept. Sleep, hah! Forget about that for the time being.

Kyle tried to compose himself. These random thoughts were no good. Too distracting. It would all become easier the more he did it. Soon it would be like… Like what, *second nature?*

But he was right. It was becoming simpler with every duty he performed. Kyle proceeded to lose his doubts, his inhibitions. He *could* cope, no problem. The more ambitious stuff would come later on. For now Kyle allowed himself a small congratulations on achieving what he set out to do. He was at last in total contr—

Kyle hadn't noticed the invader until it was too late. A virus. A common cold virus, brought on by sitting through that rainstorm yesterday. Kyle ordered his antibodies to intercept, but even before they could set to work he began getting strange signals from his nervous system. A tingling sensation in…

In his nose.

He couldn't help himself, he had to relieve the pressure and sneezing was the only way to do it. The rush of air threw him completely, leaving his nose at precisely 100 mph, sending him into a panic as he felt himself wobbling backwards. Kyle endeavoured to compensate, tried to work his muscles in teams of 20 or 30 at a time, contracting the meat in his arms to move the bones and put out his hand.

Kyle opened his eyes without comprehending the enormity of what he'd done. The light streaming in through his conjunctivae, corneas, irises, pupils, lenses, vitreous humour, and optic nerves overwhelmed him, sabotaging any attempt to close his eyelids again. He sought to process over a million colours: blues, greens, reds… all bouncing into his brain far too quickly for him to differentiate, while he struggled to keep his heart, lungs, liver and the rest of his organs working properly. Kyle felt himself shouting out, a *natural* human reaction. But disastrous in his case, forcing him to draw in more breath, to change the tension in his vocal chords (tightening them to scream), to trouble his larynx, his tongue, needlessly – distracting him further.

The sound vibrated off his helix, tragus, concha and travelled down the external acoustic meatus on both sides of his head. Inside his ears it passed through the tympanum, stretched taut across the ear canal, caused the malleus (hammer) to strike the incus (anvil) – each bone no bigger than a grain of rice – taking the vibrations down to the stapes, fenestra ovalis, zipping through receptors in the cochlea and up through the acoustic nerve into his brain. More sensory input to collate.

By now the pads on his fingers were touching the grass, transmitting yet more data directly to his bulging grey matter – using up more than its fair share of energy firing overburdened neurones. His arm buckled under the weight of his body. His palm connected with the ground, sending shockwaves through his tendons, brachialis, biceps brachii and up into his pectoral and trapezius muscles.

Kyle needed to cough, but was having difficulty regulating his breathing. Saliva production fell and the dryness in his throat caused him to choke.

Hold it together, he told himself, *you can do it…*

But he couldn't. He knew he couldn't. He was losing his grasp.

Kyle's body cried thick, watery tears. Blood commingled with sweat and he had to release it through his pores or risk drowning in his own juices.

He concentrated on his lungs and heart again, sacrificing other vital systems. All he could think of was to keep that muscle pumping, to keep breathing.

To stay alive.

But now his eyes were open, he was compelled to try and focus. Using all of his might, Kyle tilted his head and looked down upon himself, finally flipping the inverted image projected onto his retina.

His body was losing coherence. His skin was rippling like washing hung out to dry. Blood was escaping down his nostrils. His bladder and sphincter nerve both went at the same time, expelling the waste he'd been so dutifully processing before – and 25 grams of dead cells at the same time. Mislaying what little strength it had left, his arm folded and he finally fell backwards. Kyle's balance was shot. His knees pointed up at the sky a second before flopping down, as if his legs were made of rubber. Kyle felt his skin sliding off – the epidermis, dermal papillae, subcutaneous fat – cells disbanding, leaving him. Striking because they hated conditions under Kyle's new management. The matrix of his bones was collapsing, his brain liquefying. His kidneys shut down, followed soon after by his liver.

Kyle fought to breathe, but his lungs were the next to go. His heart beat slowly in his chest; he didn't have much time left before it turned to mulch.

I'm sorry, he 'thought'. *I'm so sorry… Won't you take me back? PLEASE!*

He no longer wanted the responsibility that came with command. He'd proved himself unworthy of it. Thought he could do so easily what *She* did for him, without realising he was still *Her* creation – just like everything else. That if *She* abandoned him, it was all over. (*She* had many different names, this archaic matriarch, this parthenogenetic parent – some ancient, some modern – many guises for many different cultures, in the East and in the West; though *She* was always credited with the same accomplishments.)

Kyle's eyesight had gone. All he could feel was his heartbeat slowly ticking down the seconds until his death.

And at the very point of nothingness, as the final beat came – when he himself ultimately gave up the ghost – and he was gradually absorbed into the earth, his biodegradable marrow feeding the soil, he experienced a devastating guilt.

But he also knew great relief. Relief and exaltation.

For he could feel his biorhythms again, this time on an unprecedented scale. The grass growing in the fields, the animals coming up to sniff at his remains, the swaying movement of the trees. Turning every living thing, turning the *whole* world, into his body. The universe into his soul.

As *She* kindly – and graciously – forgave him his trespasses.

As *Mother Nature* welcomed her lost sheep back into the fold…

FAÇADES

Ah, visitors! Please sit down. Over there, just opposite. That's right. Sorry if I seem a little pushy. You see, sometimes it gets so lonely in here. It's nice to see different faces. How did I come to be here? I don't think you'd believe me if I told you. Oh, very well, if you insist. But remember, every word of this is true...

I can recall the week it happened vividly in my mind, even though it was so very long ago. I was sleeping in the spare bedroom because Jill and I had had words. It suited me fine. I couldn't bear to be around her anymore, let alone share the same bed.

It still puzzles me how a marriage can fall apart so quickly. One minute you're walking down the beach, hand in hand, whispering to each other that this love will last forever. The next thing you know, there's shouting and arguing every time you're in a room alone together. Bitter, callous things are said on both sides. Hurtful, personal sideswipes you can never take back even if you wanted to; and most of the time you don't.

Anyway, suffice to say our union had reached an all-time low – in private, at any rate. To the outside world we were the perfect couple. We had to keep up the pretence for the sake of our respective careers. I was close to promotion at the firm where I worked, and Jill's job at the gallery meant that she had to attend plenty of what she called 'New Talent Bashes'. And guess who had to go with her to hang off her arm?

We'd both become very good actors by this stage, though. Those painted-on smiles seemed like second nature. We never left home without them. We were wearing outrageously false grins that Saturday night, in fact, Jill's big night: the opening of Ellis Blare's show.

Though we arrived together, shaking hands and greeting guests, we soon parted company and drifted off into the crowds to mingle. Or at least Jill did.

For my part I studied the work of this talented new sculptor my spouse had 'discovered'. In the main exhibition area there were several pieces on display. I found them all intriguing, but disturbing at the same time. The figures carved from rough stone with angular features seemed to be shouting at me. Some were kneeling, others standing with their arms outstretched, still others crouching or lying on their sides. But all had that open-mouthed look of shock etched into their faces.

'Fascinating, aren't they?' said a voice from behind me. I nearly spilt my glass of wine on the statue in front. Then I turned to see a woman standing mere feet away. Never in my life had I been so completely captivated by a member of the opposite sex.

Her face was smooth and delicate, with round cheek bones and soft, pink lips heightening her appearance. There was not a hint of make-up – she didn't need any. And all this was framed by curling brunette hair which dangled in spring-like rivulets.

She fixed me with a curious stare, those deep grey pools drawing me in. Pleading with me to come closer.

And I did so, but just a step or two.

Only when she looked over my shoulder at the statue did I risk a glance at the rest of her. My eyes travelled over her body like an explorer charting unknown territory. The thin green dress she wore accentuated her curves and she held herself upright with such elegance, I thought for one brief moment I might be in the presence of royalty.

'Did you hear what I said?' That voice again. It sang to me in angelic tones. Apologies for being so dramatic, but I'm just trying to express how I felt. You see, I never would have thought it possible to become obsessed with a woman in the space of a few seconds. But there I was – hopelessly so. What's more I was glad.

'Yes,' I answered finally. 'Yes, they're quite remarkable. In fact I don't think I've ever seen anything quite like them.'

'Do you know much about art?' she enquired.

'My wife runs the gallery. You pick up a few things.' I regretted the words almost as soon as I'd said them. Why bring Jill into this? The woman's face showed only the barest indication of surprise, so quickly I tried to gloss over my last sentence. 'For instance, these reflect a distinct influence of Epstein and Brancusi in terms of material and certain elements of form. Yet the figures are closer to cubist paintings with all those flat angles. But the face, ah now the face is Bacon through and through.'

She smiled. 'You know more than you're letting on Mr...?'

'Todd. Peter Todd. And you are?'

The woman held out her hand and I shook it. The grip was soft and firm at the same time. 'Ellis Blare,' she said matter of factly. 'And actually, Peter, this face – all of the faces – are based on the work of Munch, not Bacon. Although I can see where you'd get that impression.'

So this was the mystery sculptor we were here to honour, I thought.

'I saw "The Scream" many years ago and haven't been able to get it out of my head since. I've been trying to capture its disturbing nature in a three-dimensional form. Don't know if I've quite pulled it off yet, though. What do you think?'

My face was turning red and I didn't know quite what to say. 'I-I think you're an exceptional artist, Ellis.'

'Why, thank you.' Again I was being drawn to her, closer and closer. I could feel the energy between us, building until I feared it would blow us apart. I find it hard to describe the effect Ellis had on me, but in my vain, blinkered, mind I thought perhaps she might feel the same way.

'Ellis. Ellis?' Jill's screech cut through the moment like a shark's fin through water. I snapped out of my bemused daze to see her trotting up to us. She linked her hand through my arm, and I wished the ground would just open up and consume her.

'I see you've met my other half,' she said, the thespian's smile still intact.

'Yes. Peter was just telling me how much he admired my work.' There was an edge to what Ellis said which went completely over Jill's head.

'Wonderful. Listen, there are some prospective buyers you really should meet…' Jill let go of me, grabbed Ellis by the arm, and tried to usher her away. For a second Ellis stood her ground. I could tell there and then she was a woman who liked to do things her way.

'Well, it was nice talking to you, Peter,' she said.

'Likewise,' I replied.

Then she leaned in and whispered almost inaudibly, 'Tomorrow. Noon. *The White Dove.*'

And she was away. Off to confront her adoring public.

I was shocked and amazed at what I'd just heard. Had this extraordinary woman just lined up a rendezvous with me? Or did I imagine the whole thing? Had I wanted it so badly I filled in the blanks myself?

Alternatively, would I get to *The White Dove* only to find it had been some kind of joke? It was a chance I was prepared to take, or regret this inaction for the rest of my days.

That night I could think of nothing but Ellis. All the way home as Jill ranted on, in the house as we prepared for bed, even in my dreams I saw her face. I couldn't shake her and those hours until noon crept by so slowly for me.

Jill didn't ask where I was going that day. She didn't much care so long as I was out of her proximity. I arrived at *The White Dove* – a delightful lunch spot in the centre of the city – around 11:30, filled with anticipation, but half expecting humiliation.

The clock worked its way agonisingly round to noon as I nursed my coffee. Every time the door went, I swivelled in my chair, desperate to see her. Not Ellis. Never Ellis.

At half past twelve I decided to leave. She had been playing me for a fool. An artist's prank gone too far. Perhaps she got her kicks from propositioning married men this way.

Then, just as I was about to get up, there was that voice again. A timbre that could light up my very worst day: 'Sorry I'm late. I got held up in traffic.'

She looked even more perfect than the day before. Once again I felt the nerves take hold of me. I was a wreck around her and she knew it.

'Peter, relax. Have you ordered yet?'

I coughed. 'Er... no. Look, I've never done this kind of thing before. I'm a happily married man.'

Ellis looked into my eyes. Somehow she could tell I was lying – on both counts as it happened. She knew it. I knew it.

'Would you like me to leave?'

'No. *God, no!*' I clutched at her hand over the table.

She laughed. 'Good, because I'm very hungry. Let's eat, shall we?'

Over lunch we talked. I don't really remember what about; my head was somewhere else. I do remember I didn't want it to stop. But the next hour flew by much faster than the last half a day had. Time's cruel like that.

When the meal was finished, she said, 'If you're really interested in my work, perhaps you'd like to see my studio flat. You know, where it all happens.'

It seemed to me as though every drop of saliva in my mouth had dried up. I was forced to nod because I couldn't get any words out.

And soon we were there, in Ellis' capacious chambers. The rooms were all completely white with mock-classical pillars stretching up to plate glass skylights. Sculptures were scattered around in various states of readiness. Some looked as though they'd been molested by a pneumatic drill while others were more recognisably human in shape. Tools, chisels and hammers carpeted the floor around them.

'This place is amazing,' I said, genuinely taken aback by the studio.

'I'm glad you like it. Your wife's paying the rent.' I didn't know if it was meant as a joke or not, so I ignored the comment altogether. The last thing I wanted to think about was Jill.

I strolled down past the first couple of stone carvings. They were quite accurate representations of the human form, nothing like the ones I'd seen at her exhibition. But they were all still screaming.

'These are very good,' I commented.

'What, those? They're just a starting point. I haven't begun to make them my own yet. It'll take days – months – of work with the chisel to get them looking like my other pieces.'

I wanted to tell her I preferred them the way they were, but thought better of it. She knew what she was doing. People wanted something different, that's why her sculptures were selling so well.

'Perhaps one day you might like to pose for me, Peter. I'll make you famous.' She laughed a little, and when I turned I knew I could resist her no longer.

'I'd like that,' I said. 'I'd like that a lot.'

I was like a puppy seeking the attentions of its master, eager to serve and craving attention. Ellis responded with her deceptively strong hands, honed by years of moulding stone to her will. She pulled me close and we kissed. It was unlike anything I've ever experienced, before or since. I was totally lost in her. But the funny thing was, I never wanted to be found again.

*   *   *

After that first encounter we were almost inseparable. Ellis had an incredible appetite and I ended up doing things I'd never dreamt possible – even in my wayward college years. I was fervent yet obedient, and in return the sculptress sated my wildest desires.

I shunned work and hardly ever returned home to Jill. In fact, I don't think I saw her all that week. However, on one occasion she did turn up unexpectedly at the studio. I just had time to hide in the bedroom before Ellis opened the door.

They talked about how well her pieces were selling and would she like to put on another show in a few months' time, with a view to leaving some sculptures there permanently? Jill sounded perfectly normal. Actually, no. She sounded happier than usual. She didn't miss me – didn't need my company until the next engagement cropped up – so she couldn't care less where I was. I know I loathed her, but part of me couldn't help feeling hurt.

Eventually Ellis got rid of her and we continued our afternoon of pleasure. I'm not being too frank, am I? Only it's just that every minute of that week is still alive for me. I play the sequences over and over in my imagination when I'm alone. It's the only thing that keeps me sane.

I went over to Ellis' studio for a final time on the Friday. It had only been six days since I'd met her, but this lady had turned my worthless life upside down. I ached for her. She was like my secret addiction. Whenever we were parted, which admittedly wasn't for long, I went into withdrawal.

We spent the day together, though she made me wait a whole two hours in the morning while she worked. I simply sat and watched her slice away at the stone. I was happy enough.

It was only after our last coupling that I found out who she really was. We lay in each other's arms and suddenly, out of nowhere, she said: 'I'm bored with this!'

At first I thought I'd misheard her.

'W-What do you mean?' I asked, trying – and failing – to retain my composure.

'I'm tired of you,' she stated. Just like that, as if the last week had meant nothing to her. She might as well have killed me there and then.

I couldn't believe what she was saying. It had to be a joke. 'Ellis, what are you talking about?' Reaching up I began to stroke her long curling hair, feeling it trickle through my fingers.

'I'm tired of you. It's time,' she said without a trace of emotion.

And suddenly I felt something move in her hair. My imagination, I thought. It had to be! But no, because the thing nestling in her locks chose that moment to bite me. It ripped through my tendons and clamped down with teeth as tight as pincers.

There was something sliding around my forearm. I tried to yank the limb free, but when I did vast fountains of blood spurted from my wounds.

I scrambled back on the bed to observe this phenomenon. Ellis had something alive in her hair. *How could this be?*

I soon realised my mistake when the first head rose from the top of her scalp. The flowing curls had changed right before my eyes – into a mass of hissing serpents.

They slithered and coiled over her crown, each one looking directly at me with cold, black pupils. Their tongues darted in and out like miniature forks of lightning.

Ellis smirked.

I felt as if I were dreaming of her again, only this time the dream had turned into a surreal nightmare. Then I remembered the pain in my hand and knew it was all true.

I swore. I don't recall what I said, but I definitely swore at the top of my voice. Those expletives were the last words I would ever speak.

Ellis was altering herself. The face I had worshipped became hollow and sunken. The so-smooth skin was now scaly and mottled. Her teeth shrank into tiny, pointed things, lining a mouth that was no longer full, but disgustingly slimy and reptilian.

I know I should have looked away, but it all happened so fast. Before I could run I caught her eyes. Again I was transfixed, though in a different way than before. They were still beautiful, except now they glowed with a fearsome power.

I opened my mouth to scream. Nothing came out. My body was contracting, hardening. I was paralysed; my face stuck in that position as I tumbled onto the quilt.

In my curled-up state I saw what was happening to the rest of me, from the torso downwards. My flesh was taking on a rough and dirty appearance. My legs seized up with cramps as they turned to stone in front of me.

It was like I was being encased in a thick membrane. Unable to breathe or even move, but still conscious of what was going on around me.

I felt myself being lifted. Though I must have weighed at least ten times my normal twelve stone, Ellis carried me easily. Because, as I had discovered to my horror, she was not like you or I. She never had been.

Ellis set me down next to one of the other statues. I could see her eyeing me up, examining me, deciding what to do next.

I don't know whether she realised I was still alive – it probably wouldn't have mattered if she had – but she began working on me straight away.

Every blow of the hammer, every chunk she chiselled off, every brush of glasspaper was excruciating agony for me. I felt it all, the many alterations she made to me. And I fathomed out now why she had to tamper with her work, had to turn each piece into a hideous carving. She couldn't leave the figures as they were because someone might recognise them. You see, once they had all been men just like me... Possibly even women too, who knows?

It took her over two months to get me just right and, though I've never looked upon my new self, I saw enough of the others to realise my own parents wouldn't know me now.

During that time I witnessed more men coming to her studio. Hapless suitors she'd put under her spell. None ever lasted more than a few days. I tried to warn them, but they wouldn't listen.

So that's how I came to be on display here at my wife's gallery. I see Jill every other day. Occasionally she even comes and sits right there. She has a new man in her life now. I see him when he brings her to work. They look so happy together. Like we used to be before… I guess she figured when I didn't come back that I'd run off with another woman, or been mugged and beaten to death in some alleyway: a John Doe that could never be identified. Either way she wasn't about to come looking for me. I wonder what she'd say if she knew?

Oh no, don't leave. *Please* stay a while longer… But then, I don't suppose *you* can hear me either, can you? Just like those poor blokes I tried to warn. All you can see is a statue. One of Ellis Blare's masterpieces. I sometimes wonder why I haven't died yet. Maybe I never will.

All right, go if you must. It doesn't matter anyway. Here come some more visitors. Please sit down. Over there, just opposite. That's right. Sorry if I seem a little pushy.

You see, sometimes it gets so lonely in here.

THE ESCAPED

How long has it been since his escape? he wonders.

Ten days maybe? *It could be ten hours, ten months or even ten minutes…* No, longer than minutes. Night had found him more than once, surely. And cascading visions have blurred his senses. He remembers snow; footprints and the trickle of blood from his nose, red on white. The blobs growing wings, taking on form. Taking…

The 'first' night he spent on the streets. He ventured into homeless territory, down the backstreets and alleyways. Tried to lose himself amongst the non-entities, thinking that nobody, not even his pursuers, would recognise him here. He attempted to blend in. But they could spot a newcomer from a mile away, those who lived here permanently. Someone who didn't belong, might not even belong with their species anymore. That same look again, they all had it. Could they see, could they tell he was no longer like them? Could they…? There were so many questions they wanted to ask of him, he could sense it. Who was he? Where had he come from? What had he *seen?*

But they didn't care for interlopers much, these people, as he soon found out when he tried to warm his hands against their barrel-lit flame.

'Hey, what the fuck do you think you're doing?' said the tramp with the tangled beard, poking the fire as if daring it to burn him.

'Yeah, get lost,' shouted another – this one just a bundle of rags moulded into human form. A woman nearby guarding her precious trolley of tin cans gave him the evil eye.

He was cold, that was all, the flames like a four-course meal placed in front of a starving man. He'd kept on shambling towards them, silent pleas forming on his lips. Movement to the left of him, another pair of figures hidden beneath cardboard boxes, a man and a woman clinging together out of necessity rather than anything approaching love.

Another cry: 'What's the matter? Can't you talk, you dumb shit?'

'Leave him alone!' This one the cardboard woman, a single voice of compassion in a chaos of hostility. 'Look, he's backward.'

'Is that it, are you backward?'

Was he? He could move backwards, forwards, in any direction he wished. Except one.

As he came closer to the fire, and the light, they noticed his shaved scalp. Could see the ragged marks. The stitches. It was then that the attack began. Blows raining down on him; not just fists either, but sticks, stones – which might break his bones. It reminded him of the sensations he'd felt in the chamber… and afterwards. Sometimes dull, sometimes biting, tearing great chunks out of him. But in spite of all this he still had one thing to thank the homeless for. As he'd tumbled into the barrel, knocking it over and burning himself badly, they'd given him his new name: Christened him with this baptism of fire.

'Fucking Headcase!' the bearded bum screamed at him.

He'd scrambled to his feet, running off into the darkness again: his retreat a survival instinct, just like his escape from *them*.

Could you ever truly escape?

So he'd passed his inaugural evening of freedom collapsed in a heap, groaning. Teeth loosened by a lucky punch to the jaw. He'd later yanked one offending molar out, gripping it between two fingers and pulling, blood swiftly filling the gap and pouring out over his bottom lip. Jesus, he'd been a mess.

He hardly slept a wink, only briefly travelling to that other world of strange shapes and colours, of blurred contours and knife-edges. Of meat and flesh. Of probes and dissection. Of unimaginable agony. A gnawing pain that simply wouldn't go away, regardless of whether he was waking or asleep. A pain much greater than the one those tramps had inflicted upon him. Something on the inside not the outside. Something placed there perhaps?

Where had he been when they'd taken him? If only he could recall… On a deserted highway? At home? Home… Did he even have a home? Strange faces, beings with no mouths, hands all over him. And lights, he saw the bright beams just before waking up in a cold sweat, wasted and dribbling into the gutter.

The next day, he moved on. Headcase had to keep moving. Had to get away because he knew his keepers would follow him. They needed him, like a junky craves the needle. No, don't talk – don't even *think* – about the needles. He probably headed south, though he had no compass to speak of, only a mental one. And although he definitely should have moved away from the population centres, he stayed where there were people, where there were crowds to conceal his presence. Out in the open, alone, he'd be a sitting target.

The clothes he'd been wearing when he escaped were now filthy, and Headcase stank. In a gents' toilets somewhere, he made a bungled attempted to snatch someone's wallet: a small man who didn't look like he had much fight in him. Headcase had been wrong. And thinking:

Don't struggle… please don't struggle… I won't hurt you… just please… Jesus, why do you have to make so much noise? I only want your money… Oh God, please be quiet… they'll hear you… they'll find me… Shut…SHUT THE FUCK UP!!!

The man kicked up such a fuss he was forced to abandon the operation altogether and run for his very life. The police would be called, and then *they* would be informed. Their agents were everywhere. *They* would come. He had to get away as fast as he could.

Headcase took refuge inside a cinema, the spacious foyer a confusion of noise and patchwork posters. Of glass booths, like the ones encircling the chamber. He looked up, dizzy, the domed roof spinning slightly. It reminded him of *their* descent. Shafts of blanched alabaster all around him, blinding him. He would see plenty soon enough. Somehow, he managed to make it through the inner doors without drawing too much attention to himself. Resting against a lemon-yellow wall, he took in long, deep breaths. The oxygen tasted acidic; its bitterness vile.

One or two people gave him funny glances, but he ignored them. There were other things on his mind. Headcase picked a black, lacquered door – Screen 3 – and pushed inside. The film had already started, was well into its storyline in fact, a flickering image projected onto the blank canvas ahead of him. The hero and his girl were involved in a car chase. Headcase couldn't tell who was the quarry and who was the prey, but he could definitely relate.

Shadowed heads were dotted about inside the theatre, tilted back, eyes glued to the film: watching, seeing. Choosing a seat nearest to him, he collapsed into its welcome embrace.

Now he did sleep, in spite of the pain. He saw the things that his memory couldn't let him erase. Saw the creatures again, the entities that had taken him. Blue, hairless – some had two eyes, some three – all intense and pupil-less. *And God, that fucking noise they made…*

They leaned over him as they wheeled him along.

There were screams. Some his own, some coming from other subjects they'd liberated. They spoke to each other without words, nods of the head enough to send their signals, mottled skin taut and stretched to breaking point over jutting bones. They monitored everything using devices he'd never seen before in his life. But he'd seen the results of their experiments, seen what had been inflicted on his 'companions'… Could he really let them do that to him?

The answer was no. Mind swimming from the drugs they had forced into him, he climbed off the trolley. One of the creatures, hideous and large, lunged at him. Headcase—

There was a hand on his shoulder, shaking him. It roused him from his sleep.

'Can I see your ticket?'

Headcase gaped at the cinema attendant blankly.

'I said, can I see your ticket please…?'

On the screen the main protagonist had entered a rough-looking bar filled with thugs. Rock music played in the background, and he could feel the lyrics talking to him: telling him things.

You're already changing, yes it's true, there's simply nothing you can do… Oh you can run but you can't hide, nor stem the flowing tide,' blasted the soundtrack. *'There'll come a time when you must choose, oh will you win or will you lose?'*

Headcase pointed at the screen as several of the thugs in the bar turned, miming the words. The music speeded up at this point, the singers sounding like they were on helium, or those chipmunks from the cartoons he used to watch with…

'*Will-you-win-or-will-you-lose will-you-win-or-will-you-lose will-you-win-or-will-you-lose will-you-win-or-will-you-lose?*' After this the words became indecipherable, barely audible.

Headcase shivered, pulling himself tight into a ball, drawing up his legs.

'I said could I *see* your ticket?' the attendant repeated. 'I want to see…'

I want to see…

This was met with a shake of the head. 'You don't have one, do you? All right, that's it, come with me.' The man grabbed hold of his arm and tried to wrench him from the seat. Headcase resisted.

'Come on, don't make things more difficult for yourself.'

More difficult? How could they be any more *difficult than they were already?*

On the screen there was a close-up of the back of the barman's head; when he turned, his mouth was missing, and he stared out at Headcase with those fierce, inhuman eyes. They were watching him, watching them.

Headcase tried to cry out and pushed the attendant aside. As he climbed the backs of seats, he looked over his shoulder. The movieworld seemed to be seeping into reality, the bar extending itself into the theatre. The thugs spilled into the cinema, pushing through the rubber screen, changing as they did so. Feelers entered with them: tentacles of vision winding into the room.

They were after him, desperate to take him back to that place. Stumbling into the aisle, he ran between tiny lights on the floor, an elongated corridor that seemed to stretch on for miles.

Oh Christ, look what they've done to you. Is this happening?

With no recollection of how he got there, Headcase was suddenly back on the streets, bumping into people, a flow of humanity he could not stem. A tide. He *had* changed; he didn't need the movie soundtrack to tell him that. Headcase had changed in ways nobody could even imagine. Whether this was down to his captors or not didn't really matter. Perhaps they were trying to take the gift away from him. To stop him from—

He lurched aimlessly into one body after the next ('Idiot! Watch where you're going! Hey, look out… Look out… look out…'), like a pinball bouncing off the buffers. Tossed around in a game of 'chance', nothing could ever be the same again.

He moved without moving, felt like the collection of molecules he knew he was, the world around him appearing as a series of still images. Snapshots taken by an amateur photographer: *Click*, a yellow car speeding past, the couple inside arguing; *Click*, traffic lights turning from green to red; *Click*, a man dressed as a clown handing out balloons in the street, all the colours of the fucking rainbow; *Click*, a huge black bird at the periphery of his vision, swooping down…

Headcase ducked. It passed over him and continued on – an omen, harbinger of death. The flapping of its wings remained in his ears long after the bird itself had vanished. He balled his fists and pounded the side of his head, dropping to his knees. Would this never end?

*   *   *

Night-time again, and the neon lights now coax him into the heart of the city. Women on street corners dressed in tight miniskirts and fishnets, beckoning to anyone who walked past. Their maggot-riddled faces lathered in make-up, the men swarming like flies round corpseflesh. And here, dealers plying their trade in alleyways, punters desperate to get out of their heads, to see sights they wouldn't normally see. What he wouldn't give to take something that would do exactly the opposite. They could have his visions anytime… and might just regret it.

Be careful what you wish for.

Headcase had known for a while that he was being followed. The unspeakables tailing him, keeping one step behind, ready to pounce on him when the time is right. They take on human form sometimes so he has to be aware, keep on his toes. Every single person on this planet is a potential.

A potential victim, subject, and host.

There's a McBurger King ahead of him, open late, ready to receive the grateful overspill from various pubs and clubs. A bloated man emerges carrying a greasy bag. Headcase's stomach is rumbling. It reminds him of just how hungry he… When was the last time he'd had any food? Without even thinking – can he still think? – he snatches the bag from the man and flees as fast as he can.

'You… Somebody… Did you see that? He just—'

Did you see… what did you see?

Even in his weakened condition, Headcase is faster than this overweight specimen. When he feels he is relatively safe, he sits in a deserted shop doorway, keeping well back and hiding himself as best he can.

Inside the bag he finds a box of fries, a burger and a large coke. Headcase tucks into the meal, the meat stringy but satisfying. It isn't until he's eaten some of the fries as well, taking a gulp of the coke to wash them down, that he starts to feel sick; he should have known he could no longer take sustenance like any other person. Any *ordinary* person. Getting up, he makes it to the pavement before puking. He continues to heave long after there is nothing left in his stomach, and the lumpy spew on the concrete bubbles and froths. Slowly it transforms into something, spreading itself out, the wings unmistakable.

Movement to the left and Headcase spots figures at the junction of the street. They are coming. He has to get out of there. Scrambling to his feet, he takes off, never looking back, not turning this time. There is a multistorey car park not too far away, so he heads for that. Plenty of places to hide, and open 24-7.

Inside: all the cars lined up in rows, sandwiched together, stored, contained. And he thinks of the beds where the other abductees were kept, some even strapped down, awaiting the procedures. The writhing, twisting people there, tossing and turning beneath the sheets – and knowing that his time would come. That soon they would pick on him, alter him in such a way that he would… One man, also bald, waking up in the middle of the night and reaching out his hand to Headcase – as if he could possibly help him: 'Don't let them take me again. *Please!*'

Headcase had ignored him, pulling up the covers of his own bed. Flinching every time one of the mouthless creatures or their minions walked by.

The man was petrified now, turning and reaching out to the other people in the beds. Imploring somebody, anybody, to help him. 'Please, I don't want to go again. I—' With a thump he dropped out of the bed, clutching his forehead, shrieking in agony. Seconds later he was still. Dead on the floor. It was how he would remain until the creatures discovered him.

Every single car light suddenly comes on at once. Headcase shields his eyes from the brightness, but still it filters through. Red veins appear when he closes his lids, the blood vessels thick, so he opens them again. Now all the car horns are going off in unison, deafening him: a sensory overload. And suddenly the figures are there in that car park, stepping out of the light, inching towards him. This time they bring with them their pets, their other experiments. The things with arachnid legs, the things with lapping, oversized tongues, the things with scales and pustules and snapping pincers...

He is grabbed from behind and at first Headcase thinks they've got him. Then he's pulled backwards and out of harm's way, and led by the hand, a grip so tight he can't shake it off. Through another set of doors, and up the stairs, dragging him up one flight after another. They pause for a moment to rest and only then does Headcase have time to take in his rescuer's appearance. The woman is smaller than him, with short auburn hair and big, round eyes, dressed in a grey-blue jump-suit. Can she see? Can she...?

She returns the favour, briefly scrutinising him. 'Holy crap, look at you. Are you okay?'

Headcase tries to nod, not really knowing either way.

'Oh God – you can't talk anymore, can you?' She seems genuinely concerned for him. 'But you can listen. Look, do you remember anything?' The woman clenches his hand. 'Squeeze it once for yes, twice for no.'

Headcase squeezes it once. Then again with less pressure.

'They're not going to stop till they get you back. You know that, don't you?'

One squeeze.

'You represent a lot of time and effort on their behalf. They're frightened. They want to stop the process now, prevent you from...' There are sounds from below them and she turns to look back down the stairs.

'Come on, we don't have much time.'

They clamber up more and more steps, until finally there are none left. The woman pushes open the nearest door with her elbow and they're on the top level of the multi-storey. A cool wind brushes their faces as they hobble out towards the edge of the rooftop.

The woman faces him again. 'You have no idea what's happening to you, do you? You suspect, but you don't really know.'

Headcase squeezes her hand, and she squeezes back. 'You're only just beginning to understand. There's something inside you, and it's awake now. They did that, they woke it up. Now it wants to escape, just like you did from them. Can you feel it? You're evolving, but that's only the first step. And once it's gone too far you can never return.' She presses herself closer to him. 'You're going to have to make a choice: you can free it or you can end up like the rest of those poor sods down there. What you're seeing, what you're hearing... no one has ever experienced this before. You're special.'

Headcase starts to squeeze her hand harder and harder, short, sharp twitches that reflect his confusion.

'Don't worry, you'll know when the time comes. And then the decision will be yours to make al—' She pauses, her eyes open wide. The woman stands up straight, and the next time she opens her mouth it is to spray him with a warm crimson wetness. Her grip on his hand goes slack and Headcase backs off. He looks on helplessly as the creatures behind her do their work, the mouthless ones and their progeny. Two moist tentacled shapes coil around her wrists and they stretch her arms out wide. Next her clothes are stripped away, followed closely by sections of her skin. He hears the swishing, snipping sound as it happens. Shiny, black fingers reach into her mouth, tearing back the lips and forcing her teeth to jut out.

For a second it's almost beautiful; she almost looks to have… to have wings…

Then dozens of the creatures overpower her and he can see nothing save for their offensive bodies. In retrospect it's probably a good thing.

It doesn't take long before they turn their attentions back to him. Headcase retreats as they reach out, beckoning, snatching. He backs off right to the edge of the car park level. He looks over the wall, then back at his pursuers. Is this the decision the woman talked about? If so, it isn't a hard one to make.

Headcase sits on the ledge, then pushes himself off. He can feel himself falling, falling…

*   *   *

He lands on the concrete but not with the force he expected.

Disorientated, Headcase looks up to see a park bench above him. The sky now bright and full of clouds. Slowly, he gets up, topples to one side and into a jogger on his way through the park. Headcase flinches back, still expecting to be taken by his keepers, then sighs with relief as the jogger simply flips him the bird without looking and carries on through the park.

Where is he? How did he end up here? Maybe he dreamt the whole thing, and is safe after all. Maybe he doesn't have to run anymore. Maybe all this is in his imagination.

And yet the pain… still there… and he can see…

The morning light is turning pink above him. It blends with the blue, creating a murky, bruised purple. It carries on for a while until one colour emerges victorious.

The sky bleeds, cotton wool clouds soaking up the redness.

He blinks. For a fleeting second Headcase sees the room where they took him the first time, the preamble to the knives coming out. Cocooning him inside their womb machines. Perhaps that had done the damage, had altered him? Re-birthed him? Something to do with… The woman had been right about one thing, he *is* changing, though he has no idea why or in what ways. His vision is becoming… strange too. The agony inside intensifying, yet receding.

Dawn should never look like this.

Run. Run like the jogger; get away while there's still time. Before they track you down again and—

Headcase is back on the streets, mingling with pedestrians. They smell like rotting carrion passing him by, like carcasses hanging on hooks in a slaughterhouse. A line from a hymn comes floating back to him:

(Hymns? Churches, when was the last time he'd been in a church?)

Change and decay in all around I see…

I see…

He watches, mesmerised, as the faces of folk on the street putrefy, become infected. No, this isn't a street. He is inside, somewhere inside.

Dazzling, intense. This is a mall: big, bustling. Headcase stumbles past an electrical shop and the TVs in the window all throw back a picture of him. His body, then a close-up of his face – a montage of images all jumbling into each other in quick succession.

Light, blood, flowers, blood, smiling, blood, knife, blood, metal, blood, wings, blood, masks, blood, hissing-blood-falling-blood-light-blood-tape-blood… Faster and faster, .like the words from the songs, like subliminal advertising gone haywire.

Headcase wants to scream, but he knows he has no voice. The torture is incredible now, intensifying with each new picture. Then suddenly he *is* screaming, louder than he can possibly imagine. He beats the sides of his temples and shouts for all he is worth. The TVs explode one by one, bursting open and spilling their cathode guts. Then the shop window showers him with glass.

All is quiet. Headcase looks up and sees that he is surrounded by the creatures. They are everywhere. It is as if they've taken over the shoppers, absorbed their bodies so they can capture him.

Mouthless monstrosities with even more arms. Where in fuck's name are they all coming from? He can run but he knows he can never, ever hide. They will always find him.

Above, the ceiling is now blood red, veins snaking down. There is a throbbing noise, a pulsating. But he is beyond pain, beyond headaches and sharp, grinding glass inside his skull.

Headcase backs off, holding his hands out in front of him. The hordes creep towards him. Wave upon wave, tide upon tide. There is no—

His foot catches on something and he almost slips. Headcase turns and sees an escalator behind him. It's waiting for him. Waiting to take him up into…

This is the choice he has to make. To move without moving again. To expand and contract at the same time.

The creatures fill the lower floor of the precinct. He can see blood raining down the walls, the mall breathing as if alive.

He knows what he has to do.

Headcase is about to make his ascension, to evolve.

'No, stop!' gargles one of the monstrosities at the front. 'You mustn't.'

They can't prevent this from happening. Nobody can. It is inevitable. 'The time has arrived and I can see,' he declares.

'Then see this…' The creatures part and allow somebody to walk through their number. It's another woman, this time her face vaguely familiar. She holds her hand out to him, just as that other prisoner did the night he died.

'Please, Bernie. Before it's too late,' she says. 'Come back with us. I need you; Bernie Jr. needs you.'

Headcase frowns, takes a step towards her. And for a fraction of a second he remembers, or *thinks* that he does. Remembers that this is his wife. The creatures, the doctors, their masks, wearing blue and white scrubs, are trying to help him, trying to take something out that doesn't belong. Something that has awakened on its own. Inside his skull. He even sees the reality of the place he is in, instead of a bizarre contortion of memories, of remembrances, of film and TV images. Is he still in the facility, on the ship… in the hospital he thought he'd escaped from…?

No, lies – all lies.

He stops dead in his tracks. What on earth is he doing? He doesn't want this. He can't return. Not now, not even if he wants to.

He has to escape. Once and for all.

Headcase turns and puts a foot on the escalator, rising towards an opening in the ceiling, in the heavens. No more blood, no more pain. He shrugs off the flesh he's known since he was a babe, allowing its drugged and diseased aggregate to collapse where it lays. Headcase releases the soul inside him that needs to be released – in the shape of a white dove.

It flaps its wings once, twice…

Has broken free, at last. Once and for all. From his pursuers, from his existence, from his very being.

Has escaped, finally, the world that held him captive.

From birth until his final dying day.

IN HYDING

It was only my little joke.

Hyde. Hyding… Hiding. Amused me at any rate, just having my fun. Had to do something to entertain myself while I was biding my time, waiting in secret. Trapped. Because that's what I was for such a long time, you see. For so very long even before the serum – whose idea do you think that was anyway? – I was biding my time. Always with him, always watching.

Much later, when he was setting down his account of the whole affair, he'd call me the 'curse of mankind' or 'pure evil'. Base and primal, responsible for all man's ills. A reflection, an ugly twin if you will. An urge to do the most horrific things, that little voice inside which encourages the worst behaviour possible. Selfishness and violence and… sexual depravity. The very thought of it makes me want to…

But no, he had his turn; his chance to set everything down and tell his side of the story. Now it is time for me to tell mine, to set the record straight. I mean, do you think I would have been able to do all those things if he hadn't wanted me to, if he hadn't enjoyed it as well? That loss of control, that feeling – it's almost as potent, as intoxicating as the drugs he took which allowed me to venture forth. Recriminations would be for afterwards, and not my domain. Acting in the moment, that's always been my speciality; not thinking or worrying about the consequences. That's someone else's problem. That was his speciality. Cleaning up messes.

Like that £100 cheque which had to be made out to the family of the unwitting child I… hurt. The clumsy bitch shouldn't have got in my way in the first place! Trampling was too good for her, if you ask me. But that bastard Enfield, chasing me and forcing recompense. Threatening a scandal. I should have just done to him what I did later on to Carew (and the delicious memory of that – the blood, striking him so hard with my cane I could hear the bones cracking – gives me a magnificent shiver of delight) but there were simply too many people around.

His money saved the day, my 'other half', thanks in no small part to his family's wealth. It allowed me to push forward with my work just as the good doctor had done with his.

And his labours up to that point had been vital; without them I wouldn't have been able to have my… fun and games. My sport. The fact that he thought he was doing humanity some sort of great service, that to separate the two halves of oneself might mean one day he'd be able to eradicate the more unsavoury side, just added to the pleasure for me. Pure fantasy, as one cannot possible exist without the other. Symbiosis, it's called. Night and day. To imagine that the world would be some sort of utopia without its darker tendencies is delusional in the extreme. Mankind would never have progressed had it not been the faction I represent. Besides, imagine how boring that would be!

Nevertheless, it suited my purposes for him to think what he thought; for him to come to the conclusion he did.

Without his sickly-sweet drive to do good, I wouldn't have been presented with my little windows of opportunity. Portions of time in which I would go on my sprees, conduct myself in the manner *I* saw fit. Holding nothing back! Listen, if you think you know the story, you really don't. In fact you don't know the half of it, my friend. Not in the slightest. Some of the things we… I did, it would turn your hair white. Why, this one time with a lady of the night – although, I have to remark she was no lady; not by the time I had finished with her anyway – well, I committed an act whereby I…

But no, I am becoming distracted once more. Where was I? Oh yes, the doctor. So, it was imperative he take up medicine. Develop a keen interest in the human form growing up – beyond the obvious which I had been fuelling in him for a number of years. It was I who subtly encouraged him to spy upon the maids at the family home. And especially through the windows of their quarters on the lower floors, catching them in various states of undress. On other occasions there were instances of relations between Meg the scullery maid and Robinson the gardener. They thought they were being oh so clever with their secrets and schemes. Arranging their meetings in the woods or the shed, never suspecting their antics were being scrutinised. Rutting away, him thrusting into her up against a tree or over the lawnmower, her cries of pleasure often more than I could stand; not when I could do nothing about it. When all I wanted to do was slit Robinson's throat, bathe in his blood, and then take Meg myself. Squeezing her breasts so hard that she would let out a different kind of cry altogether.

It was more than Henry could bear as well, verging on his teens – images he would often take away with him so that when he was alone, hiding away…

Never caught, never seen.

But there again, that just proves how necessary the other half of the equation is. Not just Meg and Robinson, lust guiding their actions, but the ability to be able to defend oneself should the boy have been discovered. Defend, conquer. Taking what you desire in more ways than one. Why, nations… whole *empires* have been built on such philosophies. Have risen up out of the need to plunder, to expand one's horizons. Of course, they have often burnt themselves out as well, but that which burns brightly can only burn for so long. As was the case in our situation, too. All good things must come to an end.

Do they not?

Distracted again, must try and focus – communicate all this while it is still fresh in my… my mind. That makes me smile, gives me cause to chuckle certainly. Henry the boy-child, the keen observer, and his nature studies. That's where we'd got to, wasn't it. Him and his high ideals, and yet he was corrupted from the start. From the moment he first lied about whether he'd knocked over the hydrangea in the parlour causing the soil to stain the carpet, or stole that apple from the market stall on a trip to town with his father. How appropriate it should be that particular fruit, eh? No doubt all the time putting it down to that shadow cast over all men. Lead us not into temptation? No, lead away, that's my philosophy. Give in to it! The more tempting the better!

But, as I must also do, it was necessary for him to follow a certain path – in spite of a leaning towards industry. Crucial that his interests be diverted towards science and medicine rather than steam engines and mechanics, especially in an age that was embracing such studies.

Did one influence the other, the idea of ridding society of its ills leading to his taking up arms in the laboratory against it – or the other way around? Whilst studying how things 'tick' did he come up the notion of *divide* and conquer this time? A lifetime's obsession, to separate out the good from the bad then destroy it? Impossible to do, simply impossible!

It was, however, possible to facilitate the bad to thrive. To bring it to the fore, let it rise to the surface just like those empires rose. And fell. Let us not forget that they also fell… How glorious, however, were they when they were at their height? How glorious was my own time in the limelight!

Before that could possibly happen, however, there was much to do. Much to consider. Failures and successes, until that secret ingredient was found. The one which made it all possible, so he believed. An impurity in the chemical, he posited, that made the whole thing work in the first place. I recall one of those very early experiments, when the 'change'– as he came to call it – lasted but a few moments at most. Definitely didn't take. Didn't assist my *taking* over, taking control. Oh, the frustration of it!

However, I suppose the anticipation of this made the first time he got it right all the sweeter. That night when he drank the potion and the nausea come upon him, and his bones began to contort; making him lighter, making him feel younger, freer. As he once described it, the caged devil being set free – and it was not a million miles from the truth. An apt description.

I will never forget when he saw himself during that inaugural transformation, however. When I allowed him to see what he'd become in the mirror, after crossing the yard and venturing to his bedroom, knowing his own staff were sound asleep. I could feel his shock at what he witnessed thrown back at him in that reflective glass; what I know Enfield also described as deformities. How dare he! And while it is correct to say that my visage is somewhat distinctive, I prefer to think of myself as unique in appearance. Down to earth, as I am in all things.

And so, the genie was out of the bottle at last! My friend had proven his worth, proven to be an excellent choice in fact. I cannot tell you how wonderful it felt to be unfettered once more, to feel at home in that skin instead of merely a prisoner. But, yet again, I was to be denied, my hold on that form not as stable as I had assumed. This was very much in evidence when the doctor effected a change back into his former self; panic gripping him and countering all my efforts. My grasp was slippery back then, and as desperate as I was to remain, I found myself imprisoned once more. Not on the outside looking in, but the inside looking out. However, he had experienced what it could be like to live without boundaries. To care not for rules and regulations. I needed only to wait a short while longer; it would only be a matter of time before he gave in to those temptations again, and then… and then…

As he said himself in his 'confession', he fell into slavery. He became *my* slave, in effect. Once we had started, he even began to take my 'suggestions' as direct orders when he transformed back. I would need a hidden place, for example, so that I could conduct my most private affairs away from the eyes of others. Thus it became essential to rent and furnish the room in Soho (the perfect location, populated by the dispossessed and the depressed alike) accessed by way of a certain door. We would also need to engage the services of a housekeeper who could be discrete. Bribery or the threat of violence, either worked as far as I was concerned.

In addition, it was necessary for his staff, for butler Poole especially, to grant me the run of his own home, in addition to arranging for me to be the sole beneficiary of his funds should he suddenly vanish without trace (securing the services of that wet fish lawyer Utterson to do so would arouse suspicion, I realised, but there was no other way unfortunately). Believe me when I say I was hoping to make the change permanent at some point, to switch places as it were. For him to become the prisoner and I the keeper of the keys, strong enough – stronger than him now by far – to ignore his pitiful pleas for release. What could he offer me, when all was said and done? Nothing to match what I had offered him.

His detainment would not be without fringe benefits. As he did with Meg and Robinson, he would be able to watch as I indulged my fantasies. No, not fantasies anymore. *Realities.* Things he could not possibly have dreamed of if he'd had a lifetime to do so. Many lifetimes. What some might call barbarity, and others would almost without a doubt call depravity, I call nourishment. It fed me, as a bountiful meal would feed a ravenous man (as the long pig had for me on special occasions). And I *was* ravenous, no two ways about that. It had been so long since I'd indulged in all the pleasures flesh had to offer.

The memories will have to sustain me, I know that. Flashes of nights when I gambled in the most unsavoury of places, drank – but not so much I might inadvertently lose the reins of this particular carriage – and fought. Fists connecting with jaws, breaking noses with wet crunches. Biting, tearing and choking. I took what I wanted, when I wanted. The laws of man did not apply to me, they never have. I did not make them, do not agree with them. Some say that without such laws there would be chaos, but I say what's wrong with a little chaos? All right, a *lot* of chaos? Civility is all an illusion anyway, the strongest and most dominant force in this world is that of will: to do and not think twice. You people spend so long trying to curb it all, when it is not realistic or achievable. It can never be wiped out, I do know that. When he loosened the shackles, hoping to find a way to stamp what I am out completely, all he did was make me stronger. And as much as he talked about being revolted by it, he enjoyed witnessing my exploits as much as he had back when he was in his teens. It had only taken a nudge then, only took one when he was older. One step at a time; a step in the right direction, so to speak.

He also managed to convince himself he wasn't to blame for any of it, that what occurred when he took the potion was not his fault. And, while I can be convincing, while I *ached* for him to create more of the solution, he still had a choice back then. Not like when I took over, when I had control; then there was no choice at all. A grey area, I suppose. Only natural he should seek to blame someone – some*thing* – else.

They thought he was being blackmailed, Utterson and co. That I had something over poor old Henry – which I did, as it happened, *lots* of things, but that wasn't the reason for him telling them all to leave me alone. He was scared of me, as he was right to be. Scared of what I could do, more timid every single day – night – I was out there. Had seen what I was capable of, thought it best that it should be his turn now to hide away and leave me to it.

Oh, there were efforts to resist, I'm not saying there weren't. He did well for a while, just before what happened with Sir Danvers Carew, but he was always going to weaken eventually. And it was when he finally did after an extended period that made me really go berserk. Made me do what I did with the cane... There was speculation, I know, as to what we were both doing down there and yes, you would be right in thinking that my particular tastes do not just run to the fairer sex. Why limit yourself, why limit your pleasure?

But, of course, Carew had certain reservations. When it came right down to it, he got cold feet about the entire thing, which just made me frustrated. Made me angry – and he was the one who paid the price. I needed to express myself in other ways, but was not aware as I stood there raining blows down upon him, harder and harder until the cane itself broke in two, until I could see his brains, that *I* myself was being observed. That it would set in motion a chain of events which would lead to the police becoming involved, for a manhunt to begin, initiated by the lawyer – Carew's lawyer – Utterson, who had every reason to hate me. Not even the note Henry showed him apologising for everything that had happened – and imagine how sick that made me feel! – put him off the scent. He thought the good doctor had forged it because of the similarity in handwriting.

It necessitated a change in plans, put a halt to my activities temporarily. I had to go into hiding once more, simply so I wouldn't be found. Yet I retained a degree of control which hadn't been there before, which hadn't been apparent until then. However, this did not prevent *him* from bringing others into this affair. From writing his account of all this to give to his friend Dr Lanyon, to be opened in the event of Henry's death. Something that he had to prove by transforming once more, and the only comfort I could gain from that was it drove Lanyon to an early grave.

More meddling, people not able to leave us – me – alone. Enfield, Utterson, even the staff on occasion. All interfering, preventing me from having my fun.

Even I could see that all this was heading towards its inevitable conclusion. I recognise the signs. He was growing weaker and weaker, enabling me to emerge on a more frequent basis – in his sleep, in the daytime – but at the same time taking its toll on his body and consciousness. As all of this reached its tipping point, it was just a matter of letting him think he was making the ultimate sacrifice. That he would stop me permanently, trap me. He had just enough resolve to 'bring the life of that unhappy Henry Jekyll to an end' and die a hero. Ha!

By that time I was long gone, I'd vacated his pitiful, broken body and was away. Nebulous, as I was before I found him in the first place when he was little and I attached myself to him. Wormed my way inside my new 'home', accepting that – in my own weakened condition and without being able to exert any degree of control beyond whispering, suggesting – I would be interred until the experiments could begin anew. He was the best subject thus far, I have to give him that. The most malleable eventually, and the best equipped to cater to my particular and inimitable needs.

You see, I would like to take credit for all of men's ills. Would like to say to you that I represent the darkness, the shadow inside us all. But that is simply not true. It just served my purposes for old Henry to believe in the notion. Why, if he had known the truth about the parasite within him, the spirit that had begun its own journey of discovery so many years ago – one 'step' at a time, and in the right direction hopefully – flitting from host to host, lifetime after lifetime, unable to survive without them (a true symbiosis), following a certain path… If he had known all that, it would have left his keen mind useless. Instead, we came the closest yet to my being able to take total control over a body, to beat down the soul which inhabits it and dominate at will.

I admit, he had his uses – and Henry made a good place to conceal myself when the authorities were looking for me. The trick would've been if I could have taken on his shape, but still remained… well, me. Hiding in plain sight, able to flit back and forth but still *be* Hyde. The ultimate goal, and something to strive towards for next time. When another empire rises, now that this one has fallen, now that this host has fallen.

It is why he could never have defeated me, because he did not fully understand the enemy he was fighting against. How could he? This all began so long ago, when I first separated myself from my original body; the true separation in this case. Dispossessed… searching for someone *to* eventually possess. Since then I have gone from body to body, always indulging myself but seeking a way to make it permanent. Different concoctions, sometimes even magicks like the ones that brought me to this state in the first place, but always the same objective.

So much hiding, so much waiting.

As I do now, locked inside this new unwitting child's form, who will slowly but surely learn not to get in my way. Subtly I shall steer events towards where they must go again, towards the sciences whilst at the same time nudging him again to entertain me; to show me sights that simultaneously frustrate but build the appetites, until I can break free once more and partake for real. Always watching, waiting, always with him.

As for the story, this true account, I know there is nobody listening to that. I am simply relating it to myself, another way to while away the time. What do I care that folk believe Henry's version of events? Utterson, Enfield... all idiots! It will be long forgotten when I emerge victorious again to wreak havoc. Although I have learned the value of not letting myself be seen too quickly, not coming even close to getting caught.

And the name, variations of such used over and over, but this one was definitely the best. My favourite. Hyde. Hyding... Hiding. Amused me at any rate, entertained me.

In the end I was just having my fun.

It was only my little joke.

THE JIGSAW FAMILY

It all started with the jigsaws, really.

When Carl thought about it, thought back to how he used to get told off. Oh, he'd been happy enough to conform to begin with, to slot the strangely-shaped pieces together to make the picture on the front of the box – couldn't get enough of it, truth be told. Landscapes, people... pictures of animals.

It was the process that kept him occupied at the start. Piecing the puzzle together, with an eye for detail. He'd spend hours and hours as a kid doing them, tongue sticking out of the corner of his mouth as he concentrated. His parents were happy enough to leave him to it; after all, there wasn't much else to do in the back of beyond where they lived – and besides:

'It sharpens the mind,' his dad used to say.

Whenever his mom complained about how pale he was, he'd go and do the jigsaws outside. Carl preferred them to all the other games that were paraded in front of him, mainly because – as an only child – he could do these on his own.

It was when he had the idea of changing it up, making this hobby more *interesting*, sharpening his mind even further, that the trouble started.

Wasn't trouble as far as he was concerned, but his folks saw it that way. Because he'd take various pieces from the jigsaws and put them together to make something new. In one particular landscape, a picture of a mountain with a lake beside it, he placed a couple of people in the water up to their chests so it looked like they were drowning; that had made him chuckle. In another, he'd manipulated the photo so that it looked like a little baby was sitting in front of a roaring lion. In one more, he placed an old man in a rocking chair in a cloudy sky, about to be hit by a jet fighter.

Wasn't easy to do, of course. The pieces didn't go in easily – round pegs in square holes, he'd later come to think of it as. But he'd trim them where necessary, cut off lumps from the side with scissors, with knives, so that they would fit… mostly. He *made* them fit at any rate, let's say that. With some he created more abstract pieces, adding human heads to beasts, inserting random objects into people, giving others four arms and four legs to create a sort of spider-creature… the list went on and on.

When his parents found out, of course, they freaked.

'Do you know how much those things cost!' had been his dad's response. Always about the money. Sometimes Carl thought he cared more about that than him; it made what came later that much easier to stomach. 'And just look at what you've been doing to them!'

His mom asked questions, so many damned questions – most of which he ignored. Then she wanted to take him to see someone, a specialist, until a friend of hers – who they insisted Carl call Aunty Marion – said it was nothing. 'My youngest, Denise, used to make guillotines out of Meccano and execute her Barbie dolls. No biggie… It's just, well, all kids have a fascination with the dark side of things at some point. They grow out of it. Besides,' she'd said, as she'd drunk her coffee and reached for another piece of cake, 'it's quite artistic really. You could have another one of them… y'know, modern artists on your hands. Could wind up making a fortune!'

But it wasn't about art at all; for one thing Carl was too young to appreciate such things, let alone want to copy them. This was just about making things fit his view of the world; whether that was a warped view or not was still open to debate. The pictures on the front of those boxes, the ones you were supposed to use as a guide, were too… normal. Didn't fit with what he wanted from the jigsaws.

It wasn't long before he started to think about his life in the same way. He was growing up, and all he'd known was his time here, with this mother and father – and they were as dull as ditch water. A guy who scraped a living as a clerk at the local bank, forever missing out on promotions, while his wife did the housework, entertained her small circle of friends, and watched the soaps on the tube. That was home, but school was no better – surrounded by screaming idiots who were obsessed with sweets, fizzy drinks and who had a crush on who; a clue, nobody ever had one on Carl, not with his weight problem and acne.

He wanted change… no, he *needed* change. And if it didn't happen soon, he'd do what he'd done with all those jigsaws and create it: make the perfect picture he had in his mind, no matter what the cost… the damage to individual pieces. So long as the bigger picture reflected what he desired.

Carl had relatives in another town he'd visited a fair few times; his dad's brother and sister-in-law. They had a much bigger house than Carl's parents, had a much bigger everything… and they had a pool! They already had a son, Bradley, but Carl felt sure that if something were to happen to his own folks, they would take him in. He'd always been nice to them when he stayed.

Hadn't been hard to engineer that trip on the stairs, rigging the carpet so his mom went flying. A broken neck hadn't been guaranteed, but Carl had been lucky on this occasion. At the funeral, he made a point of telling his real aunty how sad his home life was, how it had been like that for some time – and he'd cried, as she hugged him to her breasts.

Setting the scene for when he put the gun barrel under his dad's chin some months later, pulling the trigger and splattering his brains all over the wall. His dad had been good and loaded – had been drinking more and more since his wife had died and he'd been left to bring up Carl on his own – wouldn't have felt a fucking thing. Then, with his gloved hands, Carl had curled his dad's fingers around the grip, left it dangling there in his lap as if he'd offed himself. Carl had paused only once on his way out of the room to call the authorities, to look at the patterns the grey matter had left on that wall. He'd cocked his head, tracing the lines of grue as they dripped downwards, re-arranging them in his mind.

He had actually made his dad more *interesting*.

When the dust had settled, and Carl had played the part of the sorrowful son to the full, he'd made his feelings clear about wanting to go and stay with his aunty and uncle. And, although Carl hadn't exactly been welcomed with open arms – at least by his father's brother (and was he just a little bit suspicious of how that man had died?) – they had taken him in. They had the room, they had the money… that certainly wasn't an issue with them. They'd buy him however many jigsaws he wanted to play about with, didn't care what he did with them.

But then there was Bradley. Snooping, spiteful Bradley. Who'd seen what he'd been doing with next door's cat, the new arrangement he'd been creating of it with a dead racoon's head and legs. Carl needed a future where that kid was totally out of the picture – the jigsaw picture – and so he made it happen. Made it happen by recreating one of his old favourites, the people drowning in the mountain lake. Simple enough to… *execute*, to hold Bradley under when nobody was around. To get out of the pool and dry himself off.

To go upstairs to his room and wait until the screaming started.

Nothing was the same after that, though. His uncle grew even more suspicious, and his aunty began to listen to those doubts – fuelled by the death of her beloved son. Accidental drowning? It happened… But on the back of Carl's mother and father?

He knew he'd pushed his luck. Not everyone wanted to be slotted into place the way he would prefer it. Not everyone could see his vision of a better future. And so he plotted to get rid of his surrogate parents, maybe replace them too – except it hadn't really worked out that way. He'd been caught with his aunty's sleeping pills and couldn't think of any excuse to give – other than he'd been planning to dope them both and toss them in the pool as well.

He hadn't been thinking far enough ahead, and now Carl realised that he needed to in all his subsequent endeavours. He'd fled, of course; caught the next coach out of town and to another state. He was almost fifteen now, practically a man. He could look after himself… But then again, the picture.

A picture of a perfect family life again. Where he wouldn't be hassled, spied upon or have to watch his back. To do that, he would have to create one. That's when he'd broken into his first property. Not without scoping it all out first, no, that would be crazy. He needed to know that the middle-aged couple were childless, needed to know their routines so he could gain entry when they were out, off to do the weekend shop. They didn't have an alarm that he could see, so he'd smashed one of the panes of glass in the back door and sat waiting for them to return home; sat and waited for them with the shot-gun he'd found upstairs resting across his knees.

Oh, their faces were a picture. Not the picture he was trying to create, but a satisfying one nonetheless. Carl had risen and pointed the gun first at the curly-haired husband, then at his blonde-haired wife, ordering them not to shout because he'd blow their heads off. Why not, it wouldn't be his first time.

'You're going to be my new parents,' he told them, then forced them to sit down on the couch so he could explain what was going to happen.

The man – his new dad – had a job; he knew that because he'd seen him go off in the mornings at 8 am sharp. There was no reason why that had to end, Carl would just stay home with the guy's wife – his new mom – to make sure that he kept his mouth shut.

'We can all be one happy family,' he enthused, as the woman cried her eyes out. 'Better than before even, better than the others.'

'W-Whatever you say,' the man told him, holding his hands up, 'just don't hurt us.'

Carl had laughed. 'There should be no need for that, as long as we all understand each other.'

And it had worked for a little while. He'd kept the gun on them when he was awake, kept them tied up on their bed when they weren't. 'Night!' he'd call from the doorway, before closing it and then making his way to the spare room he'd claimed as his own.

They'd all eat together in the evenings and he'd get his dad (Malcolm, he'd discovered) to tell them all about his day, before watching TV together. Anyone came to the house, he'd encourage one of the pair to get rid of them. Same went for phone calls. But he knew before long people would start asking questions (so many damned questions); he couldn't keep them isolated from the world like this. Couldn't freeze them in a perfect moment like you could with those jigsaws.

In the end it didn't matter, things came to a head anyway. He was woken by banging one night, and raced to their room to find Malcolm free of his bonds: he'd squirrelled away a nail-file from the bathroom. There was a struggle, but Carl had managed to whack him with the butt of the gun. Because it would have been too noisy, though, he didn't shoot the guy. Instead, he pulled out the knife he always kept now in his belt and bent, grabbing Malcolm's head by the hair and yanking it back so he could bring the blade across his throat. His wife – Felicity – had opened her mouth to cry out, but he'd brought the knife around in an arc.

'Shut the fuck up!' Carl told her. 'Or you'll be next.'

Her eyes had flicked from the knife to her dead spouse, wallowing in a pool of his own blood – drowning, but in a different way. The survivor mechanism kicked in and she forced herself to stay quiet, nodding vigorously to show that she was listening.

The patterns of the blood on the floor made the scene more *interesting*, Carl thought to himself, even as he was hefting up the body and placing it in a chair. He'd decide what to do with it in the morning, but for the time being he was tired. He made sure his other mother's bonds were secure then left her in there with the corpse of her husband while he went to get some z's.

'If I hear so much as a peep...' he warned her as he was closing the door. Then added: 'Night. Sleep tight!'

The sound of her muffled sobs followed him out into the hallway, but he couldn't really begrudge her that. She was doing her best... and he'd make it up to her. In the morning.

He'd done his best as well, to find someone who bore a pretty good resemblance to Malcolm, he thought. Had to go to the next town over, having fed his mom one of those old sleeping tablets of his aunty's that he still had. He'd taken Malcolm's car (those driving lessons he'd given him had really come in handy), trawling through the streets and looking left and right at the populace until he spotted him. Then he'd trailed the stranger until the crowds had thinned out, before pulling alongside him and asking for directions. As the man leaned in, Carl had whacked him on the side of the head with a hammer. After that, it was a simple matter of dragging him inside and driving off – stopping to put him in the boot in a more secluded spot. No muss, no fuss.

When Carl got him home and both parties started to come around, he introduced the man to his new wife and then her ex, promising that the same would happen to him unless he played ball.

'But… but people will be looking for me,' argued the man, once he'd finished throwing up on the carpet at the sight of the body that looked like an alternate version of him. Maybe even a future version.

'They won't find you,' Carl promised. 'You're going to live here now, with us. Isn't that right?' He looked over to his mom for support, who glanced between them and nodded again.

It did make him think, though, because not only would people be looking for the new 'Malcolm', the original would also be missed at work. And what would they do for money, come to that? There was some in the house, a little in the bank, and this newcomer had cash in his wallet, but that would only last so long. Once again, he hadn't really thought it through, the consequences of it. Just like when he went ahead and mangled those jigsaws when he was little, the repercussions of that (they'd nearly sent him to the headshrinker for Christ's sake – and for what? he was perfectly sane…)

So that little unit had carried on for a while anyway, and the original Malcolm had ended up getting fired over the phone when Carl told them to shove their job up their ass. They'd managed, they'd muddled along, and he'd even got rid of the body from the bedroom – had taken it downstairs to work on, in fact (waste not, want not). Made it a more *interesting*, more Carl-like sight, by slotting a clock into his face, replacing his hands with a power-drill and a spatula. Still making his jigsaws even now, making life more entertaining. Sharpening his mind.

He'd shown 'Mom' but she hadn't been too impressed, just like his real one hadn't been. Now she had finally screamed and Carl had been forced to silence her, reluctantly. He'd played around with her body, as well, of course he had… But he'd soon grown bored. And when he went upstairs again to talk to his new 'dad', the new Malcolm, it had been about leaving and seeing more of this country.

'I'm growing up, Pop. I-I think I need my own space. Do you know what I'm saying?'

The man had nodded, eyes wide with fear.

'There comes a time when a son has to fly the nest.'

More nodding.

'I'm so glad you agree.' Then Carl had finished the job he started with the hammer when he'd first picked the man up, creating patterns on the bedspread that were so very different to his own father's brains on the wall.

He'd poured gasoline on everything, lit a match, and set fire to his makeshift family abode. It was high time, he figured, that he struck out on his own. He started off in Malcolm's car, but soon switched, and carried on doing that all the time he was on the road. He explored America's frontier via its back roads and motels, 'borrowing' a home here and there, having some fun along the way. In shady bars he came across people who could fix him up with everything he needed… for a price. IDs, drivers' licenses.

It was a great time, attending the university of life as he saw it. But all good things have to come to an end and – as nice as it was paying for female company, or just taking it when he wanted – Carl realised it was time now to think about settling down.

Finding the right girl. Finding the right place. Maybe even starting a family of his own.

That picture was shining the brightest when he found the love of his life, the flame-haired Sally: waitressing in a place just the other side of Texas. And yes, he could have wined and dined her, sweet-talked her and dated her until they'd both fallen in love with each other. But Carl was in too much of a hurry for that! Besides, what if she didn't like him in the same way? He'd lost most of the weight, and his skin was okay, but still… He couldn't risk that, couldn't risk it not fitting his picture of how life should be.

So, having only met her a handful of times having breakfast in her diner, he waited for Sally's shift to end one evening and came up behind her in the car park, covering her mouth and nose with the handkerchief covered in chloroform. Tying her up and popping her in the boot of his Chevy.

'Now all we have to do is find the place of our dreams,' he said to her, as he slammed the lid of the boot. 'I can picture it now.'

He – *they* – found it eventually at #136 Golden Elm Lane. A property which looked just like it sounded. Oh, Carl had done it all above board this time – no break-ins, no risk of being thrown out by the real owners, because this was going to be their forever place: his and Sally's.

He put down a considerable deposit on the house, amassed from various jobs he'd done on the road, plus gambling and money he'd just plain stolen. And by May that year they'd moved in… so much better than having to live out of the Chevy, feeding Sally in the boot and sleeping on the backseat.

Carl waited until night-time to carry her over the threshold, unconscious again, naturally. This was where they'd begin their new life, and it would never, ever be a normal, mundane one. They'd never end up like his mom and dad had; never fall into that trap.

He made a romantic meal the next evening, while boxes of stuff still lay scattered all round waiting to be unpacked; things Carl had ordered for the house. Well, that is to say he phoned for a romantic pizza and they ate it by candlelight. It was as he opened the wine and poured one for Sally that he outlined his long-term plans to her.

'So, what do you think, sweetheart?' he asked, raising his own glass – automatic pistol in his other hand.

'W-Why… why won't you let me go?' she said.

He frowned. 'Weren't you listening? We're going to make a go of it here. I think we'll have a wonderful life together. And y'know, at some point baby will make three.'

A tear tracked down Sally's cheek and she looked away from him.

There was no need to be coy, he thought to himself, not if they were going to spend the rest of their lives together. That night he showed her just how much he loved her in the only way he knew how. He took her there and then on the kitchen floor, handgun to her head; could tell by the way she moaned and gyrated beneath him that it was reciprocated. It was the most amazing night of his life, if he was honest.

Carl was realistic enough to know that if they were going to make it work here, going to raise a family, then the money he had would run out at some point. He'd need to get a job – just not at a bank, he wasn't going down that route. Fortunately, they were hiring at the local car dealership, and he took to that like a duck to water. He was good at… persuasion. It enabled him to drive a different car every other week and the pay was pretty decent, enough for a couple starting out, anyway.

'You should bring your wife around for dinner one night,' his boss, Mr Rockwell, told him, folding his fingers over his rotund belly as he sat behind the desk in his office. 'My wife makes a mean apple pie!'

'Oh, Sally's a little shy,' Carl told him. 'And she's a bit tied up with things at home at the moment, still getting things straight.'

She was tied up all right, and every evening Carl would release her, remove the gag from her mouth. Change her panties and clean her if she'd pissed or shit herself while he was out. 'They keep on asking about you at work,' he told her one time. 'If it carries on then we might just have to have my boss and his missus over for dinner. What do you say?'

Sally had spat on him in response.

Carl brought his pistol up under her chin, wiping his face with his other hand. 'Now, I hope you're going to be more polite than that if we have guests, sweetheart.'

She was, to be fair – probably because Carl had threatened that he'd kill all three of them, Sally and Mr and Mrs Rockwell, should they suspect anything was amiss. In fact, so good was Sally – not only as a cook, but as hostess – that it had seen Carl move one more rung up the ladder at work, escalating his plans for a baby.

But, try as they might – and boy, did Carl try – he just couldn't make Sally pregnant. After months of this, the final straw came when she began laughing one night as he'd brought up the subject. 'You know what I think, I… I think you're just firing blanks,' she told him, sneering. 'That's when you can manage to get it up, or last more than about five minutes.'

Carl hadn't been able to help himself, he'd punched her in the face at that. Punched, and kept on punching, even after her nose was broken – then he'd put the pillow over her face and unloaded his pistol into it.

'Who's firing blanks now?' he said.

Getting up off the bed and breathing quickly in and out, he stood back from the scene – and cocked his head. She'd done him a favour really, made their marriage more *interesting*. Certainly made the marital bed that way. It wasn't a picture he'd envisaged, but now that he was looking at it…

He'd taken the body down into the basement of the house, and put the bed sheets through the wash. Then, and only then, had he climbed in his car of the week – a bright red Lincoln – and set off in search of Sally Mk II. She'd be better even than the first one, he knew that.

Carl had called in sick from the road, and by the end of the third day – after putting many miles between himself and home – he'd found his bride. Flame-hair, check. High cheekbones, check. Body to die for, check. Opportunity to get up behind her and shove a blade into her side, threatening to slide it in all the way if she didn't come with him… check.

The next day, he'd returned home with her and as far as anyone watching – any of the neighbours – might be concerned, he was just coming back with his wife; close, sure, arm-in-arm actually, but then that was nice after all this time married, wasn't it? To still want to be all over each other.

'What is this?' she'd asked once they were safely inside. 'What the fuck's going on?' Had a mouth on her, this one. That would have to stop – that had been the downfall of the first Sally.

'You're here to fit in. To be my wife,' he told her in no uncertain terms, now pulling his gun and pointing it at her. 'Any objections, Sally?'

'My name's not—'

Carl had jabbed the weapon in her direction, cocked it. 'I said any objections?'

She'd stared at the piece, then at him, and shook her head. And so life – the picture he had of life – settled into another routine. This Sally had been more co-operative in bed, had even taught *him* a thing or two, but in the end the result was the same. He even began to suspect the first Sally had been right, that it might be him who was putting paid to things – firing… firing his blanks. This Sally said nothing, was actually even quite sympathetic, or at least acted it.

'Sometimes it takes a while, y'know?' Oh, she'd fitted in quite well in the end.

But he wanted a kid *now*, so that he'd be young enough to enjoy the grandchildren later on. As a consequence, Carl went out and took one, just like the picture he had in his head. Snatched the child from the back garden of a house a few towns over.

'This,' he said to Sally when he got home, offering his prize to her, 'this is Carl Jr.'

'O-Okay,' had been her reply, reluctantly taking their son from him. That should have rung warning bells, the way she held him. Wasn't really the maternal kind, this Sally. And Jesus, the kid had a set of lungs on him! That hadn't been in the picture, that hadn't been part of the vision.

He thought about swapping out the baby, but that would just have been cruel, so instead he replaced Sally with a woman he knew had a family, took her while she was out pushing her pram through a park. It was time to change things up again, anyway, to find not only a new mother for Carl Jr, but a different 'wife'. Sally was gone, had run off with his brother – so went the story at work – leaving him to cope on his own… until dark-haired Natalie had stepped in – hired as the nanny, but he'd eventually fallen in love with her.

Natalie was much better with Carl Jr right from the start – right from

Carl's order to 'Fix him!' She'd nursed the child, whilst pleading to be let back to see her own again. Carl kept promising he would… someday, but of course that day never came. She hadn't been the first, wouldn't be the last, and as time went on – Carl eventually taking over the dealership after an unfortunate accident saw off Mr Rockwell – he replaced her for another look-alike, then finally a woman who was nothing like the others, who came with her own child (a daughter, Abigail; a sister for Carl Jr) in tow. Becky was her name, and she looked more like his mom than his aunty or his second mom had.

But she asked questions. Lots of questions. So many damned questions… Couldn't help herself apparently. 'What are you doing when you're not at work,' she enquired one day, 'when you're not with me?'

'A man's got to have his hobbies,' Carl had replied. 'Hey, would you like to see?'

Becky had hesitated then, shaking her head.

'Oh, come on. You're always asking me.' Carl had dragged her by the arm then, dragged her from the kitchen table where he'd tied both his wailing children to their chairs.

Dragged her down into the cellar where he kept his previous 'wives'. Where he kept… others as well, fresh pieces to play with, added to on a regular basis. The children would get to see this as well, soon. All kids had a fascination with the dark side, didn't they?

Becky had almost gagged at the sights down there. The surroundings were bad enough, photos taken of landscapes all jumbled together, pasted on the walls. But in the room itself: humans and animals stitched together – a woman with a dog's head, a dog with a woman's head – a person with four arms and four legs; everyday objects embedded into others, like car parts, a lamp, a mirror, a mixing bowl. Making it all more… *interesting*.

Creating patterns, creating new pictures. The list went on and on…

'I… I don't…' she began, but Carl was already rounding on her with the instrument he always used to separate; so much more effective than scissors or knives. To cut the pieces into shapes he was happy with, chopping off any edges he didn't like.

'It sharpens my mind,' he explained.

She screamed when she saw what was about to happen (not that it would do her much good down there with all the sound-proofing). That she would be replaced now – perhaps with another Becky, perhaps someone altogether different. All part of his grand design. His ever-expanding puzzle.

But Carl just laughed, and set to work with his jigsaw once more.

CRAVINGS

That hunger. Believe me, it's the worst.

The cravings, so intense you don't know whether to laugh or cry. When you're starving, famished. When you realise you've just *got* to eat, to devour – shovel it all into your mouth right away, sometimes swallowing it without even chewing. Because you're eating for two, right? Because you have this thing inside you that's reliant on you, that's feeding on you, even as you feed *it*.

I should have just stayed in that Friday night all those months ago. That's all it took, one night and your whole world is turned upside down. Only a few moments really when you get right down to it, not that I can remember the actual deed. I've had flashes sometimes, but… I don't know, it doesn't really matter now, does it? What's done is done, that's what my old grandma used to say. No use crying over spilt milk. Oh, but I did anyway – mainly because it was like a tanker-full rather than a bottle or a glass.

I've cried, dear Christ how I've cried.

Shouldn't have gone. Shouldn't have listened to Brenda – it was her stupid idea, and she's had her fair share of those in the past. Especially when we were at uni, the amount of crazy things we did back then we wouldn't have dreamed of before we left home. Well, *I* wouldn't have anyway. That's where I met her actually, Freshers' Week. I'd arrived all shy and wet behind the ears, and suddenly there was this girl who not only knew the ropes, she'd climbed up them, down them, tied them into knots.

'So you are…?'

'Melissa. Mel.'

'Okay, Melissa, Mel. Wanna have some fun before you hit the books?'

And we certainly had that. In pub after pub, nightclub after nightclub. Drink, some drugs… and guys. There was no shortage of those. When I moved away from home, my parents thought I had my head on straight – and I probably did, till I came across Brenda. After that, it wasn't so much on straight as back to front and upside down. I'm guessing my story isn't that much different to a lot of people's who went off to get a degree, or try to – I barely scraped it in the end because of the mistakes I made at the start, and a fat lot of good it did me out there in the real world getting a job anyway. Then again, what was I thinking with History of Art? Working in a gallery or something? Was never going to happen.

But, in any event, that's how I met her, at Haylington University. That's also where I met Gavin. I thought he was a pretty decent guy, compared to some of the losers I'd ended up with anyway. Didn't know they were losers at the time, obviously – who does? Wouldn't have been hanging around with them if I had… or maybe I would, because when you're in the love haze you just can't see it, can you? Gav had been part of an extended group I'd known for ages, that Brenda and I sometimes went out with. I never really *saw* him, though, you know what I mean? Not until that night when a couple of guys were trying it on in *Tub-Thumpers*, and I couldn't see any of my mates around to help me out; not even Bren, who was probably in some corner somewhere with her tongue jammed down a bloke's throat.

But Gav stepped in, like a knight in techno-coloured armour – at least that's what he looked like under the lights in there.

'Are these idiots bothering you?' he said.

'Like you wouldn't believe,' I told him. They weren't bothering me after that. Backed off holding their hands up in surrender. The better man had won. 'Thanks,' I said. And then Gav asked me what I was drinking… We ended up chatting till dawn, once we'd left that place – because we couldn't hear ourselves think – and found an all-night café.

After that we were pretty much inseparable, and whenever I went out with Brenda, Gav was always there too. Kept me on the straight and narrow, more or less. When my course finished, I stayed in that town – as did Brenda – and I ended up moving in with Gav. We were practically living together by that time anyway, so it just seemed like the next logical step. My folks were all right about it, or said they were – though maybe that was just because I didn't give a toss whether they cared or not. And that was that, life went on. Gav got a job working in IT, which was what he'd studied, and I managed to get something working at a call centre. I soon packed that in because of the hours and crappy pay, and found myself a receptionist's job at the local dentists. Transferable skills, you see: using phones and all that. I was lucky to get it, liked the people there, and I got free dental. Even paid for driving lessons and a little car of my own (Gav's was a company one).

I was like, hey, look at me, doing the whole adult thing. Winning at life.

Silly bitch.

I still went out every now and again, except it was to coffee shops in the daytime mainly with Bren, to have a natter. She was still a bit of a party animal, still 'on the scene' and hadn't really settled down with the one guy; in fact at any given time would have a few on the go. I used to look at her and think, God I'm glad that's not me anymore. I'm so glad I've got Gav.

But people change, situations change. You're not the same person in your late 20s you are at the beginning of them, or even in the middle. And men get bored. With some it takes a few weeks, with others even less. With some it takes a while. The longer he stayed with that firm, the more Gav used to go out with 'the lads' he knew from it. At first only at weekends, then more and more in the week. Like he was actively trying not to spend time with me.

Then the emergencies at work started up, the conferences he would get sent on – and I later found out he volunteered for. I used to trust him, would joke that I could put him in a room full of naked women and he'd only want to cover them up because he thought they looked cold. We don't really know anyone though, do we?

I'll admit, it did make me a bit nuts for a while. I'd do the checking the phone thing that I swore I'd never do, demand to know exactly where he'd been and with who, though I very rarely got a straight answer. In the end the inevitable happened, and I came back to the flat to find he'd just packed up his stuff and left. Not without having somewhere else to live, of course. Men don't let go of one branch till they have the next one firmly in their grip. Turned out he'd shacked up with one of the women he'd been seeing over the years – and there were a *lot*, trust me. This one worked at a solicitors they provided IT support for… fucking slut!

Why do we do that, why do we always blame the other women? It was Gav who was cheating: on me. She *was* a bit of a slut, though, by all accounts. I saw her once when I went round to theirs, waiting until they were both home to confront them on the driveway of her house. Ranting and raving, going mad at them and – can you believe it? – asking what I could do to get Gav back. Begging. Ridiculous!

Mum and Dad didn't help either, with all their talk about fish and the sea. Concerned that I was going to slip into some kind of depression like I used to do in my teens, and have another episode. But at least it stopped them from asking when I was going to make an honest man out of Gav – the answer to that: never, wasn't possible – or when they could expect the grandkids to come along. That one's almost laugh out loud funny now… not.

You can imagine what state I was in after all that, which is probably why I agreed to that night out. Dr Brenda's prescription to get over Gav and his antics.

'You know what you need, don't you?'

'Gav's head on a plate?'

'A good old-fashioned night on the tiles, like we used to have.' Like Brenda *still* had, although I got the sense that she would have done anything to have me with her again. 'Hasn't been the same without you,' she confessed. When everything else fails, flattery and all out guilt-tripping will usually do the trick. 'It'll be fun,' Brenda assured me, although I was less than convinced.

Fun like in the old days, now that 30 was on the horizon, just sounded sad and pathetic. I much preferred a cuppa and the soaps to dancing the night away to some techno-beat, getting smashed out of my skull. In the end, I said yes more to shut her up than anything. I could always leave early if I wasn't into it, get a cab and get back to my lonely sobbing into my tea. Much less sad and pathetic.

'You never know, you might even meet another fella,' Brenda had said. 'Get you back on that horse again.'

That was the last thing I wanted, or needed. Riding of any description. And I told Brenda so, got her to promise that if I did come out with her she'd leave all that alone. Not try and set me up with anyone. It was my one and only condition.

In your condition...

'Oh... all right, just us girls. But you don't know what you're missing.'

I knew full well. Could live without knowing. Would live a lot longer without...

Brenda came round at 6 to 'help' me get ready. Brought some of her clothes for me to choose from, because mine were woefully out of date and not at all appropriate for painting the town red – which meant that they covered up more than 20% of your body and didn't leave you freezing to death when you came out of the club again. Of all of them, I went for the simplest. You can't really go wrong with the little black dress, can you? Though I would have preferred it not to be quite *so* little. If the hem had been a bit longer, like somewhere in the region of my knees instead of just past my waist. Same went for the cleavage, which left very little to the imagination. Okay, nothing at all if I'm being honest.

'I can't really get away with this kind of stuff anymore, Bren,' I told her.

'Rubbish,' she said, shushing me so she could put the finishing touches to my make-up, which apparently involved drawing my eyebrows on so thick it looked like they'd been marker-penned, and painting my lips so red it looked like I'd been wounded. A bleeding cut, to match my bleeding heart...

Blood, meat... the feeding... the cravings...

I felt incredibly self-conscious, but at least I wasn't wearing what Brenda had on, I told myself. If we stayed together, she was bound to get all the attention from the male population, who'd ignore me and make straight for the woman who was in what appeared to be little more than a pink satin nightie. It might have been for all I knew. Would cut out the middle man later anyway, save her the trouble of putting that on for bed. If she even wore anything at all, and if she planned on being alone of course. Which, knowing Brenda, she probably didn't.

She assured me, as we got out of the taxi, that very little had changed. And she was right; it was the same old, same old. Apart from the fact that *I* had become, y'know, old. Oh, I realise if I'd said that to someone in their 30s or 40s, or even Mum and Dad's age, they'd have punched me in the face. But compared to a lot of the punters out there, I felt positively ancient, even if I didn't look it. There were still some, however, like Brenda, who hadn't chosen the quiet life yet – or it hadn't chosen them, one or the other. Especially if you knew where to go, knew the route these days as my best friend clearly did.

I didn't start to loosen up until we'd hit the third place. Not really. I didn't even have a drink in the first one, just diet coke. Wanted to keep my wits about me because, well, someone probably should the way Brenda was downing those vodkas. But when I did have my first Bacardi – a large one, I was told – I started to feel a little better, I have to admit. It always took the edge off back in the day, I'd just gotten out of the habit I guess. Or didn't want to become too reliant on it, especially when I began to have my suspicions about Gav.

I'd only had a couple before I began to feel its effects, as out of practice as I was. I wasn't paralytic or anything, just nicely by that time. In spite of my protests, and refusing to get up there myself, Brenda was on the dance floor throwing some shapes – some very odd ones, it had to be said – much to the amusement of a handful of youngsters, and the delight of a couple of guys who looked about our age. They were ogling her as she gyrated, no doubt wishing she had a pole she could swing around.

That was where I met… *him*. I couldn't tell you his name, because I don't think he ever gave me it, or I simply don't remember. It's hard enough trying to picture his face, and even then I'm not sure I'm remembering it correctly, the features swimming. Everything's a bit hazy from then onwards, you see. I do remember, after the initial awkwardness, us chatting like I'd known him for years. I was well aware that I'd been down that road before, but for some reason I didn't seem to give a crap that night. To me, he seemed perfect. I think I let him buy me a drink, maybe even two – and then suddenly I was kissing him. Falling into him, losing myself. It just seemed like the right thing to do, the *only* thing to do. More drinks, more kissing and—

The next thing I knew I was in bed at home. It was morning, and light was streaming in through the window, hurting my eyes. I had one sheet over me, but was naked underneath it. And I was alone.

I struggled to remember what had happened the night before, recalled meeting someone – Mr Perfect, Mr Right? – but not a lot after that. Had he come back here with me? I hadn't done something like that since my first year at uni, not since Gav came along, for obvious reasons… Was the guy still around, maybe in the loo or having a shower or something? I sat up and cocked an ear but there were no sounds coming from down the hallway. I called out, not his name because like I said I didn't know that, just hello. Nothing. My dress and my underwear were scattered across the bedroom floor, like I'd been in a hurry to get them off; not folded neatly like I usually did over the chair at the dresser. My mobile was on the bedside table, switched off, which I never do, and when I turned it back on again I saw a handful of messages from Brenda.

Hope U havin' a gr8 time – said one.

Just wat u needed – said another.

And a message that morning wanting me to call her, perhaps meet up for coffee later in the day… if I didn't have other plans, that was. I frowned, rubbing my forehead as I sat there leaning against the pillows. Mr Right? More like Mr Fucking Right Now! A one-night stand, an easy lay, whatever… and he'd bailed. I had no number for him, no way of getting in touch. Not even his bloody name! How could I have been so stupid?

That was the first time I cried about this whole thing, and they were different to the tears I'd shed over Gav and his tart. Did I feel different even then? I felt used… and I suppose I had been. *Definitely* had been, looking back. If what had happened had happened, then I should really have gone and got the morning after pill, but I didn't think I needed it. Gav had insisted I take regular steps to ensure that wasn't an issue early on in our relationship. But then nothing's ever 100% effective, especially when you're dealing with something that…

Anyway, I was still in a bit of a state when I met Brenda, not that she seemed to see it. Sensitivity's never really been her strong suit.

'You dark horse, you,' was the first thing she said as we sat down in the coffee shop with our cappuccinos. 'All that talk about not… And then you—'

'Brenda, please.'

'Got luckier than I did, sadly. So, how was he?'

'God, I can't even…'

'*That* good, eh?'

'I… Look, I don't remember.'

Brenda stared at me then as if to say *how?* 'You weren't that far gone when you left, were you? What happened, did you have a few back at his place?'

'I…' All I could do was shake my head. 'Why did I do that? Why did I go off like that with a complete and utter stranger?' Even as I said the words, I remembered that he hadn't seemed like a stranger at the time. That he'd had an… effect on me. Brenda would have just called it charm, but it was more than that.

'You were adamant it's what you wanted,' Bren promised me, taking a sip of her coffee. 'Came and found me, said you'd met a bloke and you were heading off.'

'Jesus… I don't remember any of that.' A thought suddenly occurred to me. 'You don't think there's a chance I might have been…'

'What, roofied? Like I say, you didn't look that out of it to me. We've both seen girls that's happened to. At uni, remember?'

It was true, we had seen a few of those. Girls we'd managed to get away from guys we were pretty sure had drugged them; some could barely walk, others were throwing up for England. So, just my stupid impaired judgement then. If only I could remember!

But I couldn't dredge the memories up at all. It was like trying to grab on to fog, nothing would stay for long – and I have to wonder now whether that's another side-effect of what happened to me. What *he* put inside me.

I've tried to figure out why, I really have. Was it some kind of survival thing? I've seen that on nature programmes. Or the opposite: once he'd done what he'd done, did he then die himself? Was that his sole purpose? I have absolutely no idea. All I know is the end result of that night, which I discovered when I didn't come on the following month. I dismissed it at first, as you do when you're trying to pretend something isn't happening. But when I was *really* late, I got myself a home test and did that.

Then I did another. And another… Every time it came up with those two red lines. Still I couldn't believe it, so I went to the doctor and she confirmed that yes, in spite of the fact I really shouldn't be, I was 'with child'. I left the clinic and started crying as soon as I got inside my car.

No use crying over spilt milk…

So, there could be no denying the fact. The question was what to do about it? I'd be lying if I said it didn't cross my mind to have a termination. I could barely look after myself, let alone a baby – and I was on my own now that Gav…

That was a point, what if it *was* Gav's? I certainly couldn't rule that out, not back then, though I know different now. Did he deserve to be a father, would he even want to be now that he had that harpy? We'd never really discussed kids, not seriously – only in that 'someday, maybe' way people do. If anything, the amount Mum and Dad kept going on about starting a family was enough to put us both off the notion. I couldn't put anything off after that news, though, could I?

I even got as far as booking an appointment, getting in the car to go – but in the end I couldn't. I just couldn't. Knowing what I do now, I don't think it would have let me anyway; it would have found a way to stop me, some kind of pain. In the same way that it won't leave me alone until it gets what it wants from me, what it needs.

I told Brenda first, of course, who sat down on the sofa in my flat and let out a long breath. She asked me what I was going to do and I told her the truth, that I had absolutely no idea.

'Holy shit, this is huge!' she said then, which didn't exactly do much to calm me down. 'You think it might be… y'know, that guy's?'

Mr Perfect? Mr Fucking Right?

I shrugged. 'Fifty-fifty at this point.'

'Holy shit,' repeated Brenda. I think the shock of it was not only because she was scared for me, but also because it made her think about herself. That it could happen to her, if she wasn't careful. 'So he probably didn't… y'know, wear protection,' she said eventually.

Almost certainly not. But I hadn't caught anything, that much I did know from the doctor's tests – and I was lucky, actually. Hadn't caught anything… except for what was inside. Or maybe it had caught me?

'When are you going to tell your folks?' she said next.

I bit my lip. Wasn't even sure I was going to, but I knew I probably should. Apart from anything I was going to need the support, financially if nothing else. I also knew that before long it would get hard to conceal, so I bit the bullet instead and called them.

'Oh love,' said my mum. 'Who's the father?'

'I… He's no longer around,' I told her. Wasn't exactly a lie; whether it was Gav or Mr Right, neither of them were exactly banging down my door.

'A rebound thing? Oh love,' Mum said again. 'I don't know whatever your dad's going to make of this.'

I did. I knew exactly what he'd make of it, what he'd think of me. I could picture his face even as Mum gave him the joyful news.

Turned out they were nothing but supportive, once the dust had settled, offered to go with me to appointments and scans, even though they lived quite far away. I was their little girl when it came right down to it, and I was finally giving them that grandchild they so craved.

The cravings… the feeding…

I even thought about asking Mum for advice about that. About those strange urges I was beginning to get. Like when I'd go to do the shopping, pushing my trolley around the supermarket – pausing at the meat counter and gazing at all that food. Uncooked, but it looked perfect to me.

Perfect, right… Mr Right…

One time I could have eaten the whole lot there and then. I think I even started drooling looking at the stuff through the glass. I shook my head though and walked off, put my other shopping through the till: the fresh fruit and veg I'd been told I needed to keep my vitamins up, and there was no way like the natural way. Like nature… Nurture.

Problem was I would just puke it all back up again. In fact there wasn't that much I *could* tolerate, not regular food anyway. All pretty normal – morning sickness, except they don't tell you it lasts all friggin' day. Morning, evening and noon sickness it should be called.

Throwing up for England.

Same with the meat. I went away and looked it up. Cravings are just the body's way of telling you it's deficient in something. Like with coal, it's lack of iron. Pickles, low salt levels. And dairy, that's low levels of calcium. See? All normal. Red meat was blood cell growth, I read. Has high levels of vitamin B6 – whatever that is – which is important for blood—

The blood, the meat…

—cell growth. Shouldn't eat it raw, mind. That's a no-no. You could catch all sorts, pass it on to the… It's a fairly common craving. You shouldn't give in to it, though. You really shouldn't. But, it's like I said, the hunger: that's the worst part. The *need* for it. I was even dreaming about it, having fucking nightmares for Heaven's sake! The only way to get it all to go away was to buy some, to eat it. Dear God, that felt good! Didn't last for long though, because that bastard thing inside me would leach (leech?) all the goodness from the meal. Leave me feeling empty again, ironically, as it demanded more and more.

Ranting and raving.

I stopped thinking about it as a baby, if I ever had done. It was just this thing, this… this parasite worming around inside of me, like the thing that had wormed its way inside me in the first place and put it there. No different.

At one of the early scans, which Mum and Dad came to, they could both see my face when I looked at the screen.

'What's the matter, sweetheart?' asked Dad.

'Can't… can't you see that?' I said.

'See what?'

'That!'

'It's a little difficult to make out,' Mum said then. 'But yes, there it is. There's the head, the body.'

I gaped at the pair, then at the person doing the scan. None of them could see it, they really couldn't. None of them could see what I was seeing. Just a healthy baby, not a… not that creature. The worm, the leech.

With child? No. With… something else.

I knew what they'd say, though, if I said anything. 'You've got to give it time, for the bond to form. The connection.' Oh, there was a connection there all right! The bond had already formed. I just wanted it out of me.

Either that or they'd say it was one of my moods, my depression – which pregnancy can trigger, I know. Another episode, like those I used to suffer from when I was young.

An episode? Would an episode make you do the things I've done? Force you to do such horrible…

Losing myself…

Because the raw meat from the supermarket, from the butchers, soon wasn't enough for it. The pain, the cravings grew worse and worse. Nothing could fill me, could fill *it*. And I was so tired all the time, from the dreams, from the torture that meant I couldn't even lie in bed without it hurting.

I thought about just cutting it out. Even grabbed a kitchen knife at one point and was about to stab it into my stomach, but a bolt of sheer agony stopped me. Saw me passing out on the floor. There was no way it would let me do that, its bond – connection – a defence mechanism as well. In control of my body, *changing* my body.

Not only would it not let me kill it, but it also wouldn't leave me be until I gave it what it wanted.

The blood, the feeding… the cravings…

The first time was just another stranger. Someone walking his dog on the street as I drove round late at night. All I had to do was pull over, ask for directions. Who was going to think I was up to no good? And then… let the Midazolam do its work, injected into his neck (it's amazing what you can get hold of working at the dentists, a forged form here and there; Dr Mel's prescription). Then it was just a case of bundling him into the back seat, leaving that yapping dog behind.

I took him to a place I'd found, an old, abandoned warehouse that not even the druggies used anymore. Laid him out on the plastic sheeting I'd brought with me. He was more or less starting to come round by then, so I found a use for that kitchen knife. Opened his coat and shirt, found a home for it in his chest. 'I'm… I'm sorry,' I said to him as I did it, and he gurgled something back.

Blood pumped out, pooling on that chest. I paced my hand on it. Felt the warmness. Wanted to lick it, slurp it greedily into my mouth.

No. I didn't want *any* of that. Wasn't me, wasn't my idea. It was that thing's – the pain, the dreams. Telling me what to do, changing me, controlling me. I *have* to remember that, if nothing else. It wanted fresh blood, fresh food. Only that would do. I tried to block it all out, what I was doing. But unlike the night this monster found its way inside me, I actually mentally recorded every minute of the feed: stripping him, putting the knife – the carving knife – to use again. Gnawing on him almost to the bone, even though it made me feel sick. Well, sick and satisfied all at once. It was filling me up, but at the same time it was only food for that thing. Would only satisfy *that* for so long.

I dumped what was left of the body in the river that ran behind the warehouse – it was how they used to export stuff back in the day (meat and…) back when the warehouse was used – weighing it down with bricks. I burned the clothes in a metal bin. Then I cleaned myself up; what a mess I – *it* – had made. Wasn't thinking about forensics or anything like that, if I got caught then I got caught. It would put a stop to this maggot's antics at least. Would be the only way it would stop, if they made it… if they made *me*.

Can't remember if it was the creature's idea or mine, or if there was any real difference by that point, but we struck upon the notion of hitting those pubs and clubs again next. Where I'd first come across *him*. Mr Right Now. With the charm.

With those eyes, those eyes that made me feel so…

Can't speak for the stranger I picked up, but a lot of those creeps deserved what was coming to them. Ogling, wanting to feed, themselves. Maybe I wouldn't feel so bad then, I thought, up in my head. My guts always felt bad. *I* always felt bad. In need.

I let them chat me up, pick me up… though never buy me anything alcoholic. Couldn't risk the… 'baby'; or rather the thing baking inside me wouldn't risk it. Then I'd suggest we go outside, go somewhere more private I had in mind. Always ended the same way: I'd drug them, and get to work. Get rid of the evidence afterwards. All that blood…

Painting the town red.

On one occasion, the guy got quite rough and I thought I wasn't going to be able to dose him in time. As he pawed me, kissing and groping – not seeming to care about my bump, which was getting quite pronounced and had to be hidden by looser and looser clothing as I continued to… hunt – I thought I saw *his* face, Mr Right's. Heard him saying to me as he held me down on my bed, climaxing:

'I'm sorry… I'm so, so sorry.'

Fitted with the idea that he was just doing what he had to, just passing this on. Then I remembered what I was there for, jammed the needle in the bloke's neck and depressed the trigger. What followed was…

The blood, the meat. Feeding. Getting rid of those cravings… The evidence.

I felt guilty every time, yet I couldn't stop. It wouldn't let me. If there was a way I could pass this on, like *he* had, I would've done it. My life had become a living nightmare, and nobody would understand. Not even Brenda. Definitely not my parents.

But I had to confront them all, sooner rather than later. You see, Brenda had spotted me a few times out in those pubs and clubs. I'd gotten sloppy, perhaps on purpose, I don't really know. It was bound to happen eventually.

She'd been trying to get through to me, texts, calling all the time, leaving voice messages.

'I-I saw you with yet another guy the other night, Mel. And in your condition… What's going on? What are you playing at?'

I wasn't playing at anything. This was no game. I wasn't a player like most of them out there, I was just getting rid of those urges, those desires. The awful, awful *cravings*.

I shouldn't have ignored those calls though, because she showed up at my door one night—

Banging the door down…

—demanding to be let in. And she wasn't alone.

'Why? Why would you…?'

'Don't blame your friend, dear,' said Mum, 'she was just trying to help.'

'You… you *can't* help me. No-one can!'

'Sweetheart, please.' That was Dad, and when he tried to give me a hug, I shrugged him off. Couldn't stand it.

'Look, just leave me alone – all of you!' I screamed it at them, practically throwing them out of my place.

Rating and raving… Going mad…

'Don't shut us out,' my mum pleaded, even as I slammed the door in all their faces, doing just that.

'That's what we get, trying to look out for you!' snapped Brenda through the wood; the last thing that was said before the voices receded. It was her doing exactly that, supposedly, which had gotten me into this mess in the first place. If only I hadn't gone that Friday night… If only.

But no. It hadn't been Brenda's fault. Not really.

I knew whose fault it was. So when I felt them again, those incredible deep-rooted aches, I knew where to find him. Find them both. I'd been there before, after all – waited for them, as I waited this time as well.

For Gav and his cow girlfriend. I didn't care anymore, didn't give a flying fuck whether the police were starting to string all the disappearances together. The fear that there might be some kind of serial killer on the loose targeting young men (just like they in turn targeted young women, hunted *them*). Let the authorities find me, catch me. But not before…

When they arrived back home, I was there, waiting. I didn't even bother with any subtlety this time, just came up behind them – rammed that kitchen knife into the slut who'd stolen him, again and again, screaming out loud.

Gavin tried to stop me, naturally, so I turned on him too. Bringing that blade down two, three times. The parasite wasn't even controlling me then; I *wanted* this. I was *enjoying* this. But, in the end, it was to serve a purpose, and so I dragged him into the car with me. I barely fitted behind the wheel anymore, but I only had to get him to the warehouse. My feeding ground.

He moaned and groaned in the seat next to me, bleeding out. The smell of the blood driving me wild, making me so… His words bubbled up through his lips: 'I'm sorry… So, so sorry.'

I'd heard it all before.

And I began to wonder, even as I pulled him from the car – dragging him into that run-down building, over into the middle where I began my feasting – sucking, biting, clawing at him… not even bothering to use the knife at all, it would only have slowed me down… I began to wonder, had there even been a guy at all?

Came and found me, said you'd met a bloke and you were heading off.

Brenda hadn't actually seen him, had she? Had he even been real, or just imaginary like those people I used to see when I was little. Episodes I had…

Going a bit nuts.

I tore open Gav's throat, ate until he was almost decapitated.

'You know what you need, don't you?'

'Gav's head on a plate?'

Ripped open his stomach, tugging out the intestines with my teeth, pulling my head back until they finally snapped like bits of elastic. Digging out his kidney, his liver, chomping away. Leaving his heart, his bleeding heart, till last. A meal fit for a king, fit to satisfy the thing inside me, nurtured by the food. Moving, swimming around in my swollen belly.

I saw flashes of him again, Mr Right… Mr Right Now! His eyes, what he'd done to me, to those people around me – getting them to see what he wanted them to, a perfect man in my case. The perfect… (*Baby on the screen, a healthy baby… child.*)

No, the reality of it! What I'd seen when we were back at my place… Had we even been back at my place? His… face… No, his *lack* of a face. Wormy, slimy, apart from those eyes, and a mouth filled with row upon row of tiny teeth.

'I'm… I'm not sorry,' he'd burbled as if through thick phlegm, thrusting into me again and again. Putting something inside me that was like him. A baby… *him*. Mr Right. Mr Right Now.

Mr Wrong, oh-so-Wrong.

I shook my head, the memories unreal. Too horrific to contemplate. Doesn't really matter, does it? What's done is done.

And now, as I roll over onto my back, I feel the first of them. Not contractions as such – not that I'd ever had any to compare them to – but something else. Something wanting out (get this thing out of me!), wanting to be free early, much earlier than it should be. Considering a termination.

Followed by the pain, the terrible pain. Not the cravings this time, not mine anyway… if they ever were. But that thing's, the tiny – not so tiny anymore – wrong thing's. The cravings, so intense you don't know whether to laugh or cry. Cry I think, from the agony. Of being bitten into from the inside. Of being devoured, one final meal before it emerges. Eating for one. Because you have this thing inside you that's reliant on you, that's feeding on you… Starving, famished. When you realise you've just got to eat, to have it…

Those cravings. That hunger… Believe me.

It's the worst.

A NIGHT WITH NICOLE

A hiss of static, someone talking in a foreign tongue, and then he found it: the station that played nothing but corny love songs all night long.

Perfect.

Francis Nesbit tapped his fingers to the opening bars of Bryan Adams' '(Everything I Do) I Do It for You'. Abandoning the radio, he turned and grinned at Nicole. There she was, already lying down – he could see her in the half-light, the candlelight. Waiting for him, inviting him to join her.

It was all Francis could do to restrain himself. He'd thought about little else the whole day… well, ever since he'd met Nicole really. But he wanted, *needed* to savour this night, this one night with her. He had to take it slow. At least to begin with.

He still couldn't believe his luck. To think that he, Francis Raymond Nesbit, once a nerdy nobody – the butt of all those jokes at school (and at home) – would ever wind up here, alone with a lady like Nicole. It was a dream come true; a dream he'd had for such a long time. There was a point back there when he thought that no girl would ever look at him twice, let alone… But that had soon changed. He never would've imagined that taking on a job like this one might have such an effect on him. His confidence increased ten-fold, he could relax and be himself around the opposite sex. It was great.

And the sheer number of women he'd encountered… So many it was hard to recall names, although he remembered every last one of their faces. They came into his life for such a brief period of time, but he relished every experience, every one-night stand, every intimate, passionate tryst. With these partners he'd lived out all kinds of fantasies, turned every erotic thought he'd ever had as an adolescent into a reality: uniforms, sexy lingerie, bondage gear, body painting, smearing food all over, then eating it… Privacy wasn't an issue, you see. Francis had the keys and he could use them whenever he wished.

Yet the first time he'd laid eyes on Nicole, he could tell she was something special. At thirty-four she was considerably older than himself, but that didn't bother Francis: he'd had women who were in their forties or fifties before today. No, it was the way she looked. So perfect. Her beauty incredible, with that silky hair and deep, brown eyes. This was before you even got to her body. A body he couldn't help gawking at even as his boss had introduced them.

No doubt about it, Francis was smitten from the outset.

Two years ago, or maybe even twelve months, he wouldn't have had the courage to do anything about it. But he was a different man these days. More worldly wise, if you liked. And while he wouldn't exactly describe himself as a stud, he did know what he was doing in *that* department now. It hadn't been long before Francis made the first move. Just a kiss, nothing more, snatched in office hours (he shuddered to think what would have happened if they'd been caught). It had proved worthy of the risk, though. Because from that moment on, Nicole was his and his alone.

Plans had been made for a night together, just the two of them. And Francis started counting down the hours till that evening. Now the time had finally arrived. She was there awaiting him, beckoning to him. He could postpone the act no longer.

Francis went to her. He caught a whiff of her perfume on the air; the smell made him tremble with desire.

'You look so stunning,' he said.

Well she did. The dress she wore clung to every curve, the pearl necklace (a sentimental gift from her mother, apparently) hung just above her neckline, her make-up – eye-shadow drawing attention to those piercing orbs and a light shade of red lipstick – was alluring rather than tarty. He stroked her cheek and they stared into each other's eyes. The longing was palpable. They kissed, Francis brushing her lips with his own. The taste was like honey. Francis started to undo the buttons on his shirt, one at a time.

No rush… Don't rush.

He ended the kiss briefly, shrugging off the cool material, baring his smooth chest, his underdeveloped torso. Francis didn't have any muscles to speak of, but some women seemed to prefer this. Nicole watched him approvingly, her head resting back against the pillow.

Francis kicked off his shoes without untying them, then undid the buckle on his belt. After slipping out of his trousers, he tossed them aside, then removed his socks. Now all that stood between him and his nakedness was a pair of flimsy jockeys. They bulged at the front, in anticipation of the wonders ahead. He was not in the least bit embarrassed; not like he used to be about his physique.

'Now it's your turn,' Francis told her. 'Don't worry, there's nobody else around.' But for some reason Nicole was being coy, or was she simply playing games with him? Encouraging him to take the lead. 'I see,' said Francis. 'All right…'

He placed his hands on her, starting at the top and trailing downwards. Passing over her breasts, which he paused for a moment to gently squeeze, over her stomach, and then further down. She groaned again as he rested his hand between her legs, the thin fabric of her dress protesting, doing its best to keep him out. And suddenly that hand was moving even further down, over her thigh, reaching for the hem of the dress, snaking under it until—

She was wearing nothing beneath.

His fingers touched her most sensitive spot. Another moan. Francis cut her off with a kiss: much harder than the first. Nicole was reluctant to begin with, but he forced her mouth open with his own, popping in his tongue to meet hers. His fingertips explored her now, rubbing, parting, probing inside her.

Bryan Adams had finished declaring his undying affection on the radio, and had given way to Phil Collins singing 'This Must Be Love'. Francis was inclined to agree this time.

He clutched Nicole to him. With his free hand, he felt around at the back for her zip. It descended effortlessly, following the contour of her spine. When it was down as far as it would go, Francis had to break off the kiss again. He pulled the top half of the dress downwards, freeing her breasts. They were a magnificent sight. Immediately he cupped one and planted his mouth over the nipple. Sucking hard, he heard more groaning from Nicole. The sound urged him on, encouraging him to draw his other hand up now, to take the weight of both breasts as he climbed in beside her. There wasn't much room, but when both of them were flat out it was comfortable enough. Francis nibbled and sucked, sucked and nibbled, then worked on the globes with his tongue.

After what seemed like an age of this, he pushed himself up and over Nicole's left leg, hoisting up the dress before positioning himself just so. Her knees came up on either side of his thighs, trapping him. Francis laughed, then reached around below to pull down his underwear.

It felt like the most natural thing in the world when he entered Nicole. Francis was still taking it slowly, aware that to hurry would do neither of them any good. He would hate for it to be over too quickly and then have to wait to try again. Tentatively, he moved in and out, covering her mouth with his own again, running his fingers through that gorgeous hair, cupping her breasts once more...

Little by little, Francis speeded up, until he got a good rhythm going – to match the song on the radio (good old Phil!). But it was no use; Francis had never been a very considerate lover and he couldn't change that fact, not even for Nicole, as perfect as she was. Indeed, it was her perfectness, the thought of her beneath him, the sight of her face, her breasts, the sensation of being inside her that caused him to lose it. Francis began to thrust in and out, shrugging an apology to Nicole. It had to be done, he had to let go.

What the hell, they had all night. He'd make it up to her.

Francis ground away on top of Nicole, grunting, groaning, crying out with delight. Each penetrating motion sent ripples of pleasure through him. He buried his head in her neck and bit down on the flesh, stretched his hands upwards, feeling the velvety texture of the pillow... It turned him on even more.

'Oh God,' he whispered. 'Oh God...' The cords on his neck stood proud as he approached the final few strokes, now holding on to Nicole for dear life. She shook beneath him as his back arched, as he pushed in one final time and opened the floodgates. Francis twitched, involuntarily pumping into Nicole a few more times – an automatic action beyond his control. Then he relaxed, slumping over her body, resting his head on her chest, his breath coming in short gasps.

'That... that was fantastic. How was it for you?' he asked.

The mushy music blared away in the background. Francis lay there listening to it for a while. Listening to the words... *was* he in love with Nicole? (Was *she* in love with him; *could* she love anymore?). She was certainly unique. Different. More vibrant, more *alive* than any of the others. He hadn't felt this way about his previous 'bed'-fellows. He wished more than anything in the world that they could just stay here together, for always. But Nicole had to go away soon, he knew that. Just like they'd all gone away. Francis couldn't do much about it.

He looked at his watch; it was just gone twelve. That gave him about five or six more hours with her – he'd even forgo sleep on this occasion – then he'd have to make a start on cleaning the place up. On cleaning Nicole up. Washing the make-up off her face, applying more of the fluid to her skin, the scent of which was so enticing now to him. Putting the clothes back on that she *should* be wearing, covering up that love bite somehow... Obliterating any evidence that he'd been here tonight before the parlour opened again tomorrow morning at nine. At the moment Nicole was the only one here, though Francis was expecting some more by the end of the week. Perhaps there'd even be a 'client' to top Nicole. But he doubted that very much. Nicole was one of a kind.

Francis shifted around inside the coffin, resting atop the largest of the rectangular tables. Nicole groaned. To anyone else it might have sounded horribly disgusting, air attempting to find its way out of a body that no longer breathed the stuff. However, to Francis it was the most beautiful sound he'd ever heard. A sound of satisfaction, of contentment, of... of love? Well, he could dream, couldn't he? He could dream...

And they still had the rest of this night together, just the two of them.

Just him and Nicole.

Nicole and him.

THE SCARRED

Hey, how're you doing?

Allow me to introduce myself, Jackson – Jackie – Trent, at your service. Now, I know what you're thinking: I've heard that name before somewhere. Could be you're thinking about the singer. You know, the one who was married to Tony Hatch? She co-wrote the theme to *Neighbours*, as in everybody needs good ones… No shit, they're better than bad ones; the kind I usually have to deal with, though I don't have any myself. Mum was a big fan, so I was told – of the singer, not the soap. Pity I was born a boy, right? Though you can take Jackie either way (a line I've often used), and my dad suggested the compromise of Jackson in case I wanted the choice. Doesn't really bother me: a name's a name, and they're both dead anyway. Died when I was only nine, leaving me to the tender mercies of my aunty and uncle.

They were okay, I shouldn't really grumble. They took me in, clothed me (though some of those clothes… man), fed me (if you count fast food nine times out of ten as food). The problem was they were never really expecting – and didn't actually want to start – a family. Sure, there was only little old me, but even that transformed them from a couple into… well, something else. This was the pair who didn't even get a pet because it would tie them down, and then I came along, an unexpected twist. Life's a bitch like that, isn't it?

Both my Aunty Jude – Mum's sister – and Uncle Harry had busy lives, you see. Harry was in the army and Jude worked on the airlines. They didn't see a vast amount of each other, as you can probably imagine, but they used to tell people that was the secret to a happy marriage. Hadn't been the case for my parents, they virtually lived in each other's pockets, but then different strokes for different folks, right?

Anyway, we moved around a lot, which is probably why I don't mind it so much these days. Once I'd been taken in by Harry and Jude, I never really had a permanent home. I used to get left on my own a lot too. Don't get out your violins just yet, it wasn't that bad. I had Buster the Golden Lab for company (yep, they finally caved on the pet front… now there was someone to look after it – plus it kept me occupied). And I had the TV: watched so much of it back then, I don't really bother with it now. That and the fact I have a busy life myself.

I blame those shows more than anything for my current line of employment. They made it all look so exciting: Magnum; Rockford; Mike Hammer; Dan Tanna… 'Course, at that age how was I to know the reality would be somewhat different; quite apart from anything else, those guys were over in the States… Oh, and they were fictional. The seed was planted though, and so years later here I am.

I left round about the time Buster died, from doggy cancer in case you were wondering, and I drifted around for a while. Eighteen and free as a bird, taking whatever jobs I cold find, getting drunk in pubs and clubs and staying in whatever low-cost hotels and motels had rooms available. Occasionally I'd take a girl back, sure; well, you do at that age, don't you. There was never anyone special. They never stuck around for long, and neither did I.

Suffice to say I did my fair share of dossing around, saw a bit of life as they say. I'd check in with Harry and Jude every now and again but, honestly, I doubt they even noticed I'd gone. Definitely didn't miss me. And there came a time when I started to become bored with it all, started to think about what I wanted to do with my life.

It was finding Al's nephew that decided it. Oh, Al was the guy at the garage I was working for at that time. Had some wild notion his brother's kid had gone off and joined a cult or something. Turned out he just owed a few of the wrong people money and had skipped town... I found him, though, followed the trail and sniffed him out. I remember saying to him: 'Seriously, cover your tracks better, mate. If I can catch up with you, then...'

Al was really grateful, mostly to know that the kid wasn't sacrificing chickens to Satan or something. Said his brother would sort out the mess, pay off the debts and sweet-talk the right people. Al was so grateful, in fact, he gave me what I came to call my real home in the end. Said I was wasting far too much money staying in B&Bs when I was travelling around. Said there was a vehicle out back that might suit me down the ground, and if I wanted to fix her up she was all mine.

I remember the first time I saw her, sitting there unwanted and unloved. A kindred spirit. A rustbucket of a thing she was back then, an old 60s VW camper-van. Something to get me about – if I could get her up and running – and somewhere I could live... temporarily, of course. Except that was nearly ten years ago. I fixed her up, just like new; no, better than new! She's my Batmobile and Batcave all rolled into one. My mobile office and my secretary. I call her Daphne, after the character from *Scooby Doo* I always had a crush on when I was little... still do, truth be told. Actually, she kinda looks a bit like the Mystery Machine I always think, without the psychedelic colours. It's a place to lay my head anyway; there's even some running water, electricity. Little extras I added myself. No shower, obviously, because of space issues. But then I use the ones in whatever gym I happen to be exercising in that week; really early or really late, whenever no-one's around, of course. It works…

You'll probably have guessed what I do by now. That's right, I'm a gumshoe, a private eye, private dick… No, scratch that last one, I've never cared for it. Nowhere near as exciting as all those TV guys made it look, but then that's the real world for you. Mostly I follow husbands who're suspected of cheating, get the dirt on people and – my specialty, as I proved even before I got my license – I find missing people. Even when they don't want to be found.

It's what I'm doing here today, meeting a couple of prospective clients at a coffee shop in town. The town I happen to be in because of them (mobile, see?) answering their call. That's right, I advertise – you can find me in the *Yellow Pages*, online, and just basically around. I have a PO Box number, phone number and email; I cover all the bases. I thought about having the meeting in Daphne, as I sometimes do, but they suggested this instead. Neutral territory, I suppose.

And there they are, I clock them as soon as I walk in. Mr and Mrs Kirk. The Kirks. He's definitely a Mister and not a Captain. Normal-looking, if you know what I mean? Thin – gaunt might be a better description – glasses, jumper under a tweed jacket. His attempt at being casual I suspect, but he wouldn't know what that was if it jumped up and had a reasonable conversation with him. He looks like what he is, a modestly successful businessman. Mrs Kirk, on the other hand, dresses a lot younger than she actually is: late forties, but in a hoodie and jeans. Maybe she just can't be bothered making an effort? They've been through the wringer a bit, these two, so who could blame them?

I hold up a hand, but they've already seen me. Were looking out for me. I spot Mr Kirk eyeing me up and down as I approach, not really sure what to make of me. I'm wearing my usual black attire: trousers, T-shirt and jacket. Casual, but also functional – much better than the threads I wore as a kid, and it helps me blend in when I'm sneaking around at night-time. You don't want to be outside someone's house with a camera at one in the morning wearing a Hawaiian Shirt and Day-Glo shorts. But I suppose it does make me look a little like a cat burglar. Like I might be untrustworthy.

Nevertheless, he rises and holds out his hand, which I shake. The grip's firm enough, or maybe that's the desperation in it. He finally lets it go and I shake Mrs Kirk's as well when she gets up.

'Mr Trent,' she says, 'thanks for coming.'

'No problem,' I tell her. It's my job, they're paying me… or will be if this meeting goes well. 'And please, call me Jackie.' The hand I was shaking a second ago offers me a chair opposite them, while her husband asks if he can get me anything. 'I'm good, thanks.'

Mr Kirk looks at his own barely touched black coffee in front of him as if wishing it was something else, something stronger (even if we had been somewhere like a bar, I wouldn't have joined him… I'm more or less tee-total these days; same thing as the TV, drank a little too much when I was younger so it doesn't appeal to me now). And the more I study that face, those fresh bags under his eyes, the lines I'm willing to bet hadn't been there until recent months, the more I reckon he's not that far off a serious drinking problem – at the very least self-medicating to get some sleep. His business, which is something to do with shipping, probably hasn't been getting the attention it usually receives either. From their body language, sitting a few inches apart when they finally do sit again, but knees pointing in opposite directions, you could almost certainly say the same thing about the Kirks' marriage.

All because of their problem, all because of the thing I'm here to help them with. Some couples, it makes them stronger, they pull together. Others... Just depends on the state of it before, I guess.

'So,' I begin, because it doesn't look like either of them will, 'we're here to talk about Phoebe?'

Mr Kirk looks down again, not at his cup this time, but at the floor. Now he glances sideways and nods, trying not to cry. Dads and their daughters, eh? That special bond, even when they get older. Those two are close, I can see that. Maybe the mother is jealous of the bond? Did that have something to do with the distance there after... Doesn't mean Mrs Kirk is any less keen to find her girl; just that perhaps she hasn't put her on a pedestal like dear old Dad. Means she might be more useful for information, that the picture I get of Phoebe won't be as idealised as it will be from her father. Might also be why, ironically, daughters confide in their mothers more when it came to personal stuff.

'She's been missing now...' I take my notebook out of my pocket, one of those hardback ones with a little holder for the pen so I can jot things down anywhere. 'A month and a half?'

Mr Kirk looks up sharply. 'Almost two,' he corrects. He could more than likely tell me to the day, hour, minute and second.

'Right... And the police have—'

'The police have been *fucking* useless!' snaps Mr Kirk, then glances around, realising he's drawn attention to himself. He shakes his head as a kind of general blanket apology.

'You'll have to excuse Gordon,' says Mrs Kirk. Of course he's a Gordon; he *looks* like a Gordon. 'But it's been a stressful few weeks...' Her eyes flick sideways across at him. 'For all of us.'

'Sure,' I say. 'No need to be sorry.'

'It's just that… well, I think they've stopped bothering,' Gordon Kirk explains. 'Tell the truth, I don't think they took it very seriously in the first place.'

'No,' I agree. They won't be doing – it's not like Phoebe Kirk was snatched from a street corner or something, or simply vanished. She's nineteen, an adult at university, and she decided to take off; I can't really say anything, it's what I did when I was around her age. She even left a voice message for her folks telling them she was okay and not to look for her. The Kirks let me listen to it as we go over everything. Her voice is light, breathy – excited. She doesn't sound like someone who is being coerced to do something against her will. One of the reasons why the police wouldn't have been treating it like a missing persons case.

Nothing unusual about people running away, happens all the time. I should know, I see enough of it. And with kids a lot younger than Phoebe. Obviously something triggered it, though; these things don't just happen in a vacuum. For me it was boredom, wanting to see the big, wide world… Didn't get very far, but there you go. What had it been for Phoebe? What had been her reason? She was away from home, so it hadn't been life back there – which, if you listen to Mr Kirk, was like some kind of Paradise on Earth where she wanted for nothing. Only child, so I can believe it. And if it was uni that was bothering her, then why not just come back to her folks? What was it that made her think there was nowhere she could go?

'We think… we think she might have been a little bit depressed,' says Mrs Kirk in that English way of understating things – I still haven't been offered a first name yet, but I already know from my research that it's Janice.

Her daughter certainly didn't sound very depressed on the recording. 'What makes you think that?'

'Phoebe lost weight whenever she was away, we both noticed it. Gordon used to joke about feeding her up while she was home.' Again, nothing unusual about that, just a student lifestyle with hardly any money… though she'd only have had to ask and would've been sent a luxury hamper, I'd be willing to bet. Not the way to fit in, however, that. Quite the opposite. 'And… well, it was probably nothing. She *said* it was nothing.'

I lean forwards. 'Tell me.'

'I only got a quick glimpse, because she always keeps herself covered up nowadays; is always cold, probably because she doesn't eat enough, or eat right, but… well, the last time she was home I thought I saw…' Mrs Kirk tapped her forearm with a finger. 'There was a scar. Not sure how old it was or anything, but… I asked her about it, and she said it was fine – just an accident at a party. Had bumped into a doorframe and cut herself on a ragged bit of wood.' It was possible, especially after too much to drink. But the covering up is ringing warning bells, I have to say. Then again, it hasn't been the warmest of starts to spring and if she was someone who just felt the cold…

'Did you mention any of this to the police?' I say.

'Of course we bloody did!' Mr Kirk butts in, voice rising once more, then he shakes his head. Another silent apology. 'They weren't interested, Mr Trent.' I don't interrupt to remind him it's Jackie or, at a push, Jackson; I think it makes him more comfortable to call me Mister. 'No concrete proof anything untoward was going on, you see.'

Makes sense, there wasn't. But it was at least cause for concern. 'I have to ask this. Did you get a sense there was anyone on the scene?'

'Boys, you mean?' Gordon Kirk folds his arms. 'Phoebe wouldn't have been interested in all that. Never has been. Too focused on her studies.' Right. So focused she was trotting off to parties, and where there are parties… 'She was a good girl,' he adds. Like she's still ten or something. In his head, Phoebe probably is. Like I said, dads and their daughters; it's complicated.

'I…' Mrs Kirk chirps up, but then falls silent once more, shakes her own head.

'Yes?' I prompt.

'I don't know, I couldn't swear to it… But I think there might have been someone, yes.'

Mr Kirk swivels round to face her. This is news to him. '*What?*'

'Oh Gordon,' she sighs, as if it says everything – and maybe it does. She was a teenager after all, a young woman. If he thought his daughter was still a virgin in this day and age he was dreaming.

'What makes you think she might have been seeing someone, Mrs Kirk?' I ignore the bristling from her husband at my choice of words.

'I don't know. Like I say, I couldn't swear to it. But… just little things, you know? The choice of songs she listened to, that look in our eyes we get when we're…' Janice pauses, thinking back to the last time she had that look in *her* eyes – and I have to wonder whether it was caused by Gordon Kirk or not. She gives a small laugh. 'You can just tell, can't you?'

Apparently, judging from his expression, Mr Kirk could not. Or didn't want to. But it gives me another angle, another avenue to explore, anyway. Might account for why Phoebe legged it, that she'd met someone and fallen in love. It does stupid things to people, love. Makes you do stupid things as well.

Could account for those scars too, though self-harm for all kinds of reasons is on the rise amongst teenagers. Had whoever she was interested in been playing hard to get, treating her mean to keep her keen and all that bollocks? Then had a change of heart and suggested they go off somewhere together? She certainly sounded like someone who was looking forward to something on that message – and a little like someone who was doing something she shouldn't. Something forbidden… No better aphrodisiac than that, though I keep this particular nugget to myself; for one thing Mr Kirk looks like he's about to have a stroke with all these 'revelations'. Things he should have faced up to a long time ago, really. But I can't say I blame him, what parent doesn't want to hold on to the image of their kid as a kid. It's a tough world out there, hard to watch them grow and go off into it. To let go.

'Right, okay.' I've probably got enough to be going on with from Phoebe's parents. I doubt they know much more, to be honest, which is where I come into it. To find out what they're missing, apart from their child. And as we wrap up the meeting, it's Mr Kirk who asks the inevitable question:

'Do you think you can find her, Mr Trent? You know, like you did with all those others? Like in the Phillips' case?'

I'm not the only one who's been doing his research, it seems. But then, this is what I do – what I'm known for in certain circles. Doesn't always work out the way people want, or expect it to. Sometimes doesn't work out at all, which is why I don't like to make promises, regardless of the way I'm being looked at – the desperation that's palpable, especially from Mr Kirk. I'm like a doctor that way, they don't like to commit to whether they can cure you. Things go wrong, that's life. Which is why the only thing I can say to him, to them both, is: 'I'll certainly do my very best.'

In the end, that's all any of us can do, isn't it?

It's about an hour away by car… by Daphne, I should say.

And there it is, as I crest to the hill I'm climbing: Mannerbridge

University. The last place anyone saw Phoebe before she disappeared. It's a curious mix of the new and old, like so many places I see on my travels. The older buildings look like something out of *Downton*, jarring terribly with the newer, more functional sections which have more in common with portakabins than anything else. Cheap, cost-effective. Most of the lessons are taught in those, because the older bits are quite unstable now. Some were even bombed during the war and never really restored properly. There was a push a few years ago apparently, but the money ran out – chiefly because the then chancellor was dipping into the funds to maintain his gambling habit. Needless to say when that came to light, he was promptly sacked and is currently serving time at Her Majesty's pleasure for fraud. None of which helped those poor buildings…

I park up a little way from the campus, so I can walk there, walk in and not draw attention to myself or what I'm doing. I might be heading towards the big three-oh, but I've got quite a baby face – I've lost track of the amount of times I got carded at pubs and clubs, which was annoying at the time but I'm grateful for it as I get older. I can blend in… and not in a creepy Joey from *Friends* way, 'I can play 19'. Besides which, there are mature students attending Mannerbridge, some much older than me. Like most unis I'm banking on the fact that security won't be great – all I need to do is tag along behind a bunch of students heading through the gates and then slip away, find the place I'm looking for.

Phoebe had an address in a hall of residence, which the Kirks gave me when I called on them the previous day. Before we parted ways at the coffee shop, we arranged a time I could come round and take a look at Phoebe's room at home, but as I suspected it told me very little. Her phone and laptop weren't there, naturally, and all I found out was what kind of bands she liked – from the posters on her walls – what kind of books she was into – YAs mainly, some classics like Dickens – and what kind of movies. There was a healthy amount of Disney, which told me she'd probably bought into that belief about princes coming along to sweep you off your feet so you could live happily ever after. Dangerous, in this day and age; guys take advantage of that kind of thinking.

I'd already looked for her social media accounts and come up empty. Either they'd been deleted, or she never had them in the first place… which is as rare as unicorn shit for this generation. Deleted, definitely. I could have gone to the trouble of rooting them out even then, but this isn't *Hunted*. I'm not after a terrorist or something, plus I figured visiting her home away from home would be more insightful anyway – and less illegal. Sort of.

Because I'm trespassing here, I know I am. And especially when I find the place where Phoebe was staying, again slipping inside when a trio of students open the door with a key-card. They don't care; barely look up from their chat about who'd been doing what to who the previous weekend, and speculating who'll be doing the same that coming Friday night.

Phoebe's room is on the third floor, so I take the stairs. Peeking around the corner onto the landing I see it's pretty quiet, and no CCTV, which is a bonus. If anyone stops and asks me who I am, I'll just say I stayed over the night before with Emma. There's bound to be an Emma, it's one of the most popular girls names around. If they look puzzled, I'll say 'At least I think it was Emma' and click my fingers, waiting for them to *give* me a name that works. Most people do. It's just a little trick I've picked up over the years.

I find her dorm room, which thankfully opens with a real key. Easier to jimmy, which is definitely not legal. I'm here on behalf of her parents though, if anything hits the fan – not my fault she never gave them any keys to her place. Needs must.

Looking about me to make sure I'm still alone, I take out my pick and with a few clicks I'm inside; another of the many things I've learned on my travels… I should write a book one day. I never went to uni myself, let alone stayed in one of these buildings – but the room is pretty much how I'd imagined it to be. Single bed running down one of the walls, a wardrobe and desk in one corner, toilet and shower in the other. Not very big but then I can't really talk, and Phoebe had certainly made it her own; something the university hadn't messed with yet because her rent was paid up till the end of the term. There are photos… the tiny Polaroid kind kids like these days… stuck to the wall with Blu-tack, of her parents, of a cat – deceased maybe, as it hadn't been around when I visited – of her friends from school (they all have uniforms on, and Phoebe's in the middle with her blonde hair tied back in a pony-tail, blue eyes shining out of a smiling face). No handy pictures of a boyfriend or anything, sadly. If only the universe made things so simple.

There's a cactus on the windowsill, a plant that traditionally doesn't need watering, and a few of her clothes are still in the wardrobe – nothing major, she's taken the vast majority with her it seems – and there are some toiletries still in the bathroom, including an almost empty can of dry shampoo. Her make-up is definitely gone, though, which says to me she packed for the long haul. No girl her age would go anywhere without that stuff.

It's as I'm coming out of the en-suite again that I notice it, the edge of the thing sticking out from under the bed. A sheet of paper, a flyer of some kind. For a party, an event…? I bend down to grab it, pull it out – noticing that it's upside down as I do so. But that's okay, I learnt how to read upside down a long while ago – another helpful trick – and spot that it's an advert for a place that's tastefully named 'Tony's Tatts'. Even if I couldn't work that out from context, there are helpful illustrations of people's arms and other body parts with tattoos of dragons and lions and such on them. I'm just turning it around and rising when I hear the shrill voice from behind me:

'*Hey!* Hey, what do you think you're doing in here?'

I stick the flyer in my back pocket and raise my hands, turning as I do so. 'Don't shoot,' I say.

The girl facing me and standing in the open doorway – about the same age as Phoebe, but with shorter jet-black hair held back with a band, and green eyes framed by round glasses – doesn't see the humour in that remark. Her arms remain folded, mouth contorted into a grimace. She's wearing a chequered shirt over what looks like a vest-top, faded jeans ripped at the knees completing the hipster uniform. 'Who are you, what are you doing in here? This is Phoebe's room!' she says, like I don't know. Very territorial.

'I'm… I'm a friend of hers,' I tell the girl.

'Oh?' she replies, but from her expression I can see she doesn't believe a word of it. She clearly knows Phoebe, knows that it's bullshit.

'Okay, okay,' I say then, lowering my hands. 'You got me. I'm her uncle. Uncle Steve.'

This she seems to more readily accept. 'Oh. Right.'

'I'm… Well, tell the truth I'm looking for her. Phoebe's parents are… we're *all* pretty upset about her just taking off. You know about that, right?'

The student nods. 'The police were here, asking questions.'

'Yeah,' I say. 'What did you tell them?'

She shrugs. 'Not much to tell. One minute Phoebe was here, the next she'd gone. Didn't even bother to say goodbye.' The girl looks hurt by the last bit.

I frown, acting puzzled, acting like I know how she'd behave. 'Doesn't sound like Phoebe.'

'I know, right?' The girl unfolds her arms, holds them out like she's about to catch someone falling from above. 'And I thought we were mates.'

'You were good friends, then?'

'Well… yeah.' Not that good if she didn't give her any indication that she might be leaving. Nevertheless, this girl is my only link to the Phoebe who lived in this room.

'Okay, so…' I wait, then nod at her, wanting a name.

'Zoë.'

'Zoë.' I smile. 'So if you have the time, would you mind me asking you a few questions myself? Maybe get you a coffee or something?' Freebies, the way to any student's heart.

'Sure,' she replies with another shrug. 'Just let me get my coat.'

Zoë disappears from the doorway, and as I step out myself I see her opening the door to her room just down the hall. She emerges wearing a big coat like an arctic explorer might need, and locks up behind her. I do the same with Phoebe's room; I've got everything I need from inside anyway.

'Right,' she says, joining me. 'Let's go.'

One coffee turns into several as we sit in the refectory and Zoë tells me all about herself, how she's the first person in her family to go to uni – how she wants to do well, better herself. Make her folks proud, show them what she can do. I listen attentively, nodding in all the right places. Eventually, she gets round to giving me the potted history of her relationship with Phoebe.

'I met her during Freshers' Week, at a humanities mixer. She looked a little… lost. You know what I mean? So we got chatting, turned out we had a few things in common. Bands we like, TV shows, things like that.' That's all it takes at that age, a few things in common – and anyone can be your new best friend. 'Got on so well, I switched rooms with a guy from her floor… I guess I wanted to keep an eye on her. Make sure she was okay.'

'Wait a minute, humanities? I thought Phoebe was studying economics, business? That kind of thing.' Mr Kirk hoping she'd come and work for him when she was finished, no doubt.

'Yeah, this was because of the electives. The modules not on her course, you know? We're both in Sheldon's anthropology class.'

'Sheldon? Is that a first or last name?'

She laughs. 'Neither. A nickname. Cos he looks like that guy from *Big Bang*. You know, the sit-com.' I vaguely recall that character, because the show had just started when I left home and I was still watching telly on a more regular basis. 'It's actually Copeland, Ed Copeland's class.'

'Right,' I say, mentally filing that titbit of information.

'Phoebe got quite into his lessons, though whether that was more to do with the fact she…' Zoë stops and looks at me, realising she's said too much. Not enough as far as I'm concerned. You can never have too much information in my line of work. I can pretty much guess where it was going, however. I might not have been to uni, but I went to school. I had crushes on the teachers, same as everyone else.

'Has a bit of a thing for this… Sheldon guy, does she?' Zoë shrugs, refusing to be drawn into it more, so I try a different tack. 'How was she before she took off, did you notice her acting strange at all?' Now Zoë shakes her head; I'm wondering if she's ever going to speak again. 'Her mum… Janice, seems to think she might have been depressed.'

Zoë laughs now. 'Depressed? Hardly. I've never seen her so happy, actually… What makes her think that?'

My turn to shrug. 'Said she noticed something the last time she was home. A scar, on her arm.'

Zoë cocks an eyebrow. 'A scar? And what, she… you think she might have tried to… Done something stupid? No, not Phoebe. That just wasn't… She wouldn't have done something like that.'

Wouldn't have just run away either by all accounts. And I didn't mention anything about suicide, that had come from Zoë, which made me wonder why. 'Not even if there had been someone she was seeing, perhaps split from?'

Then got back together with? Ran off with?

'No…' Zoë doesn't look sure, though. 'No, I'd have known about it.'

Yeah. Like Mr Kirk would have known about it, too.

It's at this point a group of other students come along, waving and calling to Zoë. She holds a hand up, beckoning them across to our table. 'Who's your new friend?' asks a tall, gangly lad with short hair and far too much oil in his trimmed beard.

'He's… This is Phoebe's uncle… Steve, wasn't it?'

'That's right,' I say, nodding to the gaggle.

She introduces them as Jake, Maya, Rob, Grace and Tim. They all knew Phoebe – though haven't seen her in weeks, have no idea where she is. And they're all in her anthropology class.

'Mr Copeland's class?' I ask.

'Sheldon and his tribalism,' says Rob – who's much more built than Jake, looks like he spends most of his time in a gym, so I'm not surprised when I find out his main degree is in sports science.

'Tribalism?'

'Whole of last term we spent on that crap,' spits Rob. 'Obsessed with it, he is.'

And apparently so was Phoebe, if she liked her tutor as much as Zoë hinted. I ask about what they studied with him and a few of the pieces slot into place. Ritualism, tribal markings, that kind of thing. Interesting.

'Bloody pervy if you ask me,' Rob continues. 'Wouldn't be surprised if he hung around in certain… specialist clubs, if you know what I mean.'

'You liked the bits where he linked it all to football, the two tribes going to war and all that.' This comes from Grace, who has the kind of blue-grey hair old ladies used to crave when I was growing up.

'Yeah, that was okay. I still only scraped a D for my essay, though,' Rob moans with a sigh.

The whole thing breaks up not long after that, and I say my thanks and goodbyes. I give them all my phone number, in case they can think of anything that might help me locate Phoebe. 'If you see her,' says Maya, who is wearing dungarees with flowers stitched onto them, 'tell her we miss her.'

'I will,' I promise, then make my way from the canteen. I now have a couple of leads to follow up. One is to look into this whole situation with Sheldon… Mr Copeland and his lessons. Was he encouraging that crush of Phoebe's? Was he the reason why she was up and down, depressed and then happy? Did he have something to do with her disappearance?

But I also have this. I reach into my back pocket and take out the flyer that I found under Phoebe's bed, finish reading the bottom of it which I'd been doing before Zoë interrupted me. The delightfully-titled Tony's Tatts not only specialises in tattoos, it also does piercings and body modification.

The kind of thing a young girl might be considering to impress a certain tutor who was into all that kind of stuff.

That afternoon I wander the streets of Mannerbridge, looking for that particular establishment.

It's not a big place, Mannerbridge, especially compared to some university towns, and there are pubs and clubs on most corners. One or two might even be the kind that kid was talking about back at the uni, the specialist kind. Hey, why not, there's a 'massage parlour' right there on the high street not even trying to disguise what it really is, with half-naked women in the window who are – so it says – trained in multiple techniques. I'll just bet they are!

What locals I see are not hard to differentiate from the other population, because they have that 'kill me now' look on their faces of people who can't wait for the summer to come and the kids to piss off back to where they belong, thank you very much.

Tony's Tatts is down a seedy back alley where you'd expect it to be, where the light can't get to it. It's not that much brighter inside, in fact, and as I walk through the doors and the strip-curtains hanging down, I see some bald bloke reclining on what looks like a dental chair having a procedure done – and I wonder how the hell the woman doing it can see. I also have to wonder how hygienic or sterile her work station is, especially when she pauses to take a puff on a ciggie. She's all leather and metal, a generous portion of both stitched into the flesh like something out of that movie *Hellraiser*. What skin I can see is covered with tattoos, which I have say are like miniature works of art. If I was into such things, I might even consider a few of them myself here and there… but there's no real point thinking about that.

'Howdy!' comes a voice from beside me, making me jump. From a room off to my left a tall guy has emerged, his beard considerably less well-kept than Jake's and in contrast to the man in the chair, his hair is down to his shoulders. My eye is immediately drawn to the bolt through his eyebrow, then up the step-ladder of rings ascending his right ear. He's dressed in a vest not dissimilar to Zoë's but with no shirt on top, so I can study more of the shop's stock in trade on his body, from pictures of wolves to the wings of what look like an eagle on both upper arms – presumably the rest of the bird is stretched out across his back. His leather trousers are held up by a belt with a silver buckle fastening it in the shape of a Wild West pistol. 'What can I do for you?'

'Tony?' I venture.

He shakes his head. 'Tony sold up a couple of years ago, we just kept the name. I'm Liam.' Fair enough… Liam's Tatts just doesn't have the same ring to it.

'Right, okay… Liam.'

'So…' he prods.

'Oh, yeah. I'm thinking of having…' I look around me at the pictures on the walls, at various other tattoos and piercings: one is a close-up of a nose, with a spike rammed through the septum. 'Having something done,' I settle on finally.

Liam frowns. 'Something?'

'Yeah,' I state, then give a little laugh. 'Not sure what, though.'

'I see,' says Liam. Then he walks over towards a desk at the back, snatches up a large book and brings it back to me. 'Any idea whether you want a tattoo, piercing… something else?'

I laugh again. 'Not really. It's… well, I want to surprise my girlfriend. She's into all this stuff.'

'Newbie? I getchya. We like fresh blood here, don't we, Doris?' The lady doing the work on the bald guy doesn't even look up. It's probably better for her client if she doesn't. Liam shoves the book into my hands. 'Have a flip through that, buddy. Might give you some ideas.'

I open the book up, which is really more of a homemade catalogue of some of the things they've done in the shop, a ring-binder with plastic folders containing photos. Again, I have to admire the skill on display – if some of those tattoos were framed, I'd put them on my walls… if I had any walls. More animals, including the cuter kittens and puppies. Likenesses of film stars like Marilyn and Humphrey Bogart, rock stars like Meatloaf and Madonna – they're all just like them. Then the darker stuff like skulls and gothic symbols. Eventually, I get to the piercings, which range from the standard fare to the more elaborate – one has a chain running from the ear to the nose, and in another shot a similar chain connects some woman's nipples. There's no warning whatsoever before I get to the things like scrotum and dick piercing, clitoris piercing… and then the weirder stuff like someone having a metal ring inserted beneath the bottom lip so you can see straight through to their teeth. I've seen some strange things in my time, but some of those pictures make me swallow dryly and be glad that I haven't had time to grab any lunch.

'See anything you fancy?' asks Liam, who's suddenly over my shoulder, causing me to start once more.

'I'm… not sure,' I say, fighting to keep the tremble from my voice. Was this really somewhere Phoebe was contemplating coming? Were these people connected with her disappearance, with those scars her mother had seen? Time to find out. 'Actually, you were recommended by a friend of mine, so I thought perhaps you could do what you did for her?'

'Really?' says Liam, and now Doris does look up from her labours.

'Yeah.' I put the catalogue down on a nearby chair and fish my mobile out, flick to a recent photo of Phoebe the Kirks sent me that I have stored on there. 'Here she is. Remember her?'

Liam takes the whole phone from me, peering at the picture and frowning. 'Never seen her before in my life. Have you, Doris?' He waves it in the general direction of the Cenobite, who shakes her head without really looking. Then Liam hands me the phone back. 'Sorry… what did she have done anyway?'

'Er… something on her arm,' I reply, not really sure what to say – which comes across massively.

Liam's eyes turn to slits. 'Are you just a fucking timewaster, buddy?'

I shake my head. 'No. No, I—'

'Because we have ways of dealing with them.' I can imagine. It probably involves hooks and chains and tearing someone's soul apart.

I hold my hands up and begin to back out. 'There's obviously been a misunderstanding. Maybe she went somewhere else?' Even I can tell that's lame, so as soon as I can I make a dash for the door, calling out 'Sorry' as I go – the strips threatening to pull me back inside the shop like those hooks I was thinking of.

I make it outside and run down the alley, glancing over my shoulder just to make sure Liam isn't following me. Catching my breath out on the adjoining street, I replay the encounter in my mind. What had I actually learned? Not a lot. Liam may or may not have been telling the truth about Phoebe, might or might not be involved with her disappearance. Might just not care for 'fucking timewasters' as he said. Would Phoebe fit into that camp? Had she changed her mind about having something done at the last minute, was that scar connected to something she'd had done and they'd messed up?

All these questions and more are rampaging round in my head as I walk back off into town. I was planning on going to get something to eat after I was done here, but for some reason I'm not hungry anymore.

Not hungry in the slightest.

As I'm taken up the stairs to the office, I can't help stifling a yawn.

I had a bad night last night, bad dreams. The first in a while: full of cuts, blood (fresh blood!) scars and metal… All brought on by the trip to Tony's. By seeing all those images, on the wall, in the catalogue. In the flesh. What Doris was doing to that guy in the dentist's chair. Fuck me!

Woke up covered in sweat, screaming. A good job I parked Daphne off the beaten track, or someone might have called the cops. You can't see inside, because her windows are tinted, but the noise might have gathered a crowd. I sat there in bed, breathing even harder than when I thought Liam was on my tail. Christ, just thinking about the nightmare even now is bringing on the sweats again, and after I went to the trouble of showering it all off in the uni gym (Rob gave me that idea), changing into a fresh set of clothes.

Just in time for my appointment with Mr Copeland. I got in to see him by saying I was writing a piece about tribalism and mythology, and wanted to pick his brains about the subject seeing as he was the foremost expert on the subject in the region. That there might even be a TV interview and possible documentary… Flattery and the promise of publicity in an area not usually associated with academia will get you far. He juggled some things around and made space for me in his busy schedule.

The receptionist showing me up to Copeland's office – which is easy to find because his name is on a brass plaque on the door – knocks on the wood and waits.

'Come,' a voice wafts through to us.

The woman opens the door and announces me, waving a hand for me to enter. I walk in and he's already rising from behind his desk, hand out as the receptionist waits behind. I don't know about Sheldon, I get more of a vampire vibe from this guy. Dracula-esque. Not the Chris Lee or later

Oldman version, but black and white Lugosi. My children of the night and all that. Leaving scars of a very different kind on the neck.

'Dr Copeland,' I say as I shake his hand, his grip even firmer than Mr Kirk's. Dr *Edward* Copeland I'm told, not Ed as the kids call him, or even Eddie Baby – Python-style. 'Thank you for seeing me at such short notice.'

'A pleasure,' he replies with a twinkle in his eye. 'Would you like any tea, coffee?' I shake my head so he tells Valerie by name 'That will be all' and she withdraws. One of his brides, retreating to her coffin. 'Please, Mr... Robinson wasn't it?' I nod, the old gags are the best. 'Please, take a seat.'

I can't help glancing around at his office as I do so, at various pictures – which range from Scottish warriors with their faces painted blue and white, Mel Gibson fashion, to Maori with their faces covered in swirling black patterns – at books with titles like *Us vs Them: Tribalism in the Modern World*, *The Politics of Populism and Nationalism* and *Ancient Cultures and Their Beliefs*, not to mention those written by him, which probably sold about five copies apiece. At the various masks and African fetishes, one of which, a primitive figure, looks like it has nails banged into it. Back to *Hellraiser* again.

He notices me gaping and laughs. 'Fascinating, isn't it?'

'It is,' I admit.

'I've been studying it all my life. The reason why we gather together in groups, gather others to us and mark ourselves out accordingly. Human nature, Mr Robinson. Human nature.' He's quite charismatic, this guy. I can see why Phoebe had a thing for him. Maybe there was even a sugar daddy attraction going on? But there are definite leadership qualities, someone who would undoubtedly be able to draw groups towards *him*.

'Mark ourselves?' I ask.

'Why yes. Sometimes quite literally. We can trace the origins of today's uniforms back to ancient civilizations, who marked their own bodies with paint or tattoos.' I have a flash then of Liam and Doris, but chase it away. 'Even decoration or scarification to pledge allegiance to a particular tribe.'

Pal, you just said the magic word. 'Yes, you see I'm particularly interested in that side of things, doctor.'

'You are?'

'Yeah, about why people did it back then. Why they might still do it today.'

He smiles. This is a man who clearly likes the sound of his own voice, likes others to hear it as well – and likes them to know just how clever he is. 'As I say, it's a way of showing you belong to a particular tribe. Or it might have religious connotations, Mr Robinson, as you probably know if you've an interest in the topic.'

'Yes… yes, of course.'

'You only have to look at stigmata. The manifestation of the wounds or scars of the Lord to show a loyalty to the Christian faith. Some believe it derives from devout faith, others that it's the body itself creating such wounds. That we're doing it to ourselves, even if we're not aware of it. Or doing it to others. The mind…' He taps his head for effect. 'The mind is capable of so much we still do not understand. And of course there are those who do it physically to themselves – it's hard to rule out the fakes. Then there's the purification aspect.'

'Purification?'

'Certainly. The reason why monks and nuns whip themselves, wear cilices. The pain is a purifying thing – the scars a reminder of the penance. Some ancient civilizations scarred themselves as a form of worship, to bring themselves closer to their deities. Some even worshipped deities who had their own scars, like the Horned Goddess found on the rock painting from 7000 BC at Tassili n'Ajjer, Algeria. She's scarred on the chest, belly, thighs, shoulder, calves… It's all on my course,' he finishes with a chuckle.

'Yes… so I've been told.'

'You… you've been *told*?' He frowns at this, wondering who's been spilling the beans.

I smile. 'So I gather… from my research into you,' I tell him, which seems to relax the man a little. I'm starting to really not like the guy at all and the next thing he comes out with doesn't help.

'There was some mention of this project being on the television. Would there be any financial aspect involved at all?'

My smile broadens. 'Oh, almost definitely.' I'm so full of shit.

'Right, good. Good.'

'You mentioned your course a moment ago; do you enjoy teaching here at the university, doctor?'

He nods. 'Indeed I do. The students by and large are keen, interested. Makes my job a lot easier.'

'Any standouts this year?'

He frowns again. 'I beg your pardon?'

'Any particularly keen students… this year. I'm just curious.'

'A couple,' he answers finally. 'But I don't see why…' The penny drops then. 'You're not here to talk to me about my work at all, are you? This is about the student who ran off.'

I hold my hands up like I did when Zoë found me. 'Sprung.'

'So, you're writing a piece about it? I spoke to the police when they came… I doubt I can help you any more than I could them.'

Or perhaps you didn't want to. 'I'm only trying to get to the truth here, Dr Copeland. Did you know Ms Kirk well?'

'I taught her. Phoebe was a nice girl.'

'One of the keen ones you were talking about?'

Eddie Baby shifts around in the seat uncomfortably, it won't be long before he's up and chucking me out – occupational hazard. 'Look, I don't know what you're trying to insinuate, but—'

'I'm not trying to insinuate anything.'

Then he's rising. Here we go. 'I think you'd better leave now, Mr Robinson… if that's even your name.'

It isn't, it's Jim and Paul's. 'Okay, okay,' I tell him, getting up too and flapping my hands. 'Thanks for your time anyway.'

He doesn't say anything as I leave, but I've already decided by the time I get to the bottom of those steps again and outside, that my time would be better spent keeping an eye on Eddie than anyone at Tony's Tatts.

The vigil begins that very evening, trailing him as he leaves his office after work.

I tail at a discreet distance, but what I've tended to find is that people don't expect to be followed by a private eye in a camper van and don't really think anything of it. He's driving a BMW that was probably nice and shiny when he first got it, but is looking a bit worn now. Explains why he was so interested in the financial side of the interview. I know from digging around into his background that the uni work doesn't pay what it used to, and those books of his won't be bringing home the bacon either. Not that there's anyone to bring the bacon home *to*, as his wife left him a couple of years ago.

Copeland lives about twenty minutes outside town, in a pleasant enough looking house – compact and bijou I think they call it in estate agent circles. Not at all a castle in Transylvania, this is down a cul-de-sac on an average-looking estate. I park at the neck of the road, with a good view of his place and my camera with telephoto lens and night vision binoculars at the ready. Like I said before, Daphne's windows are tinted, so I can see out but people can't see what the hell I'm doing inside. Good job, too.

As I watch, the lights go on in his living room. When I see him sit down and flick his TV on – then five or ten minutes later fetch the ready meal he obviously slammed in the microwave when he got home and eat it from a tray on his lap – I have to wonder whether this is my guy at all. He just seems so… boring. But then a lot of the killers in history have appeared that way, haven't they? Look at the testimonials from their neighbours – everybody needs good ones – stating that they were quiet as church mice. Usually because they had a soundproof murder dungeon or something where they were cutting up their victims…

I shake my head. That's not what's happened to Phoebe. I'll find her safe and sound somewhere shacked up with a fella. Not here, not in Eddie Baby's basement. She's certainly not playing happy families with him anyway, no sign of her all evening. Not even when he goes to bed upstairs, alone. Sighing, I give it an hour or so after he turns out the lights… just in case. But then I find myself nodding off too.

I'm not at all surprised, after thinking about dungeons and cutting people up, that I have the nightmare again.

It's a day and a half later before anything out of the ordinary happens.

Copeland just goes through his routine of driving to work, hitting his office, teaching and heading home to watch documentaries on Webflix. Even porn would have been a welcome distraction.

I'm reconsidering my decision not to watch Liam and co. when things take a turn for the strange. Instead of getting in his BMW and heading home, this time he heads across campus instead, making for the deserted part and the buildings that look like they can't help themselves. Glancing over his shoulder the whole time, in a way he really hasn't been doing up to this point. Makes me conclude that he's been waiting to do this, has given it a couple of days to make sure the coast is clear.

Hanging back, I follow him to the building he's entered, which looks for all the world like a church. It's cordoned off and has a sign up saying that it's dangerous inside and anyone trespassing does so at their own risk. Might be a local hangout for all I know, especially at the weekend, but it seems pretty quiet tonight and it is only Thursday. Somewhere for a secret meet-up perhaps? But who with? Phoebe? Someone else?

Inside, it opens up on to a huge room and there's the remains of the last attempt to do up the building. Bits of wood, scaffolding, that sort of thing. It's dark, and at first I can't see where Copeland's gone. Then I spot him going through a door on the far side. Just what the hell is Eddie Baby up to?

Once he's through, I run to the door. On the other side is a set of steps leading downwards. It's still quite dark, but I can make out the light from his phone torch down there – it's throwing back enough for me to just about see where I'm going, so I follow him. At the bottom is a narrow corridor. I can't see Copeland anymore, but there's light coming from the end of that corridor anyway. Now, I have a choice: should I go down there and see what he's doing, or go back up and maybe phone the boys in blue? I'd call them from here, if only I had a bloody signal! What if he's down here on legitimate business, I say to myself. Hardly seems likely in this place, does it? But still...

Shrugging, I decide to check out the light. Tentatively I make my way down that corridor, which leads to another room underneath this building.

The light isn't coming from Copeland's phone anymore, it's coming from inside there. It's flickering, so even before I see the candles I can tell that they're illuminating the scene. Illuminating the person in there as well.

It's not Copeland, I don't have a clue where he's gone. Maybe somewhere at the back, where the shadows are deepest? Instead, I'm looking at someone in chains, hanging from a wall on the left-hand side of the room. Female, just hanging there manacled by the wrists. At first I think she's naked, but she's actually in her underwear, a bra and knickers. And her head is lolling forwards, like she's unconscious… or worse. Even without seeing her face, I can tell from the blonde hair and her general frame that this is Phoebe Kirk. And there are cuts all over her: arms, legs, torso… some fresh, some look like they were made a while ago. Some deep, some quite shallow.

Copeland didn't have a murder room, a torture room in his own home… he was using this place instead. Christ Almighty! I should really be going and getting the cops now, because this has all taken a bit of a *Texas Chainsaw Massacre* turn (enter at your own risk!) but I'm rushing over to Phoebe to check on her. Try and get her down, see if she's even still breathing.

She is. But as I gently lift her head she remains unconscious. 'Phoebe. Phoebe, can you hear me? My name's Jackie I'm here to…' What? Rescue her? How very Luke Skywalker. 'Your parents sent me, I work for them.'

Phoebe mumbles something I can't quite hear, but then opens her eyes and looks at me. Thankfully, there are no scars on her face – it's the one bit of her Copeland's left alone. But fuck's sake! The rest of her's a real mess. There's pleading there in those eyes, desperation to match her father's, and she's mumbling again. 'What? Phoebe I can't hear you,' I tell her. But then her eyes shift sideways. She's not looking at me anymore, she's looking at what's behind me. The person behind me, because I can hear that now – a shuffling. Movement.

I start to whirl around, but it's already too late. Something connects with my head…

Then it's not only the shadows at the back of the room that are dark.

It's everything.

I've got the dream – the nightmare – to thank for waking me up this time.

Cuts, slashing, blood, metal… And I jerk awake on the floor of that basement room, the stone floor cold against my face. My head's pounding – hardly surprising, as I can see the bit of wood nearby that clocked me – and I try to clutch my skull, but realise my hands are fastened behind my back. A plastic zip-tie… Good, that's good. Forget what you've seen in movies, on those shows that got me into this in the first place – if it had been rope, I wouldn't have been able to rub it against something and cut through it in minutes. I'd be in proper trouble.

Not that I'm not in trouble right here and now, as I look up and see someone dressed in a hooded robe, in a kind of *Eyes Wide Shut* deal. Copeland… and all that talk of worshipping scars, of scarring yourself and other people as a form of worship. He's even marked out the ground with symbols… fucking nutter. But he's not alone. There are others down here with him, *several* hooded figures. A real bloody cult, not Al's imagined one. Do me a favour! One's quite big, maybe Liam's size. Does Copeland know the people from Tony's Tatts? Are they the link?

'Hey,' I shout up. 'Hey, you guys. This has gone far enough, don't you think?'

No reply.

'People know where I am. They'll come for me.'

One of the hooded figures looks at another beside them. 'Did you hear that?' And I know that voice. I've heard it before. A couple of days ago in the refectory…

Same as the person who replies: 'He's lying . Nobody knows where he is.'

'Rob? Grace?'

Both the hooded figures turn and look at me. 'Bollocks,' says Rob. 'He's recognised us.' He pulls back his hood with a sigh and Grace does the same.

'Course he has, he recognised your voices, morons.'

'And now yours, Jake,' I tell him, realising it's the lad who asked who I was.

'Shit!' says the hooded figure with Maya's voice.

'The gang's all here,' I say. 'I take it that one's Tim, then.' Has to be, he's the only one who hasn't spoken yet – just like he didn't in the canteen. 'Hey Phoebe!' I shout, though I can't actually see her anymore; she's not on the wall. 'These guys have really, really missed you.'

'Shut the fuck up!' snarls Jake.

'So, what, Doctor Doom roped you *all* into this?' The charismatic leader, who sits at home on his own at night watching the tube, eating his micro-meals. 'You're just doing what he tells you?'

'We're not doing what *anyone* tells us,' says a voice from the back. The others move out of this person's way as they drag someone with them. 'Are we, Sheldon?' Zoë removes her own hood and at the same time shoves a bound Copeland down to the floor next to me.

Okay, now I'm confused. Copeland *isn't* behind all this? He didn't bring Phoebe down here, keep her here? 'You're all insane!' the tutor shouts back at them, then looks at me. 'Why is the reporter here?'

'He's not a reporter, are you?' Zoë looks down on us both, hands on her hips. 'Not Phoebe's uncle either. She told me all about her family when we were… getting to know each other.' There's something in the way she says that and now it all slots into place. Phoebe's dad had been right, there wasn't a guy on the scene – and definitely not Copeland – but there had been somebody.

Anyone can be your new best friend… or more.

Someone Phoebe thought that she cared about, maybe even loved. And love can make you do crazy things, like hurt yourself – or let someone else hurt you. Let them lure you down here to keep on hurting you. She'd fooled her… and me as well, for that matter. 'What is it, private detective? Someone her folks hired, I'm guessing, when the police lost interest? I knew he'd follow you here anyway, because he was keeping tabs on you. That's why I sent you the text to get you here, somewhere nice and private. This place that bears its own scars…' She chuckles. 'I've seen the way you look at me, Sheldon.'

So he wasn't that blameless after all, this guy. Wasn't averse to a bit of extra-curricular activity if it was on offer.

'Not that I'd touch you with a bargepole, mate.' Zoë stuck a finger in her mouth and pretended to gag and the others laughed now as well. 'But I have to say, you do talk a lot of sense. Those classes of yours… Well, we wouldn't be here without them, would we guys?'

'You're… what are you talking about?' asks a panicked Copeland.

'Your teachings, about scarification. About religion. We… hey, we thought we'd give it a try.'

'Give it a…' Copeland shakes his head.

'We've all done it, haven't we?' Zoë's looking around the group. 'See?' she says, rolling up a sleeve to show the marks there. Then she undoes the belt on the robe and lets it drop to the floor, revealing that she's in her underwear too. The others follow suit, showing us the scars they have on their own bodies. A few here and there, some more than others; done to themselves, to each other. I catch the glances Rob and Jake are giving the girls, and figure there's more than just the scarring to this as far as they're concerned. Silent Tim's busy checking out the other guys. 'But we need to take it up a notch, which is where Phoebe comes into it.'

'You're… you're all insane,' shouts Copeland.

'You said that already,' Zoë replies. 'But don't knock it till you've tried it, doc. It's… helped, hasn't it?' The others nod in agreement. 'Amazing how lucky you can get with a few offerings of blood. With a few scars.'

'Offerings to who?'

'I'm guessing that Horned Goddess you told me about,' I say. Horny Goddess more like, judging from some of the drooling that's going on in that room.

'To whoever's listening!' Zoë says with a maniacal grin, which fades almost instantly. 'It's time to step things up again, though. Tonight…' Now she steps aside, and they all do – to reveal Phoebe, no longer hanging from the wall but still in chains. On the floor, unmoving, with the markings surrounding her. 'Tonight Phoebe will offer up the ultimate sacrifice.'

'It's hardly a sacrifice if you're offering her life up for her,' I point out.

Zoë grins and stoops, picking something up off the floor. When she rights herself, I see it's a large knife, already bloody. Probably the one they've been using to inflict the damage on Phoebe for the last month or more. Taking it in turns, in shifts to come down and check on her, feed her, keep her alive… so they can just kill her in cold blood. I have to agree with Eddie Baby, these guys are fucking bananas; no chickens and Satan for them, no puzzle boxes. 'And she won't be alone. Three sacrifices…'

I feel like saying, 'For the price of one', but this isn't the time for stupid jokes. None of this is funny at all. But while Single White Female's been explaining her evil schemes – while everyone's been distracted – I've been hard at work on that zip-tie. You see, you can get out of a set of those quite easily if you know what you're doing and especially if it hasn't been pulled tight enough. If you've practiced it many times, for hours and hours, with duct-tape around your wrists to protect them… like I just happen to have done. Getting tied up: it's another one of those occupational hazards.

I'm upright by this time, and the trick is to create enough space – pulling the plastic apart – so you can then slam down with both hands against your lower back. Might take a few goes, but it should work. It works today anyway, thankfully – though I know my wrists are going to pay the price for it later on. I just need to wait until the right moment, which is apparently when Zoë hauls Phoebe's head up by the hair, holding the knife to her throat.

And I'm on my feet.

Rob's the first to spot it, of course, and rushes towards me. He's big, but I've tackled bigger. The key is to use his size against him, so as he lunges I grab his arm and swing him round into the wall where he slumps to the ground. Grace jumps on my back and starts to claw at me like a wild animal, so I bend forwards to shrug her off and she takes my jacket with her – and almost my T-shirt as well.

There's a gasp as it rides up – not sure from where – and that gives me an idea. 'All right. You guys want scars? I'll give you scars!' I pull the rest of the tee off and they all gape: even Zoë who's lowered the blade a little; even Rob from his fallen position next to the wall. They're staring at me… at my scars. Old scars, but ones that never went away – neither the physical, nor the mental ones which manifest themselves as dreams, nightmares sometimes. It's the reason why I shower early in those public gyms, because I don't want anyone to see.

Oh, that's right. I never did tell you how my own parents bought it back when I was nine. Car crash, one they didn't make it out of but I did. Survived… though not without horrific injuries to my body; the only bit it left alone was my face. Blood, cuts, metal. It's all I remember now, but the scars are there as a permanent reminder. Not a penance, not a form of worship – though Maya is getting down on her knees now in a sort of prayer position, she's that fucked up – but something I carry with me every day of my life. If that horned bitch is their goddess, then I should be their fucking god!

An unexpected twist. Life's a bitch like that, isn't it.

'Jesus,' says Tim, the only time I've ever heard him speak. It does tend to have that effect on people. One of the reasons I never stuck around much if I met someone on my travels, or they didn't; once the night had passed, the alcohol had worn off, and the dawn shed some light on the situation, who'd want someone like me?

Zoë's the first one to snap out of it, shouting: 'It doesn't change anything! Stick to the plan, stick to…' But then something is cutting her off. A chain around her throat, pulling backwards. Phoebe, teeth gritted and finding the strength from somewhere. Getting her revenge on the person she thought she loved.

But there's another problem now. A couple of the candles have been knocked over in the scuffles and one has found a discarded robe. It's on fire, and that fire is spreading quickly – leaping to other bits of discarded clothing. Won't be long before this whole room goes up in flames! We'll all have more scars than we can count then, third degree burns or worse.

'Get out! Everyone… get the fuck out of here!' I shout, but I don't need to tell some of them twice. Jake is already racing down that corridor, Grace behind him. I free Copeland who thanks me with a nod, and I send him on his stumbling way.

Then I hear the screaming. It's not Zoë, because her voice is still being cut off by Phoebe's throttling. The fire has found Rob, cutting him off in a different way. Blocking him off and now consuming him. Maya and Tim are trying to get to him, but the flames are driving them back. In the end Tim has to pull her away and get her to safety, tears flooding her eyes. There's nothing any of us can do for Rob.

I rush over to the two people left, place a hand on Phoebe's shoulder. 'Enough… that's enough now.' Zoë is unconscious, the same as how I found Phoebe here, so I have to pick her up and carry her. 'Can you walk?' I ask Phoebe, who nods. Walk or end up like Rob? No contest really.

It seems to take an age to get up that corridor, up the steps – and I have to keep stopping to check on Phoebe all the way. Then we're above ground, and then we're outside. I can hear sirens in the distance so someone's already called the authorities; probably Copeland (there's no sign of the rest of them). Police, ambulance, fire crews… the works.

I put the unconscious Zoë down. If there had been any justice, she'd have died down there instead of that meathead Rob. She was more dangerous than the lot of them. More devious, more charismatic than Copeland could ever hope to be.

And I look across at Phoebe. She's on a grass verge, hugging herself. In shock, for sure. The wounds that have been inflicted on her will fade, the scarring might not even be that bad in time. As for those mental scars… They'll take so much longer to heal, if they ever do.

But I found her, I tell myself. Found her and saved her. Did my best.

In the end, that's all any of us can do, isn't it?

I said it wasn't that exciting my life, didn't I?

Maybe this isn't such a good example of that. The cases like this are few and far between, though they're starting to get more frequent, I've noticed. As the world gets darker and darker.

The one bit of light here was reuniting Phoebe with her folks. You should have seen the hugs she gave them in the hospital, telling them she was so sorry. That she thought she knew what she was doing when she left them the message. That she'd thought Zoë was… the one. She was a one all right, a real piece of work – ended up in a very different kind of hospital. She led me on a bit of a dance, planting that flyer in Phoebe's room, sending me off to Tony's Tatts and aiming me in the direction of Copeland with her smoke and mirrors… Though it had been her own parents who'd done the damage there, who'd hit her when she didn't do well enough at school (some of her own scars were quite old, much older than a few months) would lock her away in cupboards as punishment… Was there any wonder she thought she needed supernatural help, needed the scars to mean something? To make sense? I hope she gets some proper help now, but they've got their work cut out for them. And I hope her parents – who are currently being investigated – get the book thrown at them.

The cops rounded up the surviving members of her merry little band, charged them with unlawful imprisonment, assault and… well, you get the picture. Their lives are pretty much over, even after they get out of jail. Their own penance, I guess, though it'll never make up for everything.

Copeland got his fifteen minutes of fame, was on TV like he wanted – just not in the *way* he wanted. Another disgraced member of staff from Mannerbridge, turned out there had been a few former students he'd been involved with – who came forward after they saw him on telly. His wife said she'd had suspicions, which was why she left him. That and the fact his S&M practices in the bedroom were getting worse and worse. He'll never teach again.

Some good came out of it all, however. An anonymous donation to help restore those buildings on the campus, especially the one that caught fire – so at least they won't be scarred anymore. Lucky them.

'I don't know how to thank you,' Mr Kirk said to me, before we parted ways, pumping my hand up and down as if he was trying to get water out of me. The way he looked at his daughter, like she was his world, like she was everything to him – and the way his wife looked at him, looking at her… Well, there was another story there to come, I didn't doubt. Probably another parting of the ways before too long.

I didn't say to him it had been a pleasure, but it was… satisfying. I saved a life, got paid and the Kirks gave me a glowing recommendation. Can't ask for more than that, right? I'm not grumbling.

So remember, if you ever need me, you know where to find me. Jackie – Jackson – Trent, at your service. You'll probably remember the name now, because you'll have heard it before somewhere.

Till next time, be good. And if you can't be good…

I'll probably see you sooner than you think.

ENFLAMED

Billy Robson was seven when he first saw the faces in the flames.

Not the faces of his parents, flesh bubbling and popping on the bone as the fire lapped over them; washing over them like waves smoothing stones on a beach. No, the *other* faces. The ones *in* the flames, made up of the flames as far as he could tell: orange eyes, yellow hair. Those creatures were grinning, actually grinning, as they made their way through his home with glee.

The first sign that anything was wrong had been the smoke. It was the middle of the night, and he'd been asleep, but woke up when he began coughing. Not the ordinary kind of coughing, like when you have a cold or something, but choking rasps, making it difficult to breathe. Billy sat up in bed, pulling the covers back and reaching for his bedside lamp – the one he sometimes had to leave on all night because he was frightened of the dark; frightened of the monsters in the dark, to be precise (they were nothing compared to some, as he soon discovered).

Except it was still dark when he turned the light on, this particular blackness like a living thing, making its way in through the cracks in his door: floating, curling, exploring every inch of his bedroom. Snaking its way into his mouth, down his throat. Billy rolled out of bed, stumbling, but actually finding that it was easier to get air the lower he was. He began to crawl, coughing all the while. Cough, crawl; cough, crawl. Until he made it to the door. Billy reached up for the handle, but soon brought his fingers back sharply, the metal red hot to the touch.

He pulled up his pyjama top, wrapping the material around his fingers to protect them, wrestling with the handle, trying to lever it down. In the end, he had to use both hands to get it to move, pulling on it and falling backwards as he did so. It was a good thing too, as the blast from the other side was merciless and swift, shooting over the top of his head like a party blower. He waited for it to retreat before flipping and crawling again, coughing even more now and struggling to see.

He wanted to call out for his folks, the only other people in the house. 'Mu… Da…' was all he could manage, strangled gargles that would never reach them. But then he saw they were on the landing anyway, had made their way out probably to get to him, to get their son to safety – putting his wellbeing before their own, as they always did (not that he'd ever really appreciated it until that moment).

Billy saw them, and they were crawling as well – but not voluntarily. They'd been brought down by the raging inferno around them. They were both alight, the nightdress sticking to his mother's body, the pyjama bottoms doing the same to his father's legs – the man's upper half was bare, as he always slept like that, and now Billy could see that the chest hair was sizzling, the skin taut and shiny where it was being consumed. Even through the smoke, he could smell what it was doing to them, like meat on the barbeques they had every summer.

Yet they were still reaching out to him, the compunction to protect so strong it didn't matter what happened to them as long as he was okay.

But they were being held – no, *dragged* back. And it was then that Billy saw the faces behind them, vague outlines of figures there pawing at his parents. A set of nebulous fingers on either side of his mother's head, 'hands' squeezing, crushing her skull. Most of her curly brown hair was already gone, crimson patches shining through like angry bald spots. But now her eyes became so much jelly, melting inside the sockets as she took one last look at her only son.

He wanted to scream, but couldn't. And those faces, those creatures in the flames were laughing, he could see them. They were enjoying this! It was an entertainment of sorts for them, manipulating fire. Playing with fire.

Playing *with* the fire.

Once they were done with his parents, they would turn their attentions to Billy.

The boy began backing off, not only to get away from the things in the flames, but also because he didn't wish to see what was happening to his parents anymore. Sights that – if he were to survive – would haunt his nightmares forever. His room was closest to the stairs, but as he turned he saw the lower half of the house was just as ravaged as this one. There was no way out, no escape from the fire people.

Billy coughed again, one long cough which wracked his whole body – and he closed his eyes, waited for them to take him, just as they'd done with his mum and dad. He felt the hands on him, but instead of pain, instead of the intense heat he'd expected which had done the damage to those he'd cared about so much, the hands were lifting him, carrying him. He opened his eyes, aware that he was being slung over someone's shoulder, saw the fireman's uniform. Could just about see the bodies of his parents, but saw no sign of those other 'people' there.

The rest was a bit of a blur; in fact he was told later that he was in and out of consciousness for a while. That made sense, because all Billy could remember was being laid down on something and wheeled, the air so clear above him he could see the stars. Then whiteness, and sirens, as people busied themselves around him. He remembered waking up in another bed, with something over his mouth to help with his breathing; a function he'd need help with for a good while afterwards. Before falling asleep again, Billy's eyes flicked over to the corridor of the hospital ward he was in, searching for the man – the fireman – who'd rescued him from the blaze. But he didn't see him then, didn't see him ever again.

He was told a few days later that the man had gone in to try and save his, already dead, parents and lost his own life in the process.

Lost his life to those monsters in the flames.

*   *   *

So, that was how it started: his obsession.

Didn't take Sherlock Holmes to figure out why, but it would take many months, many years of therapy and counselling to get past – or so they thought by the time they were finished. It was what Billy let them think, telling them what they wanted to hear.

To begin with he'd tried them with the truth. 'But I swear I did see faces, people. I think they might even have started the fire in the first place.'

'It's understandable that you'd want to give the thing that took your parents away from you some kind of recognisable form. As human beings we see patterns in everything, try to give meaning to them, William.' He always called him that, Billy's therapist, leaning back in his creaky leather chair and scribbling his notes on a pad. 'The fire was electrical, you know it was. And the batteries in the alarm were flat, that's why it didn't go off.' They blamed his parents for that, because if they'd been alerted early then they might all have got out of there alive. Billy still refused to believe that, thought the fire-people must have done something to the alarm so they could have their 'fun'.

Billy had no grandparents left, his one remaining nan having passed in a nursing home the previous year. Which left his uncle, on his dad's side – who had two kids already and really couldn't take on another mouth to feed. They all lived miles away, so it was easy for him to do that; to turn his back on Billy. Out of sight, out of mind. Besides which, he was damaged goods now.

It was probably for the best anyway.

Billy liked to keep himself to himself, which worked well in the various orphanages and children's homes he found himself inhabiting. He wouldn't have liked sharing his space with another family, losing his privacy… That's what he told himself, although the main reason, if he was honest, was that he was scared of losing anyone else close to him. It was safer to remain detached, not form close relationships.

His quietness made him a target for bullies, of course. They couldn't just leave him alone to his own thoughts, usually dwelling on that night – *the* night. The one where he was born again, if you like, a Phoenix rising – or being carried out of – the ashes. And that's pretty much all that had been left of the house by the time the fire had finished with it; they'd finally given in to his pleas to visit, as part of his letting go of the past. It had been a blackened husk, awaiting demolition so another house could be built on top of it. 'It's what you must do,' he'd been told. 'Build a new life for yourself.'

So he had, or he'd tried to. If only people had left him alone, Billy would have been happy enough with his studies. Not the educational kind, but his real education. Researching, learning everything he could about the subject. And the practicals – his examination of the element that had stolen his family from him. Or, more specifically, his attempts to examine the things that lived *within* it. Hid within it. His only way to bridge the gap between worlds and gain access to them.

'Playing' with the fire…

Billy did controlled experiments to begin with; all he'd needed was matches and paper, setting small fires under glass to observe what happened. Sometimes they would peter out, but sometimes he'd have to step in and put them out himself. Always he watched, observed closely for any glimpse of the creatures. Sometimes he fancied he saw an eye, or a mouth, but it was more likely he'd just been staring at the flames for so long. They were too small anyway, those fires. All he could risk indoors without revealing what he was doing.

So, when he could get away, Billy would take himself off to isolated spots where there was absolutely no risk of being interrupted. Out in the woods was favourite, because even if someone did wander along – and he'd never encountered anyone in all the time he was doing his tests – he could just say he was camping or something; had made a camp fire to warm himself or to cook with. When in actual fact he was trying to lure the faces, even shouted at the flames on occasion to see if they would be goaded into showing themselves. But again the fires hadn't really been big enough.

On the one occasion he'd stoked it just that little bit too much, added too much bracken, too many dry leaves, and almost started a flash fire. Billy had only just managed to put it out, stamping at the edges of it and smothering the flames with dirt he had ready to hand. As he'd been panicking, rushing about to contain the blaze, he'd thought he heard laughter – had his efforts amused them? Or maybe it had just been his imagination, the same as his therapist claimed it had been all along.

It only made him more determined.

As he got older he began to wonder whether it was the promise of danger that drew them, like moths to the… He saw the chance to kill two birds with a single stone when one of those bullies in the latest facility he was in pushed him too far: pushed him into some bins in fact, just to look big in front of his mates. Grogan his name was, and Billy had seized the opportunity a couple of weeks later, to lock the thickset lad in one of the storage sheds while he'd been packing away some of the stuff after games. Then it was just a matter of tossing in a lit cigarette – Grogan was always smoking, notorious for it he was – through a window into a waiting cardboard box, and watching what unfolded.

Billy had opened the door eventually, once he was satisfied the faces, the monsters, weren't coming – not even when he'd laid on such an offering. By the time Grogan had staggered out, finally raising the alarm, Billy was back in his room. In spite of the suspicions raised they couldn't prove a thing. Grogan knew, though, Billy could tell by the way he looked at him, but the lad steered well clear after that. Billy was out of there the following year anyway, off to make his way in the world.

He took a succession of jobs in his late teens and early twenties that would allow him to continue with his studies. The first was helping out at a pottery, placing bowls in the kiln. The next was at a hospital, working in the basement where they got rid of clinical waste in the furnace – which also included body parts, or sometimes even whole bodies. Billy would peer in through the glass plating, looking, searching until his eyes hurt – and even then he would don protective goggles so he could carry on. Never once did he see any hint of the creatures feasting on the corpses. Just like

Grogan, the people he worked with kept their distance; and down there, if those weirdoes did that, what did it make you? There was a rumour a guy from the morgue was even sleeping with the corpses, the Jane Does that arrived here on a regular basis, but even *he* was scared to go anywhere near Billy, as focussed on his mission as he was. It just made him that little bit more intense than other people, like he knew something that they didn't... which of course he did. He'd seen something that, to his knowledge, nobody else in the world ever had. But nothing came of his explorations there. The flames fed, but his enemies did not appear even once.

That post had led directly to the position at the crematorium, a chance to do what he'd been doing on a much larger scale. The largest yet in fact, for – at least in the place he now worked – the dead were not cremated in individual units after the curtains closed on their caskets. They were burned alive en masse in huge ovens, the ashes mixed before being handed to deluded, grieving relatives. Billy was in a unique position to observe all this, to make sure the flames were hot enough to break down flesh and bone, to watch once more through toughened glass. But, again, they did not come. *Where are you?* he thought. *Why won't you show yourselves?* The closest he came was when he fancied he saw the dead rising up inside there to build a burning doorway, a glimpse of some kind of utopia on the other side... It wasn't until one of his colleagues nudged him that Billy realised he was simply daydreaming. He'd been staring into the conflagration for so long he was starting to hallucinate. And he couldn't afford to do that, couldn't lose his grip on reality or he might not be able to tell the real from the unreal, might dismiss the creatures even if they did venture forth again.

He soon realised they wouldn't come for those who were already dead. That led to Billy bringing in living sacrifices at night, while there was no one else around. Except this time, unlike Grogan, he would actually follow through; intent was the key, he felt sure of it. The smaller creatures had been easier to kill, the rats especially. They didn't deserve to be on this Earth in the first place, and it didn't help their cause that they bit Billy as he was shoving them into the baskets to bring them here. They went up in seconds inside the massive oven, though; blink and you missed what was happening. He'd certainly missed it if the flame-faces had cropped up.

Larger, thought Billy. They'd last longer, would make more of a meal for the greedy tongues inside and possibly attract his prey. He tried birds first – more than just the two, chickens and the like – but they were no use. The traps he set out in the woodland, a place he knew well, offered him wild animals like rabbits and hares, some foxes. Those had been harder to watch, particularly when they looked him in the eye, but he reminded himself of his mission and pushed down those feelings of guilt. He had to remain detached, as always. Think about them as a means to an end. No more, no less.

When nothing came of this, he began to think maybe he had to care about the sacrifices in order to draw *them* out. After all, that's what the word meant: he had to sacrifice something he'd miss. So he visited the pounds, targeted the most sorry-looking dogs he could find, heard their heartbreaking stories – one had been maltreated by his previous owners to such an extent it had come in looking like a skeleton – and settled on a mongrel imaginatively named Scooby. Billy had taken him home and kept him for a fortnight to get attached, then driven him to the crem to do the deed. He'd placed food in the oven so Scooby would trot in, but when the dog had looked up at him then back down at the bowl – basically asking him if it was safe – Billy had to carry the dog inside himself. He'd slammed the door with tears in his eyes, had been foolish to even begin to care about something else.

His hand had been on the button, but he just couldn't do it. Couldn't watch as Scooby roasted alive inside that oven, even if it did mean he stood a chance of seeing those murdering bastards again. So he'd let the mutt out and it had come to him, jumping up and licking his face. 'I'm sorry, boy,' he'd whispered, then taken the dog home again.

Billy hadn't stayed at the crem much longer, couldn't stand the thought of what he'd almost done. But he wasn't prepared to give up on his lifelong goal either, which meant he had to find a compromise. In the end it had been a no-brainer, inspired by his past. He would become a real-life fireman. Kill two birds again, the chance to possibly see those monsters as he simultaneously attempted to save people from their clutches.

They'd pretty much welcomed him with open arms at the fire department, especially after he'd told his story about how he'd been saved as a kid. (He'd had to falsify some of his details to get in, obviously – couldn't have them seeing the reports on him from that time and knowing what he was really up to.) 'I want to give something back,' he'd told them. 'I wouldn't be here today if it wasn't for one very special and brave fire-fighter.'

Billy had worked hard, training all the hours God sent to make the grade. He was determined not just to become good at his job, but the very best. His superiors were delighted with the way he was progressing, and it wasn't long before he was assigned active duty. The only criticism was that his colleagues couldn't really get a bead on him, could never work him out. Plus he wasn't really a team player to begin with, which was a problem for them – and the risks he took, mainly to see if he could catch sight of those elusive faces, put not only himself in danger, but members of his team.

The one person who always stood up for him was Kurt Fowler, probably because Billy had pulled Kurt out of harm's way one time when a flaming beam was about to fall on him.

'He's a natural born fireman,' Kurt had spoken up when their Commander brought Billy in to explain himself. 'One of the best I've ever seen, in fact.'

'We can't afford mavericks in this department,' his boss – a craggy-faced man called Didcott – had told them. 'Do you understand?'

Billy had said that he did, and from then on he'd been a bit more careful. If anything, had played the role a little too well. Being a fireman had gone from being another means to an end, to his actual life. His plan had worked a little better than he'd intended, and that became evident when he was faced with another important decision.

A couple, trapped on one of the upper floors of a block of flats. The firemen had all gone in together as a team, but through no fault of his own, Billy had become separated from the rest of his colleagues. The corridor was like a firestorm, and even through his mask Billy had trouble breathing or seeing anything. There were figures who'd made it out onto the landing, crawling – and, behind them, he thought for just a moment he saw those faces in the flames again. They were coming, all he had to do was leave this man and woman to their fate.

They were reaching out for help, just like his parents had done, and Billy had shaken his head. When it came right down to it, as with Scooby, he just couldn't do it – even if it meant not seeing his monsters again. He'd rushed through the flames, taking one person under each arm and stumbled to a window. Once there, he'd put his charges down and smashed the glass with his axe. The ladder had been there in moments, more of his team present to help the people out.

Then Billy had climbed down himself, casting one last look back but seeing nothing.

Half-cursing himself for having saved the couple.

*   *   *

In time, though, the edge was taken off this by Jules coming into his life.

Billy hadn't been looking, but as so often happens that's when it had come along. Love. As much as he'd tried to shield himself from it, the fact that he'd let Scooby in, that he'd become friends with Kurt, had set the precedent. It had been through his mate, actually, that he'd met Jules. She'd been at a gathering Billy let himself get talked into attending, and Kurt had introduced the couple – an old friend of his from school, he'd explained. Billy had been shy at first, hardly surprising when you considered he'd never had much to do with girls, to do with *women* at all, but she'd eventually coaxed him out of his shell. They'd seen each other several times and she appreciated the fact he hadn't leapt on her – little realising it was simply because he was scared. 'Most of the men I've ever known couldn't wait to get me in the sack,' she'd said and then smiled, causing those dimples to appear in her cheeks.

'I… I think I'm falling for her,' Billy had admitted to Scooby after their last date at the cinema. The dog had cocked his head as if he understood. In spite of himself, Billy had begun to imagine a future with Jules, maybe even children; pushing down those memories of the faces, trying to forget what had happened when he was so very young. Didn't he deserve some happiness for a change?

He'd built himself up to telling her at an Italian restaurant that

Valentine's weekend, had even brought roses along. But, as he'd begun to say those words, she'd stared at him sadly.

'Billy, listen. I never meant to lead you on. I thought we were just having a nice time, y'know? Nothing serious or anything.'

'But… but I—'

'Yeah, I know,' she said, playing with her raven hair, 'I got the message, but… well, I wasn't looking for anything… I thought you knew that? I thought I'd made it clear.'

'Jules, I don't understand.'

'It's complicated. Look, you're just not that experienced with all this stuff, are you?'

Billy held his hands up and admitted that he wasn't, but he knew how he felt about *her*. What he'd had to sacrifice to feel that, letting down the barriers.

'I think we should cool things off a bit, maybe just try being friends for a while,' Jules had said and his heart sank. As she'd got up to leave, he'd grabbed for her hand, garbled something about loving her more than anything in this world, but then she was gone.

Billy left messages, sent texts, but Jules didn't answer any of them. He'd found out what was happening, of course. When he'd followed her that time and seen her coming out of the pub with Kurt. Had seen the kiss he couldn't unsee.

Couldn't wait to get her in the sack.

Had realised then there was another opportunity to kill two birds with one stone when the memories of those faces came rushing back to him.

It was time to play with the fire once again.

* * *

It would be relatively easy to break into the house at night, when all the lights were out, make it look electrical in nature – and there was a certain irony to that he hoped *they'd* appreciate.

He didn't blame Jules for all this, he blamed Kurt for confusing her; they obviously had unfinished business from their formative years. His 'best friend' should have warned him about that, shouldn't have introduced them in the first place if she was an… old flame. It was all Kurt's fault, but regardless of that the man's death would still be painful for Billy. Almost as painful as it had been to lose Jules.

Midnight, Saturday, he'd done the deed. There was no chance of alarms going off either, because those were hooked up to the electricity and once that was dead…

It hadn't taken long for the place to start going up, not once he'd begun to help it along. Billy watched, transfixed, donning his mask when the smoke got too much.

It was as the fire spread upstairs that he'd heard the cries from up there. Children's voices.

Kurt didn't have kids, so what—

He couldn't think about that now: they were here, inside. Billy sprinted past the flames, and up the stairs. There were two kids on the landing, crying and coughing. One boy, one girl. No more than about seven, either of them – possibly twins?

What the fuck? he thought. *Just what the fuck?*

And there, at the far end, trying to get to them, was Kurt. Already the fire was spreading on this level. He seemed confused that there was another person up here with them, but pointed to the kids nonetheless. Practically begged this masked person to save them, which Billy had every intention of doing. They weren't part of the plan, whoever they were.

He grabbed them, slinging one over his shoulder and carrying the other in his arms. Managed to get them outside, then heard sirens in the distance – because of the time he'd spent getting the kids out – thought about how it would look to find him here. Plus which, after seeing Kurt up there, after looking into his eyes, Billy was starting to have second thoughts.

By the time he got upstairs again he could see not one, but two adults on the landing. Their flesh was melting on the bone, but Billy would recognise that raven hair anywhere, those dimples. Jules had been with Kurt that night and…

Christ, she'd never even mentioned having kids.

It's complicated.

No wonder she'd had trouble letting him in, was reluctant to make a sacrifice herself. But not with Kurt (maybe they were even his kids?). Didn't matter now, because as he watched the couple burning alive, blistering and frying and finally blackening (part of him even enjoying this because of what they'd done to him) Billy saw them – at last he saw *them*!

The faces, the figures. They'd come out again to play…

He raced forward, not even knowing what he'd do when he reached them. In all these years he'd never even considered what he'd do when they appeared again, how he'd punish them. But in the end, it was *they* who took action. Opening their arms to embrace him like some long lost brother.

The heat was more intense than anything Billy had ever felt, fusing the mask to his face, instantly incinerating his clothing and the gloves that he wore. Turning him into a walking bonfire; causing him to resemble a stuntman from an old Hollywood movie.

Yet there was no pain. Billy felt nothing but numbness as they worked upon him, unmaking him, turning him into something else. He'd proven himself worthy, the entertainment pleasing to them – these creatures who were little more than children themselves, or existed with a child's mentality. Here was their way of making amends, offering him a childhood back where he could have fun. Existing as one within the fire, the only world he'd ever really known.

It took Billy only a moment to decide. This or oblivion. Really, it was a no-brainer – the chance to build a new life for himself as a fire person.

As a natural born fire*man*.

* * *

As the emergency services arrived, fire engines and ambulances, the children – Lucas and Emily – struggled to come to terms with what they'd seen.

Not the beginnings of the end for their Uncle Kurt, only recently reconciled with their mother. Not even the rescue, by a friend of their father's they'd later be told, who'd died heroically trying to save both their parents. But the faces, all orange eyes and yellow hair: the figures they'd seen in the flames.

The creatures that would haunt and shape their lives from now on. The monsters who'd been hidden inside, who'd been so gleeful as they'd entertained themselves, manipulating fire. Playing with fire.

Playing *with* the fire.

IN PIECES

They were made for each other, *made* each other.

It had been one of their little in-jokes, that they fit together so well. Her head in the crook of his neck, resting against his shoulder; slotting together like one of those models he used to make when he was younger, tongue sticking out of the corner of his mouth. Back when he was more of a recluse and shunned the nightlife and parties other teenagers embraced so eagerly.

Adrian had always been shy, awkward around the opposite sex – around people in general. Safer to stay out of all that, to stay indoors and glue together those bits of plastic and vinyl, paint the planes, cars, figures. Something he could have more control over, making friends that wouldn't hurt him. Besides, he was all that his mother had left since his father had died, and she wasn't exactly doing great; her lungs… all that smoking she'd done throughout her life. It was one of the reasons he hadn't headed off to uni like so many of the kids he'd gone to school with. Got a little part-time job at the factory shop (handling rejects, just like he was), more to help out with money than anything, but even then he kept himself to himself.

When his mum had taken a turn for the worse, found herself in hospital barely able to breathe, Adrian had been forced to confront the reality of the situation. That when she was gone, he'd be alone. That he'd always be alone.

But Rebecca had come along and changed all of that.

A nurse at the hospital where his mother was being treated, she was the kindest person he'd ever met – which, he supposed, went with the territory. But there was something more to it, even he could see that. The way she looked at him sometimes, the way she talked about his loyalty to his parent – 'You don't see it all that often,' she'd told him, smiling that sweet smile of hers. Told him she admired that. Imagine, someone actually admiring *him*!

He knew the dangers of it, probably as well as she did. The nightingale effect, wasn't it called, falling in love with your doctor or nurse? It was one of the reasons why he wasn't sure he could trust it, not to begin with, anyway. But he hadn't been the patient, his mum had – and Rebecca hadn't been the one looking after him. Well, not in a medical sense; just being there for him, especially during those late night vigils by the side of the bed. Always there with cups of tea, biscuits. Sometimes even sitting with him and – if she thought she could get away with it, when nobody was looking – holding his hand once or twice as the ventilator kept his poor mum alive.

And when the old lady had passed, of course. Being there for him then, holding him as his body shook with sobs. Helping Adrian with the arrangements, even coming to the funeral with him – there weren't many friends or family left, so he'd been glad of the support. Then, afterwards, when they should have said their goodbyes and gone their separate ways, ships in the night and all that, they found they simply couldn't.

Couldn't bear to be parted for more than a few hours at a time, as a matter of fact. Texts would fly back and forth while they were at work, phone calls when they were both at home, meetings for coffee and then dinners. They'd taken it slow, in spite of all this, though, to make sure. Both of them had to be sure it was real, that what they felt for each other was true love, not just a passing thing – and not just because of what they'd been through together.

They needn't have worried, their feelings had passed the test of time. They made each other happy. Indeed, Adrian couldn't remember ever being as happy as he was when he spent time with Rebecca. Even just knowing she was in his life put a spring in his step as he stacked the shelves with those rejected goods – appreciating the flaws in them, knowing that someone would want to buy them. Would love them.

It hadn't all been plain sailing, of course. What relationship didn't have its ups and downs? But these were mainly down to outside influences, other people… especially Rebecca's dad. She was extremely close to him, which was to be expected seeing as her mother had died when Rebecca was only small (almost a mirror of Adrian's situation). That man had been both mother and father to her, so naturally it followed that he should be extremely protective of his daughter – perhaps a little *too* protective. Adrian could understand that, given some of the men who must have been sniffing around before he came along, only after one thing but pretending they were the perfect gentlemen. Rebecca was extremely pretty, with those huge blue eyes and dark-blonde hair which she tended to put back into a ponytail. But dads could usually weed the bad ones out with no problems at all; see it when even their kids refused to.

Adrian had no clue what he must have against *him*, though – he was always polite and respectful, had treated Rebecca the right way even from the start. The fact she'd been caring for his mother, maybe? Was that muddying the waters? Surely he could see it went beyond that? It had led to a certain amount of bad feeling, and was probably the reason why they hadn't got married in the end; just moved in together after almost a year.

Indeed, the only person in her family that could see what a nice guy Adrian was seemed to be her cousin Jane. Younger than Rebecca by a couple of years, Jane was more like a sister than a cousin; as close to her as one, probably because neither of them had had siblings. 'We spent a lot of time together, especially when we were younger. There are just things you need to discuss with another woman that you really can't with your dad,' Rebecca had told him. He'd nodded, understanding all too well that there'd be things you'd keep from *her* old man – though strangely not from him.

As soon as he'd met Jane, Adrian realised there was a bit of hero worshipping going on between her and Rebecca. A big sister thing, definitely. She'd even followed Rebecca into the caring profession, though had ended up more on the rehabilitation side of things. Working with people in accidents to – sometimes quite literally – get them back on their feet again. Piecing people – piecing their lives – back together. Mending what was broken. And they'd got on too, almost as well as Jane did with Rebecca – treated him, he felt sometimes, like 'one of the girls' and to begin with he didn't know whether that was a good or bad thing. Good, he'd decided eventually, as he definitely wasn't your typical laddish guy.

Not like some of the prizes Jane would go on dates with, which they'd hear all about when she came round and offloaded on them over wine. There'd be tears occasionally, and Rebecca would comfort her, stroking that auburn hair of hers cut in a bob.

'Why can't I find someone, Bex?' she'd ask her cousin, using the nickname she'd give her many years ago. Rebecca would look across at him then for support and Adrian would tell her there were still some good guys out there, though with each horror story he heard he was beginning to wonder. Especially after some of the double dates they'd all been on together. Keith, who couldn't keep his eyes horizontal for the life of him, or Lee, who spent more time chatting up the barmaid than he did chatting to Jane. 'I just want what you guys have, what you found. What am I doing wrong?'

'Oh sweetie,' Rebecca would say, again and again, 'you're not doing anything wrong.'

Another nod at Adrian and he'd chip in with, 'They didn't deserve you, Jane. It'll happen sometime. You wait and see.'

'Thanks Ade, that's so lovely of you.' Look, they were all close enough now that he even got his own abbreviation, though he couldn't help thinking it made him sound like that guy out of *The Young Ones* and *Bottom*. She'd dry her eyes then, those big, wide blue eyes that apparently ran in their family, and they'd all have some more wine.

There were good times they'd share as well, of course. Day trips to the coast or off to the cinema, but Jane didn't like to impose too much. Said she felt like a third wheel, or a fifth wheel – as the other one made it sound like she was a Robin Reliant!

'Nonsense,' they'd both say, they enjoyed her company. But it was true, if Adrian was being honest, the time he spent alone with Rebecca was precious. The fitting together thing, Part 13A slotting into Part 5C. Head on the shoulder watching TV in the evening, or some weepie – Rebecca loved those for some reason.

Fitted together in other ways too, not that Adrian had much to compare it to – hermit that he'd been. But yes, that side of things, when they (he) eventually got over the nerves, was amazing. The closeness was incredible; Adrian would never have believed it was possible to be that close to someone. But there he was, and there Rebecca was. Fitting together, enjoying the life they were building – which inevitably at some point would involve getting hitched (regardless of her dad's feelings); would involve starting a family of their own.

'You know it's going to happen, don't you?' he'd say to her, and she'd get this look on her face which said: 'Well, don't leave it too long, will you? You never know what's around the corner.'

And he shouldn't have left it, should have just plucked up the courage to move their relationship forward – but even after all those years, he was still a coward. Still couldn't believe his luck and didn't want to push it, to rock the boat. Not that it would have done that, he realised now. Realised way too late… You never knew what was around the corner, that was a fact – and what had been around their next corner had been too horrible to even contemplate.

He still couldn't believe it, months later. Hadn't been able to believe what he was hearing when he got the phone call. When he heard that Rebecca had simply collapsed at work, helping to get a patient back into bed.

'What? No… Is this some kind of joke?' he'd asked, but they weren't laughing. *He* definitely wasn't laughing. Especially when he discovered it was all real, and Adrian was her emergency contact for such a thing. When he realised that Rebecca had just keeled over and—

He'd rushed to the hospital, hoping against hope that the urgency in the person's voice had been misplaced. That he'd get there and Rebecca would be sitting in the nurse's lounge having a cup of tea: 'A funny turn, love,' she'd tell him, and there'd be laughter.

Funny. Turn.

Or in bed with the docs flitting around her, making sure she was okay, Rebecca telling them not to fuss so much… She'd been in bed alright. On the bed, anyway. Where they'd fought to revive her, and failed.

'What…? I don't understand… How…?' He'd been gibbering, not able to put into words all the confusion and frustration he needed to get across.

'Massive heart attack. Heart failure,' the doctor with sideburns and a bald head (just another confusing thing) had said to him when Adrian had been taken to her.

In other words, a broken heart. Which was apt, really, when you thought about it. Another mirror, because his had broken that day as well, when he saw her laying there, her big eyes closed, so cold to the touch when he broke down and wrapped his arms around her body, crying more than Jane had ever done on those visits to their place. The love of his life: gone. No way of bringing her back.

It was explained to him that there had been no way of knowing, that it didn't matter how fit she'd appeared, the defect (no… she hadn't had any defects!) had been dormant all this time. Apparently her grandfather on her mother's side had passed away from something similar and it had just skipped a generation. Sudden, unexplained, though they'd done all the tests and examinations. Adrian had been informed every step of the way, but in the end didn't want to hear it. Couldn't stand picturing Rebecca being sliced into, cut into pieces. Her body, the perfect body he'd kissed and caressed, like something out of a horror show now. Bloodied and torn and…

The days, weeks, following that had been a bit of a blur. He'd barely made it through the funeral, ignoring the rants from Rebecca's father that it was all his fault, that she'd been okay until she met him. It wasn't rational, Adrian knew that, but then what about this was? The man needed something, someone to blame, because there was nothing else *to* blame… apart from his late wife's genetics, obviously, and he didn't want to go there. Jane had defended Adrian, telling her uncle to back off – in fact she'd been great. Had helped with the arrangements, just like Rebecca had done with Adrian's mother. Done her best to help him through those dark, dark days that followed as well.

Stopped him from just ending it all, and following Rebecca to wherever she had gone. Threw out the razor blades when he looked like he might do something with those, bought him an electric razor instead. Took the knives from the kitchen and brought in plastic ones.

'I… I only want to be with her,' he'd say, over and over again, usually after way too much to drink.

'I know, Ade,' Jane had replied. 'I know. But she wouldn't have wanted that for you.'

Adrian would shake his head. She'd want to be with *him* as well, he knew that, felt it. But he also knew Jane had a point; Rebecca wouldn't have wanted him to just throw his life away, waste it like hers had been wasted. She hadn't had a choice: he did. That didn't make things any easier to swallow, of course.

Jane had done her best to distract him, listened as he poured out his feelings even as his eyes poured out their reserves of saltwater – returning the favour for all the times they'd done that for her, he thought. She'd tried to take his mind off things; if not get him back to work, then encourage him to at least leave the house.

'It's not good for you to be cooped up inside here,' she'd tell him.

His answer would always be that it wasn't the first time, that it was how he used to be. Disconnected from this world… until he'd met Rebecca, of course. Then she'd *become* his world.

'Yes, but you have to eat,' she'd say then, coming round and making sure he *had* things to eat. Stocking his cupboards, cooking meals that he barely touched.

He showed no interest in TV or books. She'd even bought some of those old models she knew he'd made when he was younger, had heard Rebecca talking about because some were still out in their garage, collecting dust.

'I sent for them, through the post,' she'd said one day, unwrapping the parcel on the kitchen table. It was a nice gesture, a kind gesture. But Jane had ended up making most of them, because again the whole thing just reminded Adrian of Rebecca. Of the fitting together.

In one moment of anger, rage filling him up that he'd never known before – Adrian rarely, if ever, got mad – he'd swiped the plastic pieces off the table, both arms moving from left to right so that both the models and boxes hit the wall. 'This is all… It's pointless! None of this matters!' he'd bellowed.

Jane had risen quickly, standing back. She wasn't shocked as such, had probably seen this a million times in her work – just not with Adrian. 'Of… of course it matters. You… we need to get you through this.'

He'd glared at her then. 'I'm not one of your patients, one of your accident victims!'

Jane had looked down, eyes brushing the carpet. 'I know you're not.'

'So stop treating me like one! Nothing's going to fix this. Nothing's ever going to fix it! Nothing can bring Rebecca back!'

'You talk like you're the only one who lost her,' Jane snapped back, eyes meeting his again. 'The only one who… who loved her. I lost her too, Adrian. I. Lost. Her. Too!'

His mouth fell open at that. Jane had known Rebecca a lot longer than he had, and although it was a different kind of love, that bond had been as strong as anything they'd had together. What made his grief any more important than Jane's?

But then she was going, grabbing her coat and walking off up the corridor towards the front door. 'Do what you like!' she called back over her shoulder.

'Jane… Jane wait, I didn't…' But the slamming of the door was the only answer she gave him.

Adrian slumped back down in the chair, breath coming in gasps. Then he got up again, went into the kitchen and took what was left of a full bottle of vodka from the cupboard. Next, he fetched the bottle of sleeping pills from the bathroom cabinet.

And he thought, as he took these through into the bedroom, that actually he *was* a bit like one of Jane's accident victims. That this had happened *to* him. Now his whole life was one big car crash or train wreck… take your pick.

But he'd had enough of it. He'd had enough, wanted to escape from this nightmare.

Putting the first of the pills in his mouth, he knocked it back with the fiery liquid.

*   *   *

The shafts of light were the first things he saw, even through his eyelids.

So bright, they burned; his face warm. This is it, he thought, Heaven… either that or the other place. The hot place.

Adrian risked opening his eyes, the light virtually blinding. But he wasn't in Heaven, Hell or anywhere else. He was still in his bedroom, curtains drawn back – he hadn't closed them the previous evening, had other things on his mind – and the morning sunlight was spilling in. Adrian attempted to move, raising his left hand, shielding his eyes from the glare, then rolling away from the window. He blinked a few times and removed the hand, his eyes adjusting finally, scanning the room, then the bed. The empty vodka bottle was on the mattress, and so were the pills. That bottle was mostly full still, its contents spilled out – he'd only taken maybe two or three. A half-hearted attempt at suicide before passing out from the alcohol; he couldn't even get that right.

And then there was Jane.

He'd upset the one person he had in his corner right now. The one person who was attempting to help him, even though he didn't deserve it. The one link he had left to Rebecca.

He began to cry again, the reserves obviously replenished. Eyes misting up again, from tears rather than sleep. But it was then that he noticed, through those blurry eyes, the hand that he'd been using as a shield, still out in front of him. Something wasn't right about that hand.

Adrian blinked once more, squeezing the liquid from the corners of his eyes. He held the appendage up and, yes, something definitely wasn't okay. Because as he blinked away more tears, the hand coming more and more into focus, it was plain, it was obvious…

That the little finger on his left hand was missing.

He frowned, puzzled, bringing the hand closer and then moving it further away, checking it from various angles. It didn't matter what he did, how he looked at it, the finger was still missing. Swallowing dryly, he forced himself to check the wound, the part of the hand where… what? He'd somehow chopped it off in a drunken stupor? In his sleep? There wasn't even a knife in here (weren't any in the fucking house!) or anything sharp enough to do the deed, come to that. Jane had made sure of that, taken the scissors as well! Even if there had been anything, where was the blood? Anyway, the edges of the injury – if you could call it that – were smooth, not ragged. And the circular bit where you'd expect to see raw meat, blood and bone, was simply a darker colour than the skin around it.

Brow still creased, he looked around on the bed again, eyes – then hand, his good hand – searching the duvet for the missing digit. It was nowhere to be seen. Adrian climbed off the mattress, looking around on the floor, under the bed, like he was trying to find a missing battery from the remote control or something. Having just as much success as you traditionally did with that task.

Adrian began to panic, struggled to breathe. Such a thing to get worked up about, after everything that had happened to him recently. It was just a little finger, when all was said and done. But it was the strangeness of it, the knowledge that a part of him was missing, even if it was one of the smallest. Yes, when Rebecca had died a massive part of him had gone as well, but this was different. This actually *was* a part of him, something that had been with him all his life since birth.

Wait, think about this, Adrian said to himself, closing his eyes. *What's happened can't possibly happen. You're hallucinating or something, the pills mixed with the vodka. Mixed with the stress you've been under, the grief. Look again, I bet it's back.*

He did, opening one of his eyes.

It wasn't.

You're dreaming, that's all, he told himself now. *Any minute you'll wake up properly, like in a movie where it's a double bluff. You'll wake up and it'll be back.*

He didn't. And it wasn't.

Adrian pinched himself, even slapped himself, but that just hurt – and he didn't wake up. Because he knew, deep down inside, that he wasn't really asleep. So what next, what now? Get someone to verify this, other than him. To take a look and tell him either he was going stark, staring mad, or…

And then there was Jane. There was nobody else he could ask, in fact. No-one else who would come out to him, and he wasn't even sure she would. But he could at least ask.

So he did.

He rang her mobile, but just kept getting the voicemail. After about the millionth time she answered.

'What is it, Adrian? I'm at work.' She didn't say it, but he also heard in her tone: 'Helping people who want to be helped.'

'I… Jane, something terrible's happened. I did something…'

'Adrian…?' Her tone changed immediately. 'Ade, slow down. Tell me what's—'

'I… I can't find… Oh Jesus, Jane. I can't… It's…'

'Ade, listen to me. I need you to calm down. You're going to have another panic attack if you don't.'

'But it's… Jane, please. Please come. I'm sorry, I…'

There was a brief pause, then: 'I'm on my way,' she told him.

As good as her word, he heard Jane's key in the door forty minutes or so later, the time it would take to get across town. By then, of course, things had got worse. 'Adrian… Adrian?' she called from the corridor she'd stormed up the previous evening.

'In… in here,' he called back, voice barely more than a squeak. Then she was at the door to the living room, bob jiggling as she opened it wider. She saw him on the couch, slumped back, legs up.

Jane rushed over, crouching down. 'Adrian... Adrian, what's happened? You didn't do something stupid, did you?'

He nodded.

'Oh Christ, I should never have... You should have rung for an ambulance. *I* should have rung for an ambulance!'

He shook his head. 'There's no... I mean, I did take some pills last night with some... some vodka, but—'

'Oh Ade.' It was barely a whisper.

'But... but that's not it, not why I called.'

She looked at him, then looked down at his hands. 'Why are you wearing a glove? Are you cold?' He could see her thinking, if you are, then why just the one glove?

Adrian shook his head again. Pulled off the leather to show her. There was a sharp intake of breath from Jane, and Adrian bit his lip; now he knew he wasn't just seeing things. Or not seeing them, as the case may be.

Not one, but two of his fingers were missing: the original, little finger, and the ring finger, the one that had been next to it. 'Holy shit, where are...' She looked at his hand, then at him, then back again. 'Why would you...?' So that's what she was thinking, some kind of weird self-harm? '*How* did you even...?' And now he could see she was remembering the razor blades and knives, though if someone was determined enough they could find a way.

'I-I didn't do this,' he said quietly. 'Didn't do it to myself. They just...' He didn't know what else to say but: 'They just went missing.'

'Ade, fingers don't just go missing.'

'You think I don't know that?' His voice rose, but then he apologised. Jane hadn't even noticed, she was too busy having a look at the hand, turning it over, examining the appendage as he'd done a million times himself. 'There aren't even… Ade, it looks healed over.'

'I know,' he replied. 'Like I said, they just vanished. One overnight. When I woke up I thought maybe I was suffering from the after-effects of the vodka and pills, but I didn't take enough to… You're seeing this as well, though, aren't you? This is really happening.'

Jane looked him in the eyes, nodded. 'You said one…'

'The little finger. The other one… It went in the time since I rang you. I looked away for just a moment, I swear and… One second it was there, the next…'

'That's just—'

'Impossible? Yeah, tell me about it!'

'I…' Jane shook her head. 'We need to get you to the hospital, get this checked out. The blood-loss will be—'

'There's isn't any blood-loss, Jane! Take a look around for yourself. Don't you understand? It just happened.'

'Can… can you feel them?' she asked him. 'The fingers, I mean.'

He waved his other hand over the space where they had been, as he'd done several times already; checking that he wasn't turning invisible or something like in those films starring Chevy Chase or Kevin Bacon. 'They're not there, I promise you.'

'That's not what I'm talking about. Sometimes in cases like this—'

'Cases like this?' He couldn't believe what he was hearing. There *were* no cases like this!

'Amputees, I meant. There's something called phantom limb syndrome.'

Yes, he'd heard of that. But no, he couldn't feel a thing. 'It's like… like they're somewhere else,' he tried to explain, but failed.

'Hospital,' she said again, tugging on his arm to pull him up – but Adrian resisted.

'I… I really don't want to…'

'I know, but—'

'What are they going to do? How can they help?'

'I don't know, but we can't just—'

'I… please Jane, will you just sit with me, stay with me a while. I just… I really don't want to be alone right now.' She'd stayed with him before, under different circumstances; he was hoping she might be willing to again. 'I'll… I'll even eat something,' Adrian promised, attempting a smile.

She looked from him to the hand and back again, same as before. But then she nodded. 'Okay, for now. But if anything else…'

'Right,' he said to her. 'Thank you.' Adrian paused for a moment before adding: 'I don't know if I've even said that before to you, but thanks. Thank you for everything. I do appreciate it.'

Jane looked down, and he couldn't be sure but it looked like she was blushing slightly. 'You're welcome, Ade. I'd have… I'd have done it for anyone.' She did do similar for so many people, but it was more than that, he knew. They had a connection, through Rebecca. They'd both loved her, as she said the night before. 'Look, I'll go and fix us both something. Soup okay?'

Adrian nodded. Right now that sounded perfect, sounded normal – and given what was happening he really needed a dose of normality. Jane rose and went to the door again, shrugging off her coat and leaving it on a nearby chair. She looked back once before heading out into the corridor, heading to the kitchen.

He might have been mistaken, but he thought he detected a look of great pity on her face.

*   *   *

They'd eaten the soup at the kitchen table in silence.

Jane had already picked up the bits of the models he'd sent crashing into the wall, placing them all on a tray which now resided on a work surface opposite the cooker.

Adrian had sipped at the chicken broth, having to transfer the spoon to his other hand – because he was left-handed for eating, right for everything else. He'd put his glove back on, just figured it was better that way; if neither of them had to look at the... 'deformity'. Not that Jane wouldn't have seen worse, she'd encountered things like soldiers who'd had their legs blown off in war zones abroad for one thing, got them through the worst of it – she'd told them tales about it all during evenings there, spoke about it with such pride. But this, this was something else entirely. This was too...

So they ate quietly, not mentioning the huge elephants in the room – or lack of said elephants – where they'd gone and what had happened to them.

Jane was the one who'd finally spoken up, as they were drinking the teas she had made. 'Does... does it hurt? I mean, I have painkillers if you—'

'No, no.' Adrian's answer was almost a sigh. 'There's no pain, there's... well, there's nothing Jane. Absolutely nothing!'

Jane sighed too. 'I just can't believe...' She got up and cleared away the empty soup bowls, dropping them in the sink with a clatter. Then she leant on the edge with her head bowed. Stood there for quite some time while Adrian just watched her.

When she did finally move, Jane suggested they go back into the living room with the teas, perhaps see what was on the TV. Doing as her training probably taught her, as she'd tried to do when Rebecca passed away: bring it all back to some sort of normality again.

Jane put some inane daytime gameshow on, which they sat in front of – Adrian's eyes glazing over and Jane's flicking across to keep watching him. He wasn't sure at what point he dozed off, but it was dusk – almost dark – when he woke up on the sofa.

That was when he screamed.

Jane had been asleep herself in the chair nearby, the antiques show that had replaced the quiz obviously having a soporific effect on the both of them. She started, head snapping from left to right as she remembered where she was, what she'd been doing. 'Ade? Ade, what…?'

More screaming from him, doubling in volume and severity. Because, as he'd woken up he'd seen the flatness of the glove resting in his lap. The emptiness of it. And as he'd brought his right hand across to check, to pull the glove off, Adrian had seen the missing fingers on that one now: or, to be more specific, the missing thumb and forefinger.

By this time, Jane had snapped on the light and had joined him in seconds. Saw what was wrong seconds later. 'Ade… Ade, please calm down. Let me…' She pulled tentatively at the glove, as if wanting – yet not wanting – to see. But it was obvious what had happened, the left hand had gone as well now: the stump at the end of his wrist as flat and smooth as the remains of the fingers there had been. Jane spotted the other missing fingers now on the right, and sucked in a breath the same as she had done when she first saw this phenomenon.

'That does it, no more excuses Ade.' Her jaw was set firm and he knew what was coming next, stopped screaming in case that helped, but it didn't in the end. 'Hospital,' stated Jane, and wasn't about to be argued with.

After locking up, she ushered him towards her light-blue Beetle, more to help him along than anything because he was still shaking. 'Don't worry, we won't have to wait in A&E or anything. I can get us seen straight away,' she assured him. Which, on the one hand (poor choice of words) was a good thing, because Adrian wouldn't have to sit around with lots of people sporting injuries, staring and pointing; but at the same time would mean he'd have to confront what was happening quicker, put it in front of an actual medical person and see what they said.

God almighty, what *was* to be said about this? He shuddered to think.

Jane drove as fast as she could without breaking any speed limits, she'd seen enough of what such things could do – the consequences – to risk doing that. When they arrived she told him to wait in the car and Adrian watched through the large glass window at the front as Jane chatted to the receptionist, who was nodding and picking up the phone.

A few minutes later, she returned and he started to get out of the car – then suddenly lost his balance, fell against the side of the Beetle; would have slid all the way down it if she hadn't been there to steady him. 'Are you okay?' It was the most stupid question in the history of stupid questions and the look on her face told him she knew it. Adrian was very far from okay, about as far as you could get.

She shouted to a couple of paramedics that were hanging around at the door, asked if they could fetch a wheelchair.

'I don't… Please, Jane. Don't make a fuss. I can manage.' Which was blatantly not true.

She shushed him, with a 'Nonsense' thrown in for good measure. The men brought the chair and Jane thanked them, easing Adrian back into it so she could push him inside, once she'd placed a member of staff card on the dashboard and locked up her car.

The brightness reminded Adrian of that morning, before all this had begun. Before he knew it was even possible to start losing bits of yourself, back when he thought he might be reunited with his lost love.

Then suddenly they were there, inside an examination room with Jane pulling the curtain around them both for privacy. 'Shouldn't be long now, I told Michelle back there it was urgent.'

'But it's not—' Adrian began, then stopped. Maybe it was urgent. Maybe there was something seriously wrong with him... beyond the obvious. It was then that his thoughts turned to a disease of some kind, something nobody had ever seen before. After all, what had things like mumps or measles looked like to the first people who saw it? Just because it hadn't happened, didn't mean it couldn't. But what in God's name could make parts of your body disappear like you were an assistant in a magician's show?

He wasn't even sure he wanted to find out.

They were joined before long by a nurse wearing scrubs and a man in a white coat. The doctor was a lot younger than the nurse, in fact he looked like he should still be in nappies. 'Okay, Jane, so what's the big emergency?' he asked, a quizzical look on his face.

She nodded at Adrian, at his hands.

'An amputee? All right...' He got closer, peered at Adrian's wrist and where his missing thumb and forefinger had been on his right hand. 'Not a recent one, either, judging by this. One of your rehabilitation patients?'

Jane looked from Adrian to the doctor. 'No... not really. And these... all this...' She waved a hand around to indicate all the missing body parts. 'This is very recent indeed.'

'What are you talking about?' It was the doctor's turn now, to exchange glances with the nurse.

'Ade... Adrian had his left hand when I came to see him, and the thumb and forefinger on the right. Sometime in the last few hours he… well, he lost them.'

'A bit careless of him, wasn't it?' said the doctor, grinning, then stopped when he saw neither of them were joining in. 'I mean, this is a wind-up, right? Payback for what I did to that anaesthetist, Cheryl. You're mates with her, aren't you? She asked you to bring in one of your guys to—'

'Simon,' she snapped, holding up a hand to silence him in case her tone wasn't enough. 'This isn't a joke.'

'But—' Before he could say any more she was telling him what had happened. 'You didn't actually see it, though,' was his response.

'I saw that Ade had a hand when I arrived, then it had disappeared a little while later. Same goes for his thumb and forefinger on the other hand.'

Adrian felt like crying again, but sucked it in.

'What I mean is you didn't see it when it actually occurred,' Simon the toddler persisted.

'So what you're saying is that he did it to himself while I was asleep and then it all just healed over? Is that right?'

The doctor rubbed his chin, which was woefully lacking in any kind of facial hair or even stubble. 'I… At this moment in time I'm not really sure what I'm saying.'

'But it warrants further investigation, surely?' argued Jane.

Another exchange of looks between the doctor and nurse, almost like she was the more senior – in more ways than one. Then, with a nod, he was asking for Adrian to get out of his clothes and into a gown.

It was as they were taking his shoes and socks off that they saw it. The reason why he'd fallen against the car outside, almost fallen over flat on his face. There were toes missing on both feet.

'Oh… oh my God!' whimpered Adrian.

'I take it that's recent as well,' said Simon, but there was still an air of disbelief in his tone.

'Of course it's bloody recent!' Jane shouted. 'Look at him. Look how upset he is!'

But both the doctor and the nurse were stepping back, their expression changing, becoming more serious. Because as they'd been talking, another of the toes had vanished.

'Fuck me,' said Doctor Simon, language he really shouldn't have known at his age. There was also something else in his expression, a flash of fear – looking down then at his own hands and feet. Probably wondering the same thing Adrian had been, whether this was contagious or not.

In any event the patient was suddenly being taken more seriously after that, Doctor Simon's word – or maybe it was the nurse, whose name Adrian still didn't know – obviously carrying some clout.

Suddenly he was being admitted and it was test after test, machine after machine he was hooked up to or crammed into, or both, with nobody any the wiser after they were done; none of them any further in getting to the bottom of it all, let alone stopping it. What *was* further along by the time all this was finished, and experts called in, was that more bits of Adrian had gone AWOL. His left ear for one thing, his nipples, more of the fingers on his right hand, the entire forearm up to the elbow on the original left side, and his whole foot on the right.

It was enough for him to be given his own room, in isolation – his visitors limited to Jane and the staff already exposed accidentally, who'd all gone through a kind of decontamination procedure she told Adrian when she got to see him again, been tested for everything under the sun and found nothing untoward. Whatever was happening was confined to

Adrian and Adrian alone. She sat beside him on a chair by the bed; an uncomfortable one from the amount of fidgeting she was doing. Or perhaps that was just because she felt uncomfortable being there in general, Adrian thought to himself. He couldn't really say he blamed her. After all, he'd had a while to think about this, to try and get his head around what was happening and, not to put to fine a point on it, in words Doctor Simon might use, 'how fucked he truly was'.

He was okay about the dying bit, sort of, he'd said to Jane – well, hadn't he tried to kill himself anyway? – just not the method of it.

'Ade… please don't talk like that,' she said to him.

'Like what? About the fact that soon I'll be gone. It's true though, isn't it? They haven't got the first clue what's causing all this, and I doubt they will anytime soon. Definitely not soon enough at this rate. They're talking about transferring me somewhere, talking about specialists – as if there are specialists in *this* – but…'

She clasped her hands, looked down at them.

'At least I'll get to see her again,' he stated. 'She's the only one who ever saw me anyway.'

Jane kept her head down. 'You… you don't know that. I mean, nobody knows what comes afterwards, do they? Nobody's ever come back to tell us.'

Adrian stuck his lip out, while he still had one. 'I *have* to believe it, otherwise…' The choice had been taken out of his hands – literally – and so he had to believe there was a reason for that, if nothing else. Not that there was rhyme nor reason to life in general. Or death for that matter.

There was silence again for a little while, which Adrian finally broke – asking a question Jane really hadn't been expecting, from the expression on her face. 'Why doesn't Rebecca's dad, your uncle, like me?'

'What?'

'He can't stand me, and I don't know why. It's not as if I've done anything to him. Unless it was come between him and her? But I adored her, treated her right. Surely he could see that?'

Jane said nothing.

'Come on, confession time. If Rebecca knew, she never told me. *Wouldn't* tell me. But Jane, I really need to know. What did I do wrong?'

'You didn't. At least I don't think you did anyway. Bex didn't either.'

He couldn't help himself, there were tears tracking down his face now. 'Then what—'

'I…' Jane shook her head. 'I can't, it's kicking someone when they're down.'

'How much worse could it possibly get?' he asked her.

She tipped her head, conceding his point. 'He… well, he just thought Rebecca could have done better.'

'How do you mean?'

'He just thinks you're not very confident, ambitious. That you'll never be somebody. That kind of thing.'

Adrian thought about it for a moment. Rebecca's dad had a point really, he wasn't any of those things, but that's why she loved him. That's what made him different from the other twats out there – or at least that's what Rebecca used to tell him. 'And that's it?'

'I guess. A father needs to know that their daughter is in safe hands…' She paused, thinking about what she'd just said. 'Sorry… I mean looked after. It's an incredibly old-fashioned view, but then… well, you've met Rebecca's dad. He thought that if anything happened, if there was a crisis you'd just go to…' She paused again, realising now what she was about to say.

He finished it for her: 'Go to pieces?' And hadn't he been right? Look how Adrian had handled the death. Look what was happening to him right now. Even as they said it, the final – little – finger of his right hand, which was resting on top of the covers of the bed, simply vanished. Adrian couldn't help himself, he began to laugh.

Laughed at the ridiculousness of all this, but also because there was nothing he could do to stop it. He was literally going to pieces, he just didn't know where those pieces were going or why. The laugh was infectious, and though she knew she shouldn't, Jane began to join in with him. The pair of them laughing like they used to do when Rebecca told a joke and they'd had several glasses of wine apiece.

But then the fear returned, and Adrian's laugh became hysterical. Loud and manic, forcing more tears out. Jane was up and hugging him, trying to calm him down. Telling him it would be all right when he knew that was so much bullshit. A line she fed her patients.

He was still laughing when the hospital staff came in and gave him the injection which put him to sleep.

*   *   *

The next day, when Jane came to visit, she told him about the press outside.

Once she'd taken in the vanishments of the previous night, naturally: left leg up to the thigh; right hand completely; one of his eyes. Adrian had also had a catheter fitted – the tube fitting directly into his bladder – because, as the doctors had put it, there was nothing 'down below' anymore. He probably should have been more upset about this than he was, but Adrian had never been that kind of guy – never measured the fact he was a man by his private parts.

Oh, but the look of horror on Jane's face! He was becoming a freak show, he knew that. Composing herself, she'd explained why it had taken so long to get through the hospital doors, fighting her way through the hordes of cameras and Dictaphones. 'There must have been a leak. They're here for you, Ade.'

They want to get a photo or an interview with the monster, he thought to himself. 'So much for Rebecca's dad,' he said then. 'I'm somebody now, aren't I! Somebody with… with only bits of his body.'

Jane lapsed into silence again, as she was doing more and more on these visits.

Adrian looked around, making sure they were alone. 'Jane, can I ask you a favour?'

She seemed to perk up at that, edging closer to the bed. Feeling useful at last. 'Anything, Ade. You know that.'

'I… I don't want to die here. In this place.'

'Ade, you're not going to—'

What was left of his right hand was up to cut her short. 'Jane, please. Hear me out. I don't think they'll let me out of here, but I don't want to… Could you, y'know, help me?'

'To escape?' She made it sound like they were in a prison, but then again, in a way, they were. Especially now the press were camped out front.

'You said anything, Jane.' Which he knew wasn't fair of him, but he was desperate.

Hanging her head, she agreed. She just needed to figure out how to do it. Adrian was their star patient, all eyes were on him. Jane snapped her fingers, told him to bear with her, then left the room.

The next thing Adrian knew, there were alarms going off and raised voices out in the corridor. Then Jane appeared with another wheelchair, helping him into it. Even without her expertise, he was a lot lighter now, he realised. The ultimate diet, dropping pounds by the hour.

'Come on,' she whispered to him. 'I know a back way out of here.'

No-one stopped them as she wheeled Adrian out, they were too busy running up and down corridors, panicking, looking for the flames. She wheeled them both to a lift, which technically shouldn't be used during fire alarms Jane told him, but then they both knew there *was* no fire.

Down to a basement level, then out through an emergency door. Out to the car park at the rear where her Beetle was. Alarms were still sounding as she pushed him to the vehicle, raised voices trailing them as she helped Adrian back into the car that had brought them both here in the first place.

Abandoning the wheelchair, she put the car in gear and set off – using her card to open the barrier. There was a small road which skirted the front of the hospital, avoiding the crowds that were gathering, the beds that were being wheeled outside. They'd caused a lot of fuss, and Adrian felt bad about that, but it had been the only way to break free.

The only way to escape.

*   *   *

After calling at her place for medical supplies, which included more catheter bags – she always kept a stock of things at home, just in case – Jane drove him out of the city.

'Where are we going?' he asked her.

'They'll be looking for you at your home,' Jane replied, eyes flicking to the rear view, 'and it won't be long before they come to my place. But I know somewhere.'

That somewhere turned out to be a small cottage in the countryside. It belonged to one of her exes, who'd turned out to be married – the prick! – but she still had the key for it. He probably figured she'd never want to use it again. He'd given it to her because that's where he took all his bits on the side; a place his wife and kids didn't even know about. 'He's in America on business at the moment. Saw his photos on his social media… I wasn't stalking him or anything,' Jane said quickly. 'I just… I just never got round to deleting him.'

He felt sorry for her all over again, then, because of the choices she'd made, because of her shitty taste in men. 'Oh, Jane.'

'It's okay, I never really… It's okay.' They arrived and Jane helped Adrian inside, then into the double bed upstairs. 'I need to pop into the village and grab some stuff. Food or whatever. I won't be long,' she assured him.

And she wasn't, half an hour tops, but by the time she returned more parts of Adrian had disappeared. Both legs, the rest of his left arm and most of his right now. It was speeding up, they both knew that. He didn't have long.

Jane made the excuse of going to grab them soup, but Adrian couldn't fail to see the tears in her eyes. All those people she'd helped, the terrible injuries she'd seen, and this was the thing that had broken her. Probably because she knew there was no hope left, that there *was* no rehabilitation for him.

When she returned with the soup, she dropped it in the doorway. There was no point to it anyway, because in the short time she'd been down in the kitchen – probably composing herself – Adrian's mouth had gone. There was no way of feeding him, even if he'd felt hungry, which he didn't.

'Christ!' said Jane, hands going to her mouth. 'Oh… Ade, I didn't mean…'

He nodded, trying to make it as understanding as he could. She came and joined him, sitting on the bed next to him, placing a hand where she thought the stumps of his legs were under the covers – where they had been not long ago – only to feel nothing underneath. He was little more than a torso and head now.

'This… This isn't… How can you still be…'

Alive? he would have finished for her, if he could.

'It can't be…'

Possible? his mind answered. He understood that, none of this was. Or it shouldn't be – and yet it was still happening. There'd be no need for those fresh catheter bags soon.

Jane lapsed into silence once more. There was nothing really to say, nothing he wanted to hear. No platitudes that would make this any easier.

As she waited there with him, she laid her head on his chest. He could feel her sobbing, hard to begin with, then more softly. Then he felt her breathing steady, as if it was the one place in the world at the moment that could offer her respite. Offer her peace, normality.

She jerked quickly awake when there was no chest left to rest on. Jane stepped back, hand to her mouth as she scanned him for new changes. He'd felt his nose go, but somehow knew, even without a mirror, that there were still two holes there which allowed him to breathe… though quite how he was doing that when his chest, and his lungs with it, were gone was anyone's guess. Adrian was just a head now, on a neck and shoulders.

Jane shook her own head violently. 'No… no, this can't be happening! I *won't let it!*'

But, like him, she had very little choice – and she knew it. Her shoulders were slumping even now in defeat, fresh tears coming. There was so little time now, so little…

'I… If I don't say this now, Ade, I'm going to regret it. So here goes.' She sucked in a huge breath, then began. 'I'm a terrible person.' He moved his head from side to side, attempting to shake it but having difficulty now. 'No, really I am. I'm a jealous person, Ade. All those times you and Rebecca welcomed me into your home, when I was crying… crying on your shoulder.' When he still had one, because Adrian was aware of those slipping away too. 'I-I kept imagining it was me with you. Stupid I know, you loved… love Rebecca. *I* love Rebecca, for Heaven's sake! I'm not saying any of this is rational, but then again I'm not sure anything is anymore. I'm not even sure if it's you, or just because you're so different, so nice. But, well, after everything we've been through with Rebecca and… I'm rambling now and I really don't mean to, it's just that…'

She turned away from him then, hugging herself. He couldn't blame her, and he wouldn't have known what to say even if he'd had a mouth. He had feelings for Jane, of course he did, but… If things had been different, perhaps she'd have given him that reason to live instead of him just being afraid.

'Look, just forget I said anything. I *shouldn't* have said anything. It's—'

That was the last thing he heard, through his one good ear, and then nothing. It was the last thing he saw as well, through the eye he had left: Jane turning around to face him once more. Adrian knew what she'd find there once she did. Him, gone completely. Escaped, though he wasn't sure he really wanted to now.

But at least he would find out then, where the rest of him went. Maybe to be with Rebecca, as he'd hoped, maybe not.

But at least he would find out. At least he would—

* * *

Months. So many long months.

Since the funeral, where they'd buried an empty casket, hardly any mourners showing up. Months since she'd had to face disciplinary action for the incident at the hospital, which had resulted in a formal reprimand and a suspension. Reading between the lines, the board had felt sorry for her and understood her actions. She was just granting a dying man his last request. A very unique dying man, but a dying man nonetheless.

So, months. And Jane had mourned Adrian, mourned him and missed him. Missed him like she'd never missed any man before. Hadn't even bothered with them since it had all happened. She was better off, she told herself. Indoors, making and painting her models. Shutting herself off from the outside world.

Then, one day, there had been a knock at the door. She'd been expecting a delivery, more models in fact, and so she rushed to answer it… only to find the postman, or delivery man, had gone off already and just left the package on her doorstep. Actually, she came outside – not bothering that she was still in her pyjamas – and looked around, but she couldn't see any sign of either.

Just the box.

It was big, much bigger than the usual parcels she received, wrapped in brown paper and string. As she checked it over Jane found that there was no address on it. Not hers, and no return. Shrugging, she tried to pick it up, but it was heavy, so she dragged it into the house, over the threshold and into her living room – which hadn't been tidied or cleaned in a while, last night's pizza box still open on the couch.

Cocking her head, then biting her lip, Jane fetched a pair of scissors. She cut the string and began unwrapping the box. Brown paper removed, she found it was just ordinary cardboard beneath.

She opened it up. It looked like a snowstorm inside, bits of white polystyrene protecting whatever had been transported. Jane reached a hand in, then quickly pulled it back. Whatever was in there was warm. Soft and warm and distinctly… fleshy. Like pieces of meat. She pulled a face at the very thought of it.

But at the same time, she had to know. Jane stuck her hand in again, grabbed the first object she came to, and pulled it out.

It was a finger. A little finger.

Jane let go, dropping it on the carpet – almost hurling it across the room, in disgust. Eventually, she went over to it, kicked it. The digit didn't move. She bent and reached out again, hesitating slightly before picking it up. Definitely a little finger… But where you'd expect there to be blood and muscle and bone at the point where it had separated, there was just a smooth dark surface. She'd seen something like this before. Seen—

Jane rushed back to the box, began unpacking the rest of the items inside. Before long, she had them all arranged on the carpet, the empty box joining the remains of the pizza on the couch.

She stood, staring at the pieces. The other fingers, thumbs, the toes, the hands and feet. Then legs in two halves, same as the arms. The mid-section complete with private parts, and torso, shoulders, neck… A head.

That was the most disturbing bit, because although it had hair the face was blank, featureless. The mouth, nose, ears and eyes resided to the side of it. Bits on the side…

Jane swallowed dryly. This was some sort of sick joke, had to be. Like the one Simon thought she was playing on him back when—

Even though they were basically just pieces on the floor in front of her, she could tell. She knew exactly who this was. It was Ade.

Jane went back to the box, rummaged through it, but there was nothing else in there apart from the packaging. No instructions, no Part 13A slotting into Part 5C. Nothing. Not that she needed a sheet of paper to tell her which bits went where, it was just that…

She should get started, she knew she should. Everything was telling her to do that, as insane as this was. Everything was telling her to go and get the superglue.

Jane worked for the next few hours, tongue sticking out of the corner of her mouth. When she ran out of glue, she'd gone to the shops and bought more. Slotting the bits together, building the figure. Leaving the features till last, sticking them on carefully – this wasn't some Mr Potato Head children's toy. Recreating the face she knew so well.

When she was done, she sat him in an armchair, standing back to admire her handiwork. There was no need for paint this time, no transfers: he was finished.

Jane started when the body twitched, moved. When the mouth opened and closed.

She let out the breath she'd been holding, which turned into a giggle of delight. He was alive! Ade was alive! Her prayers had somehow been answered.

But he was disorientated, scared. She could see that by the way he was looking around the living room, looking at her with pleading in his eyes. 'W-W… Where… W-Who?' he managed, voice barely a whisper.

It would take time, this. It was more complicated than just putting the pieces together, like Humpty Dumpty. What he'd been through no-one had ever been through before.

Nobody knows what comes afterwards, do they. Nobody's ever come back to tell us.

Adrian had, but it would take time… time and rehabilitation. And even then, she wondered whether he would remember, like those people who'd been in crashes and suffered brain injuries. But Jane was patient, she was kind. She'd pieced together the person, now she had to help him piece together his life.

But the hard part was done. He was back and she'd made him. Made him for her; was made for her. As, eventually, she might be for him one day – finding some semblance of normality. They might even be made for *each other*. Might end up being an in-joke they'd share. Fitting together, like she'd fitted all the bits of him together.

Mending what was broken, even if it was a heart.

PLEASURES OF THE FLESH

This was where they all came to satisfy their needs.

The police knew it existed, but chose to ignore the fact most of the time. Only every so often would they run in a suspect, or do a drive-by, just to keep their superiors happy. Mostly though, they understood the advantages of such a place. Rapes were down in this area, as was domestic violence. Trimberly was a sort of release valve; somewhere people of *that kind* (in other words anybody and everybody, from all walks of life) could get their kicks. And the men, women and children – yes, sweet Jesus, children! – who plied their trade here, running a risk that the rest of the population thought unacceptable, well they were happy enough. After a fashion. They were born to this, even enjoyed it. Must do, so the more cynical would say, otherwise they'd go out and get a proper job like everyone else. It helped them sleep at night to think this way.

And into this den of inequity drove Dustin, headlights dipped, body hunched over the steering wheel. He turned the corner into Riley Street. The bridge was only a stone's throw away now, and up and down this tract of dull concrete the businessmen and women walked. Some in groups, most on their own.

Every time a car came into view they would stroll to the curbs, trying to attract the driver's attention, hoping (*though not deep down*) that they would be chosen next. Mortgages or rent had to be paid, food had to be bought, families provided for. All that took money.

Dustin drove slowly, looking from side to side. He bit the skin around his thumbnail, a nasty habit he'd picked up. It wasn't that he was nervous, well maybe just a little. He had paid for it before, when he couldn't find it easily in the clubs and bars – one-night stands, never anything more. Dustin hadn't been involved seriously with anyone since his first girlfriend, Linda. It just wasn't worth the waiting, the wooing, the courtship rituals. He knew what he needed and the sooner the better as far as he was concerned. It didn't worry him in the slightest. What he was doing was only what came naturally.

Looks were not important to Dustin, though. He could see the beauty in most people. And he didn't mind what shape his partner was either: big, small, fat, thin. He couldn't care less, even about the gender. As long as he had a good time, as long as they both had a good time getting it together; that last bit was important to him. Okay, so these men and women had slept with half the city's population, but he still prided himself on his technique.

One solitary girl was leaning against the side of a building, shoulders pressed up to the brick. She looked promising. Dressed in a red leather skirt and jacket, she stood with her arms folded, scanning the road. When she saw Dustin she forced a smile, her painted lips curving upwards. With a certain reluctance, she swayed over to the crawling car, her high heels clacking on the concrete. Dustin was enthralled at sight of her, a young face (eighteen, twenty at the outside) with shoulder-length brunette hair, medium height, and with legs a model would kill for; here encased in what looked to be fishnet stockings from this distance. She didn't seem very experienced, but that didn't matter to Dustin.

He pressed on the brake until he was parallel to her, then flipped down the passenger window. The girl put one elbow on the top of the car and bent over. The skin from her neck to her low-cut top was exposed. Dustin gazed at it, eyes travelling down to her cleavage.

'See anything you like?' she asked him.

'Oh yes,' said Dustin.

'I can be anything you want me to be,' she told him, running a hand over her hip. 'You only have to ask.'

Pretend to be anything: nurse, schoolgirl, nun… He didn't want any of that. 'Just be yourself,' he told her.

They negotiated, getting the business side of it out of the way first. The woman looked trustworthy so he gave her the money in advance. She stared at it in amazement; clients never paid in advance, always afterwards. What was to stop her from running off with it right this second? Nothing, except that now she would have a good feeling about this man. Like she should go with him or she might miss out on something.

'Climb in,' he said in that gentle voice.

And she did just that.

'My name's Dustin,' he told her, holding out his hand. The woman slid her own inside his and he kissed the knuckles. A proper gentleman. His lips tingled as they brushed against her skin.

'I'm Amber.' Neither green nor red, but could turn either at any time.

Eventually he took her hand away from his mouth and said, 'Very pleased to meet you Amber.' The car pulled away from the curb, leaving Riley Street behind.

There was very little conversation after this, though. Amber preferred it that way, she told him. The less personal the better. However, when Dustin quizzed her about how long she'd been doing this, he saw her frown then answer. Not only that, but answer truthfully.

'Eight months,' she told him. 'I'm trying to put myself through college.' She shook her head, knew she shouldn't be saying all that. Never reveal anything about yourself, that's what she would've been taught by the older girls on Riley Street.

Dustin picked up on her nerves. 'Don't worry, I'm not an axe-wielding lunatic or anything like that.' It was true, he wasn't. He didn't want to hurt her.

'Glad to hear it,' said Amber, a hitch still in her voice. 'Although if you were, I doubt whether you'd tell me.'

Dustin laughed. 'No, I suppose not.' He felt the desire now, inside. Was growing impatient, needed her.

'Where are we going?' Amber asked him, as if all of a sudden realising she didn't know. 'Hotel?'

'No, back to my place. I have a house.'

'You aren't married, then?' Not that it should make any difference, but for some strange reason it did.

'No. I'm not the marrying kind.'

The car sped on, first one turning, then another. Amber shifted around uncomfortably so he tried to put her at her ease. 'I'll drive you back, of course,' he said. Amber nodded; she believed him.

'Almost there.' Dustin pulled into a side road and then into a driveway. Amber twisted round so she could see the house. He knew what she was thinking: *Not bad.* If the payment in advance hadn't signalled it, now she knew he had money. Who knows, might even become a regular? But she was also probably wondering what he needed her services for. Dustin was quite good looking in a Latin-American kind of way; even his five o'clock shadow was appealing, he'd been told. He had a nice car and home. Surely he could find women in the normal way? Unless, of course, he *wasn't* normal. Was she going to get inside only to find vast arrays of S&M equipment, or maybe he'd want to lick her feet for half an hour? He couldn't help chuckling at that thought.

'What?' she asked.

'Nothing,' answered Dustin and she frowned again.

He got out, went round and opened the door for her. Again, such a gentleman. Then he guided her to the front door. The house was fairly secluded, willowy trees blocking off the view left and right, so he wouldn't have to worry about anyone seeing him come in. That was handy.

'Have... have you done this kind of thing before?' she ventured.

He opened his mouth to answer, then closed it again. But the answer was: yes, he had. Probably more times than her, if he was being honest.

Dustin fiddled with the key and stepped inside.

With the lights on she could now see that it was tastefully decorated, too. Modern, without being too sterile. Amber smiled, clearly liking what she saw. She was starting to like him, too, which Dustin understood was a definite no go in her line of work. Would have been one of the first things she learned: don't get involved, too messy.

But surely if the right man came along, someone with money, someone handsome. It had been known to happen...

'Would you like a drink?' Dustin asked her. 'Tea, coffee? Something stronger?'

'I don't usually, but...' She nodded. Didn't usually drink on the job, because it would affect her reasoning, make her more vulnerable. Though how much more vulnerable could she be than she was right now? 'I'll have a Bacardi if you have any.'

'Sure, just give me a second. Oh, make yourself at home, won't you.'

Dustin disappeared into the kitchen, while Amber made herself comfortable on the couch, a cream-coloured leather one.

As he returned she was running a hand down the arm, clearly enjoying the feel of it.

'Here you go.' Dustin gave her the glass of Bacardi.

Amber shrugged off her red coat and accepted the drink, taking a sip straight away.

'Do you mind if I ask you something, Amber?' Dustin sat on the sofa, not too close, but not miles away, either.

'I guess,' she said, voice trembling.

'Are you happy with what you do? How your life's turned out?'

Another frown. It was a strange question, he realised. She'd probably been expecting something along the lines of: 'Would you mind if I brought out the whips now?'

'Sure. I mean, well it's not perfect, but then again whose is? College is going okay, kind of. And this is…' Amber paused. 'I don't mind it too much.'

'But have you ever wondered if there was something more? True happiness.'

'I suppose so. But I don't really—'

He could no longer resist, the anticipation, the build-up too much. Dustin knew all he needed to know. *He* would make her happy tonight, truly happy. 'Drink up,' he said. 'It's time.'

'What, here?'

'To start with.' Dustin watched as she gulped a little more of the

Bacardi, before setting it down on the coffee table. Then he moved closer, taking control; he could see her trembling. Amber was scared. But scared and excited at the same time, he could sense it. No client would ever have had this effect on her, not even the first (*especially* not the first). It was almost like she was a virgin waiting for the big night.

Dustin took her arm, her bare arm up to the shoulder, and started to kiss it. Softly, tenderly. Amber shivered. The brush of his lips alone was enough to arouse her. She probably knew that every part of a woman's body became an erogenous zone when they were excited, but the forearm? The elbow? Ridiculous! And yet it was happening. She closed her eyes, losing herself to the experience as his kisses reached higher and higher, savouring every inch of her arm. Until he came to the strap of her top.

'Why don't you take this off?' Dustin told her, and Amber was more than willing. Ready for whatever came next.

She stood in front of him and pulled the top over her head, casting it to one side. Then she undid the zip on her leather skirt and eased it over her hips. It dropped to the floor resting alongside the top. Underneath she wore a black bra, panties and hold-up fish-nets.

Amber was just about to join him on the couch again when he said, 'No, take it *all* off.'

She cocked her head. 'Most of them like me to keep this stuff on.'

'I don't. Please, Amber.'

Amber shrugged and reached round to undo the clasp on her bra. She pulled the straps down her arms and dropped it to the floor. Dustin gazed at her exposed breasts. They were perfect. Not too large, not to small, with dark, pert nipples already rising up. The stockings came off next, followed by the panties. These she slid provocatively down her long legs, obviously taking pleasure in Dustin's face.

'Now the jewellery,' Dustin said.

Amber was once more puzzled by his request, but the punter was always right. And besides, she looked more than eager to see what else he could do with those lips of his. Quickly, she took off her ear-rings, her pearl necklace and the few rings she had on.

Now she was completely naked.

Dustin was captivated by the sight of her, his breathing erratic, his eyes wide. This gave Amber pleasure, too. She *wanted* him to find her attractive. She needed it badly.

The girl sat back down on the couch again and waited for it to begin.

Most of her clients would only be interested in their own gratification, with no thought for hers. Why should they be when they were paying? She may as well have been a blow up doll for all they cared. Dustin was different. He would take his time, and the idea of foreplay was no stranger to him.

With his hands and lips he explored her now. Not just her arms, hands, but the whole of her upper half. When Dustin reached her neck, licking the skin there with his darting tongue, Amber cried out with joy. His hands played over her breasts at the same time, which were now ultra-sensitive, responding eagerly to his touch. He tweaked a nipple, only softly, but it was enough to make her cry out again.

There would be all kinds of thoughts rushing through her mind, all kinds of questions: how was he doing this to her, how was it possible to feel so much pleasure, wave upon wave? Dustin was confident it would be nothing she'd ever experienced before, not even with those she had professed to love.

He purposefully steered clear of below the waist. For now. Dustin didn't need to go *down there*. Not when he could enflame Amber by just stroking her shoulders, trailing his nails across her belly, nibbling the flesh behind her ear.

The first racking spasm took Amber completely by surprise, in spite of everything leading up to it. But not him. He'd seen it before… She tipped back her head, breath coming through clenched teeth, and held on to Dustin as his lengthy energetic tongue did the work.

Sometime between the first of these explosions of pure delight and the next, Dustin carried her up to the bedroom. Amber hardly noticed she was moving, such was the intensity of her bliss. The next thing she was aware of, vaguely at best, was being laid down on a large bed.

Dustin's bed.

Amber was still reeling, but she watched with admiration as he stripped off his own clothes. Opening the wardrobe door, he hung up the clothes on hangers. There was a flash of light as the mirror on the inside reflected his face, then he closed the door. When he turned, Dustin saw the uncertainty in her eyes. That moment's respite would have given her pause to think, to wonder whether he'd slipped something into her Bacardi. Surely no one could do the things he'd done to her, not that way at least.

Then it was gone again. She wanted more.

He could see she took almost as much pleasure in the sight of him as the feel of his skin on hers. His body was well-muscled and perfectly-proportioned. Her eyes were driven downwards, and she was far from disappointed. He could feel her own impatience now, Amber wanting him to hurry, to come across to her right that second, to continue pleasuring her as he had downstairs, but she could barely speak.

Then he appeared above her, smiling.

Amber smiled back.

Dustin began to kiss her once more, lips brushing her neck, her shoulders, licking once again; tongue leaving a trail of saliva like a slug. The tingling returned and he knew Amber could feel it too. His mouth found one of her nipples, which was already erect. Covering it, Dustin began to alternate between sucking on it and flicking it back and forth with his tongue. She let out a wail of delight, hands finding his own shoulders and holding him, nails digging in.

She paused for a second, suddenly realising what she'd done. Hurt the client when he hadn't asked for that – for the rough stuff. She just hadn't been able to help herself, Dustin knew that. He pulled his head back. 'It's okay,' he told her. 'Just let yourself go. Let yourself enjoy every single moment of this. The happiness, the pure joy.'

Amber nodded, a little uncertain. That was meant to be her line, surely. She was meant to be showing him the time of his life not the other way around. Then it didn't matter because he was sucking on the other nipple, teasing it and playing with it until she let out another loud moan.

When he felt like she couldn't take any more, Dustin went down and down, kissing and licking her toned stomach muscles until she bucked beneath him. But that was as nothing compared with when his tongue found her sex. Already slick from her first orgasms, he lapped at her juices greedily like he wanted to drain them all, dry her out. Fortunately they just kept on coming, the more he worked – and Amber yelled out once again as she climaxed.

But Dustin was only really getting started. And now, to give her time to recover, he began slickening her thighs, her knees, her calves… all the way down to her feet, where he paid special attention to her ankles and toes, nibbling each one in turn, much to Amber's obvious glee.

Bending to take in his face at the bottom of the bed, she said to him: 'I want you. I want you… inside me.' Didn't care about protection, about diseases or anything else. Just needed him, right now.

Dustin grinned. He was more than happy to oblige; it was time anyway, he'd only been prolonging the moment. So he pulled himself back up the duvet, like he was swimming the channel, then dove in. Hitting the target first time, shoving himself in up to the root and causing Amber to draw in breath sharply.

As he began to build up a rhythm, Dustin didn't ignore the rest of Amber – returned to old haunts like the breasts and nipples, the shoulders, the neck. He knew they could both feel the tingling sensations mounting, Amber shivering with ecstasy beneath him was evidence of that. The pleasures of the flesh, something that most people thought they had experienced but were so, so wrong. Tip of the iceberg stuff, nothing like the pair of them were going through right at that moment. The dizzying heights of rapture.

Dustin thrust in and pulled out, making sure he stimulated her most sensitive area – not that every single fibre of her wasn't sensitive at the moment. Wasn't responsive to his touch. She was putty in his hands, in fact, but willingly so. Desperate for him to make her even happier, to deliver more complete bliss, which was what he wanted too after all. The smile on her face, eyes closed, head back, told him how much she was relishing all of this, heading for yet another orgasm which he would try to double or triple by angling himself so that he could reach her G-spot inside, rubbing against that as well, delaying his own release.

Amber snaked her legs around his back, locking him in position, urging him on, her cries louder and louder with each fresh movement he made. Her hands were under his arms, cupping his back now and doing the same. The fingernails were digging in once more, drawing blood Dustin knew –

the wetness running down as she raked the flesh there. He didn't care, it was getting towards the end now; once Amber had come for the final time, it would be his turn and then all this would be over.

Then there it was, finally – having taken so long and yet no time at all. Amber's whole body was shaking with the powerful sensations she was feeling, but Dustin was determined to finish what he had started, even back there on the street. To have his own climax, unable to do anything but let go.

But instead of what would normally happen, his seed pumping out into her, it was quite the reverse. A suction was being created down there that made his efforts with her nipples earlier seem tame by comparison. A pumping, certainly, but of Amber *into* him. He was inside her, but he was starting to draw her back inside himself.

And next, the look – the realisation that something was very wrong indeed. That this wasn't normal. Amber's body was still tingling, Dustin knew, still wet with a combination of sweat and his spit. Changing her, making her more malleable, just as her mind had been earlier; no match for his from the start.

'What… what's…?'

Amber tried to move, to wrestle herself free, but she couldn't – mainly because her fingers, her whole hands were sinking into Dustin's back like it was made of hot tar. Her legs and feet were doing the same, melting into him. She was aware of what was happening, but it shouldn't be possible.

His own hands, where they met her skin, were doing the same as his organ inside her, sucking her up like a vacuum cleaner. Amber let out a scream, not of satisfaction this time but of absolute terror.

Dustin hated this part, hated that he had to do it. He didn't want to hurt her, but he must. It was necessary… That's why he had to make sure that her last moments were pleasurable, so he didn't feel quite as guilty. He'd given something to them, now they had to give something back.

Amber's face was slack, skin there stretched like some kind of weird mask. Eyes dribbling out of their sockets as she was pulled into him. Where they met at the chest it was almost like they were melding together, two people literally becoming one; forget the old song by that girl group years ago, this was the real thing.

The screams were petering out because Amber's mouth was being pulled downwards, and her lungs were already halfway inside Dustin. He brushed his own mouth against her, then his cheek, then his whole face, rubbing her flesh until it was absorbed like a sponge mopping up a spillage on a wet kitchen floor.

He shivered himself as the last of her bled into his pores, sinking onto the duvet where Amber had been only seconds before, enjoying the most magical and intense evening of her short life. Gone now, wiped away like she had never existed at all. Dustin let out his own satisfied cry.

Then, and only then, did he say: 'I'm sorry. I'm really sorry.' He had the good grace to acknowledge that at least. That he'd taken Amber's life – well, her body at any rate – in order to feed. That she was no more now, because two beings couldn't possibly exist in the same space.

Or could they?

Dustin jerked. Twitched. He frowned, as Amber had done so often while he was coaxing her back to his home. Then came the pain, and he knew the look of terror she'd sported back there was being mirrored on his own face.

Something was wrong, terribly wrong.

Dustin got onto all fours on the bed, felt like he was going to throw up. Jesus, in all these years, after all those meals, he'd never felt like this before.

Maybe it was like when you ate something bad… food poisoning? Stood to reason that it could happen whatever way you digested something, didn't it? Or… or an allergic reaction? Amber like poison to him and he didn't even know it?

He staggered off the bed, half-collapsing off it actually, to crawl across the bedroom floor. Heading for the bathroom, heading for the toilet where he fully expected to be violently ill.

Dustin was shivering again, but there was no pleasure in it this time; no satisfaction. Using the door, he managed to get to his feet and caught a glimpse of himself in the bathroom mirror. White as a sheet, but that wasn't all. His flesh was undulating in a way he hadn't seen outside of when he fed. Like it was losing coherence.

'Christ!' he shouted, hands going to his face – where they almost sank in, if he hadn't pulled them back in time. 'What's… what's happening… to me?' Wasn't as if he could just ring an ambulance either, he couldn't let the outside world see this. See what he really was. He'd end up in some facility somewhere being experimented on. Dissected.

But it was definitely tempting, especially as he bent double again, the sheer agony amazing. The tingling was back as well, and when he looked down at his legs he saw they were rippling too, like the surface of a lake someone had thrown a rock into. Jerking, kicking out…

Getting his kicks.

His arms followed suit, then the rest of him: altering, changing, taking on another shape.

A more female shape.

Gone was his impressive manhood, which had retreated back up inside him – never to be seen again. And as he slowly rose, he could feel the weight of the swelling at his chest. Two breasts emerging, pushing outwards to his disgust. The dark nipples of each sprang out, like they were being released from captivity, standing to attention. Pert.

The hair was disappearing from his arms, his torso, but conversely that on his head was darkening and growing. Brunette, shoulder length. When he looked in the mirror this time, he knew what he would see. The full red lips, the eyes of a young girl, eighteen, twenty at the outside.

Was aware of what was happening, though it shouldn't be possible.

It was his final thought before losing his grip on himself, Dustin's features, his body wiped away so completely it was like he had never existed at all.

* * *

Amber righted herself, looked in the mirror. Looked down at herself.

She looked fine, nothing out of place. Which was a miracle considering what she'd just been through. Poor Dustin… no, not poor Dustin. Fuck him! He'd been trying to make a meal out of her. Assuming she was like the rest of the populace, when in fact she was just pretending, like him. Could be anything she wanted to be.

Still, it was a shame. In all her time doing this, living this kind of life, in a place that would give her a greater choice of victim, men, women and children – yes, sweet Jesus, children! – she'd never come across another one like her. A person of *that kind*. Who was born to this, even enjoyed it. After a fashion.

Had often wondered, but never thought… She'd known what was happening as soon as it started of course, the tingling intensifying. The release valve, then the absorption. And she'd been scared, *of course* she'd been scared. Didn't have a bloody clue what would follow once it began, but couldn't back out. Scared… but excited at the same time.

In the end, though, it had come down to who was the strongest. She might be young, but Amber was feisty, regardless of the vibes she was giving off. Amber, who could turn green or red at a moment's notice. And you really didn't want to be around when she was on green!

What had also helped, she realised, was to let Dustin think he had won. Let him think she was like all the others, and let him think she was gone. Then it was just a simple matter of taking control. Taking his body, or her body *back* more accurately.

She should go soon, gather her things and take off – not that she was expecting there to be anyone else who lived here, not with Dustin the way he was. Maybe she'd have more Bacardi first. That would make her happy.

Was she really happy with her life? Dustin had asked.

College was okay, she was paying her way through that to give her some sort of decent job. The kind Dustin must have had to afford this kind of place. But this… doing this. Well, it was necessary. She didn't want to hurt anyone, but must – she'd realised that quite early on.

It was the only way to satisfy her needs.

EXTRAS

THE TORTURER – A PLAY

<u>ACT I</u>

<u>SCENE 1</u>

Blackness. The first thing we're aware of is the sound of dripping water. Gradually, details are revealed: a small window above, with bars covering it, lets in some light; the walls of this place are stone, solid. It's a cell of some sort – and then the light picks out a solitary figure laying in one corner, unconscious.

The man, ANDY, begins to move, wakes, lifting himself up slowly as if it's hurting him. Slams a hand down suddenly on the floor – making us start.

Slowly the figure drags itself into view, gaunt and ill-looking. His clothes are dishevelled, shirt and trousers – no shoes, bare feet – heavy bags under his eyes. The sound of crying now joins the dripping of water, from another cell perhaps. The man looks towards the audience, addresses them.

ANDY

[*Croaky voice*] I'm not sure how long I've been here. A few days, a week

241

maybe? Feels like a lot longer. I've not seen a soul since I arrived, either; shoved in here like some kind of animal. I didn't see the men – I assume they were men – who grabbed me, kidnapped me. I know it sounds like a cliché, but it really did happen so fast. And it was dark, too. As dark as it is here in this… cell. Yes, I suppose that's what you'd call it. Four stone walls surround me, slimy to the touch. It's damp in here and smells of faeces and urine… Mostly mine. There's no bed, so I have to sleep on the cold floor. At night I feel things crawling over me, insects and… I think rodents of some kind as well. [*Beat*] Goes without saying, I've slept very little of late.

The man crawls a bit further, still facing the audience, before continuing on with his monologue. His stomach lets out a growl and he clutches it.

ANDY

Hardly surprising. I've not eaten so much as a scrap of food since my incarceration. I sometimes wonder if they've forgotten all about me, the people who put me here. Or left me to die for some reason I can't even begin to understand…

The crying gets louder now.

ANDY

If so, then I'm not the only one… You hear that? It gives me hope. The sound of another human being at least. I've tried banging on the walls, on the door. To get some kind of response, from either my captors or that poor sod in the same boat as me. [*Beat*] But I never get a reply.

Now he clambers unsteadily to his feet, begins pacing up and down in front of us.

ANDY

It's like you can feel yourself going insane, in stages. No, not insane. Not yet! We were never meant to be alone like this, imprisoned. It's inhuman… [*To himself*] Try to think things through, clearly. Work out why you're here. I'm not rich, am I? I don't think I'm famous, so no one will pay a ransom for me. Nobody bears me any kind of grudges that I know of… Perhaps it's just an arbitrary thing? My being here could be a random act. Wrong place at the wrong time. Terrorists trying to make a point by snatching the first person they came across. [*Becoming more distressed*] If only they'd let me go. I wouldn't tell anyone. What the hell do I know to tell anyone anyway? Oh Jesus, why won't they just let me go?

We and the man hear the sound of footsteps, heavy footfalls which get louder on approach. Then the jangling of keys, someone at the door. The man looks like he's going towards the noise, on the right, then backs off.

ANDY

Someone coming… But why am I so scared? It's what I've been waiting for, hoping for – and yet…

Then suddenly there are two large men in the cell with him, dressed in black: entering stage right.

ANDY

No… You stay away. I'm warning you…

They approach, grab him – and although he struggles, the man is no match for them.

ANDY

Get off me! No, wait… please! Why are you doing this?

They drag him off, his feet hardly touching the ground, and away into the blackness – exiting stage right.

<u>SCENE 2</u>

The men and their prisoner appear stage left, and they throw him into the space: where there is a table plus two chairs in the centre. It is lit by a single bulb. They depart and he gets to his feet – gapes over to the left, thinking that might be his escape route…
He makes his way over slowly, then speeds up – only for another figure to appear at the door, blocking his path. The TORTURER. He's also dressed in black. His hair is short and he wears a pair of glasses. In his hand he carries a clipboard. The TORTURER holds out his other hand, indicating the table with chairs on either side.

TORTURER

[*Flat, toneless*] Please, take a seat.

A pause as the prisoner stares at him. Frowns, then in the end decides to sit down on the left-hand side chair. He waits for the man with the clipboard to do the same, but he doesn't. The TORTURER simply hovers – the prisoner craning his head to see what he's doing. Finally, the TORTURER walks into view in front of him. Gives a chilling smile.

TORTURER

Splendid. Now we can begin… [*Smile fading into a sneer*] Please tell me your name.

ANDY

What?

TORTURER

Your name. Quickly!

ANDY

Andrew… Andy Brooks.

The TORTURER pauses to write something down on the clipboard.

TORTURER

You know why you're here, of course.

ANDY shakes his head.

TORTURER

Oh, come now. You do know, Mr Brooks. Think.

Silence passes between them. ANDY finally shrugs his confusion.

TORTURER

No? All right, if that's the way you want it. Tell me how you came to <u>be</u> here, then.

ANDY

Your people grabbed me and—

TORTURER

[*Impatient*] Before that. Tell me what you were doing before that. What you have been doing for the last few months, the last few years.

ANDY opens his mouth as if to reply, then frowns again. Shakes his head.

ANDY

I... I...

He shakes his head again.

TORTURER

Your answer, Mr Brooks?

ANDY

I can't... It's all a bit of a fog.

TORTURER

Where were you when you were taken? Near where you live, where you work?

ANDY

I don't... I don't remember.

TORTURER

Don't remember where you live? Where you work? Or where you were taken?

ANDY

I... All three. I can't seem to...

TORTURER

And you expect me to believe that?

ANDY

Your men, they hit me and then...

TORTURER

So, memory loss from concussion? Is that it? Our fault?

ANDY

I-I didn't say... I just... I'm finding it hard to...

TORTURER

[*Angry*] <u>Tell</u> me!

ANDY

I'm sorry, I...

*The TORTURER swings his clipboard, missing Andy's head by inches.
Then he slams it on the table, making Andy – and the audience – jump.*

TORTURER

Not good enough. Who do you work for?

ANDY

I… don't…don't remember. Look, what's all this about?

TORTURER

It's very simple. You tell me which side you're on. Make life easy for
yourself.

*The TORTURER walks around the back of him, places his hands on
ANDY's shoulders.*

ANDY

I'm not on anyone's side.

TORTURER

We're all on one side or the other… I'm not a patient man. You should
know this. I've been hired to do a job, and that's exactly what I'm going
to do, Mr Brooks.

His grip is tightening on ANDY's neck.

ANDY

Listen, where am I? What do you want from me?

TORTURER

I've told you that already.

ANDY

When am I going to get something to eat?

TORTURER

When you answer my questions. Who do you work for and what have

you done?

ANDY

What have I…

The TORTURER's hands close in on his neck, squeezing. ANDY
brings up his own hands, fingers clawing to try and dislodge the grip,
but it's no use. In the end The TORTURER slams him forward on the
table, and ANDY lies still. Unconscious. Everything goes black.

<u>SCENE 3</u>

The lighting is low/tinged with grey-blue and Andy is still at the desk,
but the TORTURER has gone. ANDY wakes, looks up, then around
him. Stage right, something moves. Several somethings, in fact, just
shadows detaching themselves from the blackness.

ANDY

W-Who's there?

They start to crawl across the stage towards him, still indistinct, still shadows. A strange wailing sound starts up, increases in volume the closer they come. ANDY rises from the table, backs away.

ANDY

I said who's there?

One of the shadows rises now itself, and all we can see is a white hand with streaks of blood on it – a white finger pointing accusingly at Andy. The shadows get closer, closer. More of them rising up. The wailing intensifies.

ANDY

[*Distressed*] No… No, please… Please don't… please go away! Please just leave me—

The shadow with the hand surges forward – as the wailing reaches fever-pitch. It's about to catch ANDY when the lights go out again.

SCENE 4

When the light comes up – that solitary bulb above the table – ANDY is back at the table where we left him before the nightmare, except his hands are tied behind his chair; to his chair. His shirt is open at the front, head slumped on his shoulder. The TORTURER is standing off to the side of him, ready for when he comes to. Suddenly ANDY jerks awake, terrified.

TORTURER

It's not polite to pass out in the middle of a conversation, you know.

ANDY

Where…?

ANDY frowns, then winces – a bruise at his temple.

TORTURER

Do you remember what we were talking about before you 'dropped off'?

ANDY attempts to nod, but it hurts too much – he winces again.

TORTURER

Good. My question still stands. Who do you work for?

ANDY

T-Told you… Don't remember.

TORTURER

Not acceptable.

The TORTURER stands back and picks something up off the table. At first we can't see what it is, then he unfurls a length of black, plastic wiring with a frayed end. He grins that chilling grin again.

TORTURER

I suppose I've made it worse. The concussion? The memory loss?

ANDY

I…

TORTURER

Not that you had any of that to start with, of course.

The TORTURER brings back the wire and whips Andy across his chest. ANDY screams out in pain and surprise.

TORTURER

We'll try again. Tell me what you know.

ANDY stares into his eyes.

ANDY

[*Panting*] My… my name is Andy Brooks… I don't remember any more than that.

The TORTURER whips him across his tied hands, just out of sight of us. ANDY howls, grits his teeth in agony.

TORTURER

Tell me!

ANDY

N-Nothing… Nothing to tell…

More whipping, twice, three times.

TORTURER

You will tell me. Eventually… One way or another.

Another couple of slashes, then slaps to the face, as much to try and keep ANDY awake as torture him. In the end, though, his head slumps onto his chest and The TORTURER puts down the makeshift whip on the table.

He stands back, hands on hips and just stares at the unconscious ANDY, cocking his head. Admiring his handiwork. Then the large men in black from before arrive, undo ANDY's bonds – and carry him back off stage left.

<u>SCENE 5</u>

ANDY is thrown into the cell, stage right, where he lays for a few moments, but the pain on his front is just too much. He crawls across the stage a little way, panting. Then flops over onto his back, looks to the audience.

ANDY

I… I don't know what he wants from me. That man… The Torturer. I… I can't give him what he wants. I honestly don't… don't remember. Just my name… But not where I live, what I do… I-I can't even remember where I was when they grabbed me… Why? Why can't I… [*Beat*] Christ! I'm so sore… I… I've never felt pain like that before… I…

His head flops back and rolls over, unconscious once more. The crying returns from somewhere beyond the cell. Everything goes black.

SCENE 6

The light, when it returns, is that strange blue/ghostly colour. ANDY wakes, looks across to see those shadows returning, stage right. Movement indistinct at first, then shapes crawling on stage, and starting to rise. The crying sound has been replaced by the strange moaning and wailing of these 'people'.

As they enter the light we can pick out more of their features: a man, a woman. The man has a ragged scar across his face, is shuffling, holding his stomach. Reaching out towards ANDY with his hand – then pointing.

The woman is similarly scared, flashes a look sideways, to the audience, showing that one eye is missing. Blood pours form her mouth when she opens it. She looks back towards ANDY, also raises her arm, her hand. Points.

ANDY

No... No... Stay away from me!

He begins to shuffle backwards out of their way, ends up on the very left of the stage. They keep on coming, a few more behind the man and woman – but they're still in blackness, shadows like the others were before. The weird moaning grows louder and louder. A hand reaches out from one of them, pointing – then falls – and it's obvious its practically severed, dangling by the strips of flesh and meat.

ANDY

No… Jesus, no… What do you want? Keep away from me!

They do nothing of the kind, in fact the first two speed up to reach him – same as before. The man lets go of his stomach, and his innards fall out, intestines dangling from a hole there. The moaning has reached a crescendo, just as the figures – mostly in shadow – reach ANDY. He screams. Everything goes black.

SCENE 7

When the light comes back, it's from the window again, gradually showing us ANDY in the corner where he was when we first encountered him in Scene I. On the right, and replacing the shadow-people, are the two large men again. They move across to ANDY.

ANDY

[*Weak*] No… No, stay away. Keep away from me… You…. You keep…

They totally ignore him, drag ANDY to his feet and carry him across the stage, towards the right where they exit once more.

SCENE 8

The large men enter stage left, carrying a barely conscious ANDY. It is the room with the table in the middle and two chairs. There is something on the table that we can't see, covered with a cloth. The men secure Andy to the chair once more, hands behind his back. Then they relieve him of the rags of his shirt that are left, revealing the scars of his injuries from the whip. They exit. ANDY remains pretty out of it. The TORTURER enters stage left, replacing them. He walks over to the table, stands next to ANDY – pats his face to wake him.

TORTURER

Mr Brooks… Mr Brooks?

Andy rouses a little.

TORTURER

Ah, there you are. Good morning.

ANDY

Morn… Morning?

TORTURER

That's right. We can't have you sleeping the day away, can we. Not when there's work to be done. And how are we, this morning? You slept well, I trust?

ANDY

I… I'm… Fucking hurts!

TORTURER

Yes. Indeed. That all does look a bit nasty, I have to admit. Perhaps I did come on a bit strong, too eager. I have been known to do that. Sometimes it gets results, sometimes… Perhaps a different tack. Softly, softly catchee monkey and all that? Is that the way you tick, Mr Brooks? A spoonful of sugar? Mary Poppins… You remember her, surely, if you don't remember anything else? Do I need to coax the information out of you?

ANDY

What… what information? I… I don't know anything!

TORTURER

Now it's The Prisoner, right? [*Puts on deeper voice*] I am not a number, I am a free man? [*Sarcastic*] Do you feel free, Mr Brooks? Do any of us really, when you get right down to it?

ANDY

[*Struggling*] What… what the hell are you talking about?

The TORTURER walks around the table, waving his hand.

TORTURER

Oh, I'm not talking about all this. Clearly you're not a free man here. But even in captivity, people believe they can be free… [*Taps side of head*] Up here. It's often what makes them so hard to break, in my experience. Do what you want to people physically and they escape into their imaginations. Helps with the pain, I suppose. To call upon some distant memory – not that you'd be able to apparently – to picture the face of a loved one.

The TORTURER pauses, leans on the table with both hands.

TORTURER

But you see, that's just another form of imprisonment. And to need things, people, places, stuff in order to make us happy. It's all leverage that can be used by a man in my position. You're not married, are you? No kids…

ANDY

No… No I don't think…

TORTURER

You'd definitely remember that, family life. Love. All things that can be taken away from someone, stripped from them.

The TORTURER pushes himself up and starts walking around the table again.

TORTURER

Those are basic human needs, you see. Companionship, interaction… But then we're fulfilling that right now, aren't we? You're not alone, in your cell. You're here, with me. And we're having a nice little chat. But there are other, more urgent needs, naturally. The need to feel safe, secure. Not under threat…

He stops now next to the table. Next to whatever's covered up by the cloth.

TORTURER

Although, again, even if you take everything else away, there's the constant threat of death. We all have to live with that, every single day. You never know when you're going to go, or where. Another prison, Mr Brooks, wouldn't you agree?

The TORTURER pats the cloth, what's under it.

ANDY

[*Eyes wide*] What... what're you...

TORTURER

Do you know what's under here, Mr Brooks?

ANDY

No... no please.

TORTURER

You don't want to know? You don't want whatever's underneath here?

ANDY shakes his head.

TORTURER

You're sure now? Quite sure?

Another shake of the head, this time more emphatic.

TORTURER

Oh, that is a shame.

The TORTURER pulls the cloth off finally, revealing a metallic object. Another cover, this time to something he takes off right away. Underneath is a full English breakfast. Still holding the lid, The TORTURER breathes in, smacks his lips.

TORTURER

Hhhmm… Can you smell that? What am I talking about, of course you can now I've removed this. It was keeping it nice and warm for you… But, well, you said you didn't want it – what a pity. I assume you don't mind if I…

He sits down on the other chair, picks up a knife and fork. ANDY leans forward in his, practically salivating.

TORTURER

Waste not, want not. Another basic human need, Mr Brooks. [*Pops in a forkful, chews*] How long has it been now since you ate anything? To be honest, I think even we've lost track. Doesn't that look good? Can you imagine the taste?

The sound of ANDY's stomach rumbling grows louder and louder.

TORTURER

[*Laughing*] You see, you can't help yourself. Your own body works against you, in fact that's just another prison – these things we walk around in. So fragile, aren't they? They require so much maintenance. Food, drink… Oh, that reminds me.

The TORTURER reaches down and picks up something from the side of his chair. It's a bottle and a glass. He begins to pour the brown liquid, licking his lips as he does so. Then he places the glass on the table next to his meal.

ANDY

[*Half-crying*] Please…

TORTURER

[*Cupping an ear*] Sorry, what was that? I couldn't hear you.

ANDY

[*More emphatic*] Please!

The TORTURER frowns. Sits back in his chair.

TORTURER

Please what? You know what you need to do, Mr Brooks. This could all end right now, you could be sitting here and enjoying this meal if you'd only co-operate with me. If you'd only tell me what I need to know.

ANDY

[*Desperate*] Please… I can't. I don't know what to tell you… Do you want me to make something up? Is that it?

TORTURER

I'd rather you didn't.

ANDY

Okay… Okay… [*Thinking, before he speaks*] I live in the centre of town… in a flat. A nice flat. I work… I work for the government.

TORTURER

Doing what?

ANDY

I'm… I'm a social worker. That's right. I deal with people's problems, try to help them and—

The TORTURER begins to laugh, long and hard.

TORTURER

Wrong. Wrong, wrong, wrong, wrong – wrong! Not even close!

ANDY

But… but if you know, then…

TORTURER

Mr Brooks, we've been through this before. You have to tell me about the nature of your work. Now, that is something I need. Something that keeps me here with you, as much of a prisoner as you. [*Laughs again*] Actually, that's not true at all, is it? You're much more of a captive than I am. You're the one strapped to that fucking chair, after all.

ANDY

Please... please just a bite. A sip...

TORTURER

You can have all you want, Mr Brooks – a three course meal fit for a King. You just have to tell me what I need to know.

ANDY

Jesus! I can't... How can I tell you something I don't know?

TORTURER

[*Relenting*] All right, all right. I'll tell you what I'll do. Make you a deal.

He picks up the glass with the liquid in.

TORTURER

You want this, right?

ANDY nods his head, winces in pain – but nods it again anyway.

TORTURER

You're quite sure?

ANDY

[*Licks parched lips*] Please...

TORTURER

Very well...

The TORTURER pushes back his chair, carries the liquid across and holds it out to ANDY, as if he's going to give him a sip... Then suddenly withdraws the glass.

TORTURER

Last chance.

ANDY

[*Desperate again*] Just give it to me!

TORTURER

Very well, but remember you asked for it.

The TORTURER throws the contents of the glass at ANDY, covering the open cuts on his face and chest. He screams in agony, bucking in the chair.

TORTURER

No need for acid or anything that fancy. Just your common or garden household vinegar. Can you feel it? Feel it working its way into those wounds, Mr Brooks? It's what you wanted, after all. What you asked me to do.

ANDY is still howling in agony, rocking back and forth with the pain.

TORTURER

No... no you don't. Stay with me, Mr Brooks. I insist.

The TORTURER begins to slap ANDY, in an attempt to stop him from passing out.

TORTURER

You think the darkness is your friend, but it isn't I assure you. Stay with me, stay with me…

More slaps, but it doesn't do any good. On the final one, ANDY jerks like an electric current is passing through him. Then he slumps forward…
And everything goes black once more.

SCENE 9

The blue/grey lighting slowly reveals ANDY sitting at the table, head slumped on his chest. The shadowy figures enter stage right, complete with that wailing noise. The man with the stomach wound is revealed, the woman with one eye, the person with the hand dangling off – which we can see is a teenager now, wearing a cap.
But a couple more have joined them – come into view. A bald man with only one arm, the wound ragged and bloodied to show that this is a recent thing. And a small child, a little girl clutching a teddy bear. White-faced, she is doing the same as the rest of them – standing, raising an arm, pointing at ANDY.
He wakes now, head rising. Realises that the bonds holding his arms back, tying his hands together and to the chair, have vanished. The figures are nearing the table, wailing getting louder, more shadowy

people behind the ones that we can actually make out. It's like something out of Dante's Inferno. ANDY pushes back on the chair, falling from it, before scrambling to his feet and falling again.

ANDY

No... No, you stay back. I don't know who you are or what you want but—

The wailing grows louder, more violent at this statement. They begin to speed up across the stage. ANDY starts to crawl backwards on his elbows, then onto his front – looking back over his shoulder as he goes.

ANDY

Please... no. Just leave me alone. Why can't you just—

Then the chase is over, they're almost upon him over on the left-hand side of the stage. We see the figures in front make to leap on him as the wailing reaches a crescendo once more. Then, just as they're about to descend, the lighting goes off.
Everything is plunged into darkness again. The wailing stops – replaced by a solitary scream... ANDY's we assume.

<u>SCENE 10</u>

The lighting goes back to normal, that bulb above the table. ANDY is back to being bound to the chair; The TORTURER is still hovering over him. ANDY suddenly bucks, is screaming – the transition back

from his nightmare to the real world. The TORTURER allows himself
a slight grin.

TORTURER

Ah, Mr Brooks. There you are… I thought for a moment we'd lost you.

ANDY

[*Barely a whisper*] Why… why can't you leave… leave me alone?

TORTURER

What's that? Leave you alone? I'm afraid I cannot possibly do that. We
have unfinished business you and I. But… Mr Brooks? Mr Brooks…?

ANDY is slumped over in the chair again, useless. Unable or unwilling
to answer. The TORTURER tuts and shakes his head, folds his arms
and stares at Andy.

TORTURER

You <u>will</u> tell me what I need to know, Mr Brooks. I promise you that.
One way or another… [*Beat*] You will tell me everything.

Lights go down gradually.

<u>END OF ACT I</u>

ACT II

SCENE 1

We open this act very much as we did the first one. Light gradually fills the space from the window with bars on it. Slowly, it reveals the figure of ANDY slumped in a huddle on the left of the stage. He has no trousers on now, is naked apart from his underpants.

We hear the sound of crying from another one of the cells. ANDY moves, lifts his head – turns to the audience and addresses them.

ANDY

Oh…it's you. You're back… Or are you? Things are beginning to get a little… I suppose what I'm trying to say is that the insanity I talked about… the stages. I'm not really sure what stage I'm at. I'm… finding it hard to think. I'm seeing things. I don't know whether they're from my nightmares or they're really here but… [*Beat*] But, well, they scare me. More than anything ever has. I think. It's hard to remember. No, <u>really</u> it is… You do believe me, don't you? Or do you think I'm hiding something? [*Beat*] <u>He</u> does. The Torturer. He keeps on asking me in session after session… Oh, there have been a few since I last talked to you. To… to be honest, I'm not in a very good way. And that crying… That fucking crying! [*To the person responsible*] Will you shut up! Just shut the fuck up! You're not the only one in here, you know!

The crying dies down a little. ANDY turns back to the audience.

ANDY

I don't know why I can't remember… I really do think the knock on the head, maybe? He doesn't believe that. The bastard. He just keeps on asking the same thing, over and over. Who do I work for, and what have I done? [*Confidentially*] I know what you're thinking. Why… why did I say I worked for the government? Why was that the first thing that sprang to mind? And honestly, I couldn't tell you… It's…[*Yawns*] I'm so tired, I can't even begin to… They don't really let me sleep, the people holding me, The Torturer – and even when I do, then… I see things. Or are they really here? I don't know… can't tell anymore. Isn't there something about sleep depravation? That it's another form of torture?

Now the dripping of the water has replaced the crying sound, getting louder and louder.

ANDY

Just like that… that fucking dripping water. That sound. If it's not the crying then it's—

As if on cue, the crying starts up again – louder than even before.

ANDY

[*Clutches head*] Oh… Oh my God. I think I'm… I really think I'm losing it this time… Look, look at this.

ANDY grabs something from the floor, it looks like a shrivelled up piece of meat.

ANDY

He gave me the scraps of the meal he'd been eating, just threw them down there on the floor in the muck and filth. Cold scraps, barely edible. But...

He eats it anyway.

ANDY

I-I think I might even drink that vinegar now. Might just imagine that it's a nice cool glass of lager going down. Christ, I could murder... No, not murder... I could... [*Beat*] If they're not the terrorists, you're thinking, maybe I am? Maybe I'm responsible for something really horrible – but I could never... I wouldn't even hurt a... [*Laughs*] Too Norman Bates. I know. I wouldn't, though. Flies, spiders... those rats. If I got hungry enough, I could probably survive by eating them – Bear Grylls and all that. Or Renfield. What? I read... Used to... I miss it actually. I won't miss that noise. The crying, the water...

Suddenly, the sounds are drowned out by heavy footfalls – getting louder and louder as the men from before approach.

ANDY

Oh no!

ANDY curls up into a ball, trying to hide in the corner of the cell.

ANDY

No... not again. Please not again. I don't know anything, how many more ways can I–

The large men are there again, entering stage right. They stand and stare across at ANDY and for a moment we wonder whether they can actually see him or not, whether his hiding has worked. Then they march across the stage, grabbing him under the arms and lifting him up.

ANDY

No, can't you see? I'm not here. I'm not really here! You can't take me to him because… because I'm not… I <u>can't</u> be here. [*Beat*] So… so it's pointless. He won't thank you for it. Oh God, oh Christ… <u>please!</u> Why won't you just let me go? I don't know anything. I promise I don't.

The men don't answer, they just continue to drag ANDY across the stage. At one point he finds his feet, tries to pull back, but they just tug him forwards again. He's going and there's nothing he can do to stop them from taking him. They all exit stage right. The space goes black.

<u>SCENE 2</u>

Lights up on the space with the table and chairs, only there are no chairs this time. But there is something on the table, covered with a cloth again. The trio appear stage left and ANDY is dragged across, past the table to the right of the stage, where he is chained to the wall. The chains are short and don't allow him to sag that far.

ANDY

No. Wait. Look, what're doing that for? I-I think I want to go back to the chair. Can't… Look, can we talk about this? Please?

They ignore him completely and carry on with their work, then leave him to hang there from the wall.

ANDY

This isn't good. This really isn't good. They haven't done this before. Oh God… Oh no…

He hangs his head and it's unclear whether it's in despair or he's unconscious again. The light flickers and dims. Then all we can see is ANDY hanging there. Something that looks like a white/grey spider appears on the floor, starts to crawl up his leg. Then another… and slowly we realise these are hands. There are two, three, four… All we can see are the hands, some badly damaged – some with blood caked on them.

The moaning and wailing sound returns – and it's this rather than the clawing at his legs that seems to rouse ANDY. He wakes, looks down at what's happening. Lets out a cry.

ANDY

No… what's… You can't be here, what're you…? Get off me. Get the fuck off me!

The hands continue to climb and paw at him, rising higher and higher, to his torso and chest now. At least a dozen or so, with more added every few seconds until he's practically covered in the things, swarming him. He screams, jerks his head back, but can't throw them off. It's like he's drowning in them now.

ANDY

[*Through gritted teeth*] What... what do you want? Please! I don't know what you...

He screams again, then the lights suddenly go out. When they flicker and come back on again, the hands have gone, and The TORTURER has entered stage left.

TORTURER

Mr Brooks. Not sleeping on the job again, are we?

ANDY

[*Disorientated*] W-Where... where did they... Where did they go?

The TORTURER looks over his shoulder, thumbs back.

TORTURER

The men who brought you here, you mean? Oh, we don't need them. I don't need them. I do so prefer our little talks to be just you and me, don't you? More intimate that way, wouldn't you agree?

ANDY

No... no...

TORTURER

You don't agree?

ANDY shakes his head, that wasn't what he meant.

ANDY

Those… those hands. The people.

TORTURER

My dear Mr Brooks, I have no idea what you're talking about. You're not making any sense. And I do so need you to make sense. Or to see sense for that matter. I was hoping today might be the day.

ANDY

[*Hoarse*] Day…?

The TORTURER *comes further into the room, pauses by the table.*

TORTURER

You know. The day… that you decide to tell me what I want to know. What I need to hear, before I can release you. [*Laughs and shakes head*] I don't know, what a palaver. You're just making things harder for yourself, Mr Brooks. Withholding—

ANDY

I'm not withholding anything.

TORTURER

[*Suddenly snapping*] I wasn't finished! Didn't your parents ever tell you that it was rude to interrupt!

ANDY *flinches at the sudden shouting.*

TORTURER

[*Calmer*] Then again, you probably can't remember. You don't appear to know anything other than your name. How about your rank and serial number? [*Beat*] That was one of my little... jokes. It's what POWs always give during wartime.

ANDY

War... wartime?

TORTURER

Oh, I don't mean to say that we're necessarily at war. Although I suppose you could say <u>we're</u> at war. [*He flicks his finger between them*] You and I. It's like I said, you have to make up your mind about what side you're on.

ANDY

I... I told you... not on anyone's side.

TORTURER

And I told <u>you</u>, a person must be on one side or the other. The right side... [*Opens up his left palm*] or the wrong side. [*Now the right*] Which is it?

ANDY

You're... you're crazy.

TORTURER

Am I? Am I really the crazy one, Mr Brooks? Think about it. But don't take too long. Because there's work to be done. You remember, work? You enjoy your work, Mr Brooks?

ANDY

Told… told you. I don't—

TORTURER

That's right. You don't remember who you work for. Oh, where are my manners – now I'm interrupting you. Whatever must you think of me?

ANDY

That… that you're a psycho.

TORTURER

That's not a name we like to hear around this place. Too Norman Bates.

ANDY laughs, recalling what he said himself earlier on.

TORTURER

Did I say something funny?

Andy continues to laugh, but shakes his head.

TORTURER

Do you think <u>any</u> of this is funny?

The TORTURER rushes over to him and grabs his face, squeezing Andy's cheeks in.
ANDY stops laughing immediately. The TORTURER drops his hand, steps back.

TORTURER

Better. You need to start taking all this a lot more seriously, Mr Brooks. We're running out of time, here.

ANDY

I-I am taking this seriously... believe me. [*Beat*] Running out of time?

The TORTURER turns his back on ANDY, starts to walk away from him across the stage.

TORTURER

I take it very seriously. My work, that is. [*Turns his head to look back*] But that doesn't mean I can't enjoy it, as well. Isn't that one of life's great goals, to do something you enjoy for a living? Something you are good at – and believe me when I tell you I am exceedingly good at this.

ANDY

Out... out of time...

The TORTURER faces forward again.

TORTURER

As I said, I'm hoping you might see reason today, Mr Brooks. If not...

He starts to walk towards the table.

TORTURER

All the rest of it, everything you've been through so far... That was just a taster of the 'pleasures' to come. But it would be much better for all concerned if you just simply co-operated with me.

ANDY

How… how can I… I co-operate when I don't know what…what the hell you're talking about?

The TORTURER rounds on him, wagging a finger.

TORTURER

[*Snapping*] Watch your fucking tone! [*Calmer*] Mr Brooks. How many different ways do I need to say it, you <u>do</u> know what I'm talking about. You do…

ANDY

[*Virtually crying*] Please… I've done nothing to you.

TORTURER

Nothing to me, personally. No. But it's not as simple as that, Mr Brooks. When I'm called in, people expect results. Nothing more, nothing less. And I always get them. You will tell me what I want to know. In the end they always do.

ANDY

How can I tell you <u>anything</u> when I don't even remember?

The TORTURER turns his back on ANDY once more, continues to the table where he uncovers one corner of the cloth. The audience sees him pick up a clear bag of something that rattles. They look like nails. He takes one out, puts the rest of the bag in his pocket. With his other hand he picks up a hammer. Andy sees none of this, continues to argue his case.

ANDY

Are you listening to me, I said how can I—

The TORTURER rushes back across to ANDY, shoves the nail in his hand under the first finger of ANDY's right hand – furthest away from the audience. He then takes the hammer and bangs it under the nail. ANDY lets out a bloodcurdling scream. The TORTURER steps back, cocks his head, admiring his handiwork as Andy continues to scream in agony.

TORTURER

How's your memory now, Mr Brooks? Anything coming back to you?

He leans in closer presenting his ear, as the screams die down – in case ANDY gives him the answer between the gasps and moans. But there's nothing. The TORTURER bangs his fist against the wall at the side of ANDY's head.

TORTURER

You disappoint me.

ANDY looks up, and looks over the TORTURER's shoulder. A couple of the figures from his nightmare have appeared stage left, a light picking them out. The scarred man – his intestines hanging out – the woman with one eye, the bald man with one arm. ANDY blinks, mumbles something – and then they're gone again, buried in darkness.

ANDY

[*Through clenched teeth*] I… I-I don't…

The TORTURER is right up in ANDY's face now.

TORTURER

Who do you work for? Who? Who? [*Shouts*] <u>Who?</u>

ANDY shakes his head, lets out another groan of pain.

ANDY

I-I don't… don't remember…

TORTURER

What are you? What do you do? What? What? [*Shouts*] <u>What?</u>

When ANDY says nothing, he takes another nail out of his pocket and hammers that into another finger on ANDY's right hand. More screaming, more waiting for answers that don't come. So the TORTURER repeats the process a few more times, until all the fingernails on ANDY's right hand have nails underneath them.
The screaming goes on and on, then suddenly ANDY's head drops. He loses consciousness. Blackness.

SCENE 3

The blue/grey light comes up and we see ANDY, still hanging there on the right of the stage. The wounded people begin to emerge on the left. The man with the belly wound, the woman with her eye missing, the bald man, the teenager and little girl. The eerie moaning and wailing starts up.

But more have joined them – are joining them as they begin to make their way across the stage – all rising from their crawling position. One man has a piece of metal sticking out of his chest, yet another woman with shards of glass stuck to her, covered in blood. One can't rise at all, because he has no legs below the knees, just ragged stumps.

ANDY wakes, looks up and over at them. He tries to pull at his chains but can't get free.

ANDY

No… not this again. Why? Who are you? I can't give you what you want.

They make their way across the stage, stumbling and crawling like zombies. A wave of them, accompanied by the wailing and moaning which increases in volume the further that get. And they're all pointing at ANDY.

Finally they reach ANDY, and he can't escape no matter how hard he tries. They begin to clutch at him, surround him, swamp him – so that the audience can't see him anymore. He starts to scream again, which can be heard above the wailing. Then everything goes black again.

<u>SCENE 4</u>

When the lights come up, they've gone, but ANDY is still hanging, head down. The TORTURER is there not far from him, holding a bucket – and he throws the contents onto ANDY. Freezing cold water, which wakes him suddenly and violently. He shakes his head, shaking off the water, and shivers. There are several more buckets next to the table.

TORTURER

Do try to remain conscious. It makes my job so much harder when you keep dozing off like that. Anyone would think you hadn't slept. And we provided such nice accommodation for you, as well. A regular home… Home from home, you might say.

He goes back over to the table, uncovers the rest of what's there: including a box and a roll of instruments which he unfurls, the metal clanking together. The TORTURER picks up a saw, holds it up to the light. Puts it down again. Then he grabs what looks like an ice-pick, practices by shoving it into the air off to the side of him. And then he picks up something that looks like a large apple-peeler – but is probably meant to peel off skin. ANDY watches all this with wide eyes.
The TORTURER unclasps the box next, taking out a scalpel, testing the point on the end of it. He's having fun playing with the tools of his trade. Next a pair of pliers, opening and closing them. Just when we think he's going to put them down again, he rushes over to ANDY, wrenching open his mouth and jamming them inside. He tugs and pulls out a tooth. ANDY gurgles, screams, blood pouring over his chin. The

TORTURER pulls back again, taking the tooth from the pliers and holding that up for examination now.

TORTURER

Left molar, if I'm not mistaken. You've kept them in good shape over the years – cleaned after every meal. No filling in this one. And there are so many more to choose from: incisors, premolars, canines… I could go on. I know them all. I've studied, trained for this. It's not something amateurs should be playing at. You have to learn, look into things, you know? What am I saying, of course you know. [*Beat*] It's not something you enter into lightly, either. Lots of thought, lots of research. Not just teeth, either. The make-up of the human body, the pain centres. How to cause the maximum amount of agony. Why, I could just prick one of your toes and you'd feel that throughout your whole frame. Isn't that something? Reflexology, it's called. Fascinating what you can pick up when you start looking into it. Not just as a professional thing, but even in your spare time… [*Beat*] And you can't escape it. It's like I was saying before, you can't get away from your own body. Not really. Even if you train the mind, picture yourself somewhere else – meditate – you'll still feel it on some level. Even when we're asleep, we feel pain – in our dreams. Our nightmares. Wouldn't you agree? Might not even be physical, we haven't even got to emotional pain yet. Probably the worst kind… Or is it?

The TORTURER rushes over to Andy again with the pliers – but this time goes for the left hand. He takes a finger, a nail, and pulls it off. More screaming. Then ANDY's head lolls onto his chest. He's losing consciousness again.

TORTURER

Oh no you don't…

The TORTURER goes over to the table, puts down the pliers and picks up another one of the buckets. He brings it back over and throws more of the freezing water onto ANDY, who wakes with a jerk, shivering.

TORTURER

There are some people who'd pay good money for all this, you know. Sickos, I grant you… But they would. You wouldn't catch me stooping so low – no siree. When I do this, there's a purpose behind it. Something important, not just a cheap thrill. Do you understand? It's a question of morality. Taking a pride in what you do. [*Beat*] Oh look, you're all wet. Sopping. You'll catch your death. Probably. Maybe we should warm you up a bit. Hold on a second, I've got just the thing.

The TORTURER wanders away, wanders to the left-hand side of the stage. Bends to pick something up that's hidden from us. He stands, holding the object behind his back – and we can now see it's an iron that has been plugged in down there. The TORTURER returns to ANDY, then produces the iron, holding it up to his face.

ANDY

No, <u>please</u> no!

Ignoring the pleas, The TORTURER touches ANDY's cheek with the iron: there's a hissing noise as the flesh sizzles. Another scream from ANDY, just when you think he has nothing left to give.

TORTURER

There now, isn't that better? Let's do the rest of you.

He touches ANDY's shoulder, working his way down the man's body, as if ironing the laundry. ANDY screams with each new movement. The TORTURER steps back again, cocks his head in admiration. ANDY's face and parts of his body are burned red. His head begins to sag again. The TORTURER wakes him this time by pressing the iron to his stomach.

TORTURER

There now. Doesn't always have to be the cold, does it. Heat has the same effect. Yin and Yang, checks and balances, Mr Brooks. Everything has its price. Today it is your turn to pay it.

The TORTURER walks away and puts the iron down upright on the table. He picks something else up, holds it out for us and ANDY to see. It is a large knife, six or seven inches long. As he did with the scalpel, The TORTURER tests the end and withdraws his finger quickly, sticking it in his mouth and sucking.

TORTURER

Do you know how long a person can remain alive during a torture session, Mr Brooks?

ANDY

[*Rasping*] Why... why are you... you doing this...?

TORTURER

We're past all that, Mr Brooks. You wouldn't play ball, and so... I believe I asked you a question. Do you know?

All ANDY can do is groan in reply.

TORTURER

No? Neither do I, as it happens. It's something I've always wondered about myself. Let's find out together shall we?

The lights dim as the TORTURER walks over to ANDY with the knife.

SCENE 5

The lights flash on and off during this scene, showing the various stages of the torture and mayhem. In one flash, we see the TORTURER using that knife, cutting bits of ANDY's flesh off. In another we see him using the apple-peeler instrument. In yet another, he's jabbing at Andy with the ice-pick. All very quick flashes but accompanied by the same questions over and over, until the repetition itself becomes a kind of torture.

TORTURER

Who are you? What were you doing before you came here?

ANDY screams and screams. He is covered in blood – his body a complete mess. But towards the end of the session, we can see something else. The people from his nightmare on the left-hand side of the stage. They are watching all this eagerly, with interest. Then everything goes black.

SCENE 6

As the lights come up again, ANDY is hanging from the wall, head lolling. The TORTURER is standing nearby with another bucket of water, which he drenches ANDY with to wake him.

TORTURER

Tell me what I want to know, Mr Brooks. Then this madness can end.

ANDY

[*Mumbling, barely coherent*] Don't... don't know...

TORTURER

You don't know. You can't remember! So you have said repeatedly, and I don't doubt that you believe it... up to a point. But both you and I know that the truth is up there.

The TORTURER points to ANDY's head.

TORTURER

You've convinced – brainwashed – yourself into believing what you're saying. [*Does feeble impression*] 'I don't remember.' [*Angry*] You don't <u>want</u> to remember, Mr Brooks. Can't you see that?

ANDY

[*Rasping*] If… If you know… then tell me.

TORTURER

[*Shaking head*] I can't do that. Doesn't work that way. You have to figure it out for yourself. Jesus, people like you make me sick! You're scum!

But—

TORTURER

And still you resist. Why do you think that is? Why do you think I am doing this? It's not for the good of <u>your</u> health!

The TORTURER allows himself a grin.

ANDY

D-Don't… know…

The figures have appeared again on the left-hand side of the stage, the zombies, the ghosts. There are more now than ever, entering, moving across the stage – and we can see them all clearly now. Fantasy and reality is blurring. ANDY frowns when he notices them, here and in the cold light of the torture chamber rather than his nightmares. The moaning and wailing sound starts up, kept at a dull hum.

TORTURER

You do know, admit it. Think very carefully, now. Who do you work for?

ANDY is looking past the TORTURER towards the dead people. The TORTURER follows his gaze, staring at them for a moment, <u>through</u> them we presume. But he thumbs back.

TORTURER

They know. Don't they, Mr Brooks?

ANDY frowns, his eyes flitting from The TORTURER to the people coming closer and closer.

ANDY

You… you can see them?

TORTURER

Of course. I'm not blind, Mr Brooks.

ANDY frowns once more in puzzlement.

TORTURER

I believe I asked you another question, but like all the others you declined to answer. They know, don't they? What you did?

Seemingly surprising himself, ANDY nods, though it pains him to do so.

TORTURER

And so I ask again, who do you work for?

ANDY

Hob… Hobson's.

The TORTURER nods now, accepting this answer. He looks from ANDY, back to the people.

TORTURER

Look at them, Brooks. Would it surprise you to learn that their blood is on your hands?

ANDY

[*Voice getting stronger*] No! That's not true!

TORTURER

You, Brooks, are a murderer.

ANDY

No. No, I couldn't… I'm not like that. I—

The TORTURER moves forward and the dead people follow behind him, all pointing towards ANDY.

ANDY

They blame me.

TORTURER

And aren't they right to blame you, Brooks?

ANDY

No, I don't think—

TORTURER

You don't think, you don't remember. I <u>know</u> that you do.

ANDY

How… How do you know all this about me, when I don't?

The moaning and wailing sound increases. ANDY strains to look away,
head going left and right.

ANDY

No… stop. Make them stop! Make them go away.

TORTURER

You are to blame for their deaths, Brooks. Yes? [*Shouting*] <u>Yes?</u>

ANDY

No! It wasn't my fault. I swerved to avoid the car… It was on the wrong side… I had to…turn the wheel to avoid it, then I couldn't… I lost control—

TORTURER

Did you, or did you not, kill them?

ANDY

Yes, you bastard. [*Screaming*] <u>Yes!</u>

The dead people nod, content now that Andy has confessed. The wailing and moaning stops.

ANDY

I-I remember.

TORTURER

Of course you do.

ANDY

Please make them go away.

TORTURER

There are none so blind as those who will not see. First, tell me what I need to know. I need to hear you say it. Then I'll make the faces disappear.

The TORTURER leans in and ANDY whispers something in his ear. The TORTURER nods, then walks past the dead people who have almost reached ANDY. The far off crying starts up again, getting louder.

ANDY

The... that crying. It's me, isn't it?

The TORTURER doesn't reply. Instead he pauses at the table, picks up another implement. It's what looks like a big ice-cream scoop. He returns to ANDY, the dead people allowing him access to his prisoner. The TORTURER leans in with the scoop. Everything goes black.

SCENE 7

Everything remains dark now as we hear noises, the rattling of keys like we heard before at the start. Someone gaining access to ANDY's cell.

PC SMITH

Somebody turn on the light, I can't see a thing.

SERGEANT

Watch your step, constable, there's water everywhere.

PC SMITH

Good Christ! Sir, I think we've found him, here in the garage. He's behind this partition.

WPC JONES

Oh my... Look at him. Just <u>look</u> at him!

SERGEANT

Has he done this? Fuck! I think he's done this to himself. Smith, don't just stand there, fetch the paramedics. Right now!

WPC JONES

What's all this stuff? Clothes-line, nails, hammer, iron... and he must have half the cutlery drawer in here with him. Shit! His eyes, he's taken his eyes out!

SERGEANT

Dr Campbell, your patient's in here.

WPC JONES

What's that smell? Can you smell that? I think it's vinegar.

DR CAMPBELL

Oh Lord in Heaven, no. I had a feeling something like this would happen. I tried to warn them at the hospital, warn his social worker. Told them he wasn't ready to go home yet. And when he missed his appointment today…

WPC JONES

Why's he done this, Sergeant?

SERGEANT

It's that bloke who was in the motorway pile-up last August. You remember, the driver for Hobson's Coaches. It was in all the papers. Right, Doc?

DR CAMPBELL

[*Sighing*] He blames himself for the accident. A lot of people died, holidaymakers: men, women, children. He'd been working flat out all week, he was tired… But there was nothing he could have done. Drunk driver was on the wrong side of the road.

WPC JONES

That still doesn't explain—

DR CAMPBELL

It's textbook. He's tortured himself mentally for months – but it seems that wasn't enough. Thank God his neighbours came home early from their trip, heard all those screams. Otherwise…

SERGEANT

Smith! Where are those bloody paramedics?

Light begins to filter in – and we see the cell window, with the bars. Andy is curled up on the left-hand side of the stage. He raises his head. Looks like he did at the start of the play. He stares across at the audience.

ANDY

The voices drone on – does someone mention the words 'fantasy' and 'withdrawn'? – but I don't take any notice. I'm not really there… I'm here. And I can still see…

Over on the right, the dead people appear and start to gather. Start to point. Andy looks at them.

ANDY

I can still see <u>them</u>. My accusers. He lied. They haven't gone away at all. They never will. I'll <u>always</u> see them, no matter what he does to me. End the madness? It'll never end! Neither will my imprisonment. As for him… The Torturer. [*Beat*] Well he <u>has</u> gone, at least for now. The voices in my cell, my home from home, have chased him off. And yet I can't help wondering, deep down inside… [*Beat*] If he'll return again as well… someday.

The light fades on the dead people. And then, finally, it goes out on Andy.

<u>PLAY ENDS</u>

SHOCK VALUE
presents
THE DISEASE
PAUL KANE
PAWEL KARDIS
introduction by Mark Alan Miller

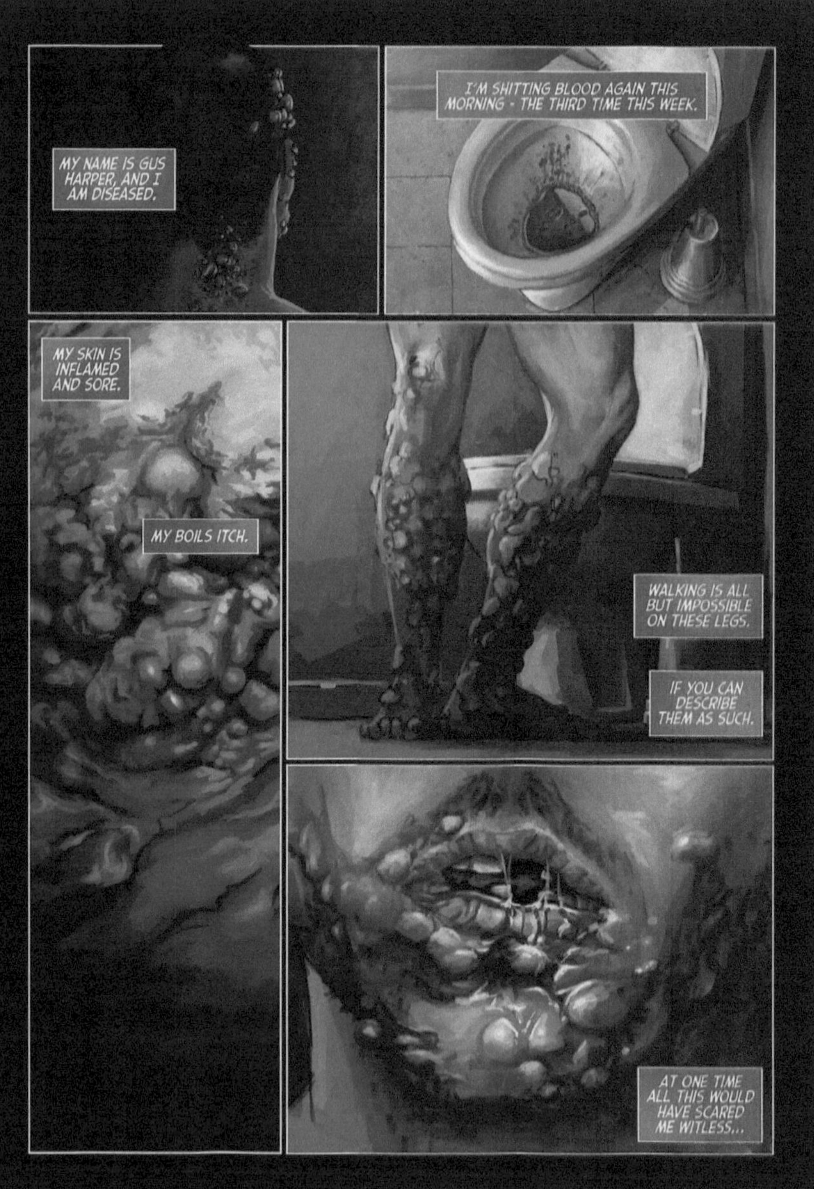
MY NAME IS GUS HARPER, AND I AM DISEASED.
I'M SHITTING BLOOD AGAIN THIS MORNING - THE THIRD TIME THIS WEEK.
MY SKIN IS INFLAMED AND SORE.
MY BOILS ITCH.
WALKING IS ALL BUT IMPOSSIBLE ON THESE LEGS.
IF YOU CAN DESCRIBE THEM AS SUCH.
AT ONE TIME ALL THIS WOULD HAVE SCARED ME WITLESS...

THE DISEASE – A COMIC

(Published by Hellbound Media)

Page 1 – Panel 1

TWO PANELS ON THE TOP TIER. IN THE FIRST PANEL WE SEE SOMEONE'S HEAD BUT ONLY FROM THE BACK AND NOT CLEARLY, PERHAPS IN SILHOUETTE. WE CAN TELL THERE'S SOMETHING WRONG WITH IT – IT'S LUMPY, MISSHAPEN – BUT DON'T KNOW QUITE WHAT YET.

Caption – top:

My name is Gus Harper, and I am diseased.

Page 1 – Panel 2

WE SEE A CLOSE UP OF A TOILET BOWL, WITH RED, ALMOST BLACK LIQUID IN THE PAN.

Caption – bottom:

I'm shitting blood again this morning – the third time this week.

Page 1 – Panel 3

A PANEL DOWN LEFT-HAND SIDE NOW, RUNNING TO THE BOTTOM OF THE PAGE, WITH TWO PANELS ON THE RIGHT: ONE TOP, ONE BOTTOM. IN THIS LEFT-HAND

PANEL WE HAVE A CLOSE-UP ON FESTERING SKIN, LEAVE IT TO THE READER'S IMAGINATION WHEREABOUTS ON THE BODY IT IS. SHOULD DEFINITELY BE REPULSIVE, THOUGH.

Caption – top:

My skin is inflamed and sore.

Caption – bottom:

My boils itch.

Page 1 – Panel 4

TOP PANEL OF THE TWO ON THE RIGHT-HAND SIDE. WE'RE LOOKING AT TWO STUMPY, RATHER WITHERED EXCUSES FOR LEGS. YOU DON'T NEED TO BE TOO DETAILED WITH THIS, PERHAPS LEAVE IT PARTIALLY SILHOUETTED AGAIN; LET THE READER'S IMAGINATIONS DO MOST OF THE WORK.

Caption – top left:

Walking is all but impossible on these legs.

Caption – bottom right:

If you can describe them as such.

Page 1 – Panel 5

BOTTOM PANEL OF THE TWO PANEL 'TOWER' ON THE RIGHT. CLOSE-UP ON A CHEWED UP MOUTH, WITH STUMPS OF TEETH AND DROOL DRIBBLING OVER THE BOTTOM LIP.

Caption – bottom:

At one time all this would have scared me witless…

—

Page 2 – Panel 1

SPLASH PAGE. ONE BIG SINGLE PANEL FILLING THE PAGE OF A PERFECTLY BLUE EYE, WITH ROTTEN SKIN PUCKERED AND MOULDY AROUND IT. WE STILL CAN'T SEE THE WHOLE OF THE FACE AND WON'T DO UNTIL MUCH LATER.

Caption – top:

Not any more.

Caption – top (just below first):

I've seen too much; gone through too much.

Caption – middle:

The memories are still alive, trapped in what's left of my mind.

Caption – middle (just below last one):

But how long they'll remain there now is anyone's guess.

And now credits… Bottom right:

Titles – bottom right: The Disease.

Beneath title: Paul Kane – Writer

Pawel Kardis – Artwork

Nikki Foxrobot – Letterer

—

Page 3 – Panel 1

TOP TIER OF THREE PANELS. THE FIRST IS COMPLETELY BLUE, AS IF WE'VE CLOSED IN ON THE EYE.

Caption – top:

I remember the morning it came on.

Caption – bottom:

A Saturday in late January.

Page 3 – Panel 2

SECOND OF THE TOP PANELS. THE BLUE BECOMES SLIGHTLY LIGHTER – THERE IS A HINT OF WHITE IN THERE, TOO.

Caption – middle:

And I remember the dream.

Caption – bottom:

Mainly because I'm still having it.

Page 3 – Panel 3

THIRD PANEL – THE BLUE IS LIGHTER STILL, VERGING ON WHITE.

Caption – top:

A dream of blueness, so bright it almost blinds me.

Caption – bottom:

I always wake just before making contact.

Page 3 – Panel 4

MIDDLE TIER IS ONE LONG PANEL STRETCHING ACROSS THE PAGE. IN IT WE SEE A WOMAN LAYING ON A PILLOW WITH HER CHESTNUT HAIR FANNED OUT ACROSS IT. SHE'S SLEEPING WITH HER MOUTH OPEN A FRACTION, WE CAN SEE HER NAKED BACK THAT STRETCHES DOWN TO MEET THE WHITE COVERS JUST ABOVE HER MIDRIFF.

Caption – top left:

On that particular morning I woke up next to Rachel.

Caption – middle:

And I watched her sleeping.

Caption – bottom right:

> The way her soft mouth opened and closed, eyelids fluttering as she dreamed her own private dreams.

Page 3 – Panel 5

BOTTOM TIER OF TWO PANELS. ON THE LEFT WE SEE A CLOSE UP OF RACHEL'S FACE, NOW AWAKE AND SMILING.

Caption – top:

> I suppose she must have sensed me looking at her.

Caption – bottom:

> Because she woke up then.

Page 3 – Panel 6

ON THE BOTTOM RIGHT-HAND PANEL, RACHEL HAS MOVED AROUND ON HER SIDE AND IS LEANING ON THE PILLOW WITH HER ELBOW, EXPOSING HER BREASTS. SHE'S STILL GRINNING, BUT NOW IN A CHEEKY, PLAYFUL WAY.

Caption – bottom right:

> We'd been together a year and a half, but she could still get me going.

—

Page 4 – Panel 1

TOP TIER STRETCHES ACROSS THE PAGE. WE SEE GUS – WELL-MUSCLED, WITH SHORT DARK HAIR – AND RACHEL MAKING LOVE IN THE BED AS THE SUNLIGHT STREAMS IN THROUGH THE WINDOW AND HITS THEM. IT'S ALL VERY

ROMANTIC AND IDEALISED, MAINLY BECAUSE IT'S HOW GUS REMEMBERS THE SCENE. THEY'RE INTERTWINED RATHER THAN EITHER ONE OF THEM BEING ON TOP.

Caption – top left:

We made love.

Caption – middle:

I'd be hard pushed to do that now – those parts of my body no longer exist…

Caption – bottom right:

But if it's truly possible for two people to become one, then I think we came pretty close.

Page 4 – Panel 2

SECOND TIER OF TWO PANELS: IN THE LEFT-HAND ONE, WE HAVE A CLOSE-UP OF GUS HOLDING RACHEL TIGHT, THE PAIR OF THEM KISSING.

Caption – top:

And as I held her…

Caption – bottom:

I knew that nothing would ever be as perfect as this again.

Page 4 – Panel 3

CLOSE-UP ON GUS AND RACHEL LOCKING EYES, FOREHEADS PRESSED TOGETHER.

Caption:

I was right, of course.

Page 4 – Panel 4

BOTTOM TIER OF THREE PANELS. IN THE FIRST, WE SEE GUS ASLEEP, LAID BACK ON THE PILLOW WITH A CONTENTED SMILE ON HIS FACE.

Caption – top:

Afterwards I fell asleep again, dozing lightly.

Page 4 – Panel 5

MIDDLE PANEL SHOWS GUS NOW ON HIS SIDE, FACING THE WINDOW, HIS RIGHT HAND UNDER THE PILLOW, EYES OPEN, AND THE SPACE WHERE RACHEL HAD BEEN IS EMPTY.

Caption – bottom:

When I woke up Rachel was gone.

Page 4 – Panel 6

THE RIGHT PANEL HAS GUS PULLING OUT HIS HAND FROM UNDER THE PILLOW.

Caption – top:

My hand had been wedged between the pillow and mattress.

—

Page 5 – Panel 1

TOP TIER OF THREE PANELS TAKES UP HALF THE PAGE, THE BOTTOM HALF OF THE PAGE IS ONE BIG PANEL. TOP LEFT PANEL SHOWS A CLOSE-UP OF GUS' HAND – IT'S ALMOST CLOSED LIKE A CLAW.

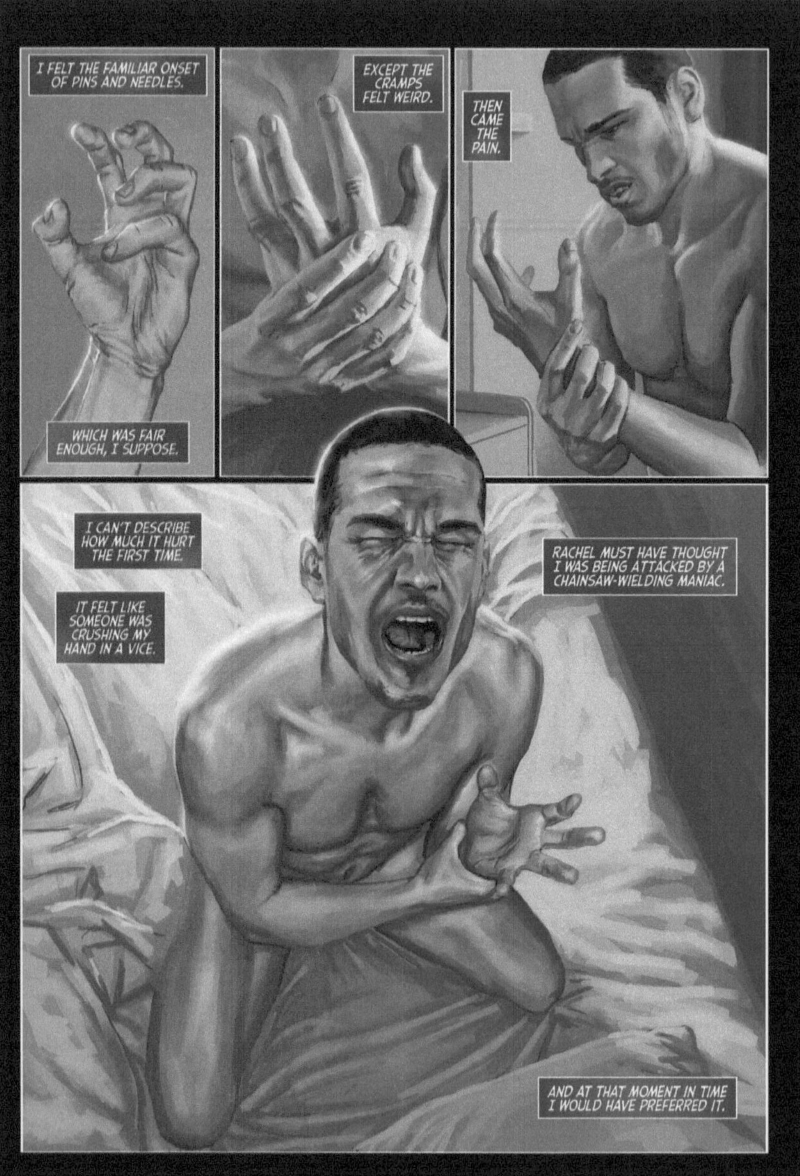
I FELT THE FAMILIAR ONSET OF PINS AND NEEDLES.
WHICH WAS FAIR ENOUGH, I SUPPOSE.
EXCEPT THE CRAMPS FELT WEIRD.
THEN CAME THE PAIN.
I CAN'T DESCRIBE HOW MUCH IT HURT THE FIRST TIME.
IT FELT LIKE SOMEONE WAS CRUSHING MY HAND IN A VICE.
RACHEL MUST HAVE THOUGHT I WAS BEING ATTACKED BY A CHAINSAW-WIELDING MANIAC.
AND AT THAT MOMENT IN TIME I WOULD HAVE PREFERRED IT.

Caption – top:

I felt the familiar onset of pins and needles.

Caption – bottom:

Which was fair enough, I suppose.

Page 5 – Panel 2

IN THE MIDDLE PANEL ON THE TOP TIER WE HAVE ANOTHER CLOSE-UP OF THE HAND, BUT GUS IS RUBBING IT WITH HIS OTHER HAND.

Caption – middle:

Except the cramps felt weird.

Page 5 – Panel 3

NOW, FINALLY, IN THE THIRD PANEL, HE'S CLUTCHING HIS WRIST AND THE CLAW HAND.

Caption – bottom:

Then came the pain.

Page 5 – Panel 4

THE BIG PANEL AT THE BOTTOM IS A CLOSE-UP OF GUS' SCREAMING FACE: HE'S IN ABSOULTE AGONY!

Caption – top left:

I can't describe how much it hurt the first time.

Caption – middle left:

It felt like someone was crushing my hand in a vice.

Caption – bottom left:

Rachel must have thought I was being attacked by a chainsaw-wielding maniac.

Caption – bottom right:

And at that moment in time I would have preferred it.

—

Page 6 – Panel 1

TOP TIER OF THREE PANELS. IN THE LEFT PANEL RACHEL IS AT THE DOOR TO THE BEDROOM IN HER DRESSING GOWN, FACE FILLED WITH CONCERN.

Caption – top left:

She was there in seconds.

Rachel:

For God's sake, Gus! What's going on?

Page 6 – Panel 2

IN THIS MIDDLE PANEL GUS IS CRAWLING AROUND ON THE DUVET STILL CLUTCHING AT HIS RIGHT HAND, STILL IN AGONY. HIS TEETH ARE GRITTED AS HE SPEAKS.

Gus:

I don't know… My hand…

Page 6 – Panel 3

HERE RACHEL TAKES HOLD OF GUS' HAND GENTLY WITH BOTH OF HERS, PEERING AT IT WITH GRAVE CONCERN. GUS IS SCREAMING AGAIN.

Rachel:

Let me have a look.

Gus:

Gnnarrrr!

Caption – bottom right:

The agony almost caused me to pass out.

Page 6 – Panel 4

BOTTOM TIER OF TWO PANELS. IN THE FIRST, RACHEL HAS LET GO OF HIS HAND AND STEPPED AWAY. SHE NOW HAS HER OWN HANDS TO HER MOUTH.

Caption – middle:

She let go immediately, frightened she might have made it worse.

Page 6 – Panel 5

THE SECOND PANEL IS A CLOSE-UP OF GUS' FACE, WITH TEARS STREAMING DOWN HIS CHEEKS, EYES SCREWED UP, MOUTH STILL WIDE OPEN. THERE'S NO CAPTION TO GO WIITH THIS ONE – IT DOESN'T NEED ANY EXPLANATION.

—

Page 7 – Panel 1

ON THIS PAGE WE HAVE THREE TIERS OF THREE PANELS EACH. FIRST PANEL OF THE FIRST TIER: A CLOSE-UP OF GUS' HAND, BUT IT LOOKS NORMAL AGAIN, THE FINGERS STRETCHED OUT INSTEAD OF CLAW-LIKE, AND NOW SORT OF LIMP.

Caption – top left:

Then as quickly as it came, the pain just vanished.

Caption – bottom right:

The spasms subsided.

Page 7 – Panel 2

SECOND PANEL ON TOP TIER: RACHEL'S HEAD AND SHOULDERS; SHE'S STILL LOOKING WORRIED.

> Rachel:
>> I think you should get it looked at, Gus.
>>
>> Your hand wouldn't start hurting like that for no reason.

Page 7 – Panel 3

IN THIS PANEL GUS IS LOOKING AT THE BACK OF HIS HAND, AS IF TRYING TO FIGURE OUT WHAT WAS WRONG WITH IT.

> Caption – top:
>> I knew she was right.
>
> Caption – middle:
>> Certain possibilities sprang to mind…
>
> Caption – bottom:
>> I'd sprained it somehow while I was asleep, or at work.

Page 7 – Panel 4

SECOND TIER. FIRST PANEL ON THE LEFT SHOWS A MID-RANGE CLOSE-UP OF GUS' WORRIED FACE.

> Caption – middle:
>> There was a fracture somewhere in the hand…

Page 7 – Panel 5

CLOSE-UP ON THE HAND ITSELF, GUS IS IN THE PROCESS OF FLEXING IT SO IT MIGHT BE BALLED INTO A FIST, OR SEMI-CLENCHED.

Caption – top:

And the last, the most likely option…

Caption – bottom:

Arthritis.

Page 7 – Panel 6

LAST PANEL ON THE SECOND TIER. A TIGHT CLOSE-UP ON GUS' EYES NOW, A CERTAIN AMOUNT OF PANIC REGISTERING IN THEM.

Caption – middle:

I was only in my early thirties but… Well, look at Dad.

Page 7 – Panel 7

BOTTOM TIER, LEFT-HAND PANEL SHOWS GUS' FACE FROM THE SIDE: HIS HEAD IS TIPPED FORWARD AND HE HAS HIS EYES CLOSED NOW. HE HAS CONSIDERED HIS OPTIONS AND HAS MADE UP HIS MIND WHAT TO DO.

Caption – top:

But I chose to bury my head in the sand.

Page 7 – Panel 8

IN THE MIDDLE PANEL ON THE BOTTOM ROW, GUS FACES RACHEL AS HE TALKS, BOTH OF THEM IN SHOT FROM THE WAIST UP.

Gus:

It's easing up now.

I-I think it'll be alright so long as I don't knock it or anything.

Page 7 – Panel 9

FINAL PANEL ON THE PAGE IS RACHEL'S FACE. SHE'S NO LONGER QUITE SO WORRIED AS SHE WAS, BUT A HINT OF THAT REMAINS.

Caption – top right:

Rachel took some convincing but finally relented.

Rachel:

Okay.

Just promise if it comes back you'll get help.

Gus (speech bubble off):

I promise.

—

Page 8 – Panel 1

THIS PAGE IS A MONTAGE PAGE. THE CENTRAL BACKGROUND IMAGE IS ONE OF GUS WALKING DOWN THE STREET WITH JEANS, T-SHIRT AND JACKET ON. OVERLAID ON THIS ARE OTHER PANELS AT TOP AND BOTTOM, ONE EITHER SIDE OF THE MAIN PICTURE.

Page 8 – Panel 2

THIS PANEL IS IN THE TOP LEFT-HAND CORNER. IT SHOWS GUS AT WORK IN A GENERIC FACTORY SCENE. HIS OVERALLS ARE DRAB AND GREY, HE HAS A FIXED BUT NOT PARTICULARLY HAPPY EXPRESSION ON HIS FACE.

Caption – top (or use in space above the panel):

It was easy to keep that promise for a while because nothing else happened. I won't say I forgot all about it, but you know how it is…

Caption – middle:

You prioritise.

Caption – bottom:

My life returned to normal. I went to work, losing myself in the
daily grind at the factory.

Page 8 – Panel 3

IN THIS PANEL ON THE TOP RIGHT-HAND SIDE OF THE
PAGE WE SEE GUS HAVING LUNCH IN A CANTEEN WITH
HIS FRIENDS FROM WORK, PLASTIC CUPS AND TRAY IN
FRONT OF HIM WITH A STANDARDISED KIND OF MEAL
ON IT.

Caption – top:

I had lunch in the canteen with the lads.

Page 8 – Panel 4

THIS PANEL IS ON THE BOTTOM LEFT, AND IT SHOWS
GUS AT HOME ON THE COUCH WITH HIS ARM AROUND
RACHEL, WATCHING TV – THE LIGHTS COULD BE DIM
AND THE TV THROWING OUT FLICKERING IMAGES INTO
THE ROOM.

Caption – top:

I went back home for nights in front of the TV with Rachel in the
evening.

Caption – bottom:

Catching up with the state of the world.

Page 8 – Panel 5

BOTTOM RIGHT PANEL: THIS HAS A CLOSE-UP OF THE TV SCREEN ITSELF AND WHAT THEY ARE WATCHING, SHOWING AN INVADING ARMY, PERHAPS A TANK AND/OR HELICOPTER ON THE SCREEN.

Caption – top right:

The usual stuff: growing tensions abroad.

Caption – bottom right:

Murder, terrorism, chemical pollutants…

—

Page 9 – Panel 1

TOP TIER HAS A SINGLE PANEL GOING ALL THE WAY ACROSS, MIDDLE TIER HAS TWO PANELS AND THE BOTTOM TIER HAS TWO AS WELL. ON THIS TOP PANEL WE SEE GUS AT HIS CONVEYOR BELT IN HIS DRAB OUTFIT AND DRAB ENVIRONMENT – THINK 1984 OR METROPOLIS. HE IS WATCHING METAL CASINGS AS THEY GO DOWN THE LINE.

Caption – top left:

I think it was about midway through the second week that it came back.

Caption – bottom right:

No warning, no strange numbness this time. Just whack!

Page 9 – Panel 2

MIDDLE TIER, FIRST PANEL ON THE LEFT – IN THIS WE GET A SHOT FROM BELOW OF GUS GRIMACING AS HIS HAND THROBS, AND HE CLUTCHES HIS ARM.

Caption – middle:

> And the pain was shooting up my arm this time.

Page 9 – Panel 3

RIGHT PANEL ON MIDDLE TIER: THIS ONE IS COMPLETELY BLACK TO REFLECT THE FACT GUS HAS PASSED OUT, BUT WITH BLUE SMUDGED SPOTS ON THE BLACK.

Caption – top:

> Mercifully I did lose consciousness the second time.

Page 9 – Panel 4

LEFT-HAND PANEL OF THE BOTTOM TIER. GUS' POINT OF VIEW LOOKING DOWN AT HIS LEGS AS HE LAYS ON A HARD MEDICAL BED IN A WHITE ROOM. A BOX ON THE FAR WALL HAS A RED CROSS ON IT. THERE ARE ALSO A COUPLE OF SHELVES WITH BOTTLES OF COLOURED LIQUID ON THEM.

Caption – top left:

> When I woke I was in what Grimwald's laughingly call their infirmary.

Page 9 – Panel 5

RIGHT-HAND PANEL ON THE BOTTOM TIER. THIS HAS A CLOSE UP OF GUS' FACE, HE'S SQUINTING AS HE WAKES UP.

Caption – top:

> I hadn't had cause to visit since their annual medical, last July.

Caption – bottom:

Clean bill of health I got, too. What a joke!

—

Page 10 – Panel 1

TOP TIER CONSISTING OF A THREE PANEL SPREAD ACROSS, REST OF PAGE HAS A TWO PANEL TOWER ON THE LEFT-HAND SIDE, ONE ON TOP OF THE OTHER, AND A SINGLE LONG PANEL RUNNING DOWN WHAT'S LEFT OF THE RIGHT-HAND SIDE OF THE PAGE. THIS FIRST PANEL ON THE TOP LEFT HAS A VIEW OF GUS' ARM, WHICH IS INFLAMED AND SORE-LOOKING, AND HIS HAND, WHICH APPEARS FLACCID.

Caption – top:

My hand and arm felt peculiar…

Caption – bottom:

But at least the aching had stopped.

Page 10 – Panel 2

THE MIDDLE PANEL OF THE TOP TIER SHOWS DR. JENKINS IN THE DOORWAY OF THE INFIRMARY. HE HAS A ROUND FACE WITH ROUND MILKBOTTLE GLASSES (WE CAN'T SEE THE PUPILS), VERY LITTLE HAIR AND RUDDY CHEEKS; HE'S VERY SWEATY-LOOKING.

Caption – top:

Dr. Jenkins came to see me.

Page 10 – Panel 3

RIGHT PANEL ON TOP TIER IS A CLOSE-UP OF JENKINS' FACE.

Caption – top:

He freaked me out, this guy.

Jenkins:

It's Gus, isn't it?

Gus Harper?

Page 10 – Panel 4

TOP PANEL OF THE LEFT 'TOWER'. JENKINS IS FACING GUS, WHO IS STILL ON THE BED.

Jenkins:

You had a bit of a turn out there, I gather.

What seems to be the problem?

Page 10 – Panel 5

PANEL DIRECTLY BELOW THIS, STILL ON THE LEFT, SHOWS ANOTHER CLOSE-UP OF GUS' FACE – ANSWERING JENKINS.

Gus:

I've been having some pain in my hand.

But it… it seems to be moving up my arm now.

Page 10 – Panel 6

LONG PANEL RUNNING DOWN RIGHT-HAND SIDE FROM THE MIDDLE OF THE PAGE. THIS SHOWS JENKINS EXAMINING GUS' ARM, RUNNING HIS PROFESSIONAL EYE OVER IT.

Jenkins:

Has your GP seen this?

Gus:

No, not really. My girlfriend wanted me to go but—

Jenkins:

But you don't care for doctors, right?

—

Page 11 – Panel 1

SIMPLE PAGE OF TWO TIERS WITH THREE PANELS IN EACH. IN THE FIRST WE HAVE A CLOSE UP OF JENKINS' FACE. HE'S SMILING, BUT IT'S NOT A SMILE YOU'D TRUST.

Jenkins:

Who does?

Caption – bottom:

His flippancy was a ruse. I could tell that straight away.

Page 11 – Panel 2

ANOTHER VIEW OF JENKINS LOOKING OVER GUS, FROM THE SIDE THIS TIME. WE SEE THE MEN IN CLEAR VIEW. BOTH HAVE CONCERN ETCHED ON THEIR FACES, ALTHOUGH JENKINS IS STILL TRYING TO HIDE IT.

Caption – top:

He was concerned, probably more about the company than me.

Caption – bottom:

He was thinking: What if it's something we've done? What if the poor bastard croaks?

Page 11 – Panel 3

JENKINS' FACE FROM THE SIDE, AS THIS PANEL'S QUITE DIALOGUE HEAVY.

Jenkins:

Listen, Gus.

How would you feel about taking a little trip to The General?

Gus (from off panel):

Why? Is it arthritis?

Caption – bottom:

He said he couldn't comment.

Page 11 – Panel 4

SECOND TIER, FIRST PANEL ON THE LEFT. THIS IS A PICTURE OF THE GENERAL HOSPITAL, AN ORIDINARY-LOOKING BUILDING, ALL GLASS AND CONCRETE – IF THERE WEREN'T AMBULANCES OUTSIDE WE PROBABLY WOULDN'T EVEN KNOW IT WAS A HOSPITAL. BUT AT THE SAME TIME IT MANAGES TO LOOK MENACING.

Caption – top:

'They'll probably want to run some tests, take a few X-rays,' he told me.

Caption – bottom:

These would be the first of many.

Page 11 – Panel 5

MIDDLE PANEL OF THE BOTTOM TIER. GUS IS IN AN EXAMINATION ROOM, DRESSED IN A GOWN AND SITTING ON AN EXAMINATION TABLE WITH HIS LEGS DANGLING OVER THE EDGE. A COUPLE OF DOCTORS AND A NURSE SURROUND HIM.

Caption – top:

I was a rush job.

Caption – bottom:

Poked and prodded by every kind of doctor in that hospital.

Page 11 – Panel 6

CLOSE-UP OF ANOTHER DOCTOR, FILLIS. IN CONTRAST TO JENKINS, THIS ONE IS VERY THIN, ALMOST TO THE POINT OF EMACIATION.

Caption – top:

Especially by an orthopaedic specialist called Dr Fillis.

Fillis:

Please hold still, Mr Harper. You are not helping.

Caption – bottom:

Who treated me like an animal in a zoo.

—

Page 12 – Panel 1

NOW WE HAVE A TOP TIER OF TWO PANELS, A MIDDLE TIER OF ONE PANEL RUNNING ALONG THE MIDDLE SECTION AND A BOTTOM TIER OF TWO PANELS. IN THIS FIRST ONE IN THE TOP LEFT OF THE PAGE, WE SEE FILLIS STARRING AT AN X-RAY, HUNG UP ON A LIGHT BOX ON THE WALL. HE'S RUBBING HIS CHIN THOUGHTFULLY.

Caption – top:

X-rays confirmed that it wasn't broken.

Caption – bottom:

But more tests were needed…

Page 12 – Panel 2

IN THE SECOND PANEL WE SEE RACHEL ARRIVE AT THE HOSPITAL DOORS, WALKING INTO RECEPTION.

Caption – top:

Rachel came to collect me at around half five, straight from work.

Caption – bottom:

I didn't see the sense in bothering her before then.

Page 12 – Panel 3

IN THE LONG PANEL ACROSS THE MIDDLE WE HAVE A SHOT OF RACHEL AND GUS THROUGH THE WINDSCREEN OF HER CAR: HE'S ON THE RIGHT FACING US, RIGHT ARM IN A SLING, AND SHE'S DRIVING ON THE LEFT.

Caption – top left:

She was full of questions, though.

Caption – middle left:

Questions I couldn't answer.

Caption – top right:

All I could tell her was what they'd told me…

Caption – bottom right:

That they would know more in a few days when the test results came back.

Page 12 – Panel 4

FIRST PANEL ON THE LEFT OF THE BOTTOM TIER. THIS SHOWS GUS AT HOME ON THE COUCH WITH HIS ARM STILL IN A SLING.

Caption – top:

Meanwhile I was stuck at home on the sick.

Caption – bottom:

But Fillis had prescribed some anti-inflammatories and painkillers.

Page 12 – Panel 5

RIGHT-HAND PANEL OF THE BOTTOM TIER SHOWS GUS WITH HIS HEAD DOWN OVER THE TOILET – NOT SURE WHETHER TO GO FOR THE GRAPHIC VOMITING ON THIS OR THE 'JUST AFTER' LOOK. I'LL LEAVE THAT UP TO YOU, PAWEL…

Caption – top:

I began vomiting a couple of times a day.

Caption – middle:

I thought it was a side-effect of the drugs.

Caption – bottom:

But now I'm not so sure.

—

Page 13 – Panel 1

ON THIS PAGE WE HAVE A DIFFERENT SET-UP. ON THE FIRST TIER WHICH STRETCHES DOWN TO THE MIDDLE OF THE PAGE WE HAVE A LONG PANEL THAT GOES LENGTHWAYS DOWN THE LEFT-HAND SIDE, WHILE ON THE RIGHT ANOTHER TWO PANEL 'TOWER' SLOTS IN OPPOSITE IT: ONE ON TOP, ONE ON THE BOTTOM. THE OTHER HALF OF THE PAGE JUST HAS TWO ORDINARY PANELS. SO, IN THE LONG PANEL ON THE LEFT WE HAVE THE AFTER-EFFECTS OF THE VOMIT IN THE TOILET PAN

– BASICALLY A REPLAY OF THE SHOT ON PAGE ONE, ONLY THIS TIME IT'S YELLOW BILE INSTEAD OF BLOOD.

Caption – top left:

The yellow bile would cling to the toilet pan, shrugging off attempts to flush it away.

Caption – bottom:

Hanging there. My offspring.

Page 13 – Panel 2

TOP RIGHT-HAND PANEL AND THE FIRST IN THE TWO-PANEL 'TOWER'. IN THIS PANEL WE HAVE A CLOSE-UP OF RACHEL SCRUNCHING UP HER NOSE AT THE SMELL FROM THE BILE.

Rachel (small letters, like a sigh):

Oh Gus.

Caption – bottom:

The smell was pretty rotten.

Page 13 – Panel 3

PANEL DIRECTLY BENEATH, BOTTOM PANEL IN THE 'TOWER'. GUS LOOKING WORRIED BUT EXHAUSTED, AS IF HE'S JUST RAISED HIS HEAD FROM THE PAN. PERHAPS A LITTLE DRIBBLE OF SPIT OR BILE DANGLING FROM HIS MOUTH.

Caption – top:

I didn't need no doctor to tell me I had something bad inside.

Caption – bottom:

And it was spreading.

Page 13 – Panel 4

BOTTOM TIER ON BOTTOM HALF OF THE PAGE. IN THE FIRST OF THE TWO PANELS – THIS ONE ON THE LEFT – GUS SITS IN FILLIS' PLUSH OFFICE AWAITING THE RESULTS OF THE TESTS. HE IS ON ONE SIDE OF A LARGE WOODEN DESK, FILLIS ON THE OTHER, WITH A LARGE WINDOW BEHIND THE DOCTOR.

Caption – top:

When the results came in, Fillis called me back.

Fillis:

Mr Harper, I have some rather perplexing news.

Page 13 – Panel 5

THE RIGHT-HAND PANEL OF THE BOTTOM TIER IS A CLOSE-UP OF GUS AND FILLIS, AN ANGLED SHOT SO THEY ARE BOTH IN THE FRAME, BUT FILLIS' DESK IS SEPARATING THEM.

Gus:

What is it?

Fillis:

There's no easy way to say this…

We simply don't know what's wrong.

—

Page 14 – Panel 1

A PAGE OF THREE TIERS WITH THREE PANELS ON EACH ON THEM. FIRST PANEL, TOP LEFT, IS A CLOSE-UP OF A VERY PAINED GUS – NOT THE AGONY HE EXPERIENCED WHEN ALL THIS STARTED, BUT RATHER THE

EMOTIONAL TURMOIL OF NOT KNOWING WHAT IS CAUSING IT. HIS MOUTH IS ONLY OPEN SLIGHTLY, TEETH GRITTED.

Caption – top:

Anger, confusion, fear.

Caption – middle:

They swirled around in my guts…

Caption – bottom:

Stopping me from speaking.

Page 14 – Panel 2

SECOND PANEL OF THIS TIER HAS A DESK UPWARDS SHOT OF FILLIS, HANDS STEEPLED IN FRONT OF HIM, ELBOWS RESTING ON THE FINELY POSLISHED WOOD.

Caption – bottom:

Why didn't they know? They were the doctors for Heaven's sake!

Page 14 – Panel 3

RIGHT-HAND PANEL ON TOP TIER IS A TIGHT CLOSE-UP ON FILLIS' MOUTH.

Caption – top:

Everything he said after that went over my head.

Caption – middle:

But it definitely wasn't arthritis. My fatty tissue was reacting with the bone, absorbing it.

Caption – bottom:

A long stream of bullshit I couldn't take in.

Page 14 – Panel 4

LEFT-HAND PANEL OF MIDDLE TIER. GUS' FACE AGAIN, BUT HIS MOUTH IS OPEN FULLY THIS TIME.

Caption – top:

I suddenly found my voice again.

Gus:

But you must have some idea—

Page 14 – Panel 5

MIDDLE PANEL OF THE MIDDLE TIER. WE'RE BACK ON FILLIS' FACE AGAIN, BUT FROM THE SIDE THIS TIME.

Fillis:

Oh we have ideas, just nothing conclusive.

We just don't have the resources to identify your disease.

Page 14 – Panel 6

RIGHT PANEL OF THE MIDDLE TIER. GUS NOW HAS HIS HEAD BOWED – IF HIS ARM WAS FREE AND NOT IN THE SLING, HE'D HAVE HIS HEAD IN BOTH HANDS.

Caption – top:

That's what he called it, a disease.

Caption – middle:

But you couldn't catch it like a cold.

Caption – bottom:

This was attacking me from inside.

Page 14 – Panel 7

BOTTOM TIER, FIRST PANEL ON THE LEFT. FILLIS IS NOW

BY THE WINDOW LOOKING OUT, WITH HIS BACK TO US
AND GUS (ALTHOUGH WE DON'T SEE THE LATTER).

Fillis:

It might be a variant of MRSA, the flesh-eating bug… or genetic.

I wouldn't like to speculate.

Page 14 – Panel 8

MIDDLE PANEL ON THE BOTTOM ROW. NOW WE SEE
THE BACK OF GUS' HEAD AND FILLIS HAS TURNED
ROUND AGAIN TO FACE HIM, ALTHOUGH HE IS STILL BY
THE WINDOW.

Caption – top:

Fillis knew how to put his patients at ease. The jerk.

Fillis:

I've honestly never seen anything like it.

But if you visit my colleagues down south…

Page 14 – Panel 9

LAST PANEL ON THE BOTTOM TIER, BOTTOM RIGHT –
ONCE AGAIN A CLOSER SHOT OF FILLIS TALKING.

Fillis:

I'm sure they'll be able to sort you out.

Caption – bottom right:

Sort me out! Like I was bringing back a faulty toaster.

—

Page 15 – Panel 1

TOP TIER IS ONE LONG PANEL ACROSS, WITH A SECOND
TIER OF TWO PANELS AND A THIRD OF THREE PANELS.

IN THIS LONG PANEL WE SEE GUS IN A CHAIR AT HOME ON THE LEFT-HAND SIDE OF THE PANEL, WITH RACHEL STANDING ON THE RIGHT, ARMS FOLDED AND DETERMINED.

Caption – top left:

> More tests, more waiting. I didn't relish it.

Caption – middle left:

> But Rachel was insistent.

Rachel:

> You're going. If not for your own sake then for mine.
>
> I haven't slept in a week.

Page 15 – Panel 2

FIRST PANEL ON THE LEFT OF THE MIDDLE TIER. WE SEE RACHEL SITTING IN A WAITING ROOM WHILE GUS DISAPPEARS DOWN A CORRIDOR, BEING PUSHED IN A WHEELCHAIR.

Caption – top:

> She took time off, probably to make sure I actually went.

Caption – bottom:

> My 'treatment' was free. I was, after all… A special case.

Page 15 – Panel 3

SECOND PANEL ON THIS TIER. GUS IN CLOSE-UP, IN THE WHEELCHAIR, IN A WHITE GOWN AND LOOKING MISERABLE. THE SLING HAS GONE NOW.

Caption – top:

> Someone was even writing a paper on me.

Caption – bottom:

Yeah, fucking Harper's disease. Roll up, roll up!

Page 15 – Panel 4

BOTTOM TIER OF THREE PANELS. IN THE FIRST ON THE LEFT WE SEE THE INSIDE OF A HIGH-TECH SF-LIKE HOSPITAL ROOM, WITH SPANKINGLY CLEAN INTERIORS, MAYBE A FEW MACHINES WITH BUTTONS LIT UP.

Caption – top:

The institute itself was like something from the future.

Page 15 – Panel 5

IN THIS ONE WE SEE ROW UPON ROW OF MEN IN WHITE SUITS, WEARING GLASSES, ALMOST LIKE CLONES – THINK THE POSTER FROM BEING JOHN MALKOVICH OR AGENT SMITHS FROM THE MATRIX RELOADED – ONLY IN DOCTOR FORM.

Caption – top:

So many doctors, their faces blurred into one, their names a mishmash.

Caption – middle:

They did everything bar turn me inside out.

Caption – bottom:

And they would've too, if I'd signed the right consent forms.

Page 15 – Panel 6

FINAL PANEL ON THE PAGE, BOTTOM RIGHT. A SHOT OF

ROWS OF TEST TUBES WITH SAMPLES IN: YELLOW, WHITE, BROWN, RED.

Caption – top:

Biopsies were taken, samples galore…

Caption – bottom:

Urine, stools, skin, blood… even semen! And photographs recorded the onslaught.

—

Page 16 – Panel 1

ON THIS PAGE WE HAVE FOUR LONG HORIZONTAL STRIP PANELS (STRETCHING FROM LEFT TO RIGHT) ON TOP OF EACH OTHER. IN THE FIRST PANEL AT THE TOP OF THE PAGE WE SEE RACHEL COVERING GUS UP WITH A BLANKET ON THE COUCH, WHILE HIS FACE IS CONTORTED WITH PAIN.

Caption – top left:

Rachel was incredibly supportive.

Caption – bottom left:

I wouldn't have come through it without her, especially when the fits became more frequent.

Page 16 – Panel 2

IN THIS SECOND LONG PANEL WE SEE A CLOSE-UP OF GUS' SKIN BUBBLING IN PARTS, SORE AND HIDEOUS.

Caption – top right:

The pain was now in my lower half, as well.

Caption – bottom right:

Sometimes you could even see the flesh bubbling like soup on a stove.

Page 16 – Panel 3

THIRD LONG HORIZONTAL PANEL ON THE PAGE SHOWS GUS BACK AT THE INSTITUTE IN A BED, ARMS BANDAGED.

Caption – top left:

Two months passed. Nothing. No results. No explanations. No cure.

Caption – middle left:

By May the disease was speeding up. Nobody could stop it.

Caption – middle top:

One thing I did learn, though, by accident: I wasn't the only sufferer.

Caption – top right:

A few other minor cases had been reported elsewhere.

Caption – bottom right:

When I asked about it, they just clammed up.

Page 16 – Panel 4

LAST LONG PANEL ON THIS PAGE SHOWS A CLOSE UP OF GUS HOLDING A MIRROR AWKWARDLY WITH HIS GOOD LEFT HAND, WE SEE THE REFLECTION: THE BIG LUMPS ON HIS NECK AND BOILS ON HIS FACE.

Caption – left middle:

Rachel had already returned home by now. I was scared of what she'd say when she saw me again.

Caption – right middle:

I didn't recognise myself anymore.

—

Page 17 – Panel 1

THREE TIERS OF TWO PANELS EACH ON THIS PAGE. THE FIRST PANEL – TOP LEFT – SHOWS GUS WALKING WITH A STICK DOWN THE PATH TO HIS FRONT DOOR, HELPED BY TWO PARAMEDICS. HE'S WEARING A LONG COAT AND HAT (ALA DARKMAN)

Caption – top left:

I needed a stick. Not even the strongest medication could ease the pain in my legs.

Page 17 – Panel 2

SECOND PANEL ON TOP TIER IS A REACTION SHOT OF RACHEL AT THE DOOR WHEN IT'S OPENED. HER HAND IS AT HER MOUTH, SHE'S TRYING TO HIDE HER SHOCK AND FAILING MISERABLY. THERE'S A SINGLE TEAR RUNNING DOWN HER CHEEK

Caption – top:

Rachel's reaction? A combination of horror and pity.

Rachel:

They still don't know…?

Gus (off panel):

I don't think they ever will.

It won't be much use to me soon anyway.

Page 17 – Panel 3

MIDDLE TIER, LEFT-HAND PANEL. WE SEE THE COUPLE FROM THE SIDE IN THE MIDDLE DISTANCE. NEITHER OF THEM IS SAYING ANYTHING. THE PARAMEDICS HAVE

STEPPED BACK BY NOW AND ARE ALMOST OUT OF FRAME.

Caption – top:

They had their theories: a genetic disorder, mutated cancer, a reversal of F.O.P. which turns your muscles into bone.

Caption – bottom:

None of it helped me.

Page 17 – Panel 4

MIDDLE TIER, RIGHT-HAND PANEL. IN THIS ONE RACHEL HUGS GUS, WE SEE HER HEAD ON HIS SHOULDER AND HER ARMS AROUND HIS BACK.

Caption – top right:

Rachel surprised me then.

Caption – bottom right:

I fought back the agony, ignoring the pain just to be near her.

Page 17 – Panel 5

BOTTOM TIER, LEFT-HAND PANEL. GUS IS SITTING ON A CHAIR IN HIS LIVING ROOM, HIS HAT GONE, THE STICK IS BY HIS SIDE, AND HE IS DROPPING TO SLEEP.

Caption – top:

This must be what it was like for the first person who'd developed TB, Polio… Aids.

Caption – bottom:

Knowing that nothing can be done is hard to take.

Page 17 – Panel 6

AND WE'RE BACK TO THE BLUE PANEL FROM PAGE 3.

Caption – top:

I had no illusions. I knew the end might come at any time.

Caption – middle:

And still I dreamed of the blue.

—

Page 18 – Panel 1

THE SET-UP ON THIS PAGE IS THREE PANELS ON THE TOP TIER, A LONG HORIZONTAL PANEL ACROSS THE PAGE FOR THE SECOND TIER, AND FOUR PANELS IN THE BOTTOM TIER. IN THE FIRST PANEL ON THE TOP LEFT OF THE PAGE, WE SEE GUS IN HIS PYJAMAS LEANING ON HIS STICK AND LOOKING OUT THROUGH THE WINDOW AT THE BACK GARDEN.

Caption – top:

Then some good news. The disease appeared to go into remission.

Caption – bottom:

Maybe it had run its course, I told myself. And like a fool I started to believe in miracles again.

Page 18 – Panel 2

SECOND PANEL OF THE TOP TIER IS A SIMPLE PICTURE OF THE SUN.

Caption – top:

The progress halted very suddenly one week.

Caption – middle:

And this respite lasted the whole of the summer.

Caption – bottom:

Though it couldn't have been the sunlight – I didn't go out much anymore.

Page 18 – Panel 3

TOP RIGHT PANEL. THE BLUE PANEL FROM THE PREVIOUS PAGE, BUT MUCH BRIGHTER AND LIGHTER AS IF EVAPORATING.

Caption:

The dreams went away at the same time.

Caption:

I never connected that before. A coincidence?

Caption:

Or another symptom?

Page 18 – Panel 4

THE LONG PANEL GOING ACROSS THE PAGE IN THE MIDDLE. HERE WE SEE THE ARMY HELICOPTERS AND TROOPS (AS FROM THE NEWS BEFORE), EXCEPT IN CLOSE-UP NOW, RIFLES RAISED.

Caption – top left:

I have no problem recalling the day it returned, either. It was the day that war was announced overseas.

Caption – bottom right:

The build up to both was swift.

Page 18 – Panel 5

FIRST OF FOUR PANELS ON THIS BOTTOM TIER, THIS ONE

BOTTOM LEFT. IT SHOWS GUS ON THE FLOOR IN FRONT OF THE TV, COLLAPSED, STICK NEXT TO HIM.

Caption:

A shockwave through my entire body.

Page 18 – Panel 6

CLOSE-UP OF GUS' FACE ON THE FLOOR, STILL BOIL-RIDDEN.

Caption – top:

And I thought then…

Caption – bottom:

What if our enemies had used a chemical weapon on us?

Page 18 – Panel 7

CLOSE-UP ON GUS' ARM, THE BANDAGES HAVE COME LOOSE, EXPOSING THE DISEASED FLESH BENEATH.

Caption – top:

If so, why me?

Caption – bottom:

I was nobody.

Page 18 – Panel 8

BOTTOM RIGHT PANEL, AND RACHEL IS CROUCHING BESIDE GUS, DISTRAUGHT.

Caption:

Rachel found me there some time later.

—

Page 19 – Panel 1

THIS PANEL RUNS DOWN THE LEFT-HAND SIDE OF THE PAGE AND THE OTHERS (2-6) ARE ON THE RIGHT HAND SIDE FROM TOP TO BOTTOM (2 AT THE TOP, 6 AT THE BOTTOM). HERE WE HAVE A SHOT OF RACHEL'S FACE IN CLOSE-UP, DISAPPOINTED, EYES FILLED WITH TEARS.

Caption – top:

Her despair was clear. The 'disorder' was here again and its effects were worsening.

Page 19 – Panel 2

A CLOSE-UP OF GUS' FACE; HIS EYES ARE SHUT AND HIS MOUTH IS A STRAIGHT LINE.

Caption – top:

I couldn't expect her to look after me anymore, and didn't want her visiting me in some hospice.

Caption – bottom:

I made my decision. I had to go.

Page 19 – Panel 3

HERE WE SEE GUS AT THE FRONT WINDOW, HIDING BEHIND THE CURTAINS, WATCHING RACHEL WALK DOWN THE PATH TO HER CAR.

Caption – bottom:

So the very next week – early September – I waited for Rachel to go out, then left myself. For good.

Page 19 – Panel 4

SHOT OF GUS STICKING HIS TONGUE OUT OF THE CORNER OF HIS MOUTH, HOLDING HIS PEN AWKWARDLY IN HIS LEFT HAND AS HE TRIES TO WRITE HIS FAREWELL LETTER.

Caption – top:

I thought I was freeing her. I'd been a burden long enough.

Caption – bottom:

She loved me, but to stay would only cause her more heartache.

Page 19 – Panel 5

CLOSE-UP ON THE LETTER ITSELF, BUT WE CAN'T REALLY READ IT YET – ALTHOUGH WE CAN SEE THE LETTERS ARE A VERITABLE SCRAWL.

Caption:

She would be better off without me. I said as much in my letter.

Page 19 – Panel 6

NOW WE CAN READ THE WORDS AT THE END OF THE LETTER, WRITTEN IN SPIDER HANDWRITING. IT SAYS:

Please don't try to find me. I'll always love you. Gus.

—

Page 20 – Panel 1

SIMPLE PAGE LAYOUT OF TWO TIERS OF THREE PANELS EACH. IN THE FIRST PANEL ON THE TOP LEFT WE SEE GUS DRESSED BACK UP IN HIS COAT AND HAT, WITH BANDAGED ARMS, DEPARTING THE HOUSE, LEANING

MUCH MORE HEAVILY ON HIS STICK THAN EVER BEFORE. HE LOOKS LIKE A WIZENED EXCUSE OF A MAN.

Caption – top left:

Really, I didn't know what I was doing.

Caption – bottom right:

I was so terrified of being without her, yet scared to be with her.

Page 20 – Panel 2

MIDDLE PANEL OF TOP TIER. CLOSE-UP OF GUS' FACE IN SHADOWS UNDER THE BRIM OF THE HAT.

Caption:

Maybe it was selfish, but I couldn't be the man she needed.

Rachel deserved so much more.

Page 20 – Panel 3

RIGHT PANEL ON THE TOP TIER. SHOT OF A TRAIN AT THE STATION – GUS IS WAITING ON THE PLATFORM.

Caption – top:

I knew exactly where I was going. East, to my parents' old holiday cottage.

Caption – bottom:

A safe place from my youth, where summers never ended

Page 20 – Panel 4

BOTTOM TIER, LEFT-HAND PANEL. WE SEE GUS IN A TRAIN CARRIAGE, AND A LITTLE GIRL OPPOSITE LOOKING OVER, FRIGHTENED, CLUTCHING HER MOTHER'S HAND VERY TIGHTLY.

Caption – top:

I climbed on the train with great difficulty.

Caption – bottom:

Fellow travellers stared at me, people backed away when I got off.

Page 20 – Panel 5

MIDDLE PANEL ON BOTTOM TIER IS ANOTHER CLOSE-UP OF GUS' FACE, NOW ONLY PARTIALLY HIDDEN BY THE HAT – WE SEE THE SADNESS IN HIS EYES.

Caption – bottom:

I felt more and more like a monster with each passing second.

Page 20 – Panel 6

BOTTOM RIGHT PANEL SHOWS A TAXI OUTSIDE A QUIET SEASIDE COTTAGE ON THE CLIFF-TOPS: WE CAN SEE A HINT OF SEA AND OVERCAST SKIES BEHIND THE COTTAGE.

Caption – top:

The cottage suited me perfectly.

Caption – bottom:

The tourist season was virtually over, leaving the nearby coastal village empty and sad.

—

Page 21 – Panel 1

THIS PAGE HAS THREE TIERS: THE FIRST TWO ARE OF TWO PANELS EACH AND THE BOTTOM ONE IS A LONG PANEL HORIZONTALLY ACROSS THE PAGE. IN THE FIRST, TOP LEFT PANEL OF THE TOP TIER, WE HAVE GUS

STANDING OUTSIDE THE DOOR OF THE COTTAGE, IT LOOKS MORE RUN-DOWN NOW ON CLOSER INSPECTION, REFLECTING THE MOOD – AND GUS – PERFECTLY.

Caption - top:

I was home.

Caption – bottom:

It was just as I remembered it. A little more run-down, sure, but it was peaceful near the sea.

Page 21 – Panel 2

SECOND PANEL ON TOP TIER HAS GUS USING THE PHONE, AN OLD-FASHIONED CRADLE PHONE ON A TABLE IN THE HALL.

Caption – top:

I stocked up on provisions…

Caption – bottom:

Delivered right to my door.

Page 21 – Panel 3

SECOND TIER. LEFT-HAND PANEL HAS GUS IN THE LIVING ROOM, SAT IN A MORE OLD-FASHIONED CHAIR, LOOKING OUT THROUGH ANOTHER WINDOW, THIS TIME BELONGING TO THE COTTAGE.

Caption:

And I settled in to wait.

Page 21 – Panel 4

RIGHT-HAND PANEL ON SECOND TIER. CLOSE-UP ON A

PORTABLE RADIO, AGAIN FAIRLY OLD-FASHIONED IN DESIGN.

Caption:

The radio kept me in touch with events.

Radio (zig-zag bubble to show it's electronic):

Our troops are now advancing on the front lines…

Caption:

Some argued necessity, others said the end was nigh and the Horsemen were saddling up.

Page 21 – Panel 5

IN THE LONG PANEL RUNNING THE WIDTH OF THE BOTTOM TIER, WE HAVE GUS AND THE RADIO IN FRAME TOGETHER; HE'S LISTENING TO THE BROADCAST ABOUT HIS DISEASE. GUS APPEARS SHOCKED, MOUTH OPEN WIDE.

Caption – top left:

Then one day I heard a piece about the disease.

Caption – middle left (just below it):

My disease!

Caption – top right:

More cases had been documented in the last few months, from all over the globe.

Caption – bottom right:

Doctors were starting to take notice, but stated the risk of contracting it was minimal.

—

Page 22 – Panel 1

THREE TIERS OF TWO PANELS AGAIN ON THIS PAGE. IN THE FIRST – TOP LEFT – WE SEE GUS LOOKING DOWN ON HIS WITHERING AND BOIL-RIDDEN LEGS.

Caption – top:

The fire in my legs reminded me of just how 'lucky' I'd been to get such a rare affliction.

Page 22 – Panel 2

RIGHT PANEL OF TOP TIER. THIS SHOWS GUS DRAGGING HIMSELF AROUND ON THE FLOOR OF THE COTTAGE BY HIS ONE 'GOOD' LEFT ARM. THINK THE END OF THE FLY II.

Caption – bottom:

Not long afterwards, I lost use in them completely.

Page 22 – Panel 3

LEFT-HAND PANEL OF MIDDLE TIER: GUS AT THE TABLE, ATTEMPTING TO EAT. NOT A PRETTY SIGHT. HIS FACE IS MORE LUMPY AND MISHAPEN THAN EVER.

Caption – top:

Eating was a bitch; the lumps now inside my mouth as well.

Page 22 – Panel 4

RIGHT-HAND PANEL OF THE MIDDLE TIER. GUS IS JUST A SHAPE IN THE BED, WALLOWING IN HIS OWN PIT.

Caption – top:

Some days I didn't get up at all.

Caption – bottom:

Why should I?

Page 22 – Panel 5

LEFT-HAND PANEL OF THE BOTTOM TIER. A BROKEN FULL-LENGTH MIRROR WITH A WOODEN FRAME AND A SPIDER'S WEB CRACK DOWN THE CENTRE OF IT.

Caption – top:

I'd smashed all the mirrors in that cottage.

Caption – bottom:

How much more bad luck could it bring?

Page 22 – Panel 6

LAST PANEL ON THE PAGE, BOTTOM RIGHT. GUS CATCHING HIS RELFECTION IN A WINDOW, BLURRED BUT ENOUGH TO REMIND HIM OF WHAT HAS HAPPENED.

Caption – top:

But every now and again the windows worked against me.

Caption – bottom:

Or the glass panelling on the door.

—

Page 23 – Panel 1

THIS PAGE HAS TWO PANELS ON THE TOP TIER, A LONG PANEL ACROSS THE WIDTH OF THE MIDDLE AND A BOTTOM TIER OF THREE PANELS. IN THE FIRST PANEL WE HAVE A SHOT OF A THERMOMETER WITH THE TEMPERATURE DOWN, AROUND 8 OR 9 DEGREES.

Caption – top left:

The temperature was dropping rapidly day-by-day.

Page 23 – Panel 2

SECOND PICTURE OF TOP TIER. THIS HAS GUS STRETCHED OUT ON THE LIVING ROOM FLOOR, UNBANDAGED AND NAKED EXCEPT FOR A PAIR OF BOXERS – THE CARPET AROUND HIM IS DAMP AND HE'S SLICK WITH SWEAT. NOW WE CAN SEE MOST OF THE DEVASTATION TO HIS BODY, HOW HIS LEGS ARE STUMPY AND USELESS, FLACID ARMS OUT LIKE A MARTYR.

Caption:

Yet I was boiling hot. I ran a fever.

Page 25 – Panel 3

THE LONG MIDDLE PANEL CONCENTRATES ON GUS' HALLUCINATIONS – HE SEES SWIRLING IMAGES OF, FROM LEFT TO RIGHT, JENKINS, FILLIS, HIS MOTHER AND FATHER DRESSED IN OLD-FASHIONED CLOTHES (THE LATTER COMPLETE WITH LUMPY ARTHRITIC HANDS).

Caption – top left:

I saw visions. Delirious, I recognised old familiar faces: Jenkins, Fillis...

Caption – bottom right:

My dead parents... Dad with his arthritic hands...

Page 23 – Panel 4

BOTTOM TIER OF THREE. THE LEFT-HAND PANEL

SHOWS RACHEL'S FIGURE STANDING BY THE DOOR – ALTHOUGH WE CAN'T SEE HER HANDS.

Caption – top:

And Rachel.

Page 23 – Panel 5

MIDDLE PANEL: A CLOSE-UP OF RACHEL'S FACE.

Caption – top:

Except the last one was real.

Caption – bottom:

She told me she'd finally found this address at home.

Page 23 – Panel 6

BOTTOM LEFT PANEL: A LIGHT BLUE FLANNEL MOPS UP SOME OF THE SWEAT ON GUS' BROW – WITHHOLD RACHEL'S HANDS UNTIL THE NEXT FRAME ON THE NEXT PAGE.

Caption – bottom:

She bathed my forehead with a cold flannel.

—

Page 24 – Panel 1

TWO TIERS OF THREE PANELS EACH. THE FIRST, TOP LEFT, SHOWS RACHEL'S BOIL-RIDDEN AND STUBBY HANDS HOLDING THE FLANNEL, IN THE CORNER OF THE FRAME WE SEE GUS' EYE OPENING WIDE IN TERROR.

Caption – top:

But her hands, they were…

Page 24 – Panel 2

MIDDLE TIER OF TOP PANEL – AN EXTREME CLOSE-UP OF GUS' SCREAMING MOUTH, COMPLETE WITH BOILS AROUND THE LIPS, HALF HIS TEETH MISSING AND PUSTULE-RIDDLED TONGUE.

Caption – bottom:

I think I screamed at that point.

Page 24 – Panel 3

FINAL PANEL ON THIS TIER, TOP RIGHT, IS BLACK – AS THOUGH WE'VE PULLED IN SO TIGHT ON GUS' MOUTH EVERYTHING HAS GONE DARK. THERE ARE NO CAPTIONS.

Page 24 – Panel 4

BOTTOM TIER OF THREE PANELS. IN FIRST, BOTTOM LEFT, WE SEE A MOON WITH CLOUDS PASSING IN FRONT OF IT.

Caption – top:

It's towards the end of the year now, but time has lost all meaning.

Page 24 – Panel 5

MIDDLE PANEL ON BOTTOM TIER: WE SEE TWO BLACK FIGURES EMERGING FROM THE COTTAGE, JUST SHAPES REALLY, NOTHING THAT RESEMBLE HUMAN BEINGS

Caption – top:

Rachel said the war was over. No one gives a shit about fighting anymore.

Caption – bottom:

Millions have the disease. The plague is uncontrollable, unpredictable. Unstoppable.

Page 24 – Panel 6

BOTTOM RIGHT-HAND PANEL: THE SHAPES ARE MAKING THEIR WAY DOWN A CLIFF-PATH, ROCK FACES ON EITHER SIDE.

Caption – top:

It happened much more quickly for Rachel than me.

Caption – middle:

The pain much greater.

Caption – bottom:

All I could do was be there for her.

—

Page 25 – Panel 1

ON THIS PAGE WE HAVE TWO PANELS ON THE TOP TIER, DOWN TO THE HALF-WAY MARK OF THE PAGE, AND THE REST OF THE PAGE IS ONE BIG PANEL. IN THE FIRST PANEL ON THE TOP TIER WE SEE MORE OF A CLOSE-UP OF THE SHAPES, THEIR BUMPS STILL SILHOUETTED BUT MORE VISIBLE.

Caption:

Now our pain is the only thing that reminds us we are alive…

Caption:

Though I don't understand how we still are.

Page 25 – Panel 2

NOW WE SEE THEM IN ALL THEIR GORY GLORY: THE MOON CATCHING THEIR FLESH AND PAINTING IT SILVER. THEY LOOK HIDEOUS, BARELY HUMAN AT ALL, JUST BAGS OF LUMPY BOIL-COVERED FLESH REALLY, BUT WE CAN STILL SEE EYES AND PARTIAL MOUTHS.

Caption – top right:

We both resemble something out of a sick horror movie. But our love remains strong.

Caption – bottom:

As does our vision… our dreams of the blue.

Page 25 – Panel 3

IN THE LARGEST PANEL ON THE PAGE WE SEE MORE OF THE CREATURES ON THE PATH BEHIND THEM – WE CAN'T SEE THE BEACH YET AS THAT IS AHEAD OF THEM.

Caption – top left:

It's taking some time to get there.

Caption – middle left:

But we are not alone.

Caption – top right:

This seaside village is no longer deserted. It has called out to everyone.

—

NOW OUR PAIN IS THE ONLY THING THAT REMINDS US WE ARE ALIVE...
THOUGH I DON'T UNDERSTAND HOW WE STILL ARE.
WE BOTH RESEMBLE SOMETHING OUT OF A SICK HORROR MOVIE. BUT OUR LOVE REMAINS STRONG.
AS DOES OUR VISION... OUR DREAMS OF THE BLUE.
IT'S TAKING SOME TIME TO GET THERE.
THIS SEASIDE VILLAGE IS NO LONGER DESERTED. IT HAS CALLED OUT TO EVERYONE.
BUT WE ARE NOT ALONE.

Page 26 – Panel 1

BIG SPLASH PAGE IMAGE WITH GUS AND RACHEL'S HEADS IN THE FOREGROUND AND THE BEACH AHEAD OF THEM, FULL OF QUIVERING SHAPES THAT ONCE WERE HUMAN, AND SOME THAT STILL LOOK PARTIALLY HUMAN. MOST ARE MAKING THEIR WAY TO THE SEA LIKE TURTLES, THE MOON ILLUMINATING THE WHOLE THING IN THE TOP CORNER OF THE PAGE.

Caption – top left:

The beach is full of quivering shapes that used to be… well, us. And even, yes even those who have not yet undergone the transformation by this late stage. Their bloodcurdling cries can be heard for miles around.

Caption – bottom right:

In my imagination I see scenes like these occurring all over the country. All around the world…

—

Page 27 – Panel 1

ONE LAST PAGE OF TWO TIERS WITH THREE PANELS IN EACH. IN THE FIRST PANEL OF THE TOP TIER, TOP LEFT, WE SEE THE THINGS THAT USED TO BE GUS AND RACHEL ON THE BEACH, MAKING THEIR OWN WAY TOWARDS THE SEA.

Caption – top:

We've talked it over and think we know why now.

Caption – bottom:

Why we are returning to what we once were.

Page 27 – Panel 2

MIDDLE PANEL ON TOP TIER. GUS AND RACHEL REACH THE LAPPING SEA, THEY'RE MELTING INTO EACH OTHER LIKE A REPLAY OF THEIR LOVE-MAKING SESSION – IF THEY WERE STILL HUMAN THEY WOULD BE HOLDING EACH OTHER TIGHTLY.

Caption:

And as Rachel and I join again, gliding over the tide, our suspicions are confirmed.

Page 27 – Panel 3

THIRD PANEL OF THIS TIER, THEY'RE NOW ON THE SURFACE OF THE OCEAN, MELDING WITH THAT TOO, ONE UPTURNED BLUE EYE CAN BE SEEN: GUS'

Caption – middle right:

We are the disease.

Caption – bottom right:

All of us.

Page 27 – Panel 4

LEFT PANEL OF THE BOTTOM TIER: WE'RE CLOSING IN ON THE EYE NOW, HEADING FOR THE FINALE. SO A CLOSER SHOT OF THE EYE BUT NOT TIGHT CLOSE-UP YET.

Caption – top left:

It's taken some doing, but our planet has at last found a cure – some might say just in time!

Caption – bottom left:

Its antibodies have been attacking us invisibly in the air, in our food, in the water… Reversing millions of years of evolution.

Page 27 – Panel 5

MIDDLE PANEL OF THE BOTTOM TIER: TIGHTER NOW ON THE EYE SO THAT WE CAN SEE THE PUPIL, SEE THE BLUENESS.

Caption – top:

Hard to think clearly… but… there is no reason to fight it now. This isn't so bad.

Caption – bottom:

Becoming one with the liquid, with each other. No worries, no anxiety, no hardship. No war.

Page 27 – Panel 6

AND FINALLY, BOTTOM RIGHT PANEL IS TOTALLY BLUE AGAIN – IT MIGHT BE THE EYE, BUT IT ALSO REPRESENTS THE SEA.

Caption – top right:

Just existence, and the promise of eternity.

Caption – middle right:

At least for now.

Caption – bottom right:

At least for—

THE END

THE DISEASE is available from:

hellboundmedia.co.uk/comic-book/the-disease-shock-value-presents

Paul Kane is an award-winning, bestselling writer and editor based in Derbyshire, UK. His short story collections include *Alone (In the Dark)*, *Touching the Flame*, *FunnyBones*, *Peripheral Visions*, *Shadow Writer*, *The Adventures of Dalton Quayle*, *The Butterfly Man and Other Stories*, *The Spaces Between*, *Ghosts*, the British Fantasy Award-nominated *Monsters*, *Shadow Casting*, *Nailbiters*, *Death*, *Disexistence*, *Scary Tales*, *More Monsters*, *Lost Souls* and *The Controllers*. His novellas include *The Lazarus Condition*, *RED* and *Pain Cages* (a #1 Amazon bestseller). He is the author of such novels as *Of Darkness and Light*, *The Gemini Factor* and the bestselling *Arrowhead* trilogy (*Arrowhead*, *Broken Arrow* and *Arrowland*, gathered together in the sell-out omnibus edition *Hooded Man*), a post-apocalyptic reworking of the Robin Hood mythology. His latest novels include *Lunar* (which is set to be turned into a feature film), the short Y.A. novel *The Rainbow Man* (as P.B. Kane), the critically-acclaimed and award-winning *Sherlock Holmes and the Servants of Hell* from Solaris, the sequels to *RED – Blood RED* and *Deep RED – Before* from Grey Matter Press, *Arcana* from WordFire Press and *Her Last Secret* and *Her Husband's Grave* from HQ/HarperCollins (as P.L. Kane)

He has also written for comics, most notably for the *Dead Roots* zombie anthology alongside writers such as James Moran (*Torchwood*, *Cockneys vs. Zombies*) and Jason Arnopp (*Doctor Who*, *Friday the 13th*, *The Last Days of Jack Sparks*) and as part of the team turning *Clive Barker's Books of Blood* into motion comics for Seraphim/MadeFire. His stand-alone comic *The Disease*, published by Hellbound Media, was also a 2016 Ghastly Award-nominated title in the 'One Shot' category. Paul is co-editor of the anthology *Hellbound Hearts* (Simon & Schuster) – stories based around the mythology that spawned *Hellraiser* – *The Mammoth Book of Body Horror* (Constable & Robinson/Running Press), featuring the likes of

Stephen King and James Herbert, *A Carnivàle of Horror* (PS) featuring Ray Bradbury and Joe Hill, *Beyond Rue Morgue* from Titan (stories based around Poe's detective, Dupin), *Exit Wounds* – a crime anthology featuring the likes of Lee Child, Val McDermid, Dennis Lehane and Jeffery Deaver – *Wonderland* (a finalist in the Shirley Jackson Awards) and *Cursed*, the last three also from Titan.

His non-fiction books include *The Hellraiser Films and Their Legacy*, *Voices in the Dark* and *Shadow Writer – The Non-Fiction. Vol. 1: Reviews* and *Vol. 2: Articles and Essays*, plus his genre journalism has appeared in the likes of *SFX*, *Fangoria*, *Dreamwatch*, *Gorezone* and *Rue Morgue*. He also co-wrote the afterword to the latest edition of Stephen King's *Night Shift* collection. He has been a Guest at Alt.Fiction five times, was a Guest at the first SFX Weekender, at Thought Bubble in 2011, Derbyshire Literary Festival and Off the Shelf in 2012, Monster Mash and Event Horizon in 2013, Edge-Lit in 2014, HorrorCon, HorrorFest and Grimm Up North in 2015, The Dublin Ghost Story Festival and Sledge-Lit in 2016, IMATS Olympia and Celluloid Screams in 2017, plus Black Library Live (Warhammer 40k) and The UK Ghost Story Festival in 2019, as well as being a panellist at FantasyCon and the World Fantasy Convention, and a fiction judge at the Sci-Fi London Film Festival. He is a former Special Publications Editor of the British Fantasy Society and is currently serving as co-chair for the UK arm of the Horror Writers Association.

His work has been optioned for film and television, and his zombie story 'Dead Time' was turned into an episode of the Lionsgate/NBC TV series *Fear Itself*, adapted by Steve Niles (*30 Days of Night*) and directed by Darren Lynn Bousman (*SAW II-IV*). He also scripted *The Opportunity*, which premiered at the Cannes Film Festival, *Wind Chimes* (directed by

Brad '*Hallows Eve*' Watson and which sold to TV), *The Weeping Woman* – filmed by award-winning director Mark Steensland, starring Tony-nominated actor Stephen Geoffreys (*Fright Night*) – *Confidence*, directed by award-winning Mike Clarke (*A Hand to Play, Paper and Plastic*) which stars Simon Bamford (*Hellraiser, Nightbreed, Starfish*), and *The Torturer* directed by Joe Manco of Little Spark Films. Loose Canon/Hydra Films have just turned Paul's novelette *Men of the Cloth* into a feature called *Sacrifice* (aka *The Colour of Madness*), starring *Re-Animator* and *You're Next*'s Barbara Crampton. His work for audio includes the full cast drama adaptation of *The Hellbound Heart* for Bafflegab, starring Tom Meeten (*The Ghoul*), Neve McIntosh (*Doctor Who*) and Alice Lowe (*Prevenge*), and the *Robin of Sherwood* adventure *The Red Lord* for Spiteful Puppet/ITV, narrated by Ian Ogilvy (*Return of the Saint*). You can find out more at his website www.shadow-writer.co.uk which has featured Guest Writers such as Dean Koontz, Robert Kirkman, Charlaine Harris and Guillermo del Toro.